PRAISE FOR WENDY WEBB

The End of Temperance Dare

"[In] this solid supernatural thriller . . . Webb succeeds in escalating suspense while keeping her story grounded, but goes full-on *Exorcist* for the finale."

— *Publishers Weekly*

"Tantalizing . . . [*The End of Temperance Dare*] could well be played on a Clue game board, with macabre crimes, inexplicable disappearances, and enough eerie suspense to drive one mad."

— Minneapolis *Star Tribune*

"There's an irresistible pull to a haunted-house story told well, and *The End of Temperance Dare* is told very well indeed . . . The story takes place on the shores of Lake Superior, with very of-the-moment characters, while drawing potent atmosphere from the richly drawn location. As the plot tightens, the strange loveliness of the manor on the lake takes hold."

— *The Big Thrill*

"There were more than enough creepy moments, mysteries to solve, and even some romance thrown in . . . This book was perfect."

— *San Francisco Book Review*

"Wendy Webb is a pro at providing all the trappings of a good Gothic mystery . . . a fun read."

— *Criminal Element*

The Vanishing

"A deliciously complex blend of psychological suspense and ghost story, *The Vanishing* is pitch perfect on every note, from its mansion setting in the pine-scented northern wilderness to the secrets and specters lurking around every corner."

—Erin Hart, author of *The Book of Killowen*

"The haunting twists and turns of *The Vanishing* left me as breathless as the beautiful setting of Havenwood itself. Reminiscent of the classics *The Haunting of Hill House* and *Rebecca*, this novel grabbed me on the first page and didn't let go. A compelling, frightening, deeply satisfying tale that is as rich in setting as it is in storytelling."

—Suzanne Palmieri, author of *The Witch of Little Italy*

The Fate of Mercy Alban

BOOK OF THE MONTH CLUB, INDIE NEXT PICK, FIVE WEEKS ON THE HEARTLAND INDIE BESTSELLER LIST

"Webb has cooked up another confection filled with family secrets coming to light in the Midwest . . . Magic and mystery intertwine in Webb's engaging Midwestern gothic."

—Kristine Huntley, *Booklist*

"If Stephen King and Sarah Waters had a love child, it would be Wendy Webb."

—MJ Rose, *New York Times* bestselling author

"This second novel by Minnesota Book Award–winning writer Wendy Webb has all the elements of a downright haunting story—and it is. Be prepared to be scared—and entertained."

—Minneapolis *Star Tribune*

"If you're craving a good old-fashioned ghost story to scare you on these cold nights, this is it. There's a big house with secret passages (think Glensheen in Duluth), a body that may have left the crypt, a beautiful apparition dancing on the lakeshore in the moonlight, a hidden manuscript, a book of curses, and an old relative who may be insane."

—*St. Paul Pioneer Press*

"I haven't picked up a thriller/horror novel this good in ages. This is the kind of book that gets your pulse racing as you frantically flip to the next chapter to find out what happens."

—*No Map Provided*

"Webb is amazing at writing a spooky, gothic atmosphere that will chill you to the bone. This is definitely a novel you don't want to read late at night while you're alone."

—Swapna Krishna

"Ghosts, witchcraft, family secrets, money and power, and pure evil run through this book. I certainly enjoyed it! A fun read and sure to keep you turning the pages. And you just have to keep reading to find out who the heck Mercy Alban is—you'll be fascinated by the story this author weaves."

—*Bookalicious Book Reviews*

"This is a first by Wendy Webb for me, but if anything else she writes is even remotely like this book then she has a devoted reader and fan in me. I was hooked from the very first page, and I refused to let go. Honestly, by the time I reached the final page, I did not want it to be over. I felt like I hadn't explored every hidden passageway and secret tunnel that Alban House held, and I wanted to spend more time there. I honestly have not read a book that kept my attention like this in a long time."

—*Dwell in Possibility Books*

"I was spellbound. Webb's novel had me hooked from the get-go, and I would not put it down until I had finished the last page."

—*A Bookish Way of Life*

"Webb has crafted a modern take on a classic genre—the Gothic ghost story. Family secrets, haunted houses, family curses with a little witchcraft thrown in as well. Webb's plotting is intricate and keeps us guessing with many red herrings and switchbacks on the way."

—*A Bookworm's World*

"Filled with multiple plot lines including a budding romance, family secrets, and a hint of the supernatural, it is hard to put this book down once you start reading. The ending to this tale almost leaves you to think there might be a sequel . . . and I would love that!"

—*Always With a Book*

"*The Fate of Mercy Alban* is a chilling, good read! This book just might make you glad you don't live in an old, haunted mansion."

—*Cheryl's Book Nook*

The Tale of Halcyon Crane

Minnesota Book Award, 2011, and Indie Next Pick

"Webb offers an engaging modern gothic tale with a strong female protagonist and well-done suspense. Fans of Mary Higgins Clark and Barbara Michaels and readers who like supernatural elements in their fiction will enjoy this debut."

—*Library Journal*

"Debut novelist Wendy Webb gives both Bram Stoker and Stephen King a run for their travel budget, inventing an island in the Great Lakes that can't be matched for pristine natural beauty, richness of history, touristic amenities . . . and sheer supernatural terror . . . The novel . . . gives a more generous account of how the spirit of a beautiful place can complexly affect a human being, for both good and ill. Wendy Webb is a professional journalist, first and foremost. Like those journalistic masters Dickens and Twain before her, she knows that to write good travel prose, you must give a vivid account of both the demons you find along the way and the demons you bring along with you."

—Michael Alec Rose, *BookPage*

"This thrilling, modern ghost story will keep you reading straight through to the surprising end!"

—Midwest Booksellers Association

"Entertaining to say the least. Sensational . . . Webb's page-turner is a guilty pleasure best suited for a lakeside cabin's bed stand."

—Megan Doll, Minneapolis *Star Tribune*

"Booksellers are loving *Halcyon Crane*, which has been selected by three Independent Booksellers' associations—national and Midwestern—as worthy of special promotion . . . Webb includes all the classic ghostly elements in her novel, but she gives the book a contemporary spin with a strong female protagonist."

—Mary Ann Grossman, *St. Paul Pioneer Press*

"This is what reading is supposed to be like: A story that comes across so well, so seamlessly that it is like a brain movie that reminds you of the first books that kidnapped your attention. Webb has crazy chops as a storyteller, and plays this one exactly right. And there are scenes that are so, so visual that it is like someone is reading the book to you while you lie there with your eyes closed. This is one of my favorites this year."

—*Minnesota Reads*

"Although not usually a fan of ghost stories, I immensely enjoyed *The Tale of Halcyon Crane*. With intriguing characters, a vivid setting, and gripping storytelling, this novel contains the ideal blend of sinister and charm."

—*CityView, Iowa's Independent Weekly*

"I love a good, spooky ghost story that carries you deep into the darkest night and raises goose bumps and neck hair. First-time novelist Wendy Webb's book, *The Tale of Halcyon Crane*, does all those things with the seamless intricacy of a clockmaker and the silky smoothness of a baby's cheek. Webb hits every note just right. It's hard to read a story like this and not compare the author to Stephen King, so I'm not going to do much of that, other than to say Webb carries a lot of the same power in her words."

—*Seattle Post-Intelligencer*

"*The Tale of Halcyon Crane* is a wonderful gothic complete with ghosts and witches, graveyards and dreams. It whisks the reader up and into its magic from the first page. Captivating and haunting, this debut proves Wendy Webb is a very gifted storyteller."

—MJ Rose, *New York Times* bestselling author

"Wendy Webb immediately captured my attention with her amazingly descriptive language. I could envision exactly what Hallie was seeing, experiencing, and even feeling. The description of the fog and the affect it had on Hallie was simply chilling and set the tone for the whole story to come."

—*Library Girl Reads*

"*The Tale of Halcyon Crane* throbs with the threat of menace; this is an atmospheric, gothic story reminiscent of *Turn of the Screw* and had me racing to the finish late into the night to find out what happens next. Read this book."

—*Misfit Salon*

"Wendy Webb has created a wonderful gothic mystery in this novel, full of secrets and betrayals. It's definitely creepy—this is not a book I would want to read late at night, during a thunderstorm. I found it to be deliciously haunting with incredible atmosphere. I thoroughly enjoyed the process of reading this book, of watching this meticulously crafted tale unfold. I had to battle dueling impulses while reading—part of me wanted to rush through it, to get to the end, while the other wanted to savor every carefully drawn word. This is a book that you'll really want to experience. I'm very sad that it's over, and that Webb doesn't have an extensive gothic mystery backlist I can immediately devour. All I can say is I'll be watching Wendy Webb's future career with a lot of interest."

—S. Krishna's Books

DAUGHTERS OF THE LAKE

OTHER BOOKS BY WENDY WEBB

DAUGHTERS

OF THE

LAKE

WENDY WEBB

LAKE UNION
PUBLISHING

Text copyright © 2018 by Wendy Webb
All rights reserved.

No part of this book may be reproduced, or stored in a retrieval system, or transmitted in any form or by any means, electronic, mechanical, photocopying, recording, or otherwise, without express written permission of the publisher.

Published by Lake Union Publishing, Seattle

www.apub.com

Amazon, the Amazon logo, and Lake Union Publishing are trademarks of Amazon.com, Inc., or its affiliates.

ISBN-13: 9781503900820 (hardcover)
ISBN-10: 1503900827 (hardcover)
ISBN-13: 9781503901339 (paperback)
ISBN-10: 1503901335 (paperback)

Cover design by Damon Freeman

Printed in the United States of America

First edition

To Ben, my son, moon, and stars.

CHAPTER ONE

It was finally time for the lake to give her up. And so, one morning in late summer, her body washed gently into the shallows, as though it, *she*, had simply been floating in a peaceful, watery slumber. She was wearing a white gown, a long, billowing, delicate thing still tied with a bow at the neck, the sort of garment one might imagine wealthy women of the past wearing to bed. A tangle of auburn hair cascaded around her face. She was smiling slightly, and her startling violet-colored eyes were open just a bit, as if awakening from a dream. One arm was concealed beneath the folds of her gown. The other stretched out onto the beach, her hand grasping at the sand as if she were trying to pull herself ashore.

Her appearance was all the more remarkable since she had died nearly a century earlier.

No one who was alive when her body floated onto shore that morning knew anything about her, with the single exception of Kate Granger, who, by no coincidence whatsoever, was in a house that overlooked the very beach where the body now rested.

This dead woman's loved ones were long dead themselves, their stories, and hers, as magical or as ordinary as they were, buried with them, disintegrating into the earth or the water, becoming a forgotten part of the landscape, just as this woman had been for the past one hundred years.

But some stories, especially peculiar, hidden ones involving murder and mystery, have a way of bubbling to the surface, especially when wrongs need to be righted. They make themselves heard despite efforts to keep them silent. All in the proper time. And now was the proper time.

At the moment the body washed ashore, Kate Granger was pouring the last of the pot of coffee into her mug before curling up with the crossword puzzle in the armchair that had been her favorite as a child. She was unaware her life was about to veer off in a very strange direction.

Her father, Fred, discovered the body. Fred had been walking this particular stretch of beach with his dog every morning for more years than he cared to admit. He gained a sense of peace during these jaunts, with the music of the water lapping at the shore. It was life giving to him in more ways than one.

He had found his share of items on this beach over the years, small things given up by the lake, blown into shore on the wind and the waves. There were the rocks, of course, stones that had been polished by the sand and the water until they shone like glass. They adorned the beach like seashells, gifts from this inland sea. Folks here wouldn't readily admit it, but most thought these small stones somehow carried the spirit of the lake within them. People picked them up and carried them in their pockets or set them on their dashboards, windowsills, and desks for luck.

Rocks weren't the only things Fred found during his walks. Even as a little boy, the lake would offer things up to him for his perusal, inspection, or enjoyment. One morning, after a particularly violent storm had reared up suddenly in the night, Fred found a piece of a lifeboat and knew that the lake had taken a ship with all its astonished hands to the bottom. Once, he found a canoe floating in the shallows, still containing a picnic lunch, two life jackets, and an unopened bottle of Jack Daniel's. He did some checking around but never learned who owned the canoe or what the lake had done with them, but he knew better than to open that bottle of Jack. Still, he had never found anything like this. Never a person.

That morning had begun like any other, with Fred and his German shepherd, Sadie, descending the long, wooden stairway from his deck to the beach. Instead of running down the shoreline as she usually did, Sadie had just stood still. Tail down, head lowered, she'd stared out across the lake and growled deep in her throat, as though the lake's very presence was menacing. Fred had called to her, "Sadie! Let's go, girl!" But she wouldn't move.

He had taken a moment to scan the horizon in the direction of Sadie's gaze, and sure enough, he saw something floating there, but at such a distance, he couldn't tell what it was. A piece of driftwood? An overturned kayak? As he'd watched it float closer to shore, Fred had begun to feel a knot in the pit of his stomach. That was no kayak.

He'd squinted into the sun as he'd reached into his back pocket for the cell phone that his wife insisted he carry on these walks and dialed Johnny's number at the station.

"I don't know for sure, John, but I think I'm looking at a body out in the lake," he had said.

With the sheriff and an ambulance on the way, Fred had kicked off his shoes and, despite Sadie's protests, begun wading into the frigid water. There was an outside chance this person was still alive. He should help. But as he'd moved closer, Fred could see that he was looking at something inanimate, already beyond rescue. Fred had stood ankle deep in the water and watched as she had floated to shore, his dog barking in warning. The sheriff had arrived a few moments later.

"What've we got here . . . ?" Johnny began, but his words stopped short. He wasn't a praying man, but at that moment, his years of Catholic school kicked in and he crossed himself. Neither man spoke.

Johnny had been county sheriff for going on twenty-five years and was no stranger to a crime scene, and yet he just stood there, openmouthed, struck mute by the sight of the dead woman before him. He had seen a body or two in his time, but nothing quite like this. Maybe it was the perfection of her skin or the position in which she was lying, one hand grasping at the sand like that. Maybe it was the expression on her face. She just didn't look dead, Johnny thought. Vision shone from those lifeless eyes . . . or did it?

His thoughts were hazy and random, and highly inappropriate for a crime scene. Johnny Stratton was thinking about true love. He went from the dead woman's expression to his ex-wife's sadly familiar morning sneer and then, more pleasantly, to Mary Carlson, his first love, a sweet-smelling, good-natured redhead he hadn't seen since high school. Johnny remembered the feel of her thigh pressed against his as they drove around town in his dad's old Camaro, the softness of her small hand as their fingers intertwined, her apple-scented perfume. He wondered, as he stood there on the lakeshore looking at this dead body, whatever had become of Mary. And then he shook off those thoughts. He was at a crime scene, for goodness' sake.

Fred was similarly mesmerized. He was also thinking about his true love, the woman who was, no doubt, doing the breakfast dishes at that moment—his wife of forty-five years, Beverly. He was glad she wasn't down on the beach to see this.

Kate broke their reverie.

She was hurrying down the staircase toward the beach. "Dad?" she called out. Her voice startled the two men; they snapped their heads in her direction. "Dad? I heard Sadie barking, so I came to see if you were . . ." Her words, too, trailed off as she drew closer. Kate took one look at the lifeless face of the woman on the beach and fell to her knees, hands muffling a scream that had no sound.

"It's okay, honey." Fred hurried to her side and put an arm around his daughter. "Johnny's calling the coroner right now. Right, John? Come on, now. Let's go back up to the house and let the sheriff do his job."

"No!" Kate screamed in a whisper. She threw off her father's embrace, and before either man could stop her, she lunged toward the woman on the beach and began tearing at her dress. As Johnny and Fred were pulling Kate away from the body, the three of them stopped yet again.

"Holy Christ," Johnny whispered.

Kate's wail finally found its voice and pierced the morning calm with a sound so fierce that all the animals within earshot fell silent to listen. There, nestled in the folds of the dead woman's gown, was a baby. The tiny body was serene and still, as though it were sleeping, cradled in its mother's arms.

CHAPTER TWO

Great Bay, 1889

The morning Addie Cassatt was born, the fog so shrouded the trees, the houses, and the lakeshore itself that her mother, Marie, didn't dare make the trip to the doctor's office alone. It wasn't far into town—the Cassatts lived less than a mile from the main street—but that morning, Marie couldn't see beyond her own front doorstep. She stared into the dense, white blanket and wasn't sure what, exactly, to do. Her nearest neighbor's house had disappeared into the fog, and Marie's husband was out on the lake fishing, despite the weather and Marie's delicate condition. There was no one to help her into town or to summon the doctor to come to her. She was alone in the house and, it seemed to Marie, alone in the world. But the puddle of water at her feet told her that, one way or another, she wouldn't be alone for long. The baby was on its way.

Marie's husband, Marcus, and his brother, Gene, were sons and grandsons of men who had fished in these waters since before anyone could remember, and a little fog (let alone a very pregnant Marie) wasn't about to prevent them from a day's work. Most of the other fishermen in town thought the Cassatts were fools to go out on a day such as this one. But Marcus and Gene knew the fish liked the velvety fog. The brothers had, more than once, seen schools of them poking their faces above the surface on foggy mornings, just to get a taste of it.

None of that mattered to Marie as she lay down alone in her bed, tossing and turning from the pain that signaled the coming of her first child. Town wasn't so far away, she kept telling herself as each contraction eased. She walked that dirt road every day with the dogs and knew every dip and turn intimately. Surely she could get there on her own now. Or at least manage to make it to a neighbor's house, at least that. *Come on, now, Marie, it's just a little fog,* she thought. *Get up. Get help. This child is on its way.*

She tried to rise from her bed, but the pain intensified. She groaned as she laid her head back down onto her pillow. Marie began to swim in a strange sense of vagueness as her body became the river that her baby would cross between another world and this one.

Her thoughts weren't her own. She could see only blinding white outside her bedside window. She couldn't be sure the school, the grocer, the post office, or any of the town buildings hadn't been literally swallowed up. Was anything there? Did the world still exist? Marie was terrified of that white, dense, living thing. She believed that, if she ventured outside, it would turn her around and force her into the thick woods beyond town, and she would be wandering, lost, when the baby came. The fact that Polar and Lucy were barking into the whiteness in the backyard, down toward the lake, further unsettled her.

Help me, Mother was the last rational thought that went through her mind before the contractions took over her body.

Just down the shoreline, Marie's neighbor, Ruby Thompson, was twisting her apron into knots. She knew that fool Marcus had gone out on the lake, leaving his wife alone on such a day, with the baby so near. Fog or no fog, she was going to make sure Marie was all right.

She wrapped up one of the pies she had baked that morning and walked out into the whiteness to the long row of pines that stood between their two houses. She touched each one, inching along blindly

7

until another tree materialized before her. Being out there, enveloped by the fog, reminded Ruby of one childhood winter day when she had been caught outside during a blizzard. Several people in her tiny community had died that day, taken by the sudden storm. Young Ruby had been walking home from school when the snow began to come down, and just like today, she had crept along from tree to tree to find her way. Now, she felt a chill just thinking about that day. It wasn't so different from this one. She shuddered with relief when she finally reached the Cassatt home.

Ruby stood knocking at Marie's front door. Why wasn't she answering? *Lord,* thought Ruby, *she might be having that baby right now.* Ruby tried the door and, finding it open, walked inside.

"Marie!" she called, but there was no reply. *Where is she? Where are those damned dogs?* Ruby began searching the house, becoming more and more frantic with every empty room. Something was not right. When Ruby found the kitchen door open to the backyard, she flew through it, heedless of the blinding fog. Ruby knew her way from this kitchen down to the lakeshore and could walk it blindly, if necessary. It was necessary now.

Ruby hurried down the path, stumbling on tree roots and stones— *Why didn't Marcus properly clear this path, the lazy sod*—until she reached the lakeshore. She could see only a few inches in front of her. Which way to go? She turned to the left and began running down the shoreline, calling her friend's name.

It wasn't long before Marie floated out of the fog, almost at Ruby's feet. She was lying in the shallow water, unconscious or asleep or dead, her dress entangled around her legs. There was no sign of the baby.

Ruby's shrieks brought everyone in earshot running. Her husband, Thomas, first; then came Otto and Betsy Lund. By the time the men had carried Marie back up to the house, allowed Ruby to get her into a dry nightgown, and laid her on the bed, she had awakened from whatever it was that had entranced her.

"Where have you taken her?" Marie cried in her delirium. "Where is my baby?"

Nobody asked why she had gone to the lakeshore. Nobody said anything at all other than, "You rest now, Marie," and, "You've been through quite an ordeal," and, "There, there, now."

But words such as these cannot comfort a grieving mother. Marie's eyes darted this way and that as she tried to rise from her bed again and again. "My baby," she kept repeating. Ruby took her husband by the arm and ushered him outside.

"Look in the backyard, in the lake, anywhere you can," she whispered. "That baby's out there somewhere. Don't let the wolves get it." *It needs a good Christian burial,* she thought, but didn't voice it aloud. *Where is that doctor? He'll have something to give Marie to quiet her cries.*

Young Jess Stewart didn't tell his parents, or anyone else, that something had called him down to the lakeshore that morning as clearly as if it had spoken his name.

He was lying under his bed, staging a battle with the wooden soldiers he had received from his uncle for his fifth birthday, when he heard a noise he had never heard before. He poked his head out from behind the blanket to listen. It sounded like singing, but there were no words. And no tune, really, not like the other songs Jess knew. This was something else. Jess thought it was the most beautiful music he had ever heard. He laid his head on the cool floor, closed his eyes, and let the music wash over him.

The sound floated into and out of his ears, creating a tapestry of thoughts inside his head. He imagined being out on the lake in a rowboat with a beautiful woman. She wasn't his mother, but she had long hair like his mother's, and she looked so kind and loving that he wanted nothing more than to crawl into her lap and go to sleep, the way he had when he was a baby. But he was a big boy now, beyond such babyish things. He opened his eyes, left the soldiers in the middle of their battle, and crept to the window. Maybe he could see something. He just had to know what was making this music.

But he didn't see anything out of the ordinary. Just the fog. He couldn't quite tell where the singing was coming from, but it sounded to Jess as though it was somewhere by the lake. What was it? Who was it?

He crept to the back door, put on his jacket, and stole down the hill toward the lake. He didn't tell his mother where he was going. He knew she wouldn't let him outside in the fog, and he had some serious investigating to do out there. As he got closer to the lake, Jess found that the fog wasn't so heavy as it was by the house. He could see a few feet in front of him, but only in the direction of the water.

Jess stood and stared awhile, trying to see something, anything. Just then, a dark figure popped its head out of the water. It looked a bit like a beaver or an otter, but much larger. Did it have horns? Jess wasn't certain. He squinted and looked closer. Yes, he thought it might. Were those humps or spikes on its back? Jess was enthralled. He had never seen anything like it. Was this a sea monster?

Whatever it was, it was staring in his direction, beckoning him closer. He inched toward it, wanting a better look. They locked eyes. It was a defining moment in the life of this young boy, something he'd never forget. It was a moment that, when he was much, much older, he would often talk about with friends over too many drinks in the local tavern, only to be the subject of their good-natured jokes and mocking. But all their ribbing couldn't convince Jess he was the fool. He knew what he had seen that day. Throughout his youth, he would sit there by the lake often, calling to this strange creature. But it never returned. The memory of it haunted him all his life, its strange song ringing in his ears in the dead of night, when he'd awaken from a dream.

As a young man, Jess would pore through books about the animals of this region, looking for information about the kinds of creatures that inhabited these shores. But in all those stories and in all those illustrations, he never found any hint of recognition, nothing that reminded him of what he had seen that day. It was as though this strange creature did not exist at all.

If he had only noticed the ancient pictographs that decorated the caves dotting the shoreline just beyond his boyhood home, Jess would have found a drawing of the very creature he had seen that day. Others had seen it, long ago. That might have led Jess to further exploration of the legends and lore of the region in which he lived. He would have found a story about an ancient, magical creature that existed in these waters, a fearsome spirit that was well known to the ancient peoples there. It was said that this creature was the embodiment of the lake itself, rendering its waters capable of saving or taking the lives of those who ventured on and around it—at its own whim. Legend had it that this creature could take human form at will. Back then, the locals knew the lake played favorites, calming rough waters whenever certain people came near, kicking up sudden storms to capsize the ships of others. They so respected and feared the power of this creature and the lake itself that, before setting out into their canoes, they would first offer gifts of appeasement, hoping to please it into granting them a safe journey.

Of course, modern-day folk weren't given to such superstitions. They had a way of forgetting the past, so intent were they on the future. Legends and lore became nothing more than stories that might entertain guests sitting around the fireplace after a nice dinner. The old beliefs faded as the modern age dawned, but the spirits that inspired those legends remained, kept doing their important work, waiting for someone to believe again.

But for now, on that foggy day, young Jess Stewart stood on the shore, watching as this strange animal opened its mouth and sang. Something made Jess turn around just then, and that's when he saw the dogs. Polar and Lucy, the Cassatts' two Alaskan malamutes. They were staring out into the water, watching something. It was Addie, but he didn't know her name then. What he saw was a baby floating in the shallow water between two big rocks. When he turned back around, the strange animal was gone. The singing was silent. All that remained was a baby floating in the water.

Jess called for his parents, knowing this was much more than a five-year-old should handle alone. "Mama! Papa! Come quick!"

Phil Stewart poked his head out of the back door. Unlike that daft Marcus, he was home that day, like any sensible fisherman would be. "Jess! Get back inside the house!" his father called.

"But there's a baby . . ."

"Get in here, I said!"

Jess heard the door slam shut. Of course they didn't believe him about the baby. Parents never believed children when they had something important to say. So he scrambled back up the hill to the house to try again.

"There is a baby in the lake." He began crying with the urgency of it all. That got his parents' attention, just as he knew it would.

"What do you mean, dear? What kind of baby?" His mother, Jennie, put down her needlepoint and looked her son in the eye.

"A human baby," Jess cried, gesturing wildly toward the lakeshore. "You need to come *right now*."

Jennie and Phil exchanged concerned glances. A human baby?

Phil shook his head and was settling back down with his newspaper, but Jennie knew Marie Cassatt was heavy with child. When that thought overtook her, Jennie's entire body was filled with the sort of vibrating, humming dread that descends when someone has arrived with very bad news but hasn't yet said anything. She shot up from her kitchen chair so fast that it fell to the floor. She flew out the door and down to the lake, her husband and son following close behind.

Neither Jennie nor Phil really expected to find a baby alive in the water, let alone floating calmly with one hand in its mouth. But Jess knew that was exactly how she would be, because that was how he left her.

"I'll be damned," Phil said.

"Run," Jennie told her son as she scooped the baby out of the water and wrapped the tiny thing in her shawl. "Run down the shoreline to the Cassatts'. Tell them we're coming."

Jennie wasn't certain this baby was Marie's, but it was a pretty good bet. She also didn't know how or why the baby had wound up in the lake. Had Marie tried to drown her? That didn't seem possible. She knew how excited the Cassatts were about the birth of their first child. Was Marie herself hurt?

Phil fumbled with his pocketknife as he cut the baby's umbilical cord, and Jennie tied it off as the placenta floated away. Then the pair hurried through the fog down the lakeshore toward the Cassatt home.

When they reached the house, Phil pushed open the door, making way for Jennie, who held the baby in her arms. They were greeted with a chorus of gasps from the neighbors still congregated there, hovering around Marie.

"You folks aren't going to believe this," Phil said, with more caring in his voice than anyone had ever heard from him. Marie sat up straight in her bed, wide eyed, silent, not daring to breathe, as Jennie laid the baby in her arms.

Phil sat down on a straight-backed chair, shaking his head. "The baby was floating in the lake near our place. It was Jess here who found her. When he called out to us that a baby was down by the beach, Jennie and I thought he was just talking crazy. But he made such a fuss about it, we went to see what it was. It was a baby, all right. Clean as a whistle, happy as a clam, floating in the water as if she had been born there, which, I reckon, she was."

The neighbors were rapt, but Marie was barely paying attention to Phil's tale. She was staring into her baby's violet eyes and thanking the lake for saving her child's life. She should have known that's where her daughter would be.

Jess Stewart was standing behind his mother, grateful that the lake, or the strange creature in it, had given this baby to him. That's the way his five-year-old mind interpreted the events of the day. He had been called down to the lakeshore in the fog to receive a gift; it was that simple. He had been chosen to save her, and the way he saw it, she was his responsibility now. He didn't tell his parents, or hers, about this. They didn't need to know.

Over the next few years, Jess watched as baby Adelaide, or Addie, as everyone called her, grew. He watched as her mother pushed her into town in the baby buggy. He watched as those dogs, Polar and Lucy, pulled her around on a sled in the winter. He watched Addie take her first steps. He watched as she played in her backyard while he was walking to school. By that time, she was watching him, too.

CHAPTER THREE

Kate opened her eyes and found herself in a bedroom. Crisp morning light streamed in through a six-paned window that was open just a bit, half-covered by a white lace curtain. Kate watched from her bed as the curtain began to billow in the breeze, slowly, delicately. She was mesmerized by the way it was dancing and swaying, lifted here and there by the wind.

Her eyes drifted around the room. A dark dressing table with a bench, two drawers on each side and a rounded mirror above it. A silver hairbrush and hand mirror on the vanity. *I've always wanted a silver hairbrush,* she thought.

Kate wanted to walk to the mirror and gaze into the glass, but she couldn't. Something held her back. Instead, she snuggled deep beneath the quilts, one red, the other a feathery white. Kate felt an utter contentment that she had not recently known, if ever. *This feels good.*

The room was mostly white. Wooden walls painted white, a white ceiling. Dark-wood floors with wide planks. A colorful area rug that looked as though it was braided from old rags. A small bedside table was next to her, and on it was a collection of small rocks, a slim hardcover book, a pitcher of water, and a glass.

The smell of lilacs surrounded her.

"How is my beautiful wife this morning?" The sound of a man's voice, a voice she had never heard but somehow knew intimately, broke Kate's meditation.

Looking up, she saw a figure standing in the doorway. He was holding a large vase filled with purple and white lilacs, Kate's favorite flower. So fragrant, so delicate, so fleeting.

The man was tall, with dark hair and eyes. *Oh my goodness, he's handsome.* She had never seen his face, but somehow he was most familiar. In one glance, she saw a small boy, a teen, a young adult, and a grown man—all the faces of this man's various ages were there, in one moment, as though she had known him his entire life.

"Your wife is happy to open her eyes and see her handsome husband," a voice said, and Kate realized it was she who was speaking. But it was not her voice. And she hadn't intended to say anything of the kind.

What's happening? Kate thought, somewhere deep inside, somewhere almost unreachable. *Where am I? Where is Kate? Am I still here?* She had the sense of losing herself, falling deeply into the soul of another, all the while smiling at this man.

"Look what's in bloom." He smiled back at her, holding out the vase. He set it on the vanity and slipped into bed alongside Kate.

She felt him next to her. His scent . . . Ivory soap?

"I thought I'd pick some flowers for my wife on this fine morning," he murmured quietly. *Wife?* The word stung Kate's ear. "I love you. I love you so much, my darling girl."

"That's a handy thing." Kate heard her own delighted laughter. "Considering how much I love you, it wouldn't do to have you anything but besotted."

He rolled onto his side and propped his head up on one arm. His face was extraordinarily beautiful. Dark with light behind the eyes.

Oh, I could get used to this, Kate thought.

"What will we do today, then?" he asked her. "The morning is fast disappearing while my lazy girl sleeps. We have a whole Saturday with nothing before us. Care for a boat ride?"

"Perhaps later." Kate smiled. "Now, I'd like to just lie here for a few more minutes with a man who came bearing flowers."

"Always the sensible girl," he said, wrapping his arms around her.

She closed her eyes, buried her face in his neck, and was suddenly overwhelmed with a love the likes of which she had never felt.

Inside of herself, deep in a place that Kate could barely reach, she was crying. It was never like this with anyone, not even with Kevin, not even in the beginning. She had never felt this feeling of love, the one she had in her dream. *This is what true peace feels like,* she thought. *This is what it is to be where one's soul resides.*

Kate opened her eyes and found herself alone in the white room. She got out of bed and walked to the mirror. A strange reflection stared back at her, another woman's face, yet it was somehow familiar. She ran a hand through a long mane of deep-auburn hair, tangled and wild from sleep. She looked into the violet eyes and touched the ribbon on the collar of her white dressing gown. Where had she seen it before?

Kate's eyes shot open and she sat up in bed. Not the same dream again. It had been recurring for three weeks, since the night of her birthday.

She didn't want to think about that night right now. Instead she stretched and glanced out the window, noticing that the sun was high in the sky. *Midday? What am I still doing in bed?* As she swam toward full consciousness, the realization hit her: The body on the beach. *I've been dreaming about a dead woman who has just washed up on the beach of my parents' house.*

Kate closed her eyes and shuddered, burying her own face in the pillows as though she was a child again, when the simple act of shutting her eyes could block out the most painful of events. Then she heard voices in the kitchen: her parents, Fred and Beverly, and Johnny Stratton.

She slipped a sweatshirt over her head and padded down the hallway into the kitchen, squinting in the bright light of day.

"Well, there's my Katie," Fred chirped as Kate took a seat at the table.

"What in the world happened?" Kate coughed into her sleeve.

"Honey, you fainted on the beach back there," Fred told her.

"But I just woke up in bed," Kate said, frowning. "How . . . ?"

"Johnny and I got you up to the house."

"Up all those rickety stairs?" Kate's hands flew to her mouth.

"Aw, you're not too heavy for this old man." Fred smiled.

"Especially when it's me who does most of the carrying," Johnny said.

Chuckles all around. It seemed to Kate that everyone was in extraordinarily good spirits, considering the fact that they had just found a dead body. Two dead bodies. But an uncomfortable silence fell among them, and Kate knew the liveliness was just for show.

"I was out all of this time?" Kate asked, searching her mind for a memory that would not materialize.

Johnny and Fred shot each other a look. "You were sort of, well, delirious, you might say, when we got you back into the house," Fred said. "Mumbling all sorts of crazy things. Your mother thought bed was the best place for you."

"How long ago was that?" Kate asked, looking at the stovetop clock.

"An hour or so," Johnny said, clearing his throat.

"And you're still here?" Kate asked.

"Honey," Beverly said, pouring Kate a cup of coffee, "Johnny's going to have to ask you a few questions about the *discovery* down on the beach this morning."

Kate took a long sip, careful to steady her shaking hands. "What kinds of questions?"

"You seemed to recognize her, is all," Johnny said slowly. "Well, that's not quite all. You seemed to know the baby was there. Neither of us had seen it, until you pulled her dress away."

Johnny waited for Kate's response to the question he didn't pose. She looked at him, and then from one parent to the other, but said nothing.

"Do you know any more about this, Katie?" Johnny asked, finally. "Are you mixed up in this thing in any way?" Johnny scratched his head and fidgeted in his chair.

Kate looked around the room at these faces she'd known all her life. They knew, just like everyone in town knew, she'd been having a rough time of it lately. She had moved back into her parents' house because Kevin, her husband of five years, had had an affair. With a much younger woman in the newspaper office where they all worked. The cliché of it would have been enough to make Kate gag if the devastation of it all hadn't imploded her world.

She had left Kevin and their house and everything in it—except her beloved Alaskan malamute—and come home to regroup and get her life back together. The whole sordid mess was common knowledge. Nobody had escaped hearing about—or just plain hearing—the loud confrontation between Kevin, Kate, and Valerie—the other woman—at the Jackpine Tavern on the night of Kate's birthday. A thing like that kept the gossip mill running for months in a small town.

What had Johnny just asked her? "I'm sorry, John. What?"

"I asked what you knew about this, Kate, if anything," Johnny said, and the gentleness in his voice was enough to break her heart.

What could she say? She couldn't very well tell the sheriff that she had been dreaming about the woman who had washed up on the beach—she'd sound like a lunatic. And she was certainly not going to talk about what had really happened out on the beach, that she had looked at the dead woman and seen herself lying there. It was as though she had stumbled across her own dead body on the beach, and more horrifying than that, her baby's.

She wasn't going to tell them she nearly died of grief at seeing the baby's sweet face, so silent, so lifeless. Had she not fainted, she surely would've snatched the baby out of the dead woman's arms and held it close to her chest, the way a mother would. No, it was better not to tell anyone about that.

But she had to say something. The three of them sat there, looking at her, waiting. Kate opened her mouth to speak and then closed it again.

"I'm going to lay this right on the table for you folks," Johnny said. "Traffic tickets, DUI arrests, minor offenses—those are the kinds of things I can make go away. But something like this? A woman and her baby, dead?"

"Now, John, you're not insinuating Katie's involved in this," Beverly broke in, much to Kate's relief.

Now she had a minute to think. This was insane, all of it. How could she explain what she had done on the beach, that she had been grasping for the baby when she shouldn't have known—didn't know—there *was* a baby?

"I'm not insinuating anything," Johnny said, watching Kate intently. "It's just, the way you went after her like that. We had to drag you off her, before you fainted. My people are going to be investigating this thing, Katie. Better that I know now if there's anything more to know. I'm on your side, here, honey. If you are involved in this in any way, if you know this woman or have ever seen her before, you need to tell me now."

Johnny went on, "Just so that we're clear. You are not making a statement here. We're just old friends talking over coffee at the kitchen table. Nothing you say right now can or will be used against you. But if you know anything, *anything*, tell me now. I do not want to find out about it days or weeks down the road. If you'd like to call a lawyer, though, we can do this by the book."

Kate finally found her voice. "I don't need a lawyer. If I could be of any help to you, I would. But I really don't know anything more than what I saw, what we all saw. I was in the house doing the crossword puzzle. I heard Sadie barking. I knew Dad had taken her with him that morning, and I got worried. Sadie doesn't bark like that for no reason. So I went down to the beach to see if he was okay."

Fred smiled at his daughter.

"And that's the first time you saw the body?" John led her.

"Yes, that's the first time I saw the body," Kate stumbled over her words. "I'd never seen the woman before." The lie stung on her lips.

"And the baby?" Johnny took a sip of his coffee.

"I can't explain that," Kate said, shaking her head. "It was something about the way the woman's arm was hidden under the folds of her dress. I saw . . . I noticed . . . I don't know. A lump or something. I was really upset by the sight of her and I had this feeling. I guess you'd call it intuition. My instincts took over. I had the feeling something else—someone else—was there. I can't explain how or why."

It was mostly the truth. She looked around at the three concerned faces, all nodding.

"That's really all there was to it," she concluded.

Johnny put down his coffee cup with a sense of finality. "I'm going to leave it at that for now," he said to Kate. "But I've got a dead woman and her baby on their way to the morgue, and it's my job to find out who they are and what happened to them. Just so you know, I am going to need to get a formal statement from both of you, Kate and Fred, but we don't need to do that now. You've all been through quite an ordeal today."

"Thanks, John." Fred patted his old friend on the back. *Such are the perks of raising a family in the small town where you, your parents, and your grandparents were raised,* he thought.

Fred and Johnny had grown up together, played on the same Little League baseball teams, vied for the same girls in high school. If they'd lived in another place, a bigger city, Kate certainly would have been hauled to the police station and questioned because of her peculiar behavior on the beach that morning. That's all she'd need.

"All right, then. I've got to get back down to the station to see if they've ID'd her," Johnny said. "I don't recall any missing persons reports about a woman and a baby from around these parts, but we don't know where this lady might have come from."

Kate's mother reached across the table and squeezed her daughter's hand.

"And Kate"—Johnny turned to her as he was on his way out the door—"this goes without saying, but don't leave town."

"Am I in trouble here?" Kate asked him, standing up. "I mean, seriously, John. This is crazy. I faint at the sight of a dead body, and now I can't leave town?"

"You're not in trouble," he said to her. "But we are going to need to get your statement sooner rather than later. You leaving town isn't going to look good to those who do the looking."

"But I was planning to go to Wharton for a few days," she said, referring to a small tourist town some fifty miles down the shoreline. "Can I still do that?"

"Taking your cell phone?" Johnny asked her. Kate nodded. "Then, okay. As long as I know where you'll be."

Kate pushed her chair away from the table, said goodbye to the sheriff, and walked out onto the deck, her giant malamute, Alaska, at her heels.

"Come on, Lassie girl," she called to the dog. "Let's go for a walk."

They headed down the staircase toward the beach. *Put it behind you. It's over.* She stopped and stared at the spot where they had found the body, remembering the sight of the woman's hand grasping at the shore. Her slight smile. The baby. Alaska howled and scratched at the wet sand, digging in deep and pulling Kate away, down the beach, toward different things.

As he drove back to the station, Johnny Stratton felt his heart pounding in his chest. By all rights, Kate Granger should've been sitting in the back seat of his squad car. If it had been any other person, any other family, the scene on the beach would've been probable cause to hold her for questioning, at the very least. Johnny shook his head. He knew too much. He knew that Kate had recently left her husband because of his infidelity. That news was all over town. And he knew, from her father's own mouth, how distracted and upset and distant Kate had been these past few weeks.

And now these bodies—a beautiful young woman and what looked to be a newborn. Johnny could barely formulate the thoughts that were simmering on the edges of his mind. Not Katie Granger. He had been at her baptism. Her first communion. Her wedding. He had known her father all his life. Was there any possibility that she was mixed up in this ugly scene? The very thought of it produced a bitter taste in Johnny's mouth. Like blood.

He dialed his cell phone. "Pick up Kevin Bradford. I want to see if that bastard can ID these bodies. No, I won't take his word for it. I want a polygraph. And I want a sample of his DNA to check against the baby's. I don't care, Howard. I want him to submit to it all voluntarily. No warrant, no lawyers, no nothing. Do you hear me?"

Johnny turned his phone off and threw it across the car seat. He wasn't going to waste any time finding out whether or not his best friend's daughter had anything to do with this.

CHAPTER FOUR

As Johnny was questioning Kate's soon-to-be-ex-husband, Kate was setting her rowing shell in the water and climbing into the delicate boat, taking care not to step through its paper-thin bottom. She had tried running for a time in the midst of her problems with Kevin in an effort to shave off the twenty-some pounds she had put on since their wedding, as though a newly svelte body might help things. But running only felt good when she stopped. With rowing, Kate felt just the opposite. Every stroke, every push felt fantastic. She couldn't get enough of skimming atop the water's glassy surface, stroking, pushing, pulling her way along. Sometimes she spent two or three hours out on the secluded bay, until her body simply couldn't take any more. The act of rowing gave Kate a feeling of power and control that she had never known. Not to mention it took care of those twenty pounds.

It was also a way to commune with the lake, alone in a small boat low on the water. Kate loved being so near to it. Kayaking gave her the same feel, the closeness to the lake, but for Kate, kayaking was hard work. Rowing was a meditation, by necessity. Thoughts couldn't wander to the latest celebrity gossip or to a song played over and over in your head or to an especially cruel word from your beloved as he walked out the door. While rowing, Kate's mind needed to stay focused on the motion of it or she'd end up face first in the water. The hypnotic rhythm—pull, skim, push—over and over again, cleared the random thoughts from her mind and lulled her into a sense of peace. She needed it today.

She slipped her bare feet into the shoes that were bolted onto the push board, put her oars in the water, and used one of them to ease herself away from the dock.

Legs bent, arms extended, oars as far back in the water as she could reach, the blades were ready to slice into the water at a perfect angle. Kate sat there motionless for a time, feeling the boat bob and sway, breathing in time with the water's heartbeat. When she and the lake were breathing as one, she found her center, her perfect balance. Kate pushed off hard with her legs, pulling the oars to her chest at the same time, then, skimming the flat blades against the water's surface, back to their ready position. And again, and again. The rhythm of it, the sameness of the movement, the communion with the lake hypnotized her.

Kate's memories of the morning's events were skimming away along the surface of the water. She felt less panicked now, safer here on the water, as she always did. She noticed a deer making its way to the shoreline for a drink. Kate hoped she wouldn't startle it too much as she passed. It didn't seem to notice her. Kate always saw wildlife when she rowed; it was one of the things she loved best about the sport. When she reached the end of the bay, where the water streamed into the vastness of the lake, she stopped for a moment to catch her breath before turning the boat around with the awkward circular oar motion that always reminded Kate of the legs of a crab that has been caught on its back.

Kate pulled the oars toward her again, slowly and more methodically this time. She wasn't in a hurry to get back to the dock. She was enjoying being out here on the water on such a blue, bright day. But suddenly, inexplicably, the weather changed, as it often did on this lake. A mist began to rise out of the water, a delicate fog. It settled like a cloud just above the water's surface, giving the landscape an eerie feeling. A couple of mallards materialized out of the fog and floated toward Kate;

an island in the distance seemed to be hovering just inches above the water's surface.

She looked down and, through the mist, stared into the water. She was caught by the sight of her own hazy, wispy reflection. Brown-haired, mousy Kate. As her oar glided over the surface of the water, Kate caught sight of something beneath, or thought she did. She skimmed to a stop. It was floating to the surface, rising like a diver out of the deep. A fish? Kate leaned over the side of the boat and squinted to get a better look. She took a quick breath in when she recognized that other woman's face, the dead woman's face, floating within her own reflection. Their two faces were entwined—Kate's eyes opened, the other woman's eyes closed. Kate stared as the two faces became one.

The eyes of the dead woman's reflection shot open, those intense, violet eyes staring directly at Kate, her mouth moving, as if trying to speak. The sight of it startled Kate so much that she lost her balance and capsized, gulping a mouthful of water as the lake came into contact with her own gasping face.

On the other side of town, Johnny Stratton was talking to the coroner, Janet Green.

"Drowning, then?" he asked.

Janet nodded. "But that's not all. She has several stab wounds in the back. My guess is that somebody stabbed her and threw her in the water, or she fell in shortly thereafter, before she was dead."

"Had she not gone in the water—"

"She'd have bled out without immediate care. There's no question about the fact that this lady was murdered. But I can tell you one thing."

"What's that?"

"She had recently given birth."

"And the baby?"

Janet sighed. Children were always the worst. It took months for their faces to fade from her memory. Sometimes much longer than that. "There's no water in the lungs," she said. "The baby didn't drown. And there's no obvious signs of trauma."

"The baby was born dead, then, or died shortly after?"

"It's inconclusive at this point," Janet said. "Although if you gave birth to a baby that didn't make it, why would you dress her? The baby had a nightgown on."

CHAPTER FIVE

Great Bay, 1894

Marie didn't explain to any of her neighbors why she had gone down to the lake to give birth that day. She thought it best not to tell folks about the strange music she had heard, how it had beckoned her to the shore. She certainly didn't tell anyone that the lake itself had called to her, saying that it alone could keep her baby safe in its watery embrace, protect her from the evil fog. *Fog will take your baby,* the lake seemed to say to Marie. *It will spirit her away, and she will be gone forever when the mist lifts and the sun shines on the shore once again.*

She didn't tell folks how she had heeded the lake's call and crept down to the water's edge or how she had waded into the water. It had felt warm and velvety, despite the coldness of the air. It was soothing to Marie, and so she had waded into the shallows, walking farther and farther still, until she was standing waist deep in the Great Lake. She had lain down then and floated, enveloped in the lake's embrace, and her baby had glided into this world easily, like a glistening, pink fish.

The next thing Marie knew, she was opening her eyes in her own bed. At first she'd thought it was all a dream, until she saw the people crowded around her, their concerned faces, their comforting words.

Marie often found her thoughts drifting back to an old family legend Marie's grandmother had told her when she was a child—tales about the lake and spirits and curses and love. Could they possibly be true? No, she told herself that morning, shaking her head as if to shake away those thoughts. After her grandmother died when Marie was just a child, Marie's mother had forbidden any talk of the old stories, and she had obeyed. As she grew up, the tales had faded further and further into the past until she could barely remember them anymore.

But as her own daughter grew, the memory of those tales nagged at Marie, nudging her, creeping bit by bit out of the abyss of denial where Marie had banished them all those years ago. Every time she saw Addie in the water, the stories came closer to the surface. Marie couldn't deny the fact that, as soon as the girl could move on her own, she crawled and toddled and tumbled and ran toward the lake. Whenever Marie would turn and find Addie gone, she knew just where to look for her.

One blustery November afternoon when Addie was no more than three years old, Marie wrapped herself in a shawl and walked down to the lakeshore (yet again) to retrieve her wayward daughter. She thought she'd find the girl immersed in her favorite activity, playing by the water's edge. But this time Addie was nearly submerged in the dark and angry water, whitecaps rising over her head and falling with the wind.

During the month of November, this inland sea, which on the best of days was unpredictable and fierce, became a veritable graveyard for the unlucky fishermen who ventured out onto its waters. It was said that in November, the lake became sly and murderous. On days that seemed placid and calm, its glassy waters would beckon ships to set sail. Yet, at a moment's notice, the lake would churn up monster storms with wind, sleet, and hail, entrapping and engulfing even the largest of vessels that had been fooled into leaving the safety of port. Indeed, enormous steel tankers had found their way to the bottom of the lake in an instant, with all hands aboard, in that deadly month.

That November day, Marie dropped her shawl and ran into the waves toward her child. "Addie!" she cried as she scooped her daughter into her arms. "You'll catch your death! What were you thinking?"

"I was just playing, Mama," Addie cooed, unsure what all the fuss was about. Back on shore, when Marie draped the shawl around her tiny daughter, she felt that the girl's body was radiating heat. It was as though she had been sitting in a hot bath.

Marie hurried up the hill to the house with her child in her arms, hoping the neighbors had not seen this peculiar display. The God-fearing people who populated the town were none too tolerant of differences, especially those of a rather strange and otherworldly variety. But surely her own neighbors would never turn on Marie and her family the way they had turned on her grandmother when Marie was just a child. Not again. Not here.

Still. There was no harm in being careful. Marie did everything she could to hide Addie's peculiarities. That the girl loved to splash and swim in the water in any sort of weather was evident—nobody could miss it. While other swimmers cried that the cold water stung their skin even on the hottest of August days, it was always silky and warm where Addie swam. The girl would watch people brace themselves on shore and run into the waves, shrieking with laughter as they surfaced, while she floated on her back. Addie thought them all mad for behaving in such an odd fashion. The townsfolk shook their heads, not knowing what to make of this girl.

But Marie laughed it off. "My Addie loves the water," she would say, shaking her head. "But then again, she was born there, wasn't she?"

This made a kind of sense to the people of Great Bay. They thought Addie's immunity to the cold of the lake was some odd by-product of the circumstances of her birth. None among them ever wondered exactly why that might have been.

Neither did anyone wonder why Marie's husband, Marcus, always caught the most fish in his nets, or how he seemed to be drawn to the biggest schools time and time again, or why he never had so much as a close call out on the lake while others risked life and limb daily. They all simply thought of Marcus as an excellent fisherman, someone with a natural talent for the waves and whatever lay beneath them. Marie had thought as much, too, until Addie was born and the old legends began swirling around in her mind once again.

The year Addie turned five years old, Jess Stewart came into the yard. Addie was playing beneath a tent of her mother's clean, white sheets hanging on the line in the back of the house. She loved the way the sheets smelled when they hung out there, fresh and alive with lake scent. Ten-year-old Jess lifted one of the sheets and looked at the girl, sitting there in the summer sun.

"I've been waiting for you," Addie said to Jess. They were the first words ever spoken between them.

"I know," he replied. "I've been waiting for you, too. Shall we go fishing?"

Up she stood, then, taking his hand. When skin met skin, young Addie knew she would live the rest of her life with this boy. As their fingers laced together for the first time, the years passed in that instant, a lifetime lived right there. Addie saw her future in a flash, the way some people's lives pass before their eyes at the moment of their deaths. She saw visions of a bicycle, letters composed on a small writing desk in her room, and a wedding in the snow. She saw arms intertwined. She felt love. She saw a baby, and tears. She heard a woman's voice issuing a stern warning. She saw men shouting and heard a gunshot that echoed into the depths of her being. She saw the lake then, big and bold and comforting. She did not know what to make of all this, being only five years old. It all happened so fast, in an instant, right before her eyes.

And then it was over. The day just as normal as it had been before. The cicadas buzzing just as they had been, the sun beating down upon her just as before, the sky the same shade of robin's-egg blue. But when she looked into the eyes of Jess Stewart and he looked back at her, she knew something had changed. They had lived a lifetime together already.

Addie didn't know it then, she never knew it, but Jess felt the same thing that day when they first held hands. But the pictures that flashed before his eyes were a good deal more disturbing than those seen by the little girl. He shook them out of his head and led Addie into the life that fate had created for them.

Marie saw what was happening between the two children and wasn't surprised, on Addie's first day of school, to open the door and find Jess Stewart standing there, scrubbed and ready for the day, his unruly hair combed into neat submission.

"I thought I'd walk Addie to school," the boy announced. "I'll get her settled, show her the ropes. I'll bring her home, too, at the end of the day."

Marie folded her arms and looked the boy up and down, squinting.

"It's all right, Mrs. Cassatt," Jess said. "I'll take good care of her."

Marie remembered the morning of Addie's birth, how Jess was the one who found her. She nodded, knowing she was powerless over what had been put in motion that day five years earlier.

"Come right home after school, do you hear?" she warned him, wagging her finger. "I don't want to be worrying about where you are."

But watching her daughter walk down the lane, hand in hand with Jess Stewart, Marie knew she had nothing to fear.

It was then she remembered the book.

CHAPTER SIX

Night had fallen by the time Kate and Alaska pulled into Wharton, a tiny portside community an hour down the shoreline from her home. Best known for its quaint, New England–like atmosphere and stunning views of the islands just offshore, Wharton was home to expensive yachts, small galleries featuring the work of local artisans, gourmet restaurants, and several mom-and-pop operations like ice cream shops and smoked-fish stands that gave the town its personality. More than any other place on the lake, Wharton had always been a tourist mecca. But that's not what Kate loved about it. For Kate, and for many locals who knew its history, Wharton was a magical place.

The town had sprung up in the wilderness, far from any other city, in the 1700s, when fur trappers, missionaries, explorers, and later, wealthy businessmen learned to appreciate its oddly temperate climate and unsettlingly warm winds. Street after street was filled with grand homes boasting enormous front porches, well-manicured lawns, and flourishing gardens. In this harsh northern land where it was winter much of the year, the air in Wharton was so warm that magnolia trees grew.

Scientists postulated that the oddly warm weather had something to do with the rocky cliffs that surrounded the town on three sides. Others argued it was the presence of several islands just offshore to buffer the cold winds that blew across the lake. Legend had it that Wharton was blessed with its temperate climate by the spirit of the lake itself, because this was where it had found its true love centuries before. But in modern times, people didn't think too much of that mythical hogwash. Wharton's climate was what it was. And what it was was a tourist draw.

Many of Wharton's grandest old houses were now bed-and-breakfast inns, catering to tourists who came to shop for local artwork, to explore the islands by ferry, to kayak or row out to the "sea caves" hewn into the rocky cliffs, or to simply wander hand in hand through town with one's beloved, marveling at the romance of this charming village, set in the middle of nowhere. Visitors said the town radiated a sense of peace unlike anything they'd ever experienced. Kate came here often because of it.

As Kate pulled into town, summer tourist season was rapidly evaporating with the falling temperatures. Which was not to say that Wharton was closed up tight with the coming of winter. On the contrary. The town's unusually warm climate drew people all year long, and although tourists couldn't enjoy the lake itself in the winter, they came for quiet weekends at the inns, long walks in the temperate air, and hours of sitting outside under a blanket with a book and a glass of wine, grateful for the odd respite from the harsh winter that surrounded the town but somehow didn't penetrate it.

Kate loved this quaint harbor village. By design, no building was taller than two stories—with the exception of the grand old mansions that lined the residential streets. Visitors were always surprised to find no fast food restaurants, no big department stores, no discount retailers, no strip malls. Unlike the downtown areas of many small communities, which had devolved into ghost towns, Wharton's downtown was still thriving with the everyday business of people's lives. Residents visited their family doctor in her office on Main Street and got their prescriptions filled at the local pharmacy two doors down. They bought everything from light bulbs to window cleaner at Frank's Hardware, which had been owned and operated by the same family for three generations. They got their fresh produce at the market across the street, exchanged town gossip at the diner, and congregated at the coffee shop, all of which were located within three blocks of each other.

The myriad upscale galleries and shops surrounding those core businesses existed mainly for tourists, but everyone, tourist and local alike, loved the restaurants, which were welcoming the first of their dinner guests for the evening as Kate drove through town. She passed Antonio's, which served Italian fare. Just down the block was the Flamingo, an eclectic place with a long mahogany bar serving fine wines and microbrews and a decidedly American menu including big salads and burgers. Kate saw a crowd gathering at The Dock, located right on the water and offering local specialties like lake trout, wild rice, and Cornish pasty, and the best lake view in town.

Kate turned from the main street and made her way up the hill toward her destination, one of the grandest old homes in town. The building had begun its life more than a century earlier as the home of Harrison Connor, a young, self-made millionaire who had been savvy enough to position himself in the right place at the right time during the shipping boom at the turn of the last century. The history of the place always swam in Kate's mind whenever she came here. It was her own family history, after all.

She knew that Harrison's opulent lifestyle in Wharton was a far cry from his upbringing as a farm boy. His father, Claus, a German immigrant, had built a farm—forced it into being with the sheer power of his determination—out of a rocky, windswept field near the border of North and South Dakota. His land wasn't filled with the rich soil that turned the region into the breadbasket of the world and, as such, it didn't take well to the wheat and sunflowers he grew, but he owned it outright, along with a few cows, chickens, and pigs.

Survival on those unforgiving, desolate plains was a constant struggle, no matter the season. The intense heat of summer punished farmers in the fields who had not so much as a tree for relief. The harsh winds of winter stirred up blinding blizzards that confused and consumed men who knew the land as well as they knew their own souls. By the time Claus was thirty years old, he looked decades older, hardened by the effort of exerting his will against the land, day after backbreaking day.

Harrison, so elegantly named for his English maternal grandfather, knew he wouldn't be on the farm for long. When he was through cleaning the horses' stalls and feeding them for the night, he would sink into the fresh straw in the barn's loft and open his schoolbooks. Education was the only way to escape a life as brutal as the one his father had endured, and so he plunged into his schoolwork with a fever. Shakespeare tonight, then.

Inside the house, his mother, Gloria, was where she always was at that time of day, standing in front of pots simmering on the stove. She and her son talked about his schoolwork, books, literature, and history—things they both loved.

Gloria was determined that her son get a good education, and because of that, she had struck a bargain with her husband years earlier, a bargain she knew was destined to crumble like the lie that it was. The boy would do his chores and help out as much as possible during his school years, she told her husband. After that, he would join his father on the farm full time. She told her husband this although she knew it to be untrue, putting off the inevitable explosion when Harrison's real intentions, and Gloria's dreams for him, were finally revealed.

Claus had come in from the fields one evening not long after his son had graduated from high school to find the boy standing in the kitchen with a suitcase. Off to college, just as his mother had planned.

The enormous Claus leaped on his son then, inflicting blow after blow. He was awakened from this all-consuming violence by his wife, who stopped the beating by grabbing her husband's rifle that hung above the fireplace and firing two shots into the air. Gloria was fully prepared to shoot to kill if necessary. Luckily for Claus, it was not. Harrison left the farm that evening and never returned.

He attended the university in the large city that was a few hundred miles, yet an entire world, away from his home. He earned a business degree and, immediately after graduation, got a job with a large, locally owned shipping company, Canby Lines, hauling grain (some of which his own father had farmed, coincidentally) across the Great Lakes.

In very short order, Harrison's charm, good looks, business savvy, and, some would say, carefully honed skills of manipulation and deception catapulted him to the position of company president, reporting only to James Canby, a widower who had founded the company and had recently taken young Harrison under his wing. It didn't hurt that Harrison was romancing Canby's daughter, Celeste, a plain, shy young thing who had never had much attention from the opposite sex. With Canby's blessing, Harrison asked Celeste to marry him, thus cementing his position as heir to the company throne.

The union was carefully calculated, but Harrison looked upon it as simple survival. He would do anything to avoid going back to the farm—not that it was ever really a consideration, what with his education and business experience. Even if he had, say, lost this particular job, he could've simply walked into another, without going to the extreme of marrying the boss's daughter. But Harrison's early life had left him with certain scars that reason and clear thinking couldn't erase. Thus, when he saw that the road to his own ultimate security began with ingratiating himself with Canby and ended with marriage to Celeste, he simply took the opportunity that was so obviously in front of him.

Not long after the young couple returned from their European honeymoon, Canby suffered a massive stroke at the office. Harrison and Celeste were at his side at the end. His last words were to his young protégé:

"Take care of her," Canby whispered.

"I will, sir," Harrison promised. And then the old man was dead.

Harrison meant what he had said. That he did not love Celeste was of no consequence to him. He was indebted to her. Because of their marriage, her father's company now belonged to him. Not only was he safe from his irrational fear of sinking back into farm life—he had a recurring nightmare that he had turned into his father, German accent and all—Harrison had become the first millionaire on either side of his family tree. He began sending money to his mother every month and continued to do so until she passed away, fifteen years after her husband died of a heart attack in the fields. Those last years were nearly the happiest of her life—rivaling only her first few years of marriage to a carefree, determined young immigrant who had not yet been turned so bitter, so vengeful, so angry by the land he had chosen to farm.

Harrison always smiled when he thought of the fact that Gloria died kicking up her heels at a town dance. She sold the farm immediately after Claus's death and moved into a small apartment in town, which she decorated in the sort of lively floral prints and gaily striped patterns that her husband would never allow in their home. She did not remarry—why should she listen to someone *else* complain that she hadn't washed his stockings correctly?—and instead played the organ at the white wooden church each Sunday morning, volunteered to help with bake sales, fundraisers, and other church events, and organized town dances, held in the high school gymnasium every Saturday night. It was at one of these events, while dancing with a man young enough to be her son, that she slipped away.

She died with a smile on her face, right there in the middle of the dance floor. People thought she was smiling because she was having such a wonderful time dancing, and that was true. But it was also true that Gloria Connor was smiling because, at the moment of her passing, she was greeted on the other side by Claus, young and vibrant again, who took her by the hand, twirled her across the dance floor, and said to her, "I've had such a good time watching you these past fifteen years,

Gloria. You really knew how to live. Pity that I didn't. Shall we live it up now?"

Meanwhile, Harrison was busy using the same kind of determination that had gotten him to his lofty position to create a happy life for Celeste. She deserved as much. When he was still a young man, Harrison Connor built his enormous, Victorian-style home high on a hill overlooking the harbor in Wharton. Its most distinguishing feature was its expansive porch that wrapped around three sides of the house, offering a view of the harbor from every direction. Harrison was often seen pacing from one end of the porch to the other, spyglass in hand, watching his fleet of ships steaming toward their destinations.

Harrison might have built a house for Celeste in a larger city, but he built this home in Wharton for the same reason many other people were drawn there—the unusually warm winds. Celeste had never fully recovered from a bout of influenza that had overtaken her shortly after her father's funeral, and he thought that Wharton's warm climate would be just the thing to buoy her health. He was wrong about this.

Celeste remained in frail health throughout much of her life, especially after the birth of their only surviving daughter, Hadley. Before the girl was born, Harrison and Celeste kept company with many young couples in Wharton, entertaining, throwing dinner parties, and generally keeping up their social obligations as befitting Harrison's standing as the town's largest employer. But after the child came into their lives, all of that ceased. The pregnancy had been difficult and draining for Celeste, and she no longer had the vibrancy and energy necessary to entertain. There were mental issues as well, known only to Harrison. A kind of madness had overtaken her after the birth of their first child. She never came out of it, was never quite right again. It was as though fiction and fact comingled in her mind, and she seemed not to be able to differentiate one from the other.

But Harrison had made a promise to her father years before and would keep that promise. In public, Harrison was fiercely devoted to his wife, despite her delicate condition. Neighbors would often notice him walking the length of his front porch, pushing Celeste in a wheelchair, pointing out this ship or that one on the horizon. It was not unusual to find the two of them sitting together on a porch swing wrapped in a quilt, him reading to her, she with her head upon his shoulder. Although plenty of tongues wagged in town about other rich men and their mistresses, there was no hint of impropriety with any of the half dozen maids that kept the Connor household running, the brass polished, the woodwork gleaming, and the child dressed, fed, and escorted to and from school. What Harrison truly felt in his heart was known only to him.

Celeste died when Hadley was just a small child. Despite the doctor's report that Celeste's heart had simply given out, whispers of addiction and an overdose of medication spread through the town like wildfire. With Celeste gone, Harrison began to pursue what was really in his heart for the first time in his life. Instead of marrying any of the legion of single women in town who would've sold their souls to become his wife, he lavished all his attention on the one person he loved above anyone else: Hadley.

Picnics, boating parties, snowshoeing in winter, horseback riding, hiking along the shore, canoeing—townspeople would regularly see Harrison and Hadley trekking out of doors together and wonder why they, too, couldn't seem to derive such pleasure from the company of their families as Harry Connor seemed to.

If a child's success in life is an indication of how well a parent did his job, then Harrison Connor earned top honors. Hadley grew into a fine young woman. She finished school, went on to college (it wasn't often the case for a girl to receive such an education in those days) and created a happy life of her own. The brown-eyed beauty married a handsome man by the name of Malcolm Granger. They had two children, Fred and Harry. Fred, in turn, had a daughter, Kate, who was now pulling into the driveway of the former home of her great-grandfather.

These days, Harrison's House functioned as an upscale bed-and-breakfast with a fine restaurant and a comfortable wine bar tucked into what had once been the home's library. The room's dark-wood paneling, floor-to-ceiling bookshelves, leather chairs, and marble-topped tables made it a favorite with tourists and locals alike. Kate especially loved coming here because of the family history it contained. Pictures of Harrison, Celeste, and Hadley still hung on the walls, and most of the volumes of books in the library had belonged to them. Indeed, much of the home was as it had been in Harrison's day, having been painstakingly restored.

The house had always been in the Connor family. Hadley and her husband, Malcolm, moved back to Wharton to care for Harrison during his declining years. Hadley doted on her father until the end, repaying him for the love and affection he had lavished on her when she was a child with the kind of reverent caretaking that only such an adored daughter could give. She took ownership of the house and the family fortune after he died. Hadley herself lived well into her nineties, taken care of in her later years by her grandson, Kate's first cousin, Simon, the son of Hadley's son Harry. When Hadley finally died, in her sleep in the house that she loved, the house went to Simon, for his loving caretaking of his grandmother.

Simon and his partner, Jonathan, were in the process of restoring every inch of the enormous structure. Every fixture, doorknob, and plank of wood flooring was original, or, as Simon liked to say, a damn good fake. Much of the furniture and accent pieces were original as well (refurbished, of course) and what wasn't antique blended old and new seamlessly. The only part of the house that hadn't been restored was the third floor—a ballroom. Simon planned to get to that project in the coming winter when the tourist season wound down.

The grandeur of the place, in addition to its standout restaurant, made it the hottest ticket in town, commanding top dollar for the privilege of spending a night under its perfectly restored roof, though it was Simon's unwritten policy that close family stayed for free.

"It was our great-grandparents' home," he'd say to Kate. "You've got as much right to be here as I do. You're going to pay to stay in this house? Please. I don't think so."

But Kate didn't take him up on this generous offer too often. She and Kevin had spent their honeymoon there, and, a few times each year, they'd come and stay in one of the Jacuzzi suites for a night or two during the off-season, just for the romance of it all.

Walking through the enormous wooden front door of this house always gave Kate a shiver. It was something about the history hanging in the air, the immediate and unbroken ties to her family's past. The photos on the walls always haunted her—young, vibrant, happy people, smiling in blissful ignorance of the fact that, one day, their great-grand-daughter would be looking at those photos, while they themselves lay in their graves.

When she was in this house, Kate could clearly see Harrison and Celeste as a young married couple, their daughter being born, growing up, and eventually dying there. Kate loved walking the same hallways, sleeping in the same rooms, eating meals around the same table as her ancestors had long ago. It gave Kate the feeling that life was so fleeting, over in an instant. A moment ago, Celeste sat here, shepherding her daughter through polite dinnertime conversation as she enjoyed the expansive view of the harbor. A century passed in the blink of an eye, and now it was Kate's turn to enjoy the view. When she was here, she felt very close to those ancestors of long ago, as if they were still here, living their lives in their own time, just beyond an invisible barrier that Kate could almost, but not quite, penetrate. It seemed like, if she held her breath and became very still, she could feel them, just there. She did not know that, indeed, their spirits and others roamed these halls, sat at these tables, and floated among the guests in the dining room, unable or perhaps unwilling to leave this magnificent house for the hereafter.

That day, Simon was standing in the doorway waiting for her.

"Well, it's about time." He enveloped Kate in a bear hug as Alaska bounded inside. They stood, holding each other for a long moment before he whispered, "How are you?"

"I'm good," Kate said, but knew he wouldn't buy it.

"Yeah, I'll bet you're good." He pulled back and squinted at her. "Everyone's good after their world falls apart. Now come over to the bar and sit down and tell me everything. I've got a bottle of wine with your name on it. I'm pouring, you're talking."

CHAPTER SEVEN

After dissecting Kate's situation with her husband, Simon crinkled his nose at her.

"There's something else that you're not saying. I could tell the moment you got here. Out with it."

Somehow, he always knew. There was no use trying to keep anything from him.

"I'll tell you," Kate said. "But you're going to think what I'm about to say is really strange."

"Strange in what way?"

Kate shifted in her chair. "Strange in a 'Kate needs a straitjacket' sort of way."

"Well, this sounds good." Simon raised his eyebrows and leaned forward. "What is it?"

Kate took a deep breath, wondering if she could actually utter the words. "It's about something that's been happening to me."

"Will you just spill it?" Simon said, refilling Kate's glass. "You know you want to talk about this, so just say it, already. How bad can it be?"

"The thing is, I've been having these dreams." Kate exhaled, and then the whole story came out in one long, continuous stream. How she had been dreaming of a woman for the past three weeks, how she had found that same woman's body washed up on the beach in front of her parents' house, how she knew there was a baby in the folds of the woman's dress.

She had said it all out loud, told someone else. The strange events of the past few weeks had been given voice. Her experience was a tangible thing now, the words forming substance and becoming something greater than simply a notion in Kate's head.

"Well?" Kate asked. "What do you think?"

"Why doesn't this kind of thing ever happen to me?" Simon wailed. "The dead simply don't want to communicate with me, and I find it highly offensive."

Kate laughed out loud. "Either that, or I'm just crazy. There's that possibility, too."

"It's certainly bizarre, I'll give you that," Simon said. "You've had recurring dreams about a woman's life. Looking in the mirror in the dreams, you see her face reflected back as your own. You're her, in a way, in the dream. So it's very personal, right?"

"Right," Kate said. "It feels absolutely personal. Intimate. You're right, it's like I am her. Or she's me. In the dreams, we're the same person."

"Are you absolutely sure it's the same woman? The one dead on the beach and the one in your dreams?"

Kate nodded. "Completely sure. It's her. There's no doubt."

"Do we know when, and how, she died?" Simon wondered. "She was in the lake, so, obviously she drowned, right?"

"I don't know." Kate winced as the words left her lips and a twinge of heat radiated in the small of her back. "Johnny Stratton is investigating."

Kate gazed out of the window, looking down the street toward the water. The face of the beautiful, serene woman in her dream, superimposed over the harsh sight of that same face, dead, lifeless, on her beach, screamed inside of her head.

"Johnny's already questioned me, sort of, in connection with all of this," Kate went on.

Simon grimaced. "Why would he do that?"

"I reacted rather badly when I saw the body," Kate admitted. "It seemed to him that I knew more than I was saying."

Simon reached across the table and took her hand. "You didn't tell him about the dreams, did you?"

Kate shook her head. "I haven't told anyone but you. I'm sure he thinks I'm involved in this somehow, but I have no idea what I'm going to tell him when he starts asking more questions."

"If only you knew who she was," Simon mused, staring out the window.

With that, Alaska padded into the room, carrying her leash in her mouth.

"I guess you're being taken for a walk," Simon chuckled.

Kate stood up and stretched. "It'll feel good to get a little exercise, actually," she said. "Care to come along?"

A few minutes later, they were meandering through the darkened streets of Wharton. A whisper of autumn was in the air, and the chill refreshed Kate's spirits.

Simon and Kate talked about other things for a bit, their parents, how things were going at the inn, but their conversation drifted to the dead woman on the beach again, almost as though she was calling them back.

"I want to find out more about who she was and who killed her, but I don't quite know what to do first," Kate said. "I can't do any research without knowing more about her."

"For starters, if you have any more dreams, try to pick up any sort of clue," Simon offered. "Obviously she was a real person. Her body washed up on your beach. That's as real as it gets."

CHAPTER EIGHT

1901 Great Bay

Addie and Jess were inseparable. They ran through the fields and fished in secret spots known only to them. Addie swam in the big lake while Jess sat on the shore reading, wondering how this fool girl could possibly stand to languish in the frigid water. They talked about school and their parents and other children, babbling like siblings sharing secrets.

These years were so idyllic, in fact, that they made Jess forget about those dark images he had seen when he'd first touched Addie's hand years earlier. They flew completely from his mind on one particularly lovely summer day—the blinding blue sky, the sun beating down on his crisp, white shirt, the slight breeze that smelled of lilac, even though the flowers were long since gone. Things might have been different, if he had heeded the warning instead of lost it, there on the lilac breeze.

That lovely summer afternoon, Addie was twelve years old, and she and Jess made their way through the forest on the edge of town to their secret place, Widow's Cove. It was a small bay ringed by a high, rocky cliff, accessible only by a footpath through dense underbrush. Addie had found it the year before, when she was following a black wolf through the forest. She could never quite convince Jess that it had really happened, given the scarcity of wolves in those parts. No one had ever seen a black wolf in or near Great Bay, he kept telling her. But she insisted that it was the truth. How else could she have found that cove?

Addie imagined that wives might go there to mourn their husbands lost on the Great Lake, so secluded and hidden was the place. Jess wasn't sure about all of that, but he had to admit that he loved coming here. It was a chance to be alone with Addie, without the watchful eyes of the community on them.

On this particular day, Addie and Jess lay side by side on one of the enormous flat rocks that dotted the shallow water just off shore. The sun was baking down on their backs. Addie could just reach the cool surface of the water with the tips of her fingers, if she stretched. The water was the color of jade.

At seventeen, Jess was much more grown up than Addie. Tongues wagged in town about the amount of time the two spent together. It got so people didn't see one without the other. *Doesn't he have sweethearts his own age? Isn't it about time he started looking for a bride?* And while Jess's friends knew better than to tease him about the little girl who was always underfoot, they secretly wondered why he wasn't, at least, interested in girls his age from school. Jess was a baseball player and a good student, and with his wavy brown hair and deep-brown eyes, he had grown into quite a handsome young man. His friends knew he could date any girl in town. So why didn't he?

But to Jess, dating someone other than Addie was simply a waste of time. He had been content to wait for the girl to grow up since the minute he had seen her in the lake on the day she was born. He knew then, just as she did, that they were a destined pair, made for each other.

As she and Jess lay on the rock, Addie rolled onto her side, ran one hand across the surface of the cool water, and looked at her reflection—vague, moving, shimmering, distorted. Life was changing, just as her reflection changed and moved in the water.

"I'll be leaving for college at the end of the week," Jess said, gazing out over the lake toward the horizon.

"I know," Addie replied, still tracing patterns across the water's surface with her finger. The sun warmed her.

"Won't be so bad," Jess said. "I'm only a few hours away. I'll come home on weekends. I can take the train."

But Addie knew that he wouldn't be back often, or if he did make the trip home initially, it wouldn't last long. He'd get caught up in college life in the city; anyone would. New things to learn, new people to know. It was a whole new life. She wanted Jess to live it, to experience all there was to do and see. She was not afraid he would be lured away from her permanently. She knew he would come back for her someday. She had seen it.

"When we were kids, you waited patiently until I was old enough to be your friend." Addie smiled at him. "That took five years. I figure I've got less time than that to wait for you now. Don't worry about coming home on weekends. I'll be here when you come home to stay."

Jess rested his chin on the warm rock where they lay. He liked the idea of Addie waiting here for him, the same as she ever was.

"We can write letters to each other," Jess offered.

"That will be wonderful." Addie smiled, already anticipating a new sort of relationship, one of sharing letters and private thoughts instead of woodland adventures and lakeside chats.

"You have a way of always finding the positive in any situation." Jess smiled back at her. "How do you do that?"

Addie shrugged, and the pair looked down at the water from their rock, gazing at each other's reflections.

"Addie," Jess murmured to her watery image. "I love you."

It was the first time he had spoken the words out loud. "I love you, too, Jess," Addie said, running her fingers across both of their reflections in the water, making them distort and dance and shimmer. Addie imagined them lying there together again when Jess finally returned from college, and wondered how their images would change.

"I suppose we'd better get going," Jess said, looking up at the sun's position in the sky. "Meet me outside on Willow Street after dinner?"

Addie saw the devilish look in his eye and suspected he was up to something. "What for?"

"You'll see," Jess said, smiling. "I'm going to leave you with something to remember me by."

Addie laughed. "I have the whole earth to remember you by. The lakeshore, the woods, this cove, our town, the sky."

"Something other than that," Jess said.

After dinner, Addie walked around the corner from her house onto Willow Street, so named for a large, ancient weeping willow that stood in the center of a nearby field. There was Jess, holding the handlebars of his bicycle. Addie didn't have one; she had never been able to master the art of riding. Her father thought it unladylike and refused to teach her, and though Jess tried a number of times, Addie just couldn't get the hang of it.

"You will ride this bicycle before the sun goes down tonight," Jess called out, when he saw her. "And then you can ride it home. I'm giving it to you."

"Truly?"

He smiled. "I can't take it with me on the train. It's yours."

"My parents won't let me take this, Jess." She scowled, anticipating their objections.

"Tell them you're just using it until I get back, then," he said. "I'm asking you to look after it for me."

"I don't know." Addie eyed the contraption skeptically. "I don't think . . ."

"That's right, girl," he laughed. "Don't think. Just ride. Now hop on. We're not stopping until you can do this."

Gingerly, Addie grasped the handlebars, hiked up her skirt, and sat on the seat, one foot securely on the ground.

"I'm going to hold on until you've got it," Jess said, taking hold of the seat. He began to push. "Put both feet on the pedals," he instructed.

"Not so fast!" Addie snapped.

"We have to go fast." Jess was jogging now. "It's easier that way."

Addie was pedaling and steering, wobbly and unsure, and as soon as Jess let go, she tumbled in a heap on the side of the road. She turned to look at her teacher, frustration in her eyes.

"Try, try again!" Jess chirped and lifted the bike off the ground. Addie got up, brushing the dirt off her skirt.

"I don't think I can do this," she said.

"You absolutely can do this," he said. "Just think how much fun you'll have with it when I'm gone."

And so they tried again, and Addie fell again. And again. And again. Curious faces appeared in windows of nearby houses. Then, people became bolder, walking out of their doors onto the street, calling suggestions to teacher and student.

"Run faster, boy!"

"That seat's too high for her!"

Jess grasped the bicycle one last time. "Hop on. We're going to show these people what you're made of."

He started running, faster now, and Addie began pedaling, surer this time, and steering more confidently. She didn't realize he had let go until she was nearly all the way to the willow.

"I'm doing it!" she called out to him. "I'm riding!" And as the crowd erupted in applause, she kept going, down Willow Street and over to Main and around to Poplar Avenue.

Jess simply stood there, watching her go, his stomach twisting into knots. He was the one who was supposed to be leaving.

CHAPTER NINE

After Kate and Simon had finished dinner and cleaned up the dishes, Kate's heavy eyelids told her it was time to turn in.

She ran a hand through her hair. "I'd love to stay up and chat, but I can't keep my eyes open."

"I'm not surprised you're exhausted," Simon said.

"You're not?"

He shook his head. "Listen, you've been trying to hold it together for weeks now," he said. "First the breakup with Kevin and then the ghastly business of this woman's body washing up on the beach. The secret you've been keeping about that . . ." He tsked and let out a sigh. "It would wear on anyone. And now that you've told someone and know you're not alone, you can let down your guard. When that happens, when you finally let go and unclench, you can feel how much work it was to hold everything together. Translation: exhaustion."

Kate snaked her arms around her cousin's waist and laid her head on his chest, exhaling. "I knew coming here was the right thing to do."

"Of course it was," he said. "Now, where did you leave your bag? I'll carry it upstairs for you."

"Oh no—" Kate began, but Simon cut her off.

"Don't be silly. You head up to your room, and I'll follow in just a minute with your bag and some hot tea."

Kate gave him a weak smile. "You're so good to me."

"Of course I am." He grinned, winking at her. "I'm an innkeeper. It's what I do."

Later, after Simon had left her bag on the luggage rack and her tea on the nightstand and they had said their good nights, Kate curled up under the covers of her bed, the pillows propped up against the headboard creating a perfect backrest. She settled in and opened a novel, but soon closed it as the words blurred together in a haze of exhaustion. She took a long sip of tea, watching the flames dance in the fireplace.

Simon had put her in her favorite bedroom in the house, a suite with a giant four-poster bed and a fireplace on the opposite wall. In a nod to guests who liked modern conveniences, a flat-screen television hung above the fireplace, so one could watch a movie, the fire, or both at the same time. A corner of the room jutted out into an alcove with floor-to-ceiling windows on three sides, designed, Kate always believed, to catch the lake breezes on summer days. In the alcove were a small writing desk and a chaise—the perfect spot for reading or just watching the boats come and go in the harbor.

On the other side of the room was a vast walk-in closet—a highly unusual and exotic feature in its day—leading to a bathroom with his and hers vanities, a tile shower, and an enormous claw-foot tub.

The suite was called Hadley's Suite for its original occupant, Simon and Kate's grandmother.

When baby Hadley was old enough to move from the nursery into a room of her own, this was where Harrison put her, and this was where she had grown up. This was the room she and her husband Malcolm had used when they had returned to care for Harrison when their own children were grown and starting families of their own. This was where Hadley had retreated to grieve after the two deaths that had shaken her to her very core—first her beloved father, Harrison, and just months later, her devoted husband, Malcolm.

Hadley had taken her last breath in this room, Kate knew. She had been there. Simon had called the families, and they had rushed to Hadley's side, sitting vigil until the moment came. She slipped into the other world peacefully, even joyfully, surrounded by the living, who were grieving her passing, and the dead, who were rejoicing her homecoming. After embracing her husband and father, Hadley saw her mother hovering near the end of the bed and flew into her arms, both of them crying sweet tears of reunion.

"My darling girl," her mother repeated, over and over. "My darling girl."

As Kate snuggled deeper under the covers and closed her eyes, she didn't know that Hadley was sitting on the bed next to her, stroking her hair. Had Kate not been so exhausted, she might have sensed her grandmother's presence there and even seen her ghostly shape, somehow translucent and solid at the same time. She might have noticed Hadley's 1920s-era dress; her unlined, porcelain skin; and her shiny, dark hair.

But as it was, Kate only felt the serenity of having her beloved grandmother watching over her as she drifted off to sleep, as if standing guard against any more unsettling dreams.

"Any dreams last night?" Simon had already set two places at the bar, made coffee, and was flipping an enormous omelet by the time Kate appeared in the morning, Alaska at her heels.

"Nothing," Kate said as she climbed onto a bar stool. "If you don't count a rambling and bizarre nightmare about being naked at work."

Simon snorted.

"I guess they can't all be glimpses into the lives of dead people," Kate said, sipping her coffee and looking out the window onto the harbor, where two sailboats, colorful spinnakers unfurled, were languidly floating on the big lake. "You really do have a spectacular view here. I've always loved it."

"I think you should avail yourself of the view for longer than just this weekend," Simon said. "I've been thinking. What if you stayed on for a while?"

"I'd love to," Kate said. "But I really need to get back home." Even as she said the words, she knew they were hollow and meaningless. Home to what?

"I suppose you need to get back to work," Simon said, taking a sip of coffee and eyeing her above the rim.

"I quit my job," Kate admitted. "Kevin's liaison with an intern at our office sort of killed my love of the place, you know? A marriage and a career, both obliterated in one evening. That has to be some sort of record."

"Bastard," Simon said under his breath.

"I just can't believe it's all over," Kate lamented.

The mention of her husband's name brought everything back to her, all of it, from the day she met Kevin through that last night at the Tavern when she had confronted her husband and the woman she knew to be his girlfriend.

She met Kevin at the *Gazette*, their town's local newspaper. He edited the sports and national news sections, and she wrote features, travel pieces, and editorials.

Kevin had been working at the newspaper for more than a year when Kate was hired. She noticed him immediately, drawn to his warm smile and lingering handshake when they were introduced. Something about the moment when his hand touched hers made her shudder.

"It's customary for the new kid on the block to buy everyone drinks at the Tavern after their first day on the job," he informed her when it was nearly quitting time on her first day.

"Really? I didn't hear about that." Kate smiled at him. He wasn't one of the best-looking men she had ever seen, but with his freckled nose and crooked smile, he was attractive in a flawed sort of way. She wondered about him. Did he have a girlfriend, or worse, a wife?

"We'll convene there at five thirty. Don't be late. And bring your credit card."

Kate was nervous, wondering how much of her scant salary she'd have to shell out at the bar that evening. But when she arrived, she was surprised to find Kevin sitting alone at a table.

"I thought . . . ," she started, looking around and wondering where everyone else was.

"Okay, I made that stuff up about the new kid buying drinks," Kevin confessed with a grin. "I really wanted to get to know you better, and I wasn't sure you'd come if it was just the two of us. Will you stay?"

Kate slid into the chair next to him. "Only if you're buying the drinks," she said.

"Fair enough," he said, motioning for the waiter.

Kate smiled. Her new job had just gotten that much more interesting. The conversation between them that evening wound its way from the safe and shallow waters of what Kate might expect on the job, to favorite movies and restaurants, to deeper subjects like their childhoods and transformative college experiences. Kate was fond of saying she had fallen in love with Kevin during that first evening together, somewhere between his hilarious story about a prom night in which his car had ended up at the bottom of the Sandy River and her tale of a college escapade in which she and her friends had stolen lawn ornaments from all over town—plastic deer and ducks and flamingos—and planted them in her then-boyfriend's front lawn. But in her heart, Kate knew she had fallen in love with Kevin the moment she saw him sitting alone at the table. There was just something about the sight of him there, waiting for her. As though he had been waiting his whole life for her to walk through the door. She confessed it to Simon the next day.

"I saw him and instantly knew I was going to marry him," she'd sighed on the phone to her cousin. "I've just met my future husband. Mark my words."

Kevin and Kate didn't tell anyone else they were dating. Office romances were frowned upon at the paper, and both of them were relatively new on the job. Kate, in fact, was just beginning the three-month probationary period, customary at many workplaces, and neither she nor Kevin wanted to muddy the waters of their employment with rumors of an affair. At work, they were cool, cordial coworkers. Nobody guessed that their friendly, though somewhat formal, demeanor with each other concealed a great fire. Kevin was a master at masking his feelings; he was so good, in fact, that early on, Kate spent many days at work wondering if she had misinterpreted his ardor that first night.

They would leave the office separately, each talking loudly about hitting the gym or doing some shopping, only to meet later at her house. At that time, Kate was renting a small cottage on a lake a few miles outside of town. When she chose the house for its old-fashioned charm and its lake view, she had no idea that its remote location would make it a very convenient place to conduct a clandestine romance. Nobody would come to her house unannounced and find them together or drive by and see his car parked in her driveway.

Those early days, the first sweet, solitary, secretive weeks, Kate felt as though she were living in a dream world. She had the job she always wanted—ever since she had discovered her love of journalism during her days writing for the high school newspaper, she had dreamed of growing up and working at the *Gazette*. And now it was a reality. She loved her job and soon became known as an outstanding writer, earning praise from everyone who read her work.

Only she and Kevin knew that another dream of Kate's had come true as well, falling head over heels in love. Kate couldn't believe her good luck. She was happier than she had ever been.

When their relationship was forbidden and taboo, sharing the secret of their affair was exciting. Kevin and Kate made a game out of seeing who could break the other's composure at work, whispering seemingly innocent words that referenced a secret intimacy. Kevin started this game by putting a note on Kate's desk that simply said, "Canoe." Kate knew what he was referring to. The night before, they had canoed to a small island just across the bay from Kate's house. They hadn't secured the canoe well enough on shore. Kate looked up from the blanket they had laid on the ground to see her canoe floating freely in the middle of the lake. When they stopped laughing, Kevin had to swim out to retrieve it.

The first time Kevin told Kate he loved her, they were at the office. It was a month or so after their relationship had begun, and Kevin walked by Kate's desk to drop off a stack of papers. As he bent down, he whispered into her ear, "I love you." He ran a finger down her forearm and walked away casually, as though nothing had been said at all. It sent a jolt of electricity through Kate's body. She'd been in love with him since their first night together at the Tavern and was relieved that he had finally gotten around to admitting he felt the same way. Later, that small act, him running his finger quickly down her forearm, came to mean "I love you" between them. It became their secret way of expressing love in a public place.

Because they didn't go out together, except for the nights when the whole gang from work would stop by the Tavern for a drink, Kate and Kevin spent the majority of their time alone, playing house. They quickly settled into a routine like an old married couple, making dinner together at her place, talking about the happenings in the office, perhaps watching a movie or a television show before tumbling into bed together.

Sometimes on weekends Kevin would stay for the night, but most often, Kate would wake up and find him gone. The empty side of the

bed always left her feeling cold and deserted, but she shrugged it off—
he had to shower and change for the workday, after all.

Three months after that first night at the Tavern, Kevin proposed
to Kate. They were sitting on the dock in front of her house on a lazy,
sunny Saturday afternoon, dangling their feet in the cool water. He
pulled the ring out of his pocket and said, nervously, "This was my
mother's. I can't imagine anyone else but you wearing it. Will you . . .
I guess what I'm saying is, will you marry me?"

Kate was stunned. It had all happened so quickly. He didn't know
her family; she didn't know his. She knew that he had grown up with
a father who was in the military, but she didn't know he'd attended fifteen different schools before he graduated from high school. She didn't
know anything about his early years, a life that consisted of making
friends and losing them, over and over again. Young Kevin had quickly
learned—after watching through the back window of his father's station wagon as countless best friends disappeared, only to reappear in
the next town in the form of some other boy just his age—that people
were replaceable.

During his childhood, Kevin had honed the art of making friends
quickly and deeply, in a frantic effort to create some sort of intimacy in
his life before it was smashed to pieces when the family had to pack up
and move to his father's next post. After many years of this, it became
easy for Kevin to create relationships. Sustaining them was another
matter. He never had any practice at it. He simply left people behind
as he began new phases of his life, knowing that someone else would
arise to take their places. But Kevin never thought consciously about
these things, or how they might impact a marriage. He was not a deep
thinker. So when he asked Kate to spend the rest of their lives together,
he had no idea he was proposing the impossible.

Kate did not know any of these things that day on the dock as he
sat next to her with a ring in his hand, but she knew there was only one

response to his question. She couldn't imagine a life without Kevin in it. Unlike his, Kate's close relationships lasted a lifetime.

She said yes, he slipped the ring on her finger, and they sat on the dock together for hours, staring at the sun glinting off the water's surface and talking quietly about the rest of their lives, which, to both Kevin and Kate, had suddenly come into sharper focus.

Later, they wondered how they were going to broach the subject of their engagement at the office. Interoffice dating was forbidden, after all. And here they were, getting married. They both loved their jobs. How would they explain this? What would happen when the truth came out?

"I think we should call Stan right now and invite him to meet us at the Tavern," Kevin said, referring to Stan Corrigan, the paper's editor in chief. "We'll tell him what's been going on between us, ask for his blessing, and hope for the best."

The meeting went better than they had hoped. Stan had no idea they were dating, but he seemed delighted to hear they were planning to marry.

"Kids, that's great news," he said, hugging them both and buying a round of drinks for the table. "A married team will probably stay around awhile," he said, mostly to himself, it seemed.

Kate had the peculiar sensation that her dream life with Kevin had just been given legs and stepped into the cold world of reality. Stan knew. Soon everyone would know. It was real. It was happening. They decided to break the news to the rest of the staff on Monday.

Kate was nervous when she arrived at the office that morning. She found Kevin already sitting at his desk with the same kind of cool demeanor that had helped keep their relationship secret for the past three months. They exchanged cordial smiles.

The paper's editorial staff always had a meeting first thing on Monday to talk about the coming week. Each department would lay out their editorial plans, discussing possible stories and angles. The staff was small enough and friendly enough that the meeting was also the forum in which they acknowledged birthdays and other important events in each other's lives.

When it was Kate's turn to speak, she talked about this story and that story, chasing this source and that photograph. Then she said, "I have something else to add. I had an exciting development happen over the weekend. I'm engaged!"

Kate's news elicited, at first, open-mouthed stares from the staff, none of whom knew she was dating anyone. From there, the scene quickly evolved into a chorus of shouts and hugs. Everyone wanted to know, Who was the lucky guy?

"Kevin, maybe you could take it from here." Kate smiled at her fiancé across the table.

More open-mouthed stares. Then cries, hugs, and shouts from the staff. It was a great moment for both Kate and Kevin, who were laughing and talking and telling the stories of how they'd had to keep their relationship secret.

Stan even got into the act, saying that everyone was invited to celebrate at the Tavern after work. "The first drink's on the *Gazette*!" Stan cried.

For Kate, it was a relief to finally be able to show her true feelings for the man sitting next to her.

From that moment until their wedding day, Kate was caught up in the whirlwind that descends upon a newly engaged woman. Introducing her parents to the man of her dreams and announcing their engagement was as joyful an experience as she had ever had. First, disbelief, then the floodgates opened, along with several bottles of wine. Fred and Beverly toasted the young couple, welcoming Kevin into their family in the warmest possible way. Kevin's parents, who had settled in a small town several miles away after his father had retired from the military, were similarly thrilled.

Then, it was on to the flurry of wedding planning—shopping for a dress, choosing the photographer (a young kid from the newspaper) and the florist, the music and the venue. Steak or chicken at the reception? Open bar or cash bar? When Kate finally walked down the aisle on her father's arm toward the only man she had ever loved, she believed, deeply in her soul, that she was blessed. Now all that was left was to live the spectacular life that they had created for themselves.

Five years passed. During that time, Kevin and Kate had purchased a home and a couple of cars, settled into a familiar routine of married life, and worked their way up from reporters to editorial positions at the newspaper.

One day, Kevin came home carrying a large, square box from the office supply store in town.

"I got something for you today," Kevin said to his wife.

Kate smiled. "I'd hazard a guess that it isn't paper for the printer."

"Open it and find out," Kevin said as he set the box in front of her. Kate gingerly took off the lid and peered inside to find a little black-and-white fuzz ball of a dog, all paws and teeth and tail. She squealed.

Kate lifted the little bundle out of the box and held it to her neck, where it nibbled on her chin with its sharp little puppy teeth.

"I know you've been wanting a dog." Kevin smiled. "I saw an ad in the paper offering Alaskan malamute puppies for sale. I thought . . ."

But Kate wasn't listening. This was truly love at first sight. Much later, when she thought about that day, she knew that whatever else Kevin had done, whatever heartache he had brought into her life, he had been responsible for finding Alaska, and for that, she would always be grateful.

After the breakup of their marriage, friends would ask Kate when things had started to go wrong. Had it been coming awhile? Had she seen any signs? The truth was, Kate had been blindsided by Kevin's affair, but in retrospect, she realized that she should have seen the signs, which were as bright and prominent as the neon ones in Times Square.

Their own relationship had started out as a clandestine affair, after all, and although Kate would admit it to nobody, not even to Simon, it seemed that Kevin had enjoyed the secrecy and the forbidden nature of those early days a great deal. All that intensity cooled considerably once they were married, but Kate reasoned that it was normal, knowing that no couple could keep up such a frantic level of excitement for a lifetime.

Still, in her heart, Kate often found herself wondering if it was only the secrecy of their relationship that had truly excited Kevin. Kate didn't realize that theirs was the longest relationship Kevin had ever had. He was always antsy for the thrill, the conquest, the adventure. He wanted to learn intimate things about somebody new. He longed to hear someone else's important stories, their life scripts. To Kate, their relationship deepened with every passing day. To Kevin, it eroded.

Kate discovered her husband's affair on her birthday. Their friends, mostly people from the newspaper, had gathered at the Tavern to celebrate, but she wasn't much in the mood for partying. For several weeks, she had been feeling that something was wrong in her marriage. It wasn't anything specific, but rather a vague sense of dread that she couldn't quite define. Kevin was always making excuses to be out of the house—he went to the gym or for long walks, worked late, that sort of thing. It left Kate with a sour taste in her mouth, a literal feeling of indigestion. But it wasn't anything that seemed big enough, substantial enough, for her to make an issue out of it. The fact that her husband was busy and preoccupied wasn't so unusual, was it? He always came home to her, right?

Along with the frequent trips to the gym, Kate also noticed that her husband was overly attentive to Valerie, his new intern at the office. She was quite beautiful—jet-black hair, a perfect figure, and more than ten years younger than Kate and Kevin. He had hired Valerie to help write the news section and had talked about her to Kate in very casual terms.

But lately she was coming up more and more in conversation. Kevin told Kate that he had taken the young intern under his wing. It was his intention to show her the ropes and make things a bit easier for her on the long, hard climb up the editorial ladder.

"The kid has great potential," he was fond of saying. "I think we found a gem when we hired her."

That wasn't so unusual, either, was it? Oh, it was all professional and aboveboard. No hint of impropriety. An older, experienced mentor and a young mentee. But Kate's radar detected something, and it wouldn't stop sounding. Yet, to her rational mind, it seemed so cliché—a wife suspecting her husband and his pretty young intern were having an affair. And furthermore, Kate trusted Kevin. That's why that nagging feeling made her all the more uneasy.

It simmered and boiled in her brain, the casual coolness between her husband and the intern, the ultraprofessional manner in which he addressed her. It seemed to Kate that he was going out of his way to show everyone that there was nothing going on between them.

But the night of her birthday at the Tavern, they had all been drinking. A few beers have a way of loosening lips, and actions. After they'd all had a few rounds of drinks, Kate saw something familiar in the way her husband reacted to this young woman. She couldn't put her finger on it, but there was something about their fleeting glances, catching each other's eyes for a second or two, then looking away.

Back at Harrison's House in Wharton, Simon interrupted Kate's memories.

"Hey, you were in another world there," he said to her. "Thinking about Kevin?"

Kate nodded, not knowing quite what to say.

"I keep thinking back to that conversation we had not too long ago about him working late so often," Simon mused, sipping his coffee. "You were making so many excuses for him. I saw the signs but didn't say anything. I wish I had."

"When I found out for sure that he was cheating, I wasn't exactly the picture of dignified grace." Kate grimaced. "I'm still sort of embarrassed by what I did."

"You never did tell me exactly what went down," Simon said, leaning in. "Do you want to talk about it?"

"Everyone from work met at the Tavern to celebrate my birthday," Kate began. "After a few rounds of drinks, Valerie got up to use the ladies' room. She didn't look at Kevin at all. But a few moments later, he excused himself and followed her. That set off my radar. It was the same sort of move we'd pull in front of our friends from work. So I followed."

Simon whistled and shook his head. "You didn't."

"I did. I found them together in the hallway near the restrooms. I got there just in time to see my husband running his finger quickly down Valerie's arm as the two passed each other in the hall. Just a slight touch. To most people, it would mean nothing. But that touch was *our* secret way of saying 'I love you' when other people were around. And there he was, touching another woman in exactly the same way."

"Oh, honey," Simon said. "What happened then?"

"I confronted him. I asked him, 'What did you just do?' and he just stammered. Stammered! Valerie slunk off back to the table. But Kevin suddenly became much calmer than the situation warranted. He asked me what I thought I saw. He accused me of having too much to drink and making things up. That really sent a chill through me. I knew what I saw. I knew exactly what that gesture meant. And that's when I marched back to the table and threw a drink in her face."

"You didn't!" Simon hooted. "That's so Alexis Carrington in *Dynasty* of you."

Kate put her head down on the table, her shoulders shaking with laughter. "I threw popcorn, too!"

"God, no. Not the popcorn."

Kate remembered wheeling around and stalking back to the table, Kevin at her heels, pleading, "Kate, don't make a scene. Let's just talk about this . . ."

But it was no use. The gall of him, putting his affair on display at her birthday party. Flirting with this woman in public while their friends gathered to celebrate *her* birthday. Something snapped inside of Kate at the thought of it, and when she reached the table, she did something she never dreamed she'd do. As she threw her drink into Valerie's face, she shouted, "That's for five years of marriage that you just destroyed."

Everyone at the table was stunned into silence. Nobody said a word.

Kate had felt as though she was observing the scene, not really participating in it. She watched herself grab a half-eaten bowl of popcorn on the table and fling its contents onto Valerie's lap, hissing, "And that's for being so stupid as to think I wouldn't see what was going on between you and my husband."

Next, Kate had watched her own hand grab the drink of the person sitting next to her, saying as an aside, "Sorry, Bob, the next one's on me," as she threw it at Kevin, shouting, "and *that's* for having an affair with this skanky tramp in front of all of our friends."

Kate stormed out of the Tavern then, crying tears of bitter resentment. Kevin ran after her.

"Kate! Let's talk about this!" he called across the rain-soaked parking lot. But Kate simply opened the car door and climbed inside.

"I don't want to hear anything you have to say," she shouted as she drove away.

When she got home, she packed a few suitcases and Alaska's favorite toys, piled the dog into the car, and the two of them drove across town to her parents' house. It had felt to Kate as though she was operating on autopilot, moving through the events with a will that wasn't her own. It was so wrong, all of it—how could Kevin have had an affair? How could she be making up the bed in her old bedroom at her parents' house? How could her marriage be falling apart? Was everything she thought she knew about her life with her husband a lie?

A few days later, she called Stan to resign her position at the newspaper. He did not accept it.

"Listen, Kate, I need you," he said. "Why don't you take a few weeks off to think things through? Maybe you two can work it all out."

Kate didn't know it then, but Kevin had come into the office that Monday morning, hung his head, and told Stan—and the entire staff at the Monday meeting—that Kate had been having emotional problems since having a miscarriage. It was a convenient lie.

He'd sighed deeply and shaken his head. "You all know she accused me of having an affair, which is obviously false. But I can sympathize with her, can't you all?" His eyes had traveled to everyone sitting silently around the table. "She's still grieving for our lost baby. She's not herself; you all can see that, can't you?"

Nods and murmurs from around the table.

"I know the scene looked pretty crazy, but it's not her fault. Please just understand that she's going through a really rough time and, maybe, pray for her? For us?"

Amid tears and hugs, they all said they would, and they left the meeting pitying the steadfast and loving husband and his "grieving, if not totally sane" wife. Valerie resigned her position in light of all the fuss. Stan was sorry, if relieved, to see her go.

Nobody, of course, knew about the scene that had taken place between Valerie and Kevin after the incident at the Tavern. He had just denied their relationship in front of all their friends, and Valerie was stunned. It had been the most intimate, deep relationship of her life, even though they'd had only a few months together. Kevin knew everything about her—she had told him all her deepest feelings, secrets, and fears—and the attention that he had lavished on her was intoxicating.

Like Kate, Valerie did not know that it was the very act of that revelation, the intimacy of getting to know another person's soul, that Kevin loved. Not her, per se.

Valerie demanded to know why he hadn't just taken the scene—as unfortunate as it was—as the opportunity for them to come out of the closet as a couple, as it were. For the past few months, he had told her he was simply waiting for the right time—well, wasn't this it? Was he really going to leave his wife and marry her, as he had promised? If not now, when? Were they really going to have a life together?

When Kevin said that they needed to put all those plans on hold now, for the sake of propriety, Valerie watched his lies evaporate into thin air like fog rising from the lake. That this man would choose his mousy, boring wife over her elicited a rage deep inside Valerie's wounded soul the likes of which she had never experienced.

But Kate knew none of this on the morning that Stan asked her to reconsider her resignation.

"Sure, Stan," she said to him. "I'll think about it and call you in a few weeks, then." But she knew she'd never go back to the paper. Her work there was wrapped up in her relationship with Kevin. She couldn't possibly continue in her job without her marriage, too. And with every day that passed, she realized what a mistake that marriage had been.

After Kate and Simon finished laughing and crying about the scene at the Tavern, Simon took Kate's hands.

"Listen," he said. "I'm going to say something that sounds very callous and mean."

"That's nothing new," she snorted.

"Seriously," he said, squeezing her hands. "Don't get mad at me for bringing this up, but you got quite an inheritance when Granny died, just like I did."

"And?"

"And—I certainly hope you got a pre-nup."

"It's written on stone tablets, I think," she chuckled. "That was the one thing my dad insisted on when I told my parents we were getting married after such a brief courtship."

"Thanks, Uncle Fred." Simon smiled. "What are the terms, if you don't mind me asking?"

"It stipulates that, in case of a divorce, our marital assets would be divided—what we earned and accumulated together after our marriage, in other words—but the trust was off-limits."

Simon had a dark thought. "What about if you died?"

"The trust would go to any children we had. If we had no children, half would go to Kevin and half back to my parents."

Simon squinted at her over the rim of his coffee cup.

"I didn't want to leave him with nothing if he were a grieving widower."

As Simon brought their dishes into the kitchen, he was suddenly very glad his cousin had come to Wharton. He made a silent vow to keep her safely under his roof until those divorce papers were filed.

Johnny Stratton's team was running into a brick wall with their investigation of the murder. They knew only the cause of death. Nothing more. No missing persons reports, no clues as to who the woman was, who killed her, or how she had ended up in the lake. Kevin Bradford's polygraph proved that he had nothing to do with this woman or her baby—DNA results might tell them otherwise, but those weren't in yet.

There was no love lost between Johnny and Kate's husband, but Johnny was literally breathing easier since he saw the man's polygraph. If Bradford didn't know this woman and wasn't the father of that baby, then Kate had no motive for killing them.

Still. He knew Katie was hiding something. He had seen it clearly in her eyes that morning at Fred's kitchen table. It was a cloud, the same cloud he had seen seep into the eyes of hundreds of liars even as they were professing the truth. If it were anybody else, he would have kept after her until she told him what it was. But Katie Granger? He was tempted to just let sleeping dogs lie. And because of that, he knew he needed to step back from this case. He was too close.

He dialed the number of the precinct in Wharton.

"Nick Stone."

"Stone! It's Johnny Stratton. How are you settling into police work in a small town?"

"Keeping Wharton safe from jaywalkers and speeders," Stone said, a chuckle in his voice. "And getting to know everyone in town. It's a nice change, actually."

"That's the spirit," Johnny said, knowing why the cop had requested a transfer from the city. "But I'm calling to change all of that, I'm afraid. I've got a murder case I need your help with."

CHAPTER TEN

Great Bay, 1901

October 30

Dear Jess,

I find myself wondering about you constantly. I'll be walking through town thinking, Does he like his courses? Has he made friends? What is the university like? Most of the time, I'm not even looking at what's in front of me, so entranced am I in the world that I am imagining for you. I'm even wondering about what you're eating. Do they have different, wonderful foods in the city that we don't have here?

As you can see, I'm still a curious cat.

Life at home is the same as it has always been, with one major difference: you are not here. You can't imagine how odd the same old life seems without someone who was always there by my side. The school year has started, as you probably know, and our new teacher, Mrs. Patterson, is fond of piling on the work.

I have reluctantly had to put the bicycle away for the winter. I've so enjoyed it these months, even though my father says it's not ladylike.

Well, that's all for now. Please write and let me know how you're getting on.

Your friend,

Addie Cassatt

Addie folded the letter into its envelope and walked out of the house toward the post office, buttoning up her coat all the way to the neck, winding her scarf snugly around her head, and pulling on her hood for good measure. The first gale of the season was upon the tiny fishing village, and, as with many late fall storms on this Great Lake, it was punishing.

Snow and hard pellets of sleet plummeted down, coating everything they touched in a slick layer of ice. Worse even than that, the wind caught those tiny frozen shards in its breath and blew them in fierce gusts into the faces of those fool enough to venture outdoors. After walking in one of those ice storms, it was not uncommon to find one's face covered in razor-thin cuts.

Any sensible person would be safe and warm inside, reading by the fire or cooking in front of a hot stove. Indeed, many eyes were delivering sidelong glances from their warm rooms behind frosty windowpanes, wondering what that foolish Cassatt girl was up to now, out walking on this kind of day. But for Addie, she was finished with her letter, and that meant it was time to walk to the post office. The weather simply didn't enter into it.

She had been waiting almost two months for a letter from Jess. Why hadn't he written immediately as he'd said he would? Addie ruminated on this for a while and concluded that he must be consumed with his new life, his college classes and a roommate, everyone and everything around him fresh and new and exciting. Home must seem quite dull indeed.

Addie had imagined they would be writing letters to each other as fast as the post could take them, and through those words and descriptions, she would experience a bit of his newfound life. She had further imagined that waiting for those letters—words from a faraway love— would add some excitement to her everyday existence. It was a romantic notion of a naïve young girl. Waiting *this long* for letters that never came was a tedious exercise in frustration. At this rate, Jess's four years of college would drag out to eternity for Addie.

Head down, eyes nearly closed, Addie slogged her way through the punishing sleet to the post office. Grateful for the brief respite indoors, she mailed the letter, exchanged a few pleasantries with the postmistress, and headed back outside toward home. She was distracted midway by the waves on the lake, enormous whitecaps roiling and bubbling on the surface of the water only to crash mightily and furiously onshore. Addie loved the lake in all its moods, but perhaps its fury most of all. The anger and power of the waves made her shudder. She felt small and helpless in the face of such power, yet she knew somehow that she would always be safe within it. She scrambled down the rocky embankment toward the lakeshore, and there she sat just out of the water's grasp.

As little as a year ago, Addie might have been tempted to peel off her coat and walk into the water, knowing its anger and chill would warm her like a hot bath. But now that she was growing up, Addie didn't let herself be drawn to the lake the way she had when she was a young girl.

It wasn't suitable for a young woman to be seen playing and splashing like a baby, her mother had said when Addie turned thirteen that year. Although she still felt much like a child, Addie liked being referred to as a young woman and saw the wisdom of acting as though she was old enough for that title.

Addie always did her best thinking on the shoreline. There, with the lake's tenor lapping in her ears, Addie found herself wondering about the life she would have when Jess finished college. Would he come home to her? Would they marry as they had planned? Or would he find another girl, someone pretty and exciting and closer to his age, at the university? She knew that's what her parents hoped. But Addie could not even summon the image of Jess loving someone else. It seemed to violate the very order of things.

The waves were stronger now, louder. Amid this sound and fury, Addie concluded that all was well with the only man she would ever love, letters or no letters. She was worrying needlessly. *Have faith, girl. Things are what they will be.* She stood and turned toward home just as an enormous wave crashed into the shore where she had been sitting only seconds before, as if to weigh in on her decision. Had she not moved, it certainly would have engulfed her. The thought took Addie's breath away. As she watched the wave recede, Addie was struck with a pang of doubt at the truth of the conclusion she had just reached. Something gnawed at her as she scrambled back up to the road, and it kept gnawing at her as she walked home.

Addie had no way of knowing that, at that very moment, Jess Stewart was hundreds of miles away, sitting across the table from a young woman named Sally, who he very much hoped would be completely taken with his charms.

On his first day away from home, as he stepped into the city from the train, Jess Stewart awoke to a new life. Great Bay, and everything in it, seemed so small and far away. College, a roommate from another town, classes, parties, tall buildings, people bustling here and there—Jess was entranced by it all. But especially by the women. This new breed of girl—worldly, sophisticated, lighthearted, fun—was so different from the sensible wives of the fishermen in Great Bay. Oh, he hadn't forgotten Addie, but she was just thirteen years old. A child, really. Addie was not like these college girls. With distance, he could see it clearly. It wasn't proper for a grown man to be carrying on a relationship with a child of Addie's age. Their childhood closeness faded from his mind as he began to discover intimacy of another kind.

Back in Great Bay, Addie shuddered, and for the first time that day, she felt cold deep inside. She tightened her scarf, buttoned her coat, and pulled the hood closer around her face in preparation for the walk home.

A few weeks later, Addie came home from school one afternoon to find a letter waiting for her on the table in the hallway. She squealed and ripped it open, dropping her schoolbooks in the process.

December 1

Dear Addie,
Thank you for your letter. I'm sorry it has taken me so long to write. You can't imagine how busy I've been! This university life is exhausting!

To answer your questions, I am indeed enjoying my classes—history, literature, economics, and science—but, like you have found with your new teacher, I'm finding that my courses are a great deal of work. After classes have concluded for the day, I spend the rest of the afternoon in the library studying until dinnertime.

My roommate is a fellow from the Dakotas whose parents own a farm in the midst of the flat prairie. His descriptions of the landscape make it sound austere and empty, very different from what we're used to—no lakes nearby, a stream here and there, flat land as far as the eye can see. He says you can see miles and miles of horizon. Can you imagine great fields of sunflowers? He plays the trombone as well—enough said about that! Now you can see why I spend so much time in the library.

About the food—nothing here is as good as my mother's pasty. Write again soon and tell me about life at home.

I regret to tell you that I will not be coming home for Christmas this year. My roommate and I have been invited to the home of a man who lives here in town. It just seemed easier this way. My parents are unhappy about this, and of course I wished to see you, but the idea of a long trip in the dead of winter convinced me to remain in town.

Your friend,

Jess Stewart

Addie slumped onto her bed. Jess wasn't coming home for the holiday, after all.

She read the letter over and over before putting it in a wooden box with a velvet lining, which she thought would be a perfect place for such correspondence. She kept the box on the writing desk by the window in her bedroom and had hoped to fill it to bursting with his letters over the course of these four lonely years.

"I thought that boy would've outgrown her by now," Marcus grumbled to his wife as he donned his coat and hat to shovel the driveway one snowy morning. "Girls her age shouldn't be writing to college men."

What could they do about it, he wanted to know. Forbid her from writing? Intercept any more letters that came? Marcus lobbied for that course of action, but Marie saw the folly in it.

"He's not coming home for Christmas," Marie whispered, not wanting Addie to hear. "Maybe he's got a sweetheart at the university."

Marcus's eyes lit up at this suggestion.

Marie continued, "Whether he does or doesn't, he's going to be there for four long years. He'll come home now and then, to be sure, but by the time he leaves that place for good, Addie will be old enough to make her own decisions. Maybe he'll come home and marry her. Or maybe he will have met someone, a grown woman, who will take his eyes away from our daughter. You never know."

"Marry her!" Marcus was aghast. "She's just a child!"

"She's thirteen years old, Marcus," Marie said. "When Jess Stewart is finished with college, she'll be seventeen. That's plenty old enough."

"That's still too young," Marcus grumbled some more.

"Oh, you," Marie laughed. "Need I remind you that I was but eighteen when we married?"

The couple shared a laugh, then marveled at how many years had passed in an instant. Their daughter, meanwhile, was upstairs in her bedroom, sitting at her writing desk, believing time had slowed to a crawl.

December 12

Dear Jess,

Your letter came in the mail today. It's a bright day here on the lakeshore. The water has not completely frozen over, and it's wonderful to hear the ice patches wash into the shore here and there. Slush, slosh, slush. I remember how you used to love listening to that.

Your description of the Dakotas sounds so different from what we have here. Fields of sunflowers! Imagine! I cannot comprehend the idea of living somewhere that didn't touch the water.

I am sorry to learn that you are not coming home for Christmas, but in truth, I did not expect you to do so. Remember what I said that day at Widow's Cove?

Your intentions to come home are good, but I know
it is a long trip.

You will be a different person when you come
home to stay, but I know that, no matter how much
living you do without me, you will not forget.

Merry Christmas, Jess.

Your friend,

Addie

That night, Addie tossed and turned in her bed. Sleep would not
come. She lay on the bed in her darkened room and looked out the
window at the impossibly tall, thin jack pine trees swaying in the wind.
A light dusting of snow covered their branches, which were illuminated
by the full moon and a sky filled with stars. Addie watched as, every
now and then, a stray cloud seemed at once to hang close to the earth
and wisp over the moon. It was a perfect, crisp winter night, but her
thoughts weren't dwelling on the beauty of the landscape.

Addie was kept awake that night imagining the time when Jess
would finally return home for good. Her eyes strayed over the snow-
covered ground, and she thought of how wonderful it would be if Jess
arrived right then, driving a horse-drawn sleigh. *It's not so unusual an
idea,* she thought. Several families in the small community kept horses,
and though she didn't have one of her own, Addie loved their soft coats
and musky scent. She loved the way she could see their breath on winter
days. They seemed so intelligent with their enormous, kind eyes.

Addie imagined that Jess would pull up to her window driving
Mrs. Anderson's dappled gray horse. Addie would run out of the house
bundled in her coat, hat, and muff, and Jess would place a heavy blanket
over the two of them for the ride. Off they'd go, over the snow-covered
fields and up to the cliff overlooking the lake, where the sleigh would
glide along silently, its runners whispering through the new-fallen snow.

It was the warmth of this image, her favorite fantasy, that finally lulled Addie to sleep.

Dreams came then, dreams Addie didn't understand. She saw a jumble of images that flashed into and out of view in rapid succession as though someone were flipping through a picture book. Jess walking down a city street, dressed in a dapper new suit. A woman laughing. Jess chatting with a man she didn't recognize. A party. People clinking champagne glasses. Women wearing glittering ball gowns and dancing round and round in a ballroom.

Then everything faded into a white mist—fog. It was blinding until a face began to materialize, bit by bit. It was the face of an old woman with impossibly bright-blue eyes. She began speaking in a language Addie didn't understand. *"Ma petite fille chérie. Le danger vient."*

CHAPTER ELEVEN

After breakfast with Simon, Kate had taken Alaska for a long walk while she was thinking about her next move. She dropped Alaska at the inn before heading to the coffee shop downtown, where she ordered her favorite indulgence—a latte with a half shot of both almond and chocolate—and noticed a tall man staring at her from across the room. She smiled slightly, thinking she knew him from somewhere. But she couldn't place exactly where. When she had coffee in hand and was turning to leave the shop, he rose.

"Kate Granger?" he asked, his voice startlingly deep.

"Yes," she said after taking a sip of her coffee. "I'm Kate. And you are—?"

"Detective Nick Stone," he said. "I'm working with Chief Stratton on the case you're involved in."

Involved in. Kate's stomach seized up at the sound of it. "Are you here to take another statement?" she asked.

"Not exactly," he said, nodding toward a table by the window. "But do you have some time to sit and talk?"

Kate followed him to the table, a silence falling between them as they sipped their coffees and watched the first tourists of the day appear on the street.

As they sat there together, that same feeling of familiarity took hold of Kate. A companionable silence, that's what this was. She looked into his face, a face she knew but had never seen. His eyes were deep and brown, his skin the color of her latte. A slight black goatee framed his perfect mouth. He smiled, the kind of brilliant, high-wattage smile that movie stars flash on the red carpet, and Kate couldn't help smiling back.

"So, what can I do for you?" Kate asked, finally, holding her paper cup a bit too tightly and spilling a little of her latte out the top as a result.

"We've basically run into a brick wall with this case," Stone said. "We've got no leads, no missing persons reports that match the woman's description. No murder weapon. No suspects. We've got very little to go on."

Kate didn't respond, not knowing where he was leading.

"I'm hoping you can shed some more light on it for us," he said.

"Well, I'm sorry for your trouble seeking me out, but I don't know anything more than I've already told Johnny," Kate said, pushing her chair away from the table and rising to her feet. "Now, if you'll excuse me—"

"I shouldn't be telling you this, but the chief brought your husband—ex-husband?—in for questioning," Stone said.

"Kevin?" Kate was surprised at how the name burned on her tongue. "Why?"

"An unfaithful husband, a beautiful dead woman and her newborn baby . . ."

Kate sat back down with a thud. "You have got to be kidding me."

"Fortunately, he checked out just fine," he continued. "The chief gave him a lie-detector test. He didn't like that too much."

"I could've saved you the trouble," Kate said. Whatever Kevin had done, he was no murderer. Or was this Detective Stone insinuating that *she* was?

"Your actions on the beach that morning made some fairly ugly thoughts cross the chief's mind," he said, in answer to Kate's unspoken question. "We had to rule out both you and your husband as suspects."

Kate shifted in her chair. "And now? What do you think now? Because this is ridiculous. I didn't kill anybody. And Johnny Stratton knows it."

"What do I think?" he asked, lowering his voice and leaning toward her across the table. "I think you know more than you're letting on. I can see it in your eyes right now."

Kate looked downward, not wanting to reveal herself even further, but she felt a blush rise to her cheeks.

Detective Stone continued, "Spend as many years as I have interrogating suspects, and you can tell when a person is lying. Or covering something up."

Kate looked into the man's eyes. She had no idea what to say.

"I work out of the precinct here in Wharton, and so the chief asked me to talk to you," he went on. "Why don't you just tell me whatever it is, Kate? Don't you want to help us solve this case?"

Kate thought of the woman's face, reflected in the mirror in her dreams. "Of course I do," she said.

"Then now is the time to tell us what you know."

Kate took a deep breath. This was getting out of hand. She and Kevin, suspects in a murder? Her dreams were one thing, but this was all too real. She needed to tell the truth, now. Yet, how was she supposed to do that? Psychic dreams? She was going to come off sounding like a wacko. First the cheating scandal and her rather public display at the Tavern, and now this. If people weren't talking about her before, they certainly would be now if word got out. She stood up from the table and nodded toward the door.

"Can we walk a bit?" she asked him.

He picked up his coffee and followed. "Lead on."

Out on the street, people were weaving in and out of the shops. Boats were floating in the harbor. An altogether normal day. Kate and Detective Stone ambled together along the shoreline path.

"I've been reluctant to say anything," Kate began, looking out at the water, "because I don't want to hear it whispered behind my back at the diner or the grocery store. If I tell you what I know, can you promise me it's not going to end up on the record?"

"What record?" Detective Stone grinned. "We're just two people talking out here on the lakeshore."

Maybe this wasn't going to be so difficult after all.

"This may sound insane," she said, eyeing him with a slight smile.

"You'd be surprised what I've seen and heard in this line of work." The detective sat down on a large piece of driftwood, picking up a rock and skipping it once, twice, then three times over the calm lake. When the ripples subsided, the surface was as still as a pane of glass. "Very little is going to sound insane to me."

"Okay," Kate admitted, joining him on the log. "I *have* seen that woman before."

Detective Stone seemed to be holding his breath. He stayed quiet for a bit, waiting for Kate to continue. When she didn't, he prompted her. "Go on."

"I've been having dreams about her." Kate sighed, knowing how crazy it sounded.

The detective did not respond right away. Then he narrowed his eyes and asked, "What kind of dreams?"

"I dream that I'm her," Kate shivered. "I've never seen her before— in real life, I mean. I don't know her name, who she is, or where she lived. I just started having these dreams a few weeks ago. In the dreams, I look into a mirror, and it's not my face I see. It's hers. Night after night. I didn't think too much of it beyond my own overactive imagination until that day we found her on the beach."

As she spoke, Stone watched her eyes. They were clear, unwavering, searching for his validation. He knew she was telling the truth, her truth, however unbelievable it might be.

"You're sure it's the same woman?"

Kate nodded. "I have absolutely no doubt it's the same woman. I dreamed bits of her life. And I saw her husband."

Stone was silent for a moment, considering what Kate had said. "You saw the husband in a dream. What was it about, specifically?"

"Well"—Kate thought back—"nothing really. Just ordinary things on an ordinary day. She was waking up in the morning. Her husband was there. They were deciding what they were going to do with the day. He brought her lilacs."

Detective Stone nodded. "Is there anything else?"

"No," Kate said, searching her mind for the smallest detail. "It seemed like they loved each other very much," she added, her heart doing a flip at the thought of it. "They seemed happy."

Detective Stone nodded, considering all that she'd said. Kate expected him to simply thank her and be on his way.

"I'm sorry I didn't tell Johnny about this before," she said. "I didn't know how to find the words to say it. I knew he'd think I was crazy. It just sounded so insane."

"How's this for insane?" Detective Stone smiled at her. "Would you be willing to come back to the station with me?"

"The station? Why?"

"You said you dreamed about the husband, right? Do you think you could pick his face out of a file of mug shots?"

"Absolutely," Kate said.

"Come on," Nick Stone said, scrambling to his feet, extending a hand to Kate to help her up.

When skin met skin, Kate was barraged with images playing in her mind like a slideshow, starring her and this detective. Scenes of laughter, of deep conversations, of sitting on a front porch. The two of them walking through the snowy woods, him carrying a camera, her mittened hand holding on to his. The two of them falling into bed, arms and legs entwined. Children ran through the slideshow, as did pets, all populating scenes of a life well lived. And then it was over, as instantly as it had begun.

Kate shook her head, staring at him. *What was that all about?* He was staring at her, too, looking into her eyes, then at their hands, then back again.

"Have you been in Wharton long?" Kate managed to cough out. "I'm here often because my cousin runs Harrison's House, and I don't recall ever seeing you before."

He nodded. "I just transferred up from the Twin Cities."

"What brought you here?" Kate wanted to know.

"This," he said, gesturing out toward the lake. "The outdoors. And I thought life at a slower pace might be just the thing for me for a while."

Stone didn't tell her about the face of the fifteen-year-old boy who had pulled a gun on him and his partner one snowy night in Minneapolis and had paid for that mistake with his life, nor did he tell her about the face of the boy's mother, whose searing, abject grief over the body of her dead son had taken up residence in Stone's heart and refused to leave.

"You wanted a slower pace, but you got a crazy lady dreaming about murder victims," Kate said, grinning. "Sorry about that, Detective Stone."

"Nick," he said. "You can call me Nick."

Two hours later, Kate's head was pounding after looking at countless mug shots, viewing every male face they had on file. None of them even slightly resembled the handsome man Kate had seen in her dreams.

Nick shook his head and sighed audibly. Seeing his disappointment, Kate winced. "I'm sorry I wasn't of more help."

"I knew it was a long shot," he said. "More than a long shot. No, I was thinking about something else, another bit of information I found out today."

"Can you tell me what it is?" she asked him.

Nick took a minute to think about this. He wasn't in the habit of sharing information about a murder case with a suspect, but at the same time, Kate was the only lead they had, albeit a strange, supernatural one. Maybe sharing a bit of information would jar something loose in her brain, or make her say more than she intended.

"We did an autopsy, but it raised more questions than it answered," he said. "When we don't have an ID on a body, we use things like dental work, clothes, scars, evidence of surgery, broken bones, anything to tell us any little detail about who the person was."

Kate nodded. She had watched enough crime shows on television to know the basics.

"First of all," Nick went on, "they found no evidence of surgery of any kind. No scars, nothing like that, except for stab wounds. Usually, people have some evidence of modern medicine, whether it be a broken bone that was set or a pin in their hip or a scar from a cesarean section."

"A nip and tuck around the jawline," Kate joked.

"Exactly," Nick confirmed. "But she didn't have any of that. And her teeth weren't in the greatest shape, either. No fillings, no bridges. No evidence of any kind of dental work."

"That's odd."

"That's not the half of it. We started investigating where her clothes came from," Nick continued. "Here's where it gets really strange. Her nightgown had a tag on the back of the neck. It was made by Anderson Mills, a clothing manufacturer based here in Wharton."

"That doesn't sound so strange," Kate was confused. "Especially if she lived around here."

Nick leaned in toward Kate and lowered his voice. "Nobody had ever heard of Anderson Mills, so I did some checking online. It shut down ninety years ago."

CHAPTER TWELVE

Kate had left the police station with a promise from Nick that he'd check in with her soon. After spending some time in the coffee shop processing the day's events, she walked up the hill to Harrison's House, her mind running in several directions at once.

She found Simon in front of a blazing fire in the living room. She snuggled in next to him.

"I think I'm going to take you up on your offer to stay in town awhile," Kate said.

"Splendid," Simon said, brushing some unseen lint off his shoulder. "I wasn't going to let you go, so it's nice I don't have to use restraints."

Kate pinched her cousin's arm. "I'm just bursting to tell you this news. There's been a development in the case of the woman on the beach, and I think I can find some answers right here in Wharton."

Kate told Simon about her experience with Nick that day, looking at mug shots to identify the husband she had seen in her dreams.

Simon's eyes danced. "Nick? Who is this *Nick*?" The way he said it, the name had several syllables.

"Detective Stone. He's new in town."

He squinted at Kate. "Nick Stone. It sounds so utterly masculine."

"Oh, stop," Kate groaned.

"Handsome detective, new in the department . . ."

"How do you know he's handsome?"

"From the look in your eyes when you said his name," he said, grinning from ear to ear. "What's he like?"

Now Kate could feel her face redden. "He's . . . I don't know. Nice, I guess."

Simon squinted at her. "Is he more Tom Cruise or Tom Selleck?"

Kate grinned. "Neither. Idris Elba."

Simon's eyes grew wide. "OMG. Someone's going to be inventing reasons to scurry down to the police station. And by 'someone,' naturally, I mean me."

Kate gave his arm another pinch, harder this time. "Get me a glass of wine, already, and I'll tell you the rest of the story."

Simon hopped up and returned with a bottle of wine and two glasses.

"You know what?" he said, pouring her a glass. "I just remembered that Jonathan met him."

"Who?"

"Your detective!"

"He's not my—"

"Oh, stop with your silly denials. Anyway, I was away when he stopped by to meet us. A couple of weeks ago. Jonathan said he was delightful and wondered if we shouldn't invent some crimes around here to keep him coming back."

"A dinner invitation might be more effective," Kate said, taking a sip.

"But not nearly as much fun. Now. Back to your mystery. I have a thought. Maybe the husband is the one who killed her. Maybe that's why he didn't report her missing."

"Nick—*Detective Stone* to you—strongly suspects that's the case," Kate said, taking a sip of wine. "He told me that, in his line of work, the most obvious answer is usually the right one. A murdered mother and baby usually points to the father."

"I can't imagine it." Simon squeezed Kate's hand. "Who could kill their own wife and baby?"

Kate shook her head. "I know. But plenty of people do. You only hurt the ones you love, isn't that the saying?"

"I don't get that they can't pinpoint the time of death, though," Simon said. "I thought they could tell exactly when a person died."

"My dad told me that the lake is so deep, so cold, and so clean—no algae or other organisms—that it can actually preserve bodies." Kate lowered her voice. "He said that if you die and sink to the bottom of Lake Superior, it's like you're on ice. It's hard to tell when, exactly, you expired."

In fact, beneath the lake's glassy surface at that very moment, a graveyard of sunken ships littered the austere, rocky bottom, filled with the well-preserved remains of the sailors who had been carried to their deaths hundreds of years before. Local divers knew which wrecks were free of these tangible ghosts and which to leave in silent memorial to the unfortunate souls entombed there.

"You mean, the bodies don't look dead?" Simon asked.

"According to my dad, they look dead all right," Kate explained. "It's just that they don't—I guess *decompose* isn't the right term—but they don't break down. They're intact."

Simon shuddered and crinkled his nose. The very thought of it was upsetting on many levels. A mother and a baby, frozen forever in the moment of their deaths.

"The thing about this particular body is, it—she—is extraordinarily well preserved, even by the lake's standards," Kate went on. "She seems to have been killed just a few minutes before we found her. But that's the other thing that's not adding up. It's what I was bursting to tell you. That nightgown she was wearing was at least ninety years old. It was made by a local company called Anderson Mills, which went out of business that long ago."

"So, she was into vintage clothing?"

89

"I was thinking the same thing," Kate said. "Is that thrift shop still open on Front Street? What's it called?"

"Mary Jane's." Simon nodded. "They've got a lot of vintage clothes."

"It stands to reason they might have stuff from Anderson Mills because it was a local company," Kate said.

"You're right," Simon said. "People cleaning out their grandmothers' closets is how they get lots of their stock. I know I took boxes and boxes of Grandma Hadley's things to them."

"This woman might have bought that nightgown there!" Kate said. "Maybe somebody on staff would remember her."

Kate took a sip of wine and wondered if Nick Stone had thought of that.

Much later, after she and Simon had had dinner, ambled around town with a happy malamute, and polished off that bottle of wine, Kate was snuggled in bed. As she lay there, her vision—or whatever it was—of herself and Nick Stone played over and over in her head. It was so clear, just as clear as her memory of her conversation with Simon earlier in the living room. What did it mean? Did she know this man and not remember him? Was her mind playing tricks on her?

She punched her pillow and turned onto her side, hoping for a dreamless sleep.

CHAPTER THIRTEEN

Great Bay, 1902

Addie's screams woke her parents and the dogs, all of whom were at her bedside in an instant. The girl was sitting upright in her bed, dripping with sweat. Her ashen face was whiter than the sheets that were tangled at her feet.

"Honey, honey," Marie cooed, smoothing her daughter's hair. "You just had a bad dream."

Addie stared at her, wild eyed, not quite realizing that she was home, safe in her bed, and not still enmeshed in those confusing dream images.

Marie encircled her daughter with her arms and drew her close, rubbing her back, murmuring soft words of comfort into her ear. The dogs jumped onto Addie's bed in their attempt to do the same.

"You're safe," Marie said to Addie in her darkened room. "It was just a bad dream. Hush now, girl. "

While Marie was comforting Addie, Marcus padded into the kitchen, lit the stove, and warmed some milk. He entered the room with a steaming cup, and all of them, father, mother, daughter, and dogs, sat on the bed for a moment while Addie sipped the warm milk.

"I had such a bad dream," Addie said, finally.

"I guess you did." Marcus smiled. "You woke the whole town. Now, drink the rest of that milk and settle back down. It won't be morning for a few hours. The fish aren't even up yet."

Addie did as she was told, grateful for the familiarity of it. She was here, in her own room with her own parents. Safe. Marcus smoothed his daughter's hair, and before going back to bed himself, he rapped her doorframe three times for luck, the way he used to when she was young and afraid of the dark. "This calls the angels," he would say to her. "Now they're here, watching over you." Addie smiled at the memory of it and felt better instantly. Marie wasn't so easily soothed. Addie had never awoken in the middle of the night before in such a state, and it rattled Marie into wakefulness. It was familiar. Disturbingly so.

She tucked her daughter beneath the blankets and sat with her, stroking her hair, until the girl fell into a shallow sleep. But Marie did not return to bed. No more sleep would come for her that night. She padded through the dark house to the kitchen. The stove was still hot, so she filled up the teapot. While the leaves were steeping, she retrieved the book from the hiding place she had selected for it years before, the third drawer down in her kitchen cupboard, where she kept her mother's old lace tablecloths. Marcus certainly wouldn't go rummaging around in there and happen upon it, nor would Addie without her permission. And there it was, a slim volume with a leather cover, weathered heavily by time.

She carried both the tea and the book to her chair at the sitting-room window. Sinking down into the chair, she put the book on her lap and sighed. She must read the story now. Her own daughter was writing the next chapter.

Marie had found the trunk in a dark and dusty corner of the attic when Addie was just a girl. Her parents had brought it with them from their former home—that and not much else. They had hurriedly packed up that horrible night, stuffing everything they could reach into the trunk, herding a young Marie out the door and quickly getting on their way. She had a vague recollection of her mother slipping the book in among more sensible things like bed linens and tablecloths and warm clothes, but when she'd stumbled across the trunk again, she hadn't been quite sure she'd find it there. Her memories of that night so long ago were starting to fade with the passage of time. She definitely remembered her mother crying when they had to leave the china behind, but did she really take the book? Marie wasn't so sure until she'd been brave enough to open it a few years ago. The trunk had been tucked away in the attic since the family arrived in Great Bay.

Marie thought back to that time, the day she had first laid eyes on the boy who would become her husband, during a town celebration at the lakeshore on a particularly warm August day. She and her family had just moved to Great Bay, a tiny hamlet some two hundred miles down the lakeshore from their previous home in Canada. They had fled under cover of night after what had happened to her grandmother—Marie didn't like to think about that horrible time in their lives—and her parents had vowed to make a fresh start for young Marie in a new town, where nobody knew their dark history. Her father was soon employed by one of the richest fishing families in town, and the three of them settled into a quiet routine. Nothing out of the ordinary. Nothing to call attention to themselves.

That day in August was the annual end-of-summer celebration in Great Bay—the townsfolk gathered after a busy fishing season and gave thanks for their good fortune with a potluck supper. Everyone brought a little something to share, spread blankets on the rocky shore, and chatted about the glorious summer that had passed. While Marie's father was introduced around by his new employer, and her mother was welcomed warmly by the neighborhood women, the young people enjoyed the unusual luxury of swimming in cool—rather than icy-cold—water after a month of temperatures well into the nineties.

Even the girls, dressed in daring new bathing costumes, ventured into the water, and with the blessing of her parents, Marie joined in the fun. She was up to her knees in the lake when she was literally bowled over by Marcus. He had been playing a game of catch in the shallow water with his brother, Gene, and was running toward an errant ball that was headed straight for Marie. His eyes on it instead of the girl in his path, he ran headlong into her, and the two of them were suddenly submerged, floating for a moment in a deep drop-off that Marie had not known was there. Beneath the water's surface, Marie had opened her eyes and seen Marcus's face for the first time. With his dark curls and olive skin, she thought he was the most beautiful boy she had ever seen. They were underwater for just a few seconds, but for Marie, the moment lasted forever—the stillness, the slight music of the water in her ears, the warmth of its embrace. When they made their way back onto shore, laughing, sputtering, Marcus apologizing and offering Marie his hand, she knew without a doubt that she'd spend the rest of her life with this boy.

She and Marcus still lived in the same house her parents had bought all those years ago. As newlyweds, they had moved in with her mother after her father's death. He had been well enough to walk Marie down the aisle but died shortly thereafter, leaving her mother, Vivienne, with a sickness that could only be described as a broken heart. She was weakened by the loss, permanently it seemed. From the moment of his death until the moment of hers, she could never take a full breath in, nor could she exert herself to any degree. Even the simple act of cooking the nightly meal was too much. It was as though her life force was seeping away, bit by bit. The townspeople thought it was grief, but Vivienne knew it was more than that. Her soul was longing to be free of its confines to join her beloved husband once again. She was incomplete without him, and had no wish to walk through life as half of a whole. Before the new year dawned, she would be gone.

She had but one request on her deathbed. "Bury me at sea," she whispered to Marie just days before she died. "Don't put me in the ground. I don't belong there. I want to go back into the water."

"You don't want to be buried next to Father?" Marie's eyes stung as she quickly blinked away the tears.

Vivienne shook her head. "He's not in the ground, child. That's just the shell of his body. Your father is waiting for me, beyond. The reunion . . ." Her words evaporated into a deep sigh as she smiled, imagining it.

A burial at sea was not the Christian thing to do, but it was her mother's last wish, and Marie was determined to carry it out. So she and Marcus huddled together and came up with a plan. When the time came, they would tell the townspeople that, sick as she was, Vivienne had asked to make one last trip to their former home to see family and friends. Marcus and Marie would take her in Marcus's fishing boat, and, as far as the townspeople in Great Bay were concerned, Vivienne would perish on the trip. Meanwhile, Marcus and Marie would take her mother's body for one last sail, way out into the vastness of the lake.

Late one autumn afternoon, Vivienne called her daughter to her bedside. "It's time," she managed to say. "Take me down to the lake, child."

"But, *Maman*," Marie protested, holding a cool cloth to her mother's fevered brow. "You should rest here, in bed."

Vivienne just shook her head. "I want the last sight I see in this life to be the water."

So Marcus scooped her out of her bed—she was nothing more than skin and bones by that point—and carried her down to the lake, Marie trailing close behind. As daughter sat with mother at the lakeshore, Marcus readied his fishing boat, hoisting its single sail and making a comfy nest out of blankets and pillows.

"What do you say we go for a ride, Vivienne?" He smiled so tenderly that Marie's eyes stung with tears. He set her mother in the nest of blankets in the back of the boat, and Marie scrambled alongside her. In no time, they were off.

They sailed straight out into open water, aided by a gentle tailwind. The lake's surface was as still as glass as they skimmed along. Marie held her mother's hand and watched Marcus as he steered the boat, keeping a sharp eye on the horizon. As the setting sun illuminated the sky with fiery shades of purple, pink, and red, Marie thought: *Maybe now is not the time. Maybe she will stay with us awhile longer.* But it was not to be.

Vivienne's eyes shone with tears, and a smile lit up her face. "Pierre," she whispered, extending one trembling hand. Then she laid her head on her daughter's shoulder, sighed deeply, and it was over. Or, for Vivienne, just beginning.

"Is she gone?" Marcus asked.

Marie held her mother's wrist, but there was no pulse. She listened to her chest for a heartbeat but heard only silence. Her skin was already beginning to cool. There was no life left.

When they slipped Vivienne's body overboard, Marie did not say a prayer, not a conventional one anyway. "Sleep well, *Maman*," she said as she watched Vivienne's body sink under the water's glassy surface.

So the trunk sat, mostly forgotten, until something drew Marie to it again when Addie was a little girl. She hadn't touched the trunk since her family had tucked it into that dusty corner, decades earlier. Was the book still there? Had it ever been? She'd opened the trunk and dug through the layers of linens until her hand hit something smooth and hard. She'd slipped the book under her apron and stolen back downstairs to the kitchen, where she'd put it in the drawer with her mother's lace tablecloths.

Now it was time to read the old tale again.

"I'm sorry, *Maman*," Marie whispered, "but this can't stay hidden forever." Then she watched out the window as the moonlight glistened on the lake until the sun's first rays penetrated the darkness.

The next morning, after Marcus and his brother had headed onto the lake to gather up the day's catch—it wouldn't be too long before the encroaching ice ended their season for the year—Marie sat with her daughter in front of the fire in the living room.

"Do you remember your dream?" Marie asked.

"I don't think I'll ever forget it," Addie said with a nod, shuddering. She drew a shawl around her shoulders, shielding herself from the cold she still felt within.

Marie waited for her daughter to continue, but she didn't. Silence fell between them.

She held out the book to Addie. "It was written, or written down, you might say, by my grandmother. I think it's time you read it."

"Your grandmother?" Addie leaned forward. "Truly?"

"Truly." Marie smiled, nodding in the direction of the book.

Addie grasped it and ran one hand along the soft leather cover. It smelled of the past somehow. She opened it and saw yellowed pages of faded, handwritten words. "The Daughter of the Lake," she said, reading the title aloud. "Is this a storybook?"

"It is a storybook, yes. After you've read it, we'll talk about what kind of story."

Addie curled her legs up underneath her as her eyes settled on the first page, squinting to make out her great-grandmother's spidery, purplish scrawl, and she began to read.

The Daughter of the Lake

Long, long ago, on the shores of the greatest inland sea, lived a beautiful girl, the daughter of a French Canadian fur trapper and his young native bride. Her name was Geneviève, after the trapper's own mother, and with her jet-black hair and shining, deep-blue eyes, she was considered to be the most beautiful girl in their village, not only for her physical beauty but also for her disposition. Life was not easy in that time and place— harsh winds blew off the lake year-round, and snow piled up in the winters, when food was scarce. People worked hard to survive. Yet Geneviève was a sunny little girl, always smiling and laughing, never cross or angry. She brought great joy to her parents—she was the apple of her father's eye—and to her entire village as well.

As she grew older, Geneviève begged to accompany her father on his trapping trips. She missed him when he was away for weeks, sometimes months, at a time. She wanted to see the world, or at least her corner of it, and she longed to sit in her father's sleek and sturdy canoe as he paddled across the glistening water. But it was the one thing he denied her.

"You are too small yet," he would say. "It's too dangerous for a little one out on the big water. And the land is no better. Bears, Geneviève. Mountain lions!"

She would always accept his denials with good grace and humor, throwing her arms around him and saying, "Maybe next year, Papa."

"Next year" finally came. Geneviève had grown into a young woman and was being pursued by all the young men in the village. Evening after evening, one or another of them would appear at their door, wanting Geneviève to sit on the porch with them or accompany them on a stroll. Her father grew increasingly worried by this—he thought his girl was much too young for such things—and one evening he spoke to her mother in hushed tones. "I must travel to Wharton, a week's paddle down the shoreline, to meet with the fur trader there. I know of friendly outposts all along the route with people who will be happy to take us in. Perhaps getting the girl away from here for a time will quiet things down."

"I know she'll be safe in your care," her mother said, and it was decided. The next morning, they set off.

Geneviève sat in the front of her father's canoe, taking in the water's fresh scent. She loved how it sparkled as the sun hit its surface, and how the shoreline changed from sandy to rocky to dense woods as they paddled along. She dragged her hand in the cool water and looked at her reflection over the side of the canoe. After several days of travel, they arrived in Wharton, where they sought out the local fur trader, who offered them accommodations in his home. As her father conducted business with the man, Geneviève soaked in a hot bath prepared for her by the fur trader's wife, who understood that a girl would enjoy such an indulgence after a long trip. Then Geneviève settled into the soft featherbed in her room and fell immediately to sleep, not realizing that her father had not returned.

Later that night, she felt someone shaking her awake. "Get up, my dear," the wife of the fur trader said to her. "Something has happened. It's your father. You must come. Quickly."

She led Geneviève down the stairs to the drawing room, where her father lay sprawled on the floor. A man wearing a black suit knelt over him, and when the man looked into Geneviève's stricken face, he shook his head, his mouth a thin line.

"Papa!" she cried and fell at her father's side. "Wake up!" But she knew from the coldness of his skin that he was no longer there.

"He collapsed as we were discussing business," said the fur trader, running one hand through his hair. "At least you can be comforted by the swiftness of his death, my dear. He did not suffer."

"But—" Geneviève searched each of their faces in turn. "That's impossible! We traveled so far to get here ... He just ..." But her words were sucked down into an eddy of grief.

"Say your goodbyes, child," the fur trader's wife told her. "The undertaker and his men are here now to take him away."

Geneviève watched, both hands over her mouth, as the men brought a pine coffin into the house through the front door. She watched as they placed her father inside and winced as they closed the lid. And she watched as they began to walk out the door, her father's coffin on their shoulders.

"This is a mistake," she murmured, following the men out the door, crying, "Papa! Papa!"

But they put him into their wagon, and the horses clopped off down the street. They turned the corner and were gone. She was alone.

"Come inside, girl!" the fur trader's wife called to her.

But Geneviève ran into the night, blinded by fear and panic and grief. She had no idea where she was going until she found herself at the water's edge. There, she fell to her knees and wept for her father and for herself. How could she possibly get home now? Would she ever return to her mother or to the village she loved? What would become of her?

The sheer force of Geneviève's wail awakened a sleeping spirit, the spirit of the lake itself. What was making this incredible racket? He took a quick breath in when he saw it was the most beautiful girl he had ever seen, the same girl that he had watched crossing the lake for the past several days, delighting at the way the sun was glinting on the water. It was the same girl who had smiled so sweetly as she had trailed her hand along the water's surface while the canoe had skimmed its way toward its destination. The same girl who had marveled aloud at the vastness of the lake, its grandeur, its majesty. Her words of wonder at the lake's beauty had sounded like a prayer to the spirit of the lake, and he had let them wash over him like a wave. Not many people said them anymore.

In that time and place, the people had begun to forget the old legends and tales told to them by their ancestors, legends of fearsome spirits of the land and the water and the sky. They no longer believed, no longer prayed, and so the spirits turned a blind eye to their troubles, refusing help during times of need and delighting in confounding those who crossed their paths. But this girl, something about her was not like the others. Geneviève's beauty and the force of her grief softened the lake spirit's heart. He watched as she wept by the lakeshore and moved closer to listen.

"Papa! Why did you leave me?" she wailed. "How am I to get home? What am I to do? I am all alone in this strange place!"

The spirit of the lake knew how far she had traveled to get there—she couldn't possibly get home on her own. And the people, he thought with a sneer of disgust, couldn't be counted on to help her.

And so he waded out of the water, donning the human form that he and all of the spirits kept for occasions when they walked among the people, and said to her, "I will take you home."

Geneviève looked up into his black eyes, and for some reason, she was not afraid of this stranger. He seemed to radiate a glow, even there in the darkness.

"My canoe is nearby." He gestured to a long wooden boat. "I have blankets and a heavy coat to keep you warm and plenty of food for the journey. You will arrive safely, this I promise you."

He extended his hand to her, and she reached up to grasp it. "I don't know what I would have done if you hadn't come along."

He placed his heavy coat on her shoulders, and she drew it around her, cuddling into its warm fur lining. Then she settled into the front of his canoe on a nest of soft blankets he had arranged for her, and they were off, gliding across the still water into the night.

The spirit of the lake had only planned to ferry her safely home, but sometime during the trip, he found himself staring at her long, shining hair instead of at the horizon as she sat in the front of his canoe. He began to make excuses to stop paddling and rest on land for a while so he could have a chance to sit and look into her bright eyes and talk with her face-to-face. He asked her about her home and her family and her upbringing. She spoke so lovingly of her parents that it melted his heart, and the first moment he heard her laugh, he knew he had fallen deeply in love with her.

When they finally reached her home, they were greeted with both celebration and grief. As the village mourned the loss of Geneviève's father, they also celebrated the stranger who had been so kind to return Geneviève to the people she loved. They offered food and drink and hospitality to the stranger, who accepted it gratefully.

But Geneviève's mother looked at this man and knew that it was not simple human kindness that had compelled him to save her daughter, and perhaps not *human* kindness at all. She was closer to the old ways and legends than anyone else in her village—she had heard tales from her elders of the spirits of nature taking human form and walking among the people. There was a slight glow about them, her grandmother had said, a subtle sheen in their eyes that wasn't quite human. *Look carefully enough,* her grandmother had said, *and you'll see it.*

Geneviève's mother looked carefully at the stranger and knew what she saw. One evening, when they were sitting by the fire, when nobody else was near enough to listen, she told him she recognized who he was. He did not deny it.

"What do you want of her?" Geneviève's mother demanded.

"I am in love with Geneviève," the spirit answered. "I want her to be my wife."

"But you cannot marry my daughter!" her mother cried. "She cannot live where you live."

The spirit nodded his head. "That is why I will consent to live where she lives. If she'll have me."

Coming upon them at that moment, Geneviève sat down next to him and held out her hands for his to grasp. "If I'll have you?" She smiled.

"Since your father is not here with us, I was asking your mother for your hand in marriage." He smiled, his face glowing like the lake's surface on a sundrenched day. "If you'll have me."

Geneviève threw her arms around him and laughed, a sound that filled up his heart like the prayers of the faithful once had. And so it was done. The spirit of the lake took the human name of Jean-Pierre to honor his bride's father and married Geneviève on the lakeshore one beautiful, bright day. They settled into a small house in the village.

Along with his new name and his new bride, Jean-Pierre took on a new vocation as well, that of a fisherman. It was a way for him to at least visit his beloved home, even if he could no longer dwell there. He would paddle his canoe into a secluded spot, shed his human form, and slip beneath the water's surface, stretching out to touch each and every one of the billions of water droplets that made up this great lake. Home. And there he would stay for much of the day—fishermen were away from the village from before sunup until sundown, after all—until he would fill his canoe with fish, don his human form again and paddle toward the village and his beloved wife. If there was anything Jean-Pierre adored more than his water realm, it was only Geneviève.

Soon, they welcomed a child into the world, whom they called Violette. Jean-Pierre walked to the lakeshore with the babe in his arms and waded into the shallows to introduce his darling girl to his true home.

"She'll catch her death!" Geneviève's mother called to him, but he wasn't so sure about that. This girl was a spirit of the lake just like her father, wasn't she? When he set the girl into the water and she floated like a fish, he knew he was right. The villagers rejoiced with the young couple as two became three.

But as happy as the Lake was on land, he began to see signs that things weren't right in the water. Salmon did not spawn, trout were dying. Fishermen came home with empty nets day after day. The shoreline was receding. No waves hit the rocks, not even on the windiest of days. No sparkle shone on the lake's surface, just a dull sheen. Without its spirit, the lake itself was dying. Jean-Pierre knew what he had to do, although it broke his heart.

The spirit of the lake spent one last night with his beloved Geneviève, telling her everything. At first, she didn't believe him, but her mother confirmed the truth of what he had said. And the couple held each other until the sun came up, for what they knew would be the last time. Then the Lake, his bride, and their daughter walked down to the shore, where he waded into the shallows and bent down to his daughter. "I will watch over you even though I cannot be with you," he said. "You are the daughter of the lake. The water will always be your place of refuge."

"Will I ever see you again?" asked Geneviève, tears welling up in her eyes.

He looked up at the shining full moon. "Luna has promised to lend you her gifts," he said. "Dream, my love, and you shall find me."

And with that, he sloughed off his human form, sank down, and vanished into the water.

Geneviève watched as a great fury was stirred up then, enormous waves coming forth on a calm day, crashing violently into the rocks on shore. She could feel her husband's spirit in the icy spray, and smell his scent on the wind.

Although she sat on the lakeshore every day of her life, that was the last Geneviève saw of her husband until her dying day. She was an old woman then, lying on the bed in the same house they had shared all those years ago. He appeared to her just as he was back then, young, vibrant, glowing. He carried her to the shoreline and sat with her, stroking her hair and telling her how much he loved her, until she took her last breath. Then he gathered her body into his arms and walked into the shallows, the waves lapping gently at the shore.

CHAPTER FOURTEEN

Great Bay

Addie closed the book and sighed. "What a beautiful and sad folk tale. You said your grandmother wrote it?"

Marie nodded. "Yes, child. But it's not just a folk tale. Geneviève was your grandmother's grandmother."

Addie squinted and curled her nose. "I don't mean to sound impertinent, but that's just not true."

"No, you don't understand, my girl. I'm not saying this folk tale is true, but as you know, many of these old tales have kernels of truth in them, no?"

Addie nodded. "I guess so."

"My *grand-mère* wrote this story to . . . well, to explain certain things about our family to future generations."

Addie curled her legs underneath her. "I'm not sure I understand. What sort of things?"

"It's the women in our family, Addie. We have gifts. One is a rather otherworldly relationship with the lake—"

Addie took in a quick breath. She knew all about that. It's just what had always been. "What's the other gift?"

"We have the gift of dreaming," Marie said, stroking her daughter's hair. "I've always known you were happiest in the lake—that was evident from the day you were born—but I didn't know you had inherited the dream gift, until now. And the gift of sight."

Addie shook her head. "Why haven't you ever told me about this?"

"My mother made me vow to keep it a secret and never tell a soul," Marie said, her voice low. "Not even your father knows. But it's the truth, and now I'm telling you."

"Why couldn't you tell anyone? What's the harm?"

"The harm is other people, Addie. My grandmother was very gifted in dreaming—she got so good at it that she even interpreted the dreams of others—and she was killed because of it."

Addie's eyes grew wide, and a gnarling began to form in the pit of her stomach. She wasn't so sure she was going to like this story.

"She had the gift from the time she was a young girl," Marie went on. "When I was just a child, I remember people coming from miles around to see her at her house—this was up in the old country, of course, before my parents and I came to Great Bay.

"They'd knock at the back door, not wanting to be seen coming in the front of the house. I was young then, but even I knew that people thought it was rather blasphemous to put any stock in dreams. They would pretend not to know my grandmother on the street or in town, but nonetheless, they would all come through the back door to sit at her kitchen table from time to time, have a cup of tea, and talk to her about their dreams."

"What was she like?" Addie wanted to know.

"For one thing, her name was Violette," Marie said.

Addie smiled. She had not known this before now.

Marie went on. "She told me that she was a great beauty in her youth, with long black hair and deep, dark eyes. She told me that all the boys in town were after her, but she only had eyes for my grandfather, who was a young apprentice for the town's blacksmith. Her parents didn't approve; they thought she could do better, but she defied them and married him anyway. She was right, of course. They had eight children and were happily married for thirty years.

"By the time I came along, my grandfather had died and my grandmother was an old woman, but I still thought she was beautiful," Marie went on. "She was wild and funny and reminded me of the gypsies who would travel through town now and then. She always had something good simmering on the stove, stew or soup or mulled cider. Bread in the oven. I would make my way across town to her house whenever I could because I loved her and I was interested in hearing her stories."

Marie stopped then, looking backward in time to those idyllic childhood days. Addie sat quietly, knowing that her mother would pick up the story where she left off.

"As I said, she'd had the gift since she was a young girl," Marie continued. "It was forbidden to talk of such things openly—the church had a tight rein on people then, much tighter than it does now, and things like dream interpretation were considered heresy. You could be hanged, or worse, for something like that. She had to be very careful. But she told me that, when she was a child, she herself had a vivid dream that told her she had the gift. It told her that she would use it to help people decipher what their dreams were trying to tell them.

"She believed that dreams were messages from the spirit world," Marie whispered. "They were a communication from the beyond, or from another time, another place. She believed that people needed to trust what their dreams were telling them—for their own good.

"First, she would ask them to describe what happened in their dreams," Marie confided. "Then, she would tell them what it all meant. I truly don't know how she did it, but much of what she said was true. Or came true."

"What kinds of things?"

"I don't remember much of that, because she never let me stay in the room when she was talking with people about this," Marie said, and it wasn't quite a lie. Young Marie would scoot out of the room, it was true, but she would listen at the doorway, just as her grandmother knew she would. But now, with Addie staring at her, wide eyed, Marie knew she had to tell the whole tale. It was time. For her daughter's own good.

"On the last day I ever saw my grandmother, I was visiting when a man came to the door, asking grandmother to interpret a dream he'd had the night before. In the dream, he was walking through his own house and came upon a door he had never seen. He opened the door to find a long table filled with all kinds of food. Fruit, breads, soups, meat, cakes. A feast was laid out before him. His wife was there with a group of people, laughing and eating and having a wonderful time, until she caught sight of him. Then everything—the wife and the table, the people, the food—all of it vanished, and he was left standing in a stark, empty room, alone.

"My grandmother was not afraid to talk about the bad along with the good. In fact, she would warn people before they sat down at her table that if she saw bad things that had already happened or especially warnings of future events, she would tell them without hesitation. It might not be pleasant, it might not be palatable information, but she would tell them nonetheless. She warned them to be prepared for the worst, and also for the best. Dreams didn't just predict harsh events in the future, they also foretold marriages, babies, and bountiful crops.

"On this day, as she did every day, she told the man what she knew to be true. His dream was a warning that his wife was not who she appeared to be. She was living a secret life. He objected to this strenuously, telling my grandmother what a wonderful woman he had married. But again she told him, 'Go home and watch your wife carefully. Do not let on that you suspect her of anything. She will reveal herself to you by accident, and then you will know.' I watched in the doorway as the man stormed out of the house in a rage.

"It did not end well. I was just a child, and my parents tried to shield me from much of it, but I learned that the man did indeed find his wife in the arms of another man several days later. In a jealous rage, he killed his wife and her lover, then turned that blistering fury on my grandmother. He ran through the streets, calling her a demon who had bewitched his wife with an evil spell. Soon, a crowd of townspeople gathered and followed him to her home."

Addie's hands flew to her mouth. "Oh no!"

"Yes, child. I'll spare you the horrible details, but my grandmother did not make it out alive, because they believed she was a witch. That very day, when my father heard the news of what had transpired in the town, he packed up our family's possessions and we fled, fearing the angry crowd would turn on us, too. When we ended up in Great Bay, my mother declared there would be no more talk of dreams or spirits or enchantment. We would be a good Christian family. Nothing more."

Marie swallowed hard and continued. "I truly had forgotten about the old family story as the years went by, but when you were born, your affinity for the water . . . and now your dreams . . ."

Addie took a deep breath in. "I'm a daughter of the lake, too?"

Marie nodded. "I want you always to honor your great-grandmother and the lake by listening to the wisdom of your dreams. Promise me, Addie."

"I will, Mama," Addie promised.

"Now," Marie said, "let's talk about the dream you had last night. I have a feeling that together you and I can unlock what it was trying to tell you."

CHAPTER FIFTEEN

The next morning dawned crisp and bright in Wharton, but Kate's head was fuzzy from too much wine the night before. What had Simon been thinking, opening bottle after bottle? What had she been thinking, drinking it all? She decided to take a walk along the shoreline with Alaska to clear her head before meeting Simon back at the inn for breakfast.

She recognized a familiar figure on the lakeshore, and the sight of him stopped her short. She thought of turning around and heading back up to the inn before she had to talk to him, but Alaska started barking at a small dog that was now running toward them.

Nick Stone whirled around. "Queenie! No!"

But the dog just kept coming. Kate pulled Alaska in tight. Malamutes were famously wary of, and even aggressive toward, other dogs, and because of their size and strength, they could easily kill with one bite.

Kate positioned herself between the small dog and Alaska as Nick ran toward them. But both of their efforts failed—and to Kate's astonishment, the two dogs greeted each other like old friends. Sniffing, jumping, playing.

"Wow," Nick said, eyeing Alaska. "That's a whole lot of dog. Is she a malamute?"

Kate nodded. "She is indeed. And yours? Corgi?"

"My faithful companion, Queenie."

"Not named for the most famous corgi-phile in the world . . ."

"Queen Elizabeth," he said, laughing. "I didn't name her. She's a rescue."

The two of them, their dogs running ahead, began walking down the shoreline together.

"Her original owner was an elderly lady who died a rather suspicious death," he said, kicking a rock into the water. "Poison, as it turned out."

"Oh no."

"Yeah. It was ugly. The son-in-law. Anyway, Queenie ended up homeless. I was investigating the crime and—I don't know. I took one look at her, sitting vigil so sadly by the body of her dead owner, and I just couldn't let her go to a shelter. I took her home with me then and there. That was eight years ago. She hasn't left my side since, through thick and thin."

Kate smiled at this man, knowing how powerful an animal's love and loyalty could be. She was glad he felt the same way.

"I'd have thought you were more the police-dog type," she said.

He laughed. "I tried to convince them to send Queenie through the training, but the powers that be didn't think that a corgi would instill the same fear in criminals as a German shepherd. I think they're wrong about that, by the way. She's small, but she's a badass."

Kate chuckled. "Any new developments on the case since we talked yesterday?" she asked.

"Not that I can say," Nick hedged, not telling her about the DNA results they'd received late yesterday afternoon.

She stopped. "So, there is something."

"There might be, but I'm not in the habit of blurting out details of a murder case to a random dog walker-slash-suspect in said case."

Kate caught the note of teasing in his voice, but his words made her stomach flip. "I'm still a suspect?"

"Until we solve this case, everyone is a suspect," he said, tilting his head toward an elderly woman making her way down the street with a walker. "Her, for example."

Kate muffled a laugh. "I thought of something, actually, about that ninety-year-old nightgown," she said.

"Did you, now?"

"I did," Kate said. "It's got to be vintage. I was thinking—since Anderson Mills was based here in Wharton, the thrift shop on Front Street might have carried the nightgown. Our woman might have bought it there. Somebody might remember her."

"Not bad sleuthing, Miss Marple." He grinned. "But unfortunately, no. They have carried some items from Anderson, but not for a long time. And nobody there recognized the woman in the photo or the nightgown she was wearing."

Kate felt her spirits drop. "So you've been there already. I was going to stop in after breakfast."

"Beat you to the punch, I'm afraid," Nick said. "It's good when the detectives are one or two steps ahead of the suspects, as a rule."

Kate stopped. "You don't *really* believe I had anything to do with this, do you?"

Nick gave her a sidelong glance. "In my gut, no," he said. "And neither does Queenie, in case you were wondering about that. But, like I said—"

"I know, I know, everyone is a suspect until you solve the case," Kate said.

"And now, I've got to get back to it," he said. "Nice to see you again, Kate Granger."

He set off, Queenie at his heels, but he turned back toward Kate. Walking backward a few steps, he said, "Maybe I'll see you out here walking your dog again sometime soon."

Kate could feel the heat rising to her cheeks. "Maybe!" she called, holding up a hand to wave. And then she turned back toward the inn, walking with a buoyancy in her step that she hadn't felt in a long time.

～

She found Simon sitting at a table by the window in the dining room with a breakfast of goat cheese frittata, sausage, and steaming coffee, along with two mimosas.

"You are a very bad man," Kate laughed, taking one of the flutes.

"Thought you could use a little hair of the dog," Simon said. "I know I could. Head. Ache. I should know better. Red-wine hangovers will kill you."

"Last night was fun." Kate smiled and sat down. They squeezed each other's hands. Kate was impossibly glad to be in Wharton with Simon. It had been much too long since they had really spent time together. Five years too long.

"Listen, I've had an idea," Simon said. "You know we're planning to tackle that third-floor restoration project this winter. A ton of old boxes are up there that I just haven't had a chance to get to. I want to sift through them and find any suitable photographs or artwork or other things to display. You know I like to use original things from the house to decorate."

"And?"

"And I'd love your help with that. Since you're planning on staying in town awhile, I thought maybe I could steal you for the rest of the day. Maybe two."

"I'd love that!" Kate cried. She could think of no better way to spend time than combing through old family heirlooms and artifacts of the past. Just the thing to take her mind off the present. "I haven't been up to that third floor since we were kids."

The cousins shared a grimace. When visiting their grandparents, young Kate and Simon had feared the third floor. The house had been inhabited by elderly people for so many years that the third floor, with the steep staircase leading up to it, had long since fallen into disrepair. It was dark, dusty, and filled with the ghosts of the past—more so than either child realized—and as such, was a perfect haven for goose-bumped childhood exploration.

One of their favorite games was a variation of "chicken." Hand in hand, Kate and Simon would creep up the dark staircase, knowing that a ghastly portrait, propped haphazardly against a trunk, awaited them when they reached the top. It was the image of a particularly stern woman wearing a black dress and veil, like some sort of haunted bride of the dead. Neither child knew that it was a portrait of Celeste's mother, who was hanging on to a peculiar dislike of the Connor children and their presence in a house she still regarded as her daughter's and her daughter's alone.

The game was to see who could endure the gaze of the "lady in black" the longest. Usually it ended seconds after it began, with Simon and Kate flying—shrieking, breathless, hearts pumping—down the stairs, back to the normalcy and safety of their grandmother's welcoming home. One day, however, the game went differently.

As Simon beat the well-worn path down the stairs, Kate remained in the room, unable to move, transfixed by the portrait's gaze. Mysterious and threatening as it was to a nine-year-old girl, the woman's flat image on the canvas—her dark, hollow eyes penetrating the veil; her stern countenance; her black dress; all of it—seemed to animate, there, before Kate's wide eyes.

Kate heard the words, clear and forbidding.

"Get out. Get out of this house."

Frozen to the spot, Kate gasped but could not take in any air. She felt as though all the oxygen had been sucked out of the room. Kate tried to take a breath, and then another, then another, but nothing entered her lungs.

She found her feet and flew down the stairs in an instant, screaming in the high-pitched way that only young girls can manage, knocking Simon down when, it seemed, a full lifetime later, she finally reached the bottom.

"You win," Simon said, simply.

"I don't want to go up there again." Kate was gasping, finally able to take a breath, feeling as though she had been nearly suffocated.

And that was the end of their third-floor games.

Now, with decades of sense and reason between her and that otherworldly experience, she was anxious to see what secrets the third floor held.

Kate took a bite of her breakfast. "I had intended to start trying to find more information about my mystery woman today, but, hey, Addie can wait."

Simon looked at her for a long while. "What did you say?"

"When?" Kate was confused.

"Just now. What did you say?"

"I said that I was going to delve into this mystery today, but it can wait," Kate said.

"No, you didn't say that." Simon's eyes were wide. "I think you said, 'Addie can wait.' Who's Addie?"

Kate was silent, searching her brain. "I have no idea," she said, finally. "I wasn't thinking. I just said it."

Simon finished his mimosa in a gulp and set the flute down on the table. "Okay, that's really weird." He was excited. The two sat staring at each other. "Katie, do you think that's her name? *Your* woman's name?"

"I don't know." Kate rubbed her arms and shivered.

"Oh, that's her name," Simon said, holding out his arm to display goose bumps. "I can feel it."

"Me too," Kate said, her thoughts swirling back toward her dreams, the woman and her husband, her body on the beach.

"Addie," Simon was murmuring. "What kind of name is that, anyway?"

"It sounds sort of old fashioned, doesn't it? Could be short for Adeline or something like that," Kate said. "Maybe it came up in one of my dreams about her, and it just slipped my mind. How else would I know it?"

"How else, indeed," Simon said, raising his eyebrows with a mock sense of drama. "This little mystery just keeps getting better and better. You should come here more often. This is the most excitement I've had in months."

After breakfast, Simon and Kate made their way through Harrison's House toward the third floor. Kate loved these hallways. The walls were papered with a rich, red print and filled with family photos and portraits. The brightly colored decor—deep reds and yellows contrasted with the dark wood of the doors, doorframes, and moldings—allowed visitors to imagine this house in its heyday more than a century ago. Kate liked to think of her grandmother as a child in this house, growing up with all this opulence and beauty around her.

"We just haven't had a chance to tackle the renovation of the third floor before now," Simon lamented as they walked through the hallways. "We had intended to renovate one floor a year, but we got so busy so quickly . . ." As they reached a door at the end of the second-floor hallway, he fished an old-fashioned skeleton key out of his pocket.

"Original?" Kate wondered.

"Of course," Simon replied. "I had all of the locks replaced on the guest bedrooms, but there was just something about these old keys that made me want to keep some of them around." He held the key up for Kate to see.

"It really gives you a sense of how long ago this place was built," Kate mused. "I haven't seen a key like that in years. I can't think of the last time."

"I guarantee you, when you get upstairs, you won't remember the last time you saw that much dust, either." Simon laughed and put the key in the lock. It opened with a satisfying *chock*. Hand in hand, just as he had when they were children, Simon led Kate up the cobwebbed stairway.

The contrast was dramatic and immediate. The vibrant colors of the second-floor hallway faded as the pair ascended the stairs, which seemed as gray and dull as the thick coating of dust covering it all. Kate stopped halfway up the staircase and turned around, noting the odd juxtaposition of the reds and yellows in the hallway through the doorframe with the dull gray of the staircase on which they now stood.

"You know what this reminds me of?" Kate whispered to Simon. "The scene in *The Wizard of Oz* when Dorothy and Toto walk out of their black-and-white world into the rich colors of Oz for the first time. Only in reverse."

"If you're Dorothy, we both know who that makes me. I resent it."

Kate laughed and gave her cousin a squeeze on the arm. They reached the top of the stairs, and Kate braced for her first view of the portrait in decades. It wasn't there. She looked this way and that. Nothing.

"What did you do with the lady?" she asked her cousin.

"Oh, I brought her downstairs," he said, brushing a cobweb from his shoulder. "She hangs over my bed now."

Kate stared at her cousin, open mouthed. Simon shrieked with laughter.

"You are the most gullible person alive." He shoved her arm, giggling. "As if I'd have that scowling shrew's picture anywhere near me. I had Jonathan bring her down into the basement. I wouldn't even touch her, and yet I didn't dare throw her out."

Only then did Kate realize she hadn't yet seen Simon's longtime partner.

"Where is Jonathan?" she asked. "With everything going on, I didn't even think to ask. My God, I've been so self-absorbed. I'm so sorry."

"He's antiquing down south," Simon said quickly. "We need some more furniture for this floor, and he needed a solo trip. And you're forgiven for being self-absorbed. Now, let's get to these boxes."

Kate took hold of her cousin's hands. "No. You love antiquing. You live for antiquing. You are never happier than when you're haggling with an antique dealer."

"And?"

"And—why didn't you go with him?"

Simon smiled and squeezed her hands. "The dearest person in my world had her world fall apart, that's why. When you called wanting to come here for a few days, I wasn't about to say no. We had planned to be gone, so we didn't book anybody in the hotel for these two weeks. And so, with no guests on the horizon, it seemed like the perfect chance to get some alone time, just me and you."

Only then did it dawn on Kate she hadn't seen any other guests, either. Self-absorbed indeed.

Tears tickled the backs of her eyes. "You gave up an antiquing trip with Jonathan for me?"

"Are you kidding? I'd give up stumbling across the Hope Diamond's twin in an old trunk for you." He furrowed his brow. "Well, okay. Not that. But just about anything else."

The two shared a laugh. But Kate felt a twinge of guilt all the same.

"You're so good to me," she said.

"Of course I am," he sniffed. "It's what I do."

Kate coughed and looked around. "Boy, you weren't kidding about the dust up here," she said.

To Kate, the room seemed to be the size of a high school gymnasium, or near enough. Rows of windows closed tight with indoor shutters lined the walls. Only a small amount of sunlight filtered through the slats.

At one end of the room stood a stone fireplace that reminded Kate of fireplaces she had seen in ancient castles in Europe. There was no hearth; instead the opening was at floor level and was nearly big enough to walk into. On each side of the massive fireplace, two doors stood closed and presumably locked. The room itself contained no furniture. Littered all over the floor was a collection of boxes and old chests, containing what Kate assumed were relics of the past.

Kate and Simon stood in silence for a few moments, taking in what was in front of them. "This is one huge room," Kate whispered. "I didn't remember it being so large."

"It's a ballroom," Simon said. "I've always wanted a house with a ballroom in it. That doesn't seem like too much to ask for, does it? A simple ballroom in which to hold cotillions, galas, and so forth. Everyone ought to have one."

"I can't believe you didn't renovate this floor first," Kate laughed. "Think of the parties you could've been hosting up here all of these years."

"I know!" Simon cried. "Damn that practical Jonathan. It was his idea to get the moneymaking part of the operation going first thing."

"What a bore," Kate replied, and then she wondered, "Is the electricity working up here, or are we going to have to feel our way around in the gloom?"

"Oh," Simon said. "That might have been a good idea, to flip the switch, as it were, for this floor. We had the whole house rewired, but I don't have the juice turned on for this part of the house right now."

"That's okay, it's a bright day. Let's just open up some of these shutters, and we'll have all the light we need."

Kate's footsteps echoed on the hardwood floor as she walked to the wall of windows. "Let's see, how do these open?" she said, examining the shutters. With great difficulty, she forced open a hook that was holding two shutters together. When she finally threw them open, she gasped at what she saw.

"Simon! Look at this view!" Kate gazed through the (albeit grimy) window onto Wharton's quaint downtown area and the entire harbor just beyond it. "My God, this is gorgeous." From this lofty vantage point, Kate could see for miles.

"Old Harry didn't spare any detail from this house," Simon said. "Let's get all of them open so we can see the full effect."

They opened shutter after shutter, revealing a panoramic sight. They were high on a hill overlooking the bay. From this height, the boats on the lake looked like toys. Although tourist season was winding down, the streets were still filled with people, wandering in and out of the shops. The bright sun glistened on the water.

"This is absolutely stunning," she whispered.

"Can you imagine the kind of parties they must've had up here?" Simon wondered. "This had to be *the* invitation to get on New Year's Eve."

Kate and Simon had no way of knowing that this lavish ballroom had, in fact, rarely been used by Harrison and Celeste in the manner it had been intended. Harrison had envisioned it as the site of lavish parties and balls celebrating all sorts of community and family events; and indeed, the ghosts of more than a few high-society women in taffeta party dresses still twirled and swayed to the tunes of long-dead musicians here. But all that had ended after baby Hadley was born. Celeste's frail constitution never recovered from her daughter's birth, and she never again had the energy or the will to plan the society soirees that her husband so loved.

Instead, baby Hadley had used the third floor as an enormous playroom during the winter months. Much later in life, she told her grandchildren stories of riding her bicycle on these floors and playing all sorts of outdoor games here with friends. Many were the chilly days when Harrison would climb the stairs and find a roaring fire in the fireplace and his daughter having a makeshift tea party with invisible friends in the middle of the empty floor. Seeing her mischievous face and bright smile, he never again wished for something as shallow as a society party.

"What are you planning to do with this room?" Kate asked Simon. "The renovation, I mean."

Simon came alive with this question, as Kate knew he would. He strode into the center of the room, turned around twice, and said, "Imagine this creaky wood floor completely restored to its original glory, gleaming with rich, warm color," he said. "A fire in the fireplace. A chandelier here, family photos on the walls there. Of course, we'll have to tear off this shabby wallpaper and find something suitable."

"Do you plan to hold parties here?" Kate asked.

"Parties, wedding receptions, you name it." Simon beamed.

"Fabulous," Kate said. "This is going to be *the* place to get married in this town. You are going to be busier than you have ever been."

"About that," he said, more seriously. "Listen. I had an ulterior motive for bringing you up here. Until now, it's been just Jonathan and me doing everything, and that's been fine because we've been only moderately busy. But as you said, when this room is renovated, we're going to have to beat guests off with a stick. We're really going to need someone to handle the public relations and marketing. You. You're nicer than we are. People like you better. You'll be better with the guests."

"You mean move here? Permanently?"

"Well, yes."

"I don't know." Kate shook her head, not wanting to think about a permanent life change right now.

"Oh, don't even bother to turn down this offer." Simon enveloped her in his arms. "You *are* going to do this. You and I both know it, silly. You're going to help me run this place and make a fortune doing it. You owe it to Harry and Celeste to keep their house alive. It's coming to you after I croak anyway, per Grandma's will—"

"What do you mean, 'croak'?" Kate looked at him, concerned.

"Oh, stop it," Simon said. "I'm not dying. Today. I'm just reminding you that this house is staying in our family. And since Jonathan and I have decided not to have any kids, this place is all yours—or your future child's—when I die or when Jonathan and I get tired of running a business and want to move to Florida to languish on the beach drinking margaritas. So you've got a vested interest. And, I hasten to add, if you come to live here you'll have plenty of free time to work on that novel you've been threatening to write for your whole life."

Kate smiled, knowing he was right. It did sound like a wonderful opportunity and exactly the change she needed. She just didn't want to commit to anything concrete, not yet. In Kate's mind, her life was still in a state of flux. Before she could commit to the next phase, she needed to resolve the current one. That meant divorce papers, selling her house, and a whole host of other unattractive activities. Not to mention that she couldn't fully concentrate on anything until this otherworldly mystery was solved.

"Okay, I'll do it," Kate said, surprising herself.

"What! What do you mean you'll do it? As easy as that? I thought I'd have to torture a yes out of you." Simon laughed.

"I'll do it, but I don't want to talk or think about it right now," Kate said. "I have a lot of other things to take care of in my life. Let me do those first, before we talk more about this."

"What things?" Simon wondered. "I suppose you want to permanently jettison that idiot, Kevin."

When Kate didn't respond immediately, Simon said, "Sorry, sweetie. I didn't mean to be so harsh."

"Oh, you're not being harsh." Kate sighed. "It's funny, Simon, but when we were talking about Kevin before, it felt like our marriage was a lifetime ago. I'm so consumed with this mystery—this woman—that I'm just not even thinking about this whole Kevin thing. Isn't that odd?"

"It isn't odd, not really," Simon said, wrapping his arms around her and hugging her close. "You're using this mystery to push away the harsh realities of your life. It's a coping mechanism."

This stopped Kate short. "Am I really doing that, do you think?" Kate asked.

"Oh, definitely," Simon said. "But, listen. Who cares? Focus on something other than your marriage-in-shambles! That's a good thing. Get through these days in any way you can. It's better than wallowing in self-pity and despair, which, by the way, I would be doing in your shoes. I love a good wallow."

Kate thought about this. "Do you think I'm just pushing my feelings away? Should I be feeling more? I mean, am I going to have a hard fall after all of this denial?"

"You're not denying anything." Simon looked her square in the eyes. "You're not thinking that maybe you were mistaken about the affair, right?"

"Right," Kate said. "I know what I saw."

"And you're not thinking of sweeping it under the rug? Marriages do survive affairs."

"Not a chance. My trust in him is completely eroded. There's nothing left."

"Okay, then," Simon said. "You're just fine. Don't obsess about him or your marriage. Use this mystery—and this house for that matter—as a wonderful diversion. Think about Kevin when you're ready to think about Kevin. Until then, let's have fun with this." He opened his arms wide, gesturing toward the dusty trunks.

Kate smiled at her cousin but said nothing, tears welling up in her eyes.

"I can't fathom why Kevin would cheat on someone as wonderful as you," Simon went on. "But I can certainly fathom why you should kick his ass out of your life. When you're ready to do that, divorce his ass, sell your house in town, and make a new life here; just know that all of this is waiting for you. And if you decide that you don't want to do what I've proposed, that instead you want to go back to Kevin and work through this to save your marriage—well, honey, I'll be standing right behind you then, too. Bring him here and we'll all toast your reunion. And I promise not to put any arsenic in his glass."

"This is such a soft place for me to fall," Kate said, the tears stinging her eyes. "Do you know how wonderful you are?"

"Of course I do," Simon laughed. "I've been singing my own praises for years."

He enveloped her in a hug again, the two of them standing together like that for a long while. "Now, are you ready to get to work?" he asked.

Kate shook the tears from her eyes and pointed to the two doors near the fireplace. "Where do those doors lead?"

"Oh, that's the best yet." Simon started toward one of the doors. "You know the turrets on either side of the house?"

"These doors lead to the turrets?"

"Winding staircases and the whole nine yards." Simon opened the door closest to him. "Have a look. This is really something special."

Kate followed Simon through the doorway and up a dusty, winding staircase, which opened up into a round room with windows on all sides. Even through the decades of dust, the view was magnificent.

"They weren't used as bedrooms in Harry's day," Simon said. "Grandma used to play up here when she was little. Do you remember her saying that?"

"I do," Kate said.

"I'm thinking we'll make them into luxury suites for people who host events in the ballroom. We'll have to add bathrooms and other amenities, of course."

If only Kate and Simon had listened a bit more carefully, they might have heard the cries, or certainly felt the anguish that still lingered here, left by a man nearly a century before. A man whose actions, kept secret all these years, had caused him to take refuge in that room and weep bitter tears of regret and disbelief where no one could hear him. It was the sound a soul made when it was in the very depths of mourning, and it never dissipated, even in death.

But they weren't listening closely enough to discern it. They were immersed in the present.

"The first step," Simon was saying as they trotted down the turret stairs to the ballroom, "is going through the trunks to see what's here, what we can use, and what we should just pack away into the attic."

"Let's get started then," Kate said, pulling a sheet off an old, wooden trunk with a brass clasp. "Is this thing locked?" she wondered aloud, but a bit of fidgeting with the lock answered her question. It popped open with a little effort.

Under a burgundy-colored blanket, Kate saw that the trunk was stuffed full of scrapbooks, newspaper clippings, aging photographs, and memorabilia of a life gone by. She sank down on the floor next to the trunk and peered inside.

"What are we looking for, exactly?" Kate wondered. If all the trunks were this full of items, they'd be there sifting through them for a good, long while.

"I'm thinking about family photos and other memorabilia from Harrison and Celeste's time," Simon said. "We're renovating this house back to its original glory, if you will, so I thought that accenting it with items from that period would give guests a real sense of the past."

"I see," Kate said, fingering the items in her trunk. "You want to duplicate the feel of the main floor throughout the house."

"Exactly," Simon said. "We've got some photos and other things, old books and such, on the second floor, but I want more of them for the guest rooms and to adorn the walls of this ballroom. What I'd really love are photos from galas and balls that Harrison and Celeste hosted here, but I don't suppose we'll get that lucky."

"Who knows?" Kate said. "All we can do is look and see what's here."

"I can see right away that this trunk isn't going to have what we need," Simon said, gesturing to the trunk in front of him. "Look at this." He pulled out an old toy, a child's telephone. "This looks like it was made in the forties. These are probably our dads' toys. I'll bet everything in here is from that period."

"My trunk looks more promising," Kate said. Simon walked across the room and came to sit on the other side of it. The two sifted through the belongings of their ancestors, taking hold of items with enormous sentimental value to Celeste and Harrison but which meant little to these two cousins today. Among the relics, they found a baby's baptism gown, a delicate crocheted blanket, a tiny silver cup.

Kate held them up and examined them, murmuring comments like, "Oh, how beautiful," and "I wonder who wore this?" not knowing that Celeste had carefully laid these items away with a crippling grief and longing in her heart.

"Harrison!" Celeste's screams had echoed through the enormous, empty house in the middle of a windy autumn night. "She's not breathing! Clementine is not breathing!"

His wife's cries awoke the new father, who rushed, horrified, to the side of his first daughter's crib in the nursery, an alcove just off what was now the master bedroom that Simon and Jonathan had renovated into a spectacular master bath, complete with a steam shower and Jacuzzi tub. It was Simon's favorite thing, lazing in the scented water, enjoying a glass of wine and a good book. He had no idea that his great-grandmother had begun to lose her sanity in the exact spot where numerous water jets now massaged the kinks in his back. Although he had told Kate that he had never heard messages from the other side, if he had listened keenly enough during any one of his baths, he would have heard the soft weeping of a woman cradling her dead child, her first child. Clementine.

Harrison had burst into the room to find a horrific scene. Celeste realized her beloved infant was dead—surely, she must've realized it—but Harrison could not convince her to let go of the tiny body. She sat in the nursery's rocking chair, singing and cooing to the dead child in her arms. "Why won't she go to sleep? Why won't she stop crying?"

Harrison ran to Cook's room and rapped at the door until she answered, disheveled in her nightclothes.

"Mrs. Connor is unwell," he whispered to her. "Run and get the doctor, will you?"

Cook bundled up against the cold and ran down the hill into town, knocking for what seemed like an eternity on the doctor's back door. When he finally answered, the two of them sped off for the house and climbed the stairs to the master bedroom to find an ashen-faced Harrison staring out of the window. His wife, rocking a dead baby in her arms, was singing a lullaby.

"This child simply will not sleep if she's not in my arms," Celeste said as she smiled at the doctor. "Every time I attempt to put her into her crib, she cries so terribly! Hush now, baby, don't you cry . . ."

Harrison looked at the doctor imploringly.

"Let me take her to the hospital, Mrs. Connor," the doctor suggested, holding out his hands. "We can care for her there. We can determine why she is crying so."

Celeste could see the wisdom of this; the child was obviously ill. She handed the tiny, stiffening body over to the doctor, who in return handed her the hot drink laced with something to help her sleep that Cook had brought up from the kitchen.

"You have been through quite an ordeal, Mrs. Connor," he said. "Get some sleep now while I tend to your daughter. I will take care of things from here."

Harrison mouthed a heartfelt "Thank you" to the doctor as he gently led Celeste back to their bed. When she awoke the next morning, she did not ask about the baby. She would not speak to Harrison, nor to anyone, about what had occurred the night before. She simply packed away all the baby's things, the gown that would've been used for her baptism, the blanket her grandmother had crocheted, the silver cup. All those precious memories, packed forever into a trunk, out of sight, out of mind.

To the world, Celeste was dealing with the loss beautifully and pragmatically, like any sensible woman of the day. Infant death was not a rarity at that time and place—it seemed every family had seen this type of tragedy. But Celeste never recovered from the loss. A second daughter, Hadley; a loving husband; and more money than she would need in five lifetimes did nothing to ease her sadness. It ate away at her body. When she died, she was looking expectantly toward heaven, wondering if Clementine would finally be able to sleep now that her mother could, at long last, hold her in her arms.

But Simon and Kate knew nothing of this as they held up those tiny relics of their great-grandmother's undoing. They didn't know about Clementine. Things such as an infant's death weren't talked about in Celeste and Harrison's day. The parents were expected to carry on with a brave face, no matter the extent of their grief. So, their great-grandchildren unknowingly sifted through Clementine's belongings, among others', looking for books and photographs to display.

A few hours and several trunks later, they had finally accumulated many such items. Simon had migrated across the room to another trunk, where he found several photographs of the family that he intended to frame and hang in the guest rooms.

"Look at this one," he said to Kate. "This must be Harrison and Celeste when they were first married."

She walked over to his side of the room and regarded the photo.

"They were so good looking, weren't they?" She smiled. "How dashing he was!"

"Those are the genes that brought you all of your glory," Simon said, holding up a stack of photographs. "Here's a bunch more. Help me look through the rest of these and then we'll call it a day."

Kate sat down next to Simon and took a pile of photos. He was right, Kate thought, these shots must've been taken early on in their marriage. The couple looked so young and so happy. Dusk was starting to fall beyond the room, but still the pair kept sifting through photos, both mesmerized by the dalliance into their collective past.

Simon held one of the images in his hands, squinting to see it in the fading light. "You've got to see this one," he murmured to Kate. "It looks like Harry and Celeste with another young couple on a picnic. What a fun shot. We've got to frame this one."

Kate took the photo from Simon. It was indeed a shot of their great-grandparents, posed sitting on a blanket at the edge of the lake. A picnic basket was in the foreground, and Kate could see a bottle of wine and a plate of food in front of the couples. Along with Harry and Celeste, there was another pair, a man and a woman of approximately the same age. All four of them appeared to be in great spirits.

The image caused Kate to take a quick breath in.

"My God," she murmured, squinting at the photo to get a closer look. "It can't be. It just cannot be."

"What?" Simon asked.

Kate looked up from the image and stared at him, open mouthed. "We've got to get this picture into the light where I can see it better." She scrambled to her feet and ran to the door.

"What is it, for God's sake?" Simon called after her. But Kate didn't stop to listen. In an instant she was flying down the stairs toward the second-floor landing, just as she and Simon had when they were children. She burst out of the dimly lit staircase into the vibrantly colored hallway, squinting and blinking at the harshness of the light. Simon was following close at her heels. He found Kate standing in the middle of the hallway under a bright light, staring at the photograph in her trembling hands.

"What?" he asked again.

Kate could barely squeak out the words: "This woman in the photograph, the one with Harrison and Celeste. It's her." She grasped her cousin's arm so tightly it made him wince.

"Who?"

"It's *my* woman," Kate whispered, shaking Simon's arm and looking deeply into his eyes. "This"—she waved the photo back and forth—"is the woman in my dreams. This is the woman who washed up dead on my beach last week."

"You've got to be kidding me." Now it was Simon's turn to stare, wide eyed.

"Simon, I'm not kidding," Kate whispered. "It's her. *This is her.* And that man sitting there with her is her husband. I've seen them both in my dreams. I know it as surely as I know my own name."

CHAPTER SIXTEEN

Great Bay, 1906

Addie awoke and looked out the window—it had to be the middle of the night, as there was no hint of dawn on the horizon. But she saw the purples and greens of the aurora borealis dancing high in the atmosphere. The sight of the northern lights always calmed Addie, and she lay there, watching the show and thinking.

It had been four years since Jess had left Great Bay. As Addie had suspected after the first letters, Jess had not returned home for Christmas or summer breaks, preferring to stay in the city with his roommate and various other friends he had made. Although they did not see each other during those years, Jess and Addie exchanged many letters and in doing so, created a closeness that perhaps wouldn't have existed without the ability to write about what they saw, did, and felt. Jess enjoyed sitting down after a long day and putting his thoughts on paper. Writing to Addie allowed him to sort out how he felt about all the various things that were happening with him—classes, work, friendships. He wasn't so much opening up to Addie in those letters as he was opening up to himself.

Neither Jess nor Addie was completely honest in their letters, and neither could detect the other's dishonesty. Jess did not tell Addie about the women he had courted and, indeed, loved. Instead, he wrote about his roommate and the plans they were making for the future. They were becoming involved with a company owned by a local businessman, Jess told her, working part-time during the school year and full-time in the summers, laying the foundation for excellent jobs once they graduated. Jess's life in the city seemed to be falling into place—a college degree, a job awaiting him. Friends. Addie wondered where she fit into the plans, and although she did not know it for sure, she had good reason to wonder. As graduation neared, Jess wrote incessantly about the future, but it had been years since he had mentioned their future *together*.

Jess did not tell Addie that he had long ago dropped the childish notion that the two of them would marry. If college had taught him one thing, it was to look to the future to choose his bride, not to the past. When he married, it would be to the most suitable woman he could find, a woman who could help him in business and in life. A sophisticated, educated woman, much like the ones he had been courting with great voracity these past four years. Someone like that delightful, if vacuous, Sally Reade, who could effortlessly host the kinds of dinner parties and soirees that were so necessary to get ahead in the world of business, who would laugh blithely and flirt with the older men in the firm whom Jess was trying to impress, who would inspire jealousy and envy and cast Jess, as her future husband, in a good light.

All these thoughts were the direct influence of his roommate, who, like Jess, had begun his life as the son of a poor man and was determined, with a passion brushing against zealotry, to rise up from those humble and indeed squalid beginnings, no matter the cost. Jess saw the wisdom in this, shuddering when he thought of a life alongside his father, toiling from dawn to dusk on that smelly, disgusting fishing boat. Jess detested fish. Just the sight of one of those slithery, slippery creatures on a dinner plate brought back the nausea he felt as a child during his first time out on the boat with his father. He had spent the entire day retching over the side. That was enough of that.

His new life in the city was far more appealing. By virtue of their good looks and cultivated charm, Jess and his roommate had begun to move—by design—in the circles of the wealthiest girls shortly after arriving there, girls with ties to the most successful families in the state.

On the strength of a recommendation from their part-time employer, the owner of Canby Lines, they were admitted to a fraternity. The pair of them moved into the fraternity house and began attending the kinds of parties that Jess hadn't even imagined during his former life in Great Bay. Handsome young men in coats and ties (at first, Jess borrowed these accouterments until he had saved up enough money to purchase his own), glittering young women in party dresses, all of them drinking cocktails and touching his shoulder as they laughed about nothing at all. Jess was dazzled by this different breed of woman. He had never seen their like before—finely dressed, made up, sophisticated. They were a world away from the hard-working, sensible women of Great Bay. A world away from Addie, the child he had left behind. Just thirteen years old when Jess had left for college. That was really what Addie was. A child. Jess could see that now.

Still, that old sense of obligation continued to tie Jess to young Addie. All of their lives, Jess felt that he was responsible for Addie Cassatt. She did not have the sort of flighty, flirty nature of the women he was meeting; she was serious and deep and thought about things like the earth and the lake and nature, and how they all related to each other. They talked about these and other important things, connecting through their souls. As his college years wore on, Jess wondered if he would be able to keep his friendship with Addie that he so enjoyed while being married to another woman. Anything was possible, he told himself.

At the same time, Addie was wondering things as well. Like Jess, she had secrets of her own that her letters did not reveal. But they did not involve other boys, or thoughts that they would not share the future they had imagined. On the contrary, she still believed very much in their shared life together. Her secrets involved her dreams, which continued to plague her as the years passed. Disturbing, garbled images—Jess with other women, someone in danger at knifepoint, unseen babies crying, fog surrounding it all. Warnings from the past. In her darkest thoughts, Addie knew full well what these dreams meant to her, but those thoughts rarely made it to the surface of her young, naive mind. Teenaged girls have a way of holding fast to their illusions, even as those illusions are dissipating into the air. Denial of unpleasant reality is as powerful as the reality itself.

Addie was unconvinced of the truth of the story her mother had shown her on the morning after she'd had the first of the dreams. It seemed too fanciful, too much like a legend, to be true. And yet, didn't legends start with at least a grain of truth? And she couldn't deny her rather special relationship with the lake, could she? And there was certainly no denying her great-grandmother's horrible fate.

Addie imagined that *Grand-mère* would sit at the edge of her bed, hold her hands, and whisper kind words of consolation when the young girl awoke in the middle of the night, afraid of the images swirling around in her head. She did not know that her great-grandmother was watching all that transpired, that she was indeed sitting on the edge of her bed, whispering words into Addie's ear. But they were not words of consolation. She was saying, as forcefully as she could muster, "Take heed, girl."

During the long years of Jess's absence, Addie passed the time like any other girl in town. She rode the bicycle Jess gave her, attended school, swam in the lake in any kind of weather, helped her parents—although, as she grew, her mother no longer allowed Addie to accompany her father and uncle on fishing excursions. *Not a suitable activity for a young lady,* she would say. While this bothered Addie somewhat—she hated being told she couldn't do this or that because she was a *lady*, and more and more of her life seemed to fit into this category—she knew in her heart that her childhood was ending and young womanhood was beginning. Laughing as her hair blew in the wind on her father's boat was a childish thing that she must put away as she prepared to create a home and a life with Jess Stewart. She waited patiently for that day to come.

Finally, it came. Four years and two months after he went off to college, Jess Stewart returned to Great Bay. He had not intended to do so, not now at least, but his father had fallen ill, and his mother had implored him to come home for a visit. Jess agreed, not only because he wanted to see his family but also because he felt that paying a visit to his hometown was a practical thing to do at this time. He and his roommate had indeed been offered employment with Canby Lines in the city, and he needed to retrieve some of his belongings in order to set up an apartment.

During the journey, Jess rested his chin on his hand and gazed out the window as the train chugged along the lakeshore toward home. As he watched the countryside pass by—a herd of cattle here, a cornfield there—Jess wondered what he would say to Addie when he arrived back home in Great Bay. He was at a loss. As the train drew closer and closer to the lake and its destination, fog obscured much of the countryside, allowing Jess's mind to wander, unfettered now by the increasingly familiar sights of home.

Jess knew that he had his pick of any woman he desired in the city, all from wealthy families that could further his career. He had studied and then cultivated the casual air and genial attitude of the wealthiest boys in his fraternity. These men could laugh at the banalities of life, knowing that nothing—certainly not lack of money or connections—stood in the way of their ultimate happiness. It was not a sense of entitlement they radiated, Jess reasoned, it was the lack of burden. They were free of worry. Jess wrapped that persona around himself like a security blanket, believing that acting as though he hadn't a care in the world would make it so. It did the job, for a while. Life fell into place—the women, the friends, and ultimately, upon graduation, a great job with a solid future. Jess Stewart had succeeded in erasing the specter of his humble past.

The only thing that remained was choosing a suitable bride. His roommate had already cemented a favorable alliance with an altogether pleasant, if a bit plain and dull, woman in town, a woman who certainly could further his career, and Jess was determined to do the same for himself.

Sally Reade, the girl Jess had known since his early days in college, stood out from a wide field of competitors. She was flighty, yes, and a trifle unstable. But her family was among the wealthiest in the state. Not only would she bring a sizeable fortune into the marriage but also a great sense of fun. Oh, Jess had witnessed her bouts of sullen moping, but they were contrasted with periods of wild energy. At those times, she threw fabulous parties and floated among the crowd of guests, chatting, laughing, and keeping people entertained until all hours. She was already building a reputation as one of the finest hostesses in town. Further, her family liked Jess. They found him to be a stabilizing influence on their unpredictable daughter. Her father had said, over and over again, that Jess—strong, solid, sensible Jess—was a good match for Sally. He anchored her. Jess hadn't proposed outright yet, but everyone saw it coming on the road ahead.

As Jess considered all of this, he felt a twinge of guilt about reneging on the life he had planned throughout his youth with Addie. It was true that none of the women he courted, especially not Sally, could measure up to the intimacy he felt with Addie. Jess tried to brush it aside, but it nagged at him. He told himself that old sentimentality and childhood promises simply could not govern the actions of a successful man bound on securing his future, could they? He would not allow the silly machinations of his childhood to ruin his chances for success in the cold, harsh, adult world of business. Surely Addie would be able to see that, too. Besides, Addie was a child. In retrospect, his relationship with Addie started to look like that of siblings. She was like a little sister to him. Still, he felt a twinge of excitement at the idea of seeing her again. It had been so long.

As the train moved ever closer to the station and Jess ruminated further on his future, Addie was dressing in preparation for his arrival. She had scarcely been able to contain her excitement for days—finally, the long wait was over. She put on the new blue dress she and her mother had made for this occasion, smoothing the skirt and fiddling with the collar over and over again with shaking hands. She brushed her hair until it shone, allowing it to fall freely around her face instead of tying it in the knot she usually wore behind her head. She looked at the clock again and again. *Two hours until he arrives.*

Meanwhile, on the train, Jess was carefully planning his exit speech. He had thought about simply writing to Addie—words on paper, carefully thought out and considered—it was a much easier way of dealing with a difficult subject. However, he was aware that this young girl had loved him for her entire life. She had been waiting for him for four long years. He needed to let her down as gently as possible. *I have met someone else, a woman of substance . . . No matter how much our friendship means to me . . .* He rehearsed it over and over in his mind, always failing to find the right words. The vision of her disappointed young face created a gnawing in his stomach. He didn't want to hurt her. And yet . . .

As the train pulled to a stop at its destination, the fog settled around the station. Jess disembarked slowly, unable to see more than two feet in either direction. It had been so long . . . Where was the station? Which way was home? He was reminded of that day long ago, when he had found baby Addie in the lake. It was the same kind of blinding whiteness, the same kind of tangible cloud that felt like a living blanket had covered the entire earth.

He was standing alone, turning this way and that, watching the few other passengers get off the train and disappear into the whiteness. *I should go that way,* he thought, when a woman materialized in front of him.

The sight of her literally took Jess's breath away. He felt as though the fog itself had rushed into his lungs, snatching his ability to breathe and withholding it from him. His heart was beating so loudly that Jess was sure everyone within earshot could hear it.

The woman was Addie, of course. But she was not the young girl Jess had left behind. With all his strategizing about the future, with all his thoughts about finding a bride, he had somehow neglected one detail: Addie was growing up. While he himself didn't see much change in his own mirror during his college years, Addie had literally transformed from a child into a woman—the most beautiful woman Jess had ever seen or imagined. Her long, auburn hair fell in soft curls around her face. Her mouth curved into a slight, mysterious smile. She was wearing a deep-blue dress that showed off her tiny waist and curvy figure. Jess thought she was absolutely exquisite, completely changed. Only her piercing violet eyes were the same as he remembered.

He stared at her in stunned silence. She, too, seemed stunned, but not by his appearance. He looked a bit older, yes, but he was largely the same as the day he left. She was reacting to his awestruck countenance. He seemed overwhelmed by her, and she didn't know what to make of it. When she imagined their reunion—and she had imagined it over and over during these four years—she thought it would be a joyous encounter filled with laughter, hugs, and kisses. This was something else again. She had not expected him to be mute at the sight of her.

He extended his hand to her face and brushed the curls back, gingerly, delicately, as though she might dissipate like the fog at his slightest touch. He just kept staring as though he was seeing a ghost, his eyes searching for the young girl he had left behind. This was no little sister. What had he been thinking?

"Welcome home," she said, finally.

His face broke into an enormous smile. He took her hands into his, murmuring, "My goodness, Addie Cassatt. You've grown up."

In that moment on the train station platform, Jess Stewart's future changed. Or, more exactly, it fell back into its rightful place. He had been dangerously close to veering off course, but now he was back on it. Without giving it another thought, he immediately and absolutely abandoned his well-considered plan to marry a suitable wife from a good family in the city. Sally Reade—or the idea of Sally Reade, a fine society wife—faded from his mind in an instant, the scales fell from his eyes, and he finally saw clearly. How could he have ever considered marrying anyone other than Addie Cassatt? She was his best friend *and* a stunning woman. Thank God he hadn't let her down in a letter! He could scarcely believe his good luck. He might have ruined it all, he might never have had her. He had trained himself to fit into the high-society circles in which he now traveled, he could train Addie to do the same. Of course! Why hadn't he thought of this before?

Jess took Addie into his arms and said, "I have come home for you, Addie."

He drew her close and kissed her then, the way he had kissed so many women during the past four years. It was Addie's first kiss, and he knew this without even asking. Neither of them knew how long they stood there on the platform, enveloped in the fog, holding each other.

"I've missed you so much," Jess whispered into her ear so convincingly that he himself believed that he had.

"I've missed you, Jess," Addie said, meaning every word.

CHAPTER SEVENTEEN

"How can you be sure it's her?" Simon said, taking a bite of salad and examining the photo more closely. "I mean, this must've been taken, what, a century ago?"

"It's her," Kate said. "If I showed it to my dad and Johnny, they'd identify her as the woman we saw on the beach. But that just can't be, right? It would make her body more than one hundred years old."

"What if the woman in this photo and the woman on your beach were, say, mother and daughter, or grandmother and granddaughter?" Simon offered. "How do you know for sure it's the same person?"

"That would make sense, if I hadn't also been dreaming about the husband," Kate said, her eyes shifting to the man's handsome face. "I saw both of them, Simon."

Kate's thoughts drifted back to her dreams—there were no cell phones, no televisions, no electronics of any kind in any of the dreams. No cars. No modern music.

"I just sort of took it for granted that she was alive now—well, recently, anyway—but when I really think about it . . ."

"You think you've been dreaming about the past."

Kate considered this, staring at the photo. It seemed like the only reasonable answer. But how far in the past?

"It explains the ninety-year-old nightgown, that's for sure," Simon said.

"Our great-grandparents are sitting with them in this shot," Kate said. "They all look pretty young. Simon, you know when they were married, right? That might give us a date to go on."

"I can't rattle the year off the top of my head, but I can certainly find it in the old family Bible," he said, pushing back his chair and making his way out of the room.

"Nineteen-oh-five!" Simon shouted from the library. "Harrison and Celeste were married in nineteen-oh-five!" He bounded back into the dining room.

"The date of this photo must be close to the same time, then," Kate said. "Judging from how young Harry and Celeste are in the picture, I'd imagine it was taken shortly before or after they were married. Within, what, five years, I'd think."

"You know . . ." Simon took a bite of French bread and considered this point. "Say this is really your woman. You've got a concrete date to start researching who she was. You won't be stabbing in the dark, so to speak."

"I can just start my search from 1905 and work forward from there," Kate agreed.

"It tells you she lived around here," Simon said, pointing to the photo. "Look, they were having their picnic on the lakeshore. You can see the house in the background."

Kate eyed the photo and nodded.

"She might have just been visiting, though," Simon backpedaled. "What if she and her husband were here on vacation when this photo was taken?"

"Doesn't matter," Kate concluded. "They were obviously friends with Harry and Celeste, so her disappearance would've been newsworthy in this town on that basis alone. You don't sit around yukking it up with the richest man in town if you're a nobody. And she was murdered, that much we know, so it would have made the papers here. 'Friend of the Connor Family Found Murdered.' That's big news in a small town."

Simon took a sip of coffee and shook his head, furrowing his brows.

"What?" Kate asked.

"I think you're getting ahead of yourself," Simon said. "We know it was murder, because the police told us. But for all we know, this is the first time anyone has seen her body. She came out of the lake. It could be that, back then, people considered this a missing persons case."

"A wife who ran off," Kate mused. "You're right, Simon. We just don't know."

Something began to seep into Kate's body, weaving its way through her limbs like a thread being tightly wound around her. Tears sprang to her eyes.

"What's the matter, sweetie?" Simon reached across the table to take his cousin's hand.

"It's just that, when Johnny couldn't find any missing persons reports anywhere in the country that matched her description, I was so sad at the thought that nobody missed this woman and her baby," Kate said. "And now I know that she had . . . people. Loved ones. Friends. Look at her. She was beautiful and happy and having a great time, right here at this house. That means people missed her when she died. These people."

"Our people," Simon said, squeezing her hand.

Kate looked at him. "What did you say?"

"Our people," Simon repeated. "These are our great-grandparents laughing with her. These two couples are obviously friendly enough to sit around with a picnic basket and a bottle of wine and have a photographer there to document it all. That's what the picture portrays, anyway. If this whole impossible situation is really happening, then the woman who has been invading your dreams and, by the way, washed up dead on your beach, was someone close to our great-grandparents. She was here, in this house."

Kate looked around the room and felt a cool breeze whisper through her hair. She could almost see Harry and Celeste entertaining this young, handsome couple, right there in the same room where she and Simon now sat.

It felt as though she was caught by the intangibility of time. Could the past and present exist at once, in the same place? Were Harrison and Celeste living there now, entertaining visitors in the long-ago past? Were they enjoying dinners here in the dining room a century before as Kate and Simon were now? Was it all happening in the same moment, but a century apart?

"We found this photo in one of those old trunks upstairs," Kate started. "If this woman and our great-grandparents were close friends, as we're now postulating, it might stand to reason that there are more photos of her, or even news clippings about what happened."

"That's right," Simon confirmed. "I saw a ton of old clippings in one of the trunks. I think Celeste might have been a scrapbooker."

Kate's mind was traveling in several directions at once. "I feel like I want to look into this further, but I'm just not sure what to do first."

"Did you bring your computer?"

Kate winced. "I didn't. On purpose. Kevin has sent me a thousand emails since we split up, and I didn't want to be tempted to read any of them. I've got him blocked on my phone."

"There's a laptop set up in the library alcove for guests. You could start by doing a quick search online."

Kate's eyes danced and she raised her brows. "We do have a date to go on. I could just start searching for *Harrison Connor, 1905* and see what comes up."

"Or even *Wharton, Addie, 1905*," Simon offered.

"Better yet!" Kate smiled, pushing herself up from the table.

She hurried into the library, wondering if this mystery could be solved with just a few clicks of the mouse. But hours later, her head pounding from staring at the brightly lit computer screen, she realized it wasn't going to be as easy as that.

Simon poked his head around the corner.

"Anything?"

Kate shook her head. "I found lots of stuff about Harrison and Celeste, and obviously lots of info about Canby Lines, but beyond that, I'm hitting a brick wall."

He sighed and folded himself into an armchair. "If only you had her full name."

Kate swiveled her chair around to look at him. "I suppose I could look through the trunks again, see if there's anything with her name on it."

He wrinkled his nose. "Doubtful. Unless . . ." He held up one finger and leaned in toward Kate.

"Unless what?"

"Unless Harrison or Celeste kept a diary."

Kate stared at her cousin for a moment. "You're brilliant! Do we know if either one of them did?"

"Well, no," Simon said, leaning back in his chair. "But even if they didn't keep a full-blown diary, they certainly might have kept a datebook where they—or their household help—recorded their appointments and entertainment schedule and such. 'Mr. and Mrs. So-and-So, dinner, 5:30 p.m.' Something like that."

Kate folded her arms. "Would it still be here, though? After a century? I throw out my calendar from the previous year every January."

"Do you really? I've got my datebooks going back, oh, I don't know. Ten years? I love to look back through them. It's like a window into the past."

"I suppose I should go upstairs right now and start hunting," Kate said, leaning back to run a hand through her hair. Her hand stopped at her forehead—it was clammy to the touch.

Simon shook his head. "I don't think so. You're tired. I can see it on your face. I'd offer to help you look tomorrow, but the contractor is coming in the morning to talk about the third-floor renovation."

"That's okay," Kate said. "I don't expect you to be as heavily involved in this as I am." She paused for a moment before continuing. "Do you know what's weird?"

Simon grinned. "A better question would be what's *not* weird. But go on."

"Her body," Kate said. "I can't get the image of it out of my mind. She looked . . . I don't quite know how to say this, but she looked like she wasn't dead at all. Like she was sleeping."

"I know," Simon said. "We talked about this when you first arrived, remember? About how Lake Superior preserves bodies because of the cold."

"She was floating in that icy water for all of those years," Kate said, leaning her head back, a chill washing through her. "The other thing I was thinking was . . ." Kate attempted to finish her thought, but in that instant, she shivered. "Can you get me some coffee, Simon? I'm freezing all of a sudden."

Simon came over to her and took her hands in his. "You *are* cold. Wait right here."

He returned with a silver tray containing a bottle of cognac and two warmed glasses.

"Come on, let's go and sit by the fire," Simon directed, with a smile. "Coffee won't do it. Hot brandies all around."

When they had settled into overstuffed chairs by the fire in the library, Kate under an afghan for good measure, Alaska at her feet, she resumed her thought: "I was thinking about the body," Kate started. "And the baby's body. They're lying in the morgue right now."

"I know, sweetie," Simon said.

"And they're so, so *perfect*, if you can call a dead body perfect, that the police are looking for a missing person from this time and place." Kate shivered as she spoke. "If sh-she really is the woman in the photograph with Harry and Celeste, that means she died sometime around 1905."

"That's right," Simon said, leaning in toward Kate and feeling her forehead. "We've already talked about this, honey." He eyed her. "Listen, I think you're coming down with something."

"Yes, but . . . ," Kate started and stopped. "But how did she stay that w-w-way? How does a d-dead body stay perfectly preserved for nearly a century?"

"Kate, your lips are turning blue," Simon said. "Something's going on here, and I don't like it. I'm calling Peter Jones." He reached for the phone on the table and dialed his family doctor.

Kate was shivering beneath her afghan, trying to sip her hot brandy with shaking hands, spilling some in the process. She felt ice cold deep inside, in her core. Simon snuggled into the overstuffed chair with his cousin, throwing an arm around her in an effort to warm her with his body heat while he spoke quietly on the phone with the doctor.

Kate kept talking. "My dad says b-b-bodies are well pr-preserved in this lake because the water is so clean and cold," she mumbled. "But not like this. Not perfect. They look waterlogged and sort of spongy, he said, they don't decay, but they don't remain as beautiful . . ."

"That's right, Peter," Simon said into the phone, his voice low. "We were sitting and talking, and she just started shivering. Her lips are blue! She's freezing. And now she's sort of—I'm not going to say incoherent, but loopy. She keeps repeating things we've talked about. It happened all of a sudd—There is? So what should I—? Okay. We'll do that. Yes. I will.

"Peter says there's a virus going around," he said to Kate, who was still murmuring about bodies and cold water.

He took hold of Kate's hand. "Oh my God. You're like a block of ice." He pulled her to her feet. "Come on. I'm taking you upstairs and getting you into a warm bath. I didn't put tubs into every guestroom for nothing."

"I'm sorry to be such a b-bother," Kate murmured as Simon led her up the stairs. He could feel her legs shaking with each step.

When they got to Kate's room, he flipped on the light and made his way to the bathroom. He turned on the water in the tub and sprinkled in some soothing bath salts that turned the water bluer than Kate's lips.

"This thing has a heater in it so you can stay in the water as long as you want, and it won't get cold," he said. "Oh, come on. Fill, already!" This he directed at the tub. In a few moments the steaming tub was full. "Let's get those clothes off," he said to Kate, unbuttoning her shirt.

"Wait a minute . . . ," she mumbled.

"Oh, for heaven's sake, I'm a gay man and your blood relation," he laughed. "I couldn't be less interested in what you've got under your clothes."

"T-t-true." She managed a laugh. "But I'd like to keep some mystery."

"Then you get in there yourself," he said. "But be careful. I'll be right outside the door."

Kate peeled off her clothes and lowered herself into the tub, the water sizzling as her icy-cold body came into contact with it. Kate submerged herself up to her neck, curled herself into a fetal position, and rested her head on the side of the tub, closing her eyes and taking in the delicious scent of the bath salts.

Simon poked his head into the room. "Don't fall asleep in there."

"I won't," Kate said through a yawn.

"Seriously," Simon said, turning on as many lights as possible. He grabbed a book from the nightstand and settled onto the bench in the bathroom. "I'm not leaving you alone to have your head slip under the water. You drowning would put a damper on our visit."

Kate chuckled but couldn't open her eyes.

"You just relax, and I'll read," Simon said. "When you're ready to get out, let me know."

"I'm not so cold now," Kate said, her eyes still closed lightly. She was indeed feeling warmer, but she was swimming in thoughts that were not entirely her own.

When Kate had been lying in the tub for nearly an hour, a rosy color came back to her cheeks. Her eyes fluttered open, and she looked around.

"Well, that was dramatic," she said.

"You love to be the center of attention." Simon smiled. Then, more seriously, he asked: "How are you feeling?"

"Better," Kate said. She sat up and leaned against the tub. "I'm warm now, but I still feel pretty weak. What happened?"

"Peter says it's probably a bug that's going around town right now," Simon said. "He hadn't heard of anyone reacting like you did, but chills and fever are not uncommon. And honey, you just took the chills to a new level."

"It was so bizarre," Kate said, rubbing her arms. "Suddenly I just felt cold. Ice cold. Deep inside. I can't really properly explain the feeling. I've never experienced anything like it."

"Do you still feel it?"

Kate considered this. "A little, I guess," she said. "But nothing like it was before. I remember once at the paper, I was covering a New Year's Day celebration. This club in town called the Polar Bears raised money by plunging into the icy lake. I did it with them to write about it. It's just like what I felt tonight. It was as though I had suddenly jumped into ice-cold water."

Simon eyed his cousin. "You know, we were right in the middle of talking about how those bodies were preserved in the cold water."

"I know," Kate said. The two cousins held each other's gaze.

"That tells me you should step back from this thing a bit," Simon said. "You're getting too involved. You're internalizing. I don't like it, Kate. It feels dangerous, somehow."

Kate didn't know what to say to that, but Simon saved her the trouble. "You hop out of this tub and get into your jammies. I'll go make you a cup of tea."

"I should really walk Alaska," she said, her chin on the rim of the tub.

"Don't be ridiculous," Simon said. "I will do the honors tonight."

"You don't have to do that," Kate protested. "Alaska is my responsibility, I should . . ."

But Simon cut her off. "Stop it. It's getting cold outside, and you could catch a chill if you go out into the night air. That's the last thing you need. Besides, I actually like parading around town with a dog twice as big as an average timber wolf. Now, I'm going to get that tea."

Ten minutes later, Kate was in her pajamas and snuggled in bed as Simon came through the door with two steaming mugs and some books on a tray.

"I'm going to read you to sleep, and I've got three choices of novel for your listening pleasure," Simon said to her as he put each cup of tea on a nightstand and then slipped under the covers with Kate. "*The Widow's House, The Library of Light and Shadow*, or *The Queen's Vow*."

Kate eyed the selections. "They all sound good. You choose."

Simon opened one of the books. "Okay, missy. Lie back, close your eyes, and listen."

Kate took a sip of her tea and snuggled down into her nest of pillows. "Simon?" Kate looked up at this dear man.

"Yes, darling?"

"I love you."

"I love you, too." He smiled and pushed the hair out of her eyes.

Before Simon had finished reading the first chapter, Kate's rhythmic breathing told him that she had fallen asleep. He felt her forehead. Cool to the touch, but not cold. She would sleep off whatever it was that had taken hold of her. He slipped out of the covers and gathered them back up around Kate's neck. He kissed her lightly, set the book on the bedside table, turned out the light, and padded silently out of the room.

"Sleep well," he whispered to his cousin as he quietly shut the door. He knew he would check on her several times during the night, worried hen that he was.

CHAPTER EIGHTEEN

Great Bay, 1906

The last of the October leaves crunched under their feet as Jess and Addie walked to the Saturday-night dance at the Great Bay social hall. The wind off the lake was brisk and exciting, filled with promise of the season to come. It snaked its way into their collars and ruffled their hair, making Addie, who had fussed over her appearance for hours before Jess arrived at her door, self-conscious and shy. It was a new feeling for her, one that had grown since that kiss on the platform. This was no child's fantasy anymore.

Addie's apprehension about the evening had to do with more than just the jitters that tied her stomach in knots every time Jess was around. Many people in town had thought her a fool for waiting for Jess Stewart while he was away at college all those years. She hadn't dated anyone in his absence and made no bones about proclaiming that he would come back for her someday. They smiled politely and whispered behind her back, wondering when that fool Cassatt girl would wise up.

Tonight, everyone would see for themselves what Addie had always known.

The night was illuminated by the full moon and a sky filled with stars that looked like the flickering lights in the houses they passed.

Addie and Jess walked arm in arm through the dark streets, chatting about everything and nothing at all.

The social hall was bright and alive with music. Nearly everyone in town showed up for these Saturday-night dances in which young people got their first taste of love, older couples twirled together on the dance floor, and the community as a whole celebrated life on the lakeshore. The women of the town usually brought food and drink, everyone sharing what they had.

Jess's arrival was like that of a conquering hero. He had been in Great Bay only a couple of days and had seen few people beyond his parents and Addie. He and Addie entered the hall to shouts of *Look who's here!* and *Jess Stewart's back!* Old friends embraced him, girls whispered about his good looks, and his former teachers and parents' friends greeted him one by one with hugs and handshakes. Addie, meanwhile, was ushered away from him by her girlfriends, all of whom wanted to know every last detail. Had he changed? Had he come back to marry her? Had he proposed? She laughed off their questions, but her blush spoke volumes.

"So you really came home for her," his old neighbor Ruby Thompson said to Jess, motioning across the room toward Addie, who was laughing with a gaggle of girls. Ruby had been there the day of Addie's birth, and she had watched these two grow their whole lives.

"Yes, Mrs. Thompson, I believe that I have." Jess flashed her a conspiratorial smile. "But mum's the word. I haven't asked her yet."

"You've surprised a lot of people in this town," she told him.

"Is that so?" Jess said, slightly offended on Addie's behalf, slightly chagrined on his own. "Excuse me, ma'am," he said to her. "It's time I danced with my bride-to-be." The music began to play, and he crossed the room to where Addie was surrounded by her girlfriends.

"May I have this dance?" He smiled, extending his hand.

Addie blushed. Shyly, she took his hand, and he led her out onto the dance floor. The entire hall seemed to take a collective breath. All eyes were on them. Jess pulled Addie close. As they began to twirl around the dance floor, staring into each other's eyes, the world fell away, the music stopped, the lights extinguished, the people vanished, and all that was left was Jess and Addie, finally together again where their hearts had always been.

Later, as they walked home through the darkened streets, Jess stopped in front of the old willow tree where he had taught her to ride his bicycle all those years ago, took her hand, and dropped to one knee.

They remained that way for a moment, neither saying anything, simply looking into each other's eyes. "Addie, will you marry me?" he whispered, choked up at the enormity of the words.

"Of course I will. I married you the first instant I met you."

He knew it was true for both of them. The question was unnecessary. He remembered the day of her birth, knowing she belonged to him. And, as it turned out, he to her.

A few days later, they sat bundled up on the lakeshore, talking excitedly about their plans. Weddings in Great Bay usually occurred on bright summer days when the lake was calm, but Jess wanted to marry Addie as soon as time would allow. He had a job back in the city, after all. How much time did she need to make the preparations for the wedding? Four weeks? Six?

For her part, Addie had always loved this time of year and was thrilled to be marrying her beloved Jess in the winter season. She had long dreamed of Jess coming for her in a one-horse sleigh. In her mind, they would dash off together through the white landscape, snuggled against the wind under a woolen blanket. It was all the stuff of a young girl's romantic dreams, of course, but it was indeed coming true.

They would be married according to Addie's wishes: a late afternoon ceremony in a candlelit church with friends and family singing Christmas carols to mark the occasion. A reception would be held at the town hall next door, with an army of local women providing the food and other refreshments.

"You'll need to learn about life in the city," Jess said to her. "It's not like Great Bay."

"How so?" Addie wondered how life on this same lake, albeit on a different shore, could be a world away.

"Life here in Great Bay is very simple," Jess explained, "but in the city, you'll see that it's quite complicated. As my wife, you'll be meeting people and doing things you never imagined. Going to parties, society soirees. Hosting dinners for important people."

"Dinner doesn't sound too complicated to me." Addie smiled at him. "*Wife* sounds good, though."

"It's all about furthering my career in business," Jess told her. "You'll have as big a role in it as I do." The words reverberated with a shallow ring in Addie's ear. Her image of life as Mrs. Jess Stewart had included only the two of them, living life as one, as it had been when they were children. Now it seemed rather crowded.

"Inviting friends to share a meal is one thing, but I don't know how to host the kind of dinner party you're describing," Addie said gingerly, looking into Jess's eyes. "I've never even been to one. What if I can't do any of that?"

Jess smiled, warming her with the softness of his gaze. "I taught you to ride that bicycle, remember? You didn't think you could do that, either."

Addie laughed at the memory. It seemed so long ago now.

"I can teach you this, as well," Jess continued. "Listen, Addie, it was the same for me when I first left Great Bay. I didn't know the first thing about the 'new world' of the city until I started experiencing it. I learned to move gracefully in that world; so can you. It's really not that difficult, I promise. You simply watch the way other people are acting and act that way, too. Easy. You'll see."

"You seem so sure," Addie said. "But this 'simple' life in Great Bay is rooted in my heart, Jess. Living on the tempestuous lakeshore. Shutting the doors against the elements and curling up with family at night. Helping neighbors when they need it. Attending church picnics and Saturday socials. All of that seems like such a far cry from the life you're describing."

"But is it a life you want, Addie?" Jess turned and faced her. It had never occurred to him that Addie might not wish to share his life in the city, with all that it entailed. "Do you *want* to marry me?"

Addie smiled. "I believe you've already asked me that question."

"Marrying me means giving up life here in Great Bay," he continued. "I know you love this place, and we can certainly come back to visit, but I can't live here, Addie. There's nothing here for me. I need to be in the city, my job—"

She silenced him with a finger to his lips. "Life, for me, is wherever you are," she said. "We are supposed to walk through this world together, wherever that may take us. I've always known it. Since the first day we met."

"But I'm taking you away from all of this." He gestured toward the lake.

"You're not taking me away from anything," she told him. "You're bringing me *to* something."

Jess kissed her then. "I am such a lucky man," he whispered into her ear.

Marcus Cassatt was elated when Jess Stewart asked for his only child's hand in marriage. Oh, there was no doubt that he had been suspicious of Jess's intentions for, well, the better part of his daughter's life. But now that Jess had gone to college, secured gainful employment in a large, prosperous business, and had indeed made good on his promise and come back for the girl, there was no complaining from Marcus about losing his daughter to this man, or to the city where he lived.

"Better Jess Stewart than a fisherman like her father," Marcus said, shaking his head. "She'd have a hard life here. He can give her a better one than we've known."

But Marie was less than overjoyed at the idea of a union between her daughter and this man. Addie's dreams seemed to be telling her that life with Jess Stewart would be filled with some sort of confusion and even danger. And now that he was back in town, proposing a marriage that would mean Addie would be leaving the only home she had ever known, Marie wondered what it all meant. The dreams weren't concrete or clear enough to deny her daughter's happiness. Just vague images, one after another. Fog. A knife glinting in the moonlight. A gunshot. Nothing she could put her finger on.

And she had never seen Addie look more radiant than in Jess's company—that was real, tangible, and undeniable.

"I'll always be here for you to talk to," Marie said to Addie one evening. "Especially about your dreams. Please promise me you'll heed their warnings."

"I will," Addie promised.

There was another reason for the hasty marriage, and everyone in town knew what it was. Phil Stewart, Jess's father, was not in good health. In fact, he was dying. Cancer was taking his life, but nobody knew that, then. The townsfolk simply knew that he was seriously ill and becoming more so with every passing day. Jess was grateful that he had indeed listened to his mother and come home on the train.

Between the time Jess proposed to Addie that night at the social hall and their wedding day, six weeks hence, Jess left for the city to put his affairs in order. He needed to find a suitable place to live—a bride and, someday, a family required more space than did a single man. He also needed to spread the news of his engagement to his closest friends in town and especially to his employer, a traditional sort who was eager for all young men in his employ to find a wife and set up housekeeping.

It also meant the unpleasant business of breaking the news to Sally Reade, whose wrath proved to be surprisingly vehement. He had taken her to a restaurant, thinking the public setting would make things easier. He was wrong about this. It hadn't helped matters that she was giddy and keyed up when he arrived at her door. But later, when he squeaked out the fact that he had proposed to another woman, Sally reacted with a stunned silence—*Oh, thank God,* Jess had thought—but then, to his utter embarrassment, it mutated into a fierce rage. Before he was able to usher her out of the room, she threw every one of the plates on their table at him, shrieking obscenities, much to the horror of their fellow diners. She cried all the way home in the cab.

After he saw Sally to her front door—and had it slammed in his face—Jess took a deep breath and looked toward the future.

His company was based in the city, but upon news of his engagement, the owner presented Jess with an opportunity to accompany him in setting up an office in the small bayside town of Wharton. Jess suspected that it was an effort by the company's well-heeled boss to distance this new star employee from the unfortunate Sally Reade business, which, by now, was all over town. Jess was relieved. Beyond escaping Sally's immediate social circles, which would no doubt be closed to him and his new wife, the job itself provided an opportunity for advancement, one that Jess would not turn down.

While he loved the city, Jess found that he was enchanted by Wharton, with its warm winter winds and charming houses with large front porches and backyard gardens. He walked through the streets and thought of how much Addie would love this town. It was an easy sort of life, not a large, thriving city, which might have intimidated and even frightened her, but it was much more cosmopolitan than the tiny community of their birth. A perfect balance. Best of all, it was located on her beloved lake. He had fretted about how she would adjust to life without that massive body of water in her view, and now it was a moot point. What a wonderful place in which to start anew.

Jess bought a white wooden house with an enormous front porch that overlooked the harbor. It wasn't the grandest home in town, but it was a highly suitable residence for a young businessman and his new bride. He furnished it modestly, knowing that Addie would want to tend to the details later, herself.

Addie and Jess were married in Great Bay on a snowy December afternoon as the sun was setting on the tiny church on the main street. Heavy, wet snow had fallen the night before, draping the streets and the houses and the enormous pine trees that lined the street like sentries in a blanket of white. The wedding-eve snowstorm had Addie and her mother fretting late into the night, peering out of the icy windowpanes of their home, wondering if the snow would let up in time for guests to arrive at the church the next day.

Marie, Addie, and several of the local women had worked tirelessly creating the perfect wedding dress—just six weeks between engagement and wedding hadn't left them much time. Marie ordered the fabric from Minneapolis the very day Addie announced her engagement, and when it finally arrived, wrapped in brown paper, the ladies of the town began meeting, usually at Marie's large kitchen table, and sewed all day, every day until the dimming light forced them to stop their careful work each evening.

As the sun was setting on their wedding day, townsfolk bundled up in their scarves, boots, and woolen overcoats for the walk to the church. Those who lived farther outside of town arrived on snowshoes and by sleigh; the Carlsons even hitched up the dogsled for the trip from their farm.

When the candles were lit in the church, Addie walked down the aisle on her father's arm in a long off-white dress decorated with pure-white embroidery on both the skirt and bodice. A wide satin ribbon at the waist and bustle in the back accentuated her tiny waistline. Dressed in white, with her deep-auburn hair cascading around her face and her violet eyes shining, Addie Cassatt looked like an angel.

Her happiness was evident to all who witnessed it, no more so than to Jess Stewart himself, who was struck by the sight of the woman who was walking, no, floating, toward him. He was used to seeing Addie in the simple, practical cotton dresses worn by the hard-working wives of the fishermen in this town. Even dressed in those usual rags, Addie was stunning. But now, in this finery . . . Jess caught his breath and thanked God for his good fortune. He might have lost her in the pursuit of a more "suitable" wife. Instead, he would be the husband of a woman he truly adored and the envy of every man in town.

As the townsfolk watched this young, beautiful couple exchange wedding vows, many of the older ones were struck by the memory of the day Addie was born. The blinding fog, the way Marie had been drawn to the lake and had given birth in the water, how young Jess was the one who found the baby floating peacefully near his home. And now here these two were, pledging to spend the rest of their lives together. A thought drifted from one to another in the pews—was destiny possible? Could it be true that some people were literally made for each other? Proof of that romantic notion seemed to be standing before them. Some wives gave their husbands sidelong glances and lamented the fact that their own destinies had run so far off the track. *Did I choose the right man? Is this all there is? Did I ever have the chance to be in love?* A few people wondered about roads not taken, sweethearts who had been deemed unsuitable by parents or other circumstances, loves lost to the lake or the woods, men who left their homes one morning and, without warning, never returned.

As her son was standing at the front of the church reciting the words his parents had said to each other more than thirty years before, Jennie Stewart slipped her hand into her husband's palm and held it tight. He looked at her with watery eyes. She kissed his cheek and whispered, "I'm so glad I married you."

Throughout the years, Phil Stewart had been, and remained, a man of few words, and those that he uttered were practical ones. But on this day he surprised his wife by smiling down at her and whispering, "We've had a wonderful life together, haven't we?"

To this, Jennie couldn't respond. It had indeed been a wonderful life, every day of it, and as Jennie squeezed her husband's palm, she knew better than anyone that it was ending, and rapidly. His health was beyond prayer for a miracle, it was beyond all hope. She had seen his pain intensify, had witnessed him lying in bed for days. That he was here, dressed and smiling at his son's wedding, was miracle enough. Jennie knew that, even as their son was embarking on a new life, so too would she. That of a widow. As she sat, leaning against her husband in the candlelit church, with the sun hanging low over the lake and all that love and happiness around her, Jennie Stewart repeated the prayer that she had whispered, over and over, to God or anyone else who would listen: *Thank you for all that I have. Please make his last days comfortable.*

After the wedding, there was much laughter, eating, drinking, and song. Addie floated among the crowd, thanking everyone for coming and trying to make a point of speaking to each person in turn. She was talking with old Mr. Peterson when her new husband took her by the arm and led her across the room. "There's someone you really must meet, darling." He smiled at her. They walked through the crowd toward another young couple, about their age. Addie had never seen them before.

"Well, old boy, it's about time you introduced me to this ravishing bride of yours," the man said, beaming at Addie.

"Darling, may I present my college roommate and current employer, Harrison Connor, and his lovely wife, Celeste," Jess said with a flourish. "Harry, Celeste, my wife, Addie."

"Your wife." Addie smiled up at him. "I think I like the sound of that."

"Get used to it, my dear," Harry laughed. "It's a title you'll carry with you for a lifetime."

"I'm so pleased to meet you," Addie said to him, taking his hand in hers. "I have heard so much about you from Jess."

"Not too much, I trust." Harry laughed and slapped his friend on the back. "Many of those stories are best left in the past, eh? We're old married men now."

"Addie, I'm looking forward to seeing you in Wharton." Celeste smiled as she changed the subject. "My husband is building us a house there, and I understand you two will be taking up residence in that charming village as well."

"Yes, that's right," Addie said, clasping Celeste's hands. "I'll be so glad to know someone in Wharton. The prospect of leaving home and moving to a new town where I know no one but my husband is a bit daunting."

"We'll do our best to make it exciting for you," Harrison said, winking at her.

"Celeste, Addie's never strayed too far from home," Jess explained, pulling his wife in close to him with one arm. "I was talking with Harry about this earlier—might I prevail upon you to take Addie under your wing, so to speak, when we arrive in Wharton after our honeymoon? With my new position, I'll have many social responsibilities, and my dear country wife needs to learn the ins and outs of throwing the perfect dinner party."

"I'd be delighted," Celeste said warmly, taking Addie by the arm and leading her away from the men. "They believe it's so complicated, what we do. It's only a matter of charm and grace, and you seem to have both of those things in spades. You'll do just fine."

Phil Stewart passed away in his bed, with his wife and the minister beside him, two weeks to the day after Jess and Addie were married. The young couple were just back from their honeymoon in Chicago when word reached them. Jess had taken his wife on a whirlwind shopping trip to the big city—the train ride alone had thrilled her. Shopping in the large department stores and walking along city streets seemed like a dream to this young woman who had never so much as stepped foot out of the tiny community of Great Bay. Addie marveled at Lake Michigan, so like the Great Lake where she had grown up and yet so very different. This was just a body of water like any other. Her lake back home was alive.

On the very hour of Phil Stewart's death, boxes upon boxes had arrived on the front porch of Jess and Addie's new home in Wharton. They were filled with dresses and linens and dishes and candlesticks purchased on their honeymoon trip—everything the young couple needed to set up their new life in style.

The father's life ending, the son's life beginning, at exactly the same hour. If Jess had been a man who thought deeply about things, the juxtaposition of these two events might have occurred as odd to him. But it did not. Indeed, he never knew exactly when his father's life ended. He only knew that his was about to begin.

CHAPTER NINETEEN

She was wrapped up in his arms, her lips on his neck, her legs around his waist. He told her he loved her, sweet and low, in her ear. Then the scene changed, and all Kate could see was rain outside her window. Violent thunder, lightning, shouting voices. And then all was still. Whiteness wrapped its tendrils around the house, around her. Where was the lake? Where were the houses across the street? Where was Jess? She felt a sharp pain in her belly and knew it was time. *Fog will take your baby.*

Startled awake, Kate found sunshine streaming through her windows and a massive dog draped across her chest.

"Morning, girl," she said, scratching Alaska's soft fur. Kate lay there awhile, trying to make sense of what had happened to her the night before. Her memories were hazy—had it really even happened?

She remembered her dreams—images and sounds flying by, one after the other. The woman with the violet eyes and her husband, locked in an embrace. The lake in a torrential rainstorm, enormous waves crashing into the shore. Shouts and accusations. Hissed threats. Fog.

She shook those thoughts out of her head and slid out from under the covers. After a quick shower, she pulled on her clothes and headed downstairs to find her cousin talking quietly on the phone in the library. The conversation stopped abruptly when she walked into the room.

"You're up!" He smiled at her as he spoke into the phone, "She's awake. I'll call you later." He hung up. "Let's have breakfast!"

"Who was that?" Kate gave Simon a sidelong glance. "Were you talking about me?"

"It was Jonathan, if you must know," Simon admitted. "And yes, of course we were talking about you. The Big Chill, as it were, has us both worried. How do you feel?"

"Okay," she said. "None the worse for wear, really." Kate wrapped her arms around her chest and shivered. "But that was weird last night. Wasn't it? I mean, if it was some sort of bug that's going around, it's short lived. I feel fine now."

Simon squinted at her. "Do you really? Because you look a little pale."

"I feel okay. It's just . . ."

"Just what?"

"Things seem a little out of control. First the dreams and now this."

"I know," he sighed. "Come on, let's have some coffee. Everything seems out of control until you've had coffee."

They settled into a table by the window that Simon had already set with a basket of croissants, a bowl of strawberries, blueberries, and melon, and a pot of French press coffee. Kate poured some into her cup, added cream, and took her first sip.

"Any dreams last night?" Simon asked.

She nodded. "I didn't really understand them, though. They were just images, one after the other."

"More scenes from the life of our mystery woman?"

She nodded, remembering. "I think I'll head up to the third floor and go through some trunks today," she said, tearing off a bit of her croissant and popping it into her mouth. "I like your idea about looking for a diary or datebook."

Simon shook his head. "I don't think that's a good idea," he said. "It's dusty up there and considering what happened last night—"

"I'm fine, Simon. Really."

He scowled at her. "At least take the day off," he said. "Relax. De-stress. Will you do that for me?"

Kate smiled. "I will. You worry too much, though."

Kate took another sip of her coffee. "The thing is, I'm a little worried, too. I mean, last night might have been nothing more than a weird flu bug going around. But I'm not sure about that. It really felt linked to all of this."

"I know," Simon said.

"Dreaming about this woman is one thing, but last night was no dream," Kate said. "I know this sounds crazy, Simon, but it felt like I was experiencing what she experienced in that cold, dark water."

"And considering the fact that our fair lady ended up murdered . . ." Simon said, remembering Kate's pre-nup.

"Exactly. I'm thinking the sooner I find out what's behind it all—"

He finished her thought. "The sooner it will go away."

"That's my plan," Kate said, tearing into her flaky croissant and taking a big swallow of coffee. "But I really think I should do something before I climb up to the third floor."

He squinted at her. "What's that?"

"I'll let you know when I've done it," Kate said, pushing her chair back from the table. "I'm going to make a phone call, and I don't want you to talk me out of it."

Before Simon could protest, she hurried out of the room and into the library and picked up the phone, fishing a business card out of her pocket. She dialed.

"Stone."

"Hi!" she said, her words tumbling out of her mouth faster than she had intended. "Detective Stone! This is Kate Granger."

"Hello, Kate Granger," he said. "Queenie missed Alaska on the lakeshore this morning."

Kate smiled into the phone. "She's out in the backyard. I haven't walked her yet."

"At this hour? That's just lazy dog ownership, if you ask me," he teased her.

"Oh, believe me, she's already voiced her grievances." Kate chuckled. "But I told her to give me a break. I had a rather rough night."

"Oh?" he said, the chuckle evaporating from his words. "Nothing serious, I hope?"

Why had she blurted that out? She hadn't intended anything of the kind. "No, no," she said, backpedaling. "It's really nothing. That's not why I'm calling."

"So, then, what can I do for you?"

Kate took a deep breath. "This is going to sound like an odd question, but I'll just say it. Have you actually seen the body of our woman who washed up on the beach?"

"Why?"

"I'm just wondering. Humor me."

"I have seen it, yes," he said. "I told you the truth, now it's your turn to do the same. Why do you ask?"

"How about meeting for lunch today? I have something to show you that I stumbled across, and . . . I'm not sure. I'm not sure at all. But it might be useful in this case, and I really think you should see it."

Again, silence. He certainly wasn't a man who talked too much, Kate thought.

"I can't do lunch, but what about this afternoon?" he offered. "Say three o'clock?"

"Meet me at Harrison's House?"

"I'll see you there at three."

And then he hung up, leaving Kate with just a dial tone, wondering if she had done the right thing.

She returned to Simon pouring her a fresh cup of coffee. "What was all that about?"

Kate sat down, hard. "I did something that might have not been the smartest of all things."

Simon scowled. "Did you call Kevin?"

She shook her head. "I called that detective. Nick Stone."

"Oh?" He raised his eyebrows. "And why did we contact the delightful Mr. Stone?"

"I wanted to show him the photo we found," she admitted. All at once, Kate's reason for calling Nick Stone seemed rather silly.

Simon narrowed his eyes at her. "Do you really think that's a smart thing to do? I mean, what's he going to do with a photo taken more than one hundred years ago?"

"I don't know," Kate said. "But I know it's her in the photo, and I felt I owed it to him to tell him."

"But, why?" Simon wanted to know. "Kate, you don't owe him anything. He's investigating a murder in the here and now and thinks you might be a part of it."

She shook her head. "He doesn't, not anymore. And don't forget, he actually took me seriously when I told him about the dreams. I looked at mug shots for hours!"

"She does protest too much," Simon said, raising his eyebrows. "So when and where are you seeing the good detective? I'd love to be a fly on the wall."

"This afternoon," she said. "And you don't have to be a fly on the wall. You can be the fly in the ointment that you are because he's coming here."

Simon cackled. "And just like that, the day got a lot more interesting."

Kate reached across the table and pinched his arm. "And I'm going to spend most of it going through trunks on the third floor," she said. "After I walk Alaska."

"That dog didn't leave your side last night, I'll have you know," Simon told her. "She was on the bed watching you every time I checked on you. Which was often. I'd poke my head into your room, and she'd stare at me with this look on her face like *I've got this*."

Kate smiled and pushed her chair away from the table, feeling lucky to have two pairs of such watchful eyes on her.

An hour later, after a good walk in the chilly air, Kate was sitting on the floor of the ballroom in front of an open trunk, sifting through its contents with Alaska by her side.

"You're really determined to do this, aren't you, my dear?"

Kate didn't hear the words of Harrison Connor, nor did she see him sitting next to her as she went through the trunks that contained many more mysteries and secrets about life at Harrison's House than Kate could possibly decipher.

She moved from one trunk to another, sifting through memories and mementos.

He rose to his feet and walked to the wall of windows, scratching Alaska behind the ears as he passed. "Such disrepair," he sighed, running one finger down the dusty shutters. "I'm so glad you and Simon are tending to it."

Kate didn't hear these things, but her bodyguard did. Alaska's ears had been on high alert, and now she was staring at the windows with great interest. Not suspicion, just interest. As though she knew the ghost of Harrison Connor meant no harm.

"If you must know, darling, the datebooks are in this one," Harrison said, moving to a trunk in the corner and tapping its lid. It sprung open, the lid hitting the wall behind it with a thud.

Kate looked up with a start. She glanced from the trunk to Alaska and then back again.

"That's weird," she said, under her breath.

Kate pushed herself to her feet and crossed the room, toward the trunk.

"They're on the bottom, under the linens," Harrison said, into her ear. "Dig a little."

As though it was her idea, Kate began to pull the old, delicate tablecloths from the trunk, noticing how the lace had yellowed with age. She put each of them on the floor, one after the other, carefully smoothing any wrinkles. When she had come to the last of them, she peered down into the trunk. What she saw sent a shiver up her spine. A stack of small leather books. She drew one of them from the trunk and turned it over to look at its cover.

It read "Engagements."

This was it! A datebook! She had actually found one! She looked back into the trunk—she had found many, actually.

Kate opened the book's cover to the first page—"Engagements, 1904." So they were sorted by year. A quick scan of the pages told her it was a listing of dinner parties, galas, and other events hosted at Harrison's House—who attended, the menu, and the occasion.

She was just about to grab the entire stack when Alaska began growling, deep and low in her throat.

"Oh, good Christ," Harrison murmured. "Not this again."

"I want her out of this house," a woman said.

"That's not really up to you," Harrison said, louder this time. "You get out. This house is mine."

"We'll see about that."

Kate wheeled around—she knew that Alaska's breed rarely, if ever, growled. She saw that her dog was staring into the corner of the room, head lowered, eyes fixed, teeth bared. Kate's mouth fell open. She had never seen the gentle Alaska bare her teeth at anyone. Or anything.

"What is it, girl?" she whispered. "What do you see?"

A coldness washed over her, as though the temperature in the room had dropped drastically. It didn't feel like what had happened the night before—she wasn't cold in her core. It was the room itself that had suddenly gone into the deep freeze.

Now Alaska was looking in her direction, staring with those yellow eyes, not exactly at Kate, but just beyond her.

Kate turned her head, following Alaska's stare, and saw a dark figure, its shape shifting and moving, not distinct like a shadow, but as though it was roiling and undulating inside, like a cloudy sky just before a hailstorm.

Kate wanted to run, to tear down the stairs like she had done as a child, but she couldn't move.

And then, hands were touching her throat, scratching at her neck, constricting, choking. Kate tried to cry out but could not find her voice. She tried to grasp the hands around her neck but it was like grasping thin air.

"Get off me!" Kate shouted, with as much breath as she could muster, attempting to push away whatever it was that had set upon her.

And then Alaska leaped on her, knocking Kate onto her back and barking savagely with terrible, guttural sounds—a wolf taking down its prey. But the dog wasn't directing the aggression at Kate. Alaska was barking at Kate's invisible attacker, snapping her jaws and thrusting her head forward into the air as though she were trying to take a bite out of something, or someone, Kate couldn't see.

And then, all of a sudden, it was over. Kate lay there with her hands covering her face until Alaska stopped snarling. She peered out from between her fingers and saw the dog standing over her, calm now but alert, panting.

Kate sat up, threw her arms around the animal's neck, and buried her face in the soft fur. Alaska broke free of Kate's embrace and began pacing, settling at the door to the stairs. A couple of yowls told Kate all she needed to know.

"I'm right behind you, girl," she said, scrambling to her feet. She looked around the room and rubbed her arms with her opposite hands. She reached into the trunk, pulled out the entire stack of datebooks, and hurried down the stairs, Alaska following close at her heels.

CHAPTER TWENTY

Kate was pounding so quickly down the stairs that, when she reached the bottom, she ran into the opposite wall with a thud. She stood there for a moment, resting her forehead against it, filling her lungs with deep breaths, trying to quiet her racing heart. Kate felt just like she had when she was a little girl and she and Simon would scare themselves on the third floor on purpose. Was something more up there than just a child's overactive imagination?

Kate didn't want to find out. She shut the third-floor door and turned the key that Simon had left in the lock. Kate knew it was silly, the notion that a locked door could keep whatever was on the third floor out of the rest of the house, but she felt safer all the same.

She found Simon in the living room.

"What is it?" he said to her. "You look like you've seen a ghost."

Kate thought of telling Simon about what had just happened on the third floor and then thought better of it. She had no idea how to find the words.

"Look what I found," she said instead, holding the stack of books out in front of her.

Simon stared at the datebooks, his mouth open. "I can't believe it! Have you sifted through them?"

"I thought I'd do it after lunch," Kate said as she set the stack down on an end table. "Do you have time to break free and go?"

A short while later, Simon and Kate were walking down the hill toward town. The early fall day was crisp and bright, and Kate could see the first whisper of color in the leaves on the maples that lined their route. The cool air felt good on her skin—calming, restorative.

Kate was turning phrases over and over in her mind, trying to find the words to tell Simon about what she had experienced earlier. She knew she had to say something—he and Jonathan lived in the house, after all. But she still wasn't sure what had happened herself. In the end she just blurted it out.

"I think we've got a ghost on the third floor."

"Is it Casper? Does that make one of us Wendy?"

"No, really. I'm not kidding."

He looked at her. "Why? Did something happen when you were up there?"

"I think so," she said.

He considered this as they walked. "You know," he said, finally, "I wouldn't be surprised. Jonathan and I have had experiences since we started the renovations—things that go bump in the night, so to speak. But we've never thought too much of it."

"Why not?"

"The house has so much history. People lived and died there. So it's really no surprise that there's a spirit or two floating around. But the one thing to remember, Kate, is that they were all *our* people. Our relatives. Grandma Hadley, for one. If there are spirits at Harrison's House, they're family. They're not out to harm us."

"Except the lady in the portrait."

Simon hooted. "Well, yes. Except that old shrew, whoever she was."

Kate thought back on her experience earlier in the day. "I know what you're saying about the ghosts being family, but this seemed sort of . . . I don't know. Malevolent."

Simon stopped her. "In what way? What happened up there, Kate?"

"I know this sounds really strange, but I felt hands around my throat. Scratching. And Alaska went insane, snarling and trying to take a bite out of whatever it was. She was in full attack mode. Had it been a person, she would've shattered bones with those bites."

Simon's face went white. "You're kidding."

Kate shook her head. "No, I'm not. It was really weird. And frightening. I felt like whatever it was was trying to choke me."

Simon squinted at her, pushing her collar aside to look at her throat. He took a quick breath in, his eyes wide.

"What?" she asked.

He took Kate's hand and marched her into the women's clothing store on the opposite corner of the street. He led her back to the mirror outside the dressing room.

"Look," he said, taking her by the shoulders and pushing her toward the mirror.

Kate opened her collar and saw it—a line of scratches on the side of her neck, as though they had been made by fingernails. She stared at Simon in the mirror.

"What is this?" she asked him, her eyes wide.

He shook his head. "I don't know. Nothing like this has ever happened at Harrison's House. Nothing. Before or after Grandma died. Like I said, if we have ghosts, they're family."

"So, who or what did this to me, then?"

He hugged her from behind and rested his chin on her shoulder, staring into the mirror and their shared reflection. "And, why?"

Kate felt a chill work its way up her spine. "I had just found the datebooks," she said. "I wonder if it didn't want me to know what was in them."

But later, after Kate and Simon had finished their lunch and she was settled by herself at a table by the window in the coffee shop, datebooks strewn before her, she couldn't figure out what the third-floor ghost was trying so hard to keep her from finding.

To Kate's eye, these were just simple datebooks, records of dinners, parties, and other events. They made for interesting reading, to be sure. Menus, lists of guests, who came, who didn't. What her great-grandmother Celeste was going to wear. "18 for dinner. Cornish game hen. Blue dress, taffeta."

She was hoping to find the name *Addie*, but it was not to be. Kate saw that, back then, couples were referred to by the husband's name. "The Preston Hills," "the Olav Johnsons." She did not know that another name in the margins, "the Jess Stewarts," was the name she sought. It didn't mean anything to her, and she passed right over it, unaware.

Kate was so immersed in dinners eaten and outfits worn during the last century, she lost track of time until the buzz of her cell phone drew her back into this century.

She didn't take the call, but she did notice the hour. Nearly three o'clock! She had to get back up to the house to meet with Nick Stone. She gathered the datebooks and put them back into her tote, dropped her phone into her purse, and headed out the door.

Out of breath and panting by the time she got back up the hill, Kate found Detective Stone sitting in the living room with Simon, cups of what she presumed to be coffee or tea in front of both of them. Alaska was curled up at Nick's feet, but when Kate came in the door, the dog stretched and trotted to greet her.

"Sorry I'm late," she said, taking a few deep breaths and giving Alaska a scratch behind the ears.

"No trouble at all." Simon grinned. "I was just getting to know your detective."

Nick stood up as Kate joined them, eyeing her cousin. "Simon, will you get me something to drink?" she said, wanting him out of the room for a minute.

"Coffee or tea?" He sniffed.

"Surprise me."

When he had gone, she turned to Nick.

"Hi," she said, settling into the armchair across from him. "Thanks for coming."

"My pleasure," he said. "I've been wondering all day what this was about, actually."

Kate ran a hand through her hair. Maybe this wasn't such a good idea after all. But he was here now, and she had to tell him something. It might as well be the truth.

"I'd start off by saying this is going to sound crazy, but I think you've heard that phrase enough from me for one lifetime, and frankly, I'm tired of saying it."

He chuckled and leaned back, crossing his legs. "Go on, Kate. What's this all about?"

She reached into her purse and pulled out the photograph she had put into her wallet for safekeeping.

"I think I know why you can't find any information about our victim," Kate said, sliding the photo across the coffee table toward Detective Stone. "You're looking in the wrong century."

CHAPTER TWENTY-ONE

Nick reached into his shirt pocket and pulled out a pair of glasses.

"I'm not sure what to say about this, Kate," he said, picking up the photo to get a better look. "Could it be her? Maybe. There's a resemblance, sure. But I think that's all there is to it."

Kate was silent for a moment as he stared at the photograph.

"It really does look like her, though," he said. He shook his head as he stared at the image. "I'm assuming this is the husband you mentioned?"

Kate nodded. "That's him. This is why I couldn't find anyone resembling him in your treasure trove of mug shots."

"Where did you get this?" he asked.

"In one of the trunks upstairs," she told him. "Simon and I were looking for old mementoes to display. The other couple in the picture are my great-grandparents. Harrison and Celeste Connor, the people who built this house. We think it might have been taken sometime around 1905."

Nick leaned back and let out a sigh. "This doesn't make any sense, you know," he said, eyeing her. "The condition of the body . . . There's no way she could've died a century ago."

"I know."

Nick ran a hand through his hair. "I shouldn't be telling you this, but if we don't get a break, this is going to slip into cold-case territory. We've got a murdered woman and a baby, and every lead we've had has taken us down a dead end."

He didn't tell her that if she and Kevin hadn't been so close to Johnny Stratton himself, they'd have been building a case, however flimsy, against them.

"Johnny wants me to keep at it, but the only clue we have—the Anderson Mills tag on her dressing gown—is pointing us right into the center of your mystery."

"That's right!" Kate said. "That is, at least, a shred of proof that I'm not making all of this up. Mary Jane's thrift shop here in town hasn't carried any vintage nightgowns like that. Sure, she might have bought it someplace else but . . . How else could that tag be explained?"

"I have no idea," Nick said. "I really don't. Did you find anything else in those trunks?"

Kate smiled. "Not anything too helpful. This morning I was look-ing for datebooks. I found a bunch of them, actually."

"Why datebooks?"

"I thought I might find some names in them. 'Mr. and Mrs. So-and-So, dinner, April twenty-fifth.' To help me search online for who this woman and her husband were."

"But I don't get it. Even if you found the right name, how would you *know* it was the right name?"

"Well, I think I already know her first name. That's the thing. I was talking to my cousin and I blurted out a name when I was mention-ing the woman. 'Addie can wait,' I said to him. I was looking for that particular name in the datebooks, but I didn't find it. All of the couples are referenced by the husband's name. 'The Harrison Connors,' for example."

He nodded. "Ah, yes. That's how they did it back then, didn't they?"

"Supremely unhelpful," Kate said. "I don't know what to do now. It seems like I'm in front of that brick wall again."

Nick leaned forward, putting an elbow on his knee and resting his chin on his palm.

"You could just let it go," he said. "This is a police matter, Kate. It's not up to you to solve this crime."

"I don't agree!" she said, louder than she intended. She pushed herself to her feet and walked over to the fireplace. "I'm the one who's dreaming about her. She washed up on the beach in front of *my* parents' home. This feels really personal to me. And, forgive me, but there's no way you are going to find a living, breathing person who is responsible for her death. If her murder is going to be solved, it *is* up to me."

"But why, Kate? Just for the sake of argument, say everything we've been talking about today is true. Say the woman lying in the morgue right now is the very same woman in this photograph. She died more than a century ago! As you said, there is no living, breathing person to bring to justice, to pay for this crime."

Kate wheeled around to face him. "That's not the point!"

"Justice isn't the point? Then what is?"

Simon had come into the room, carrying Kate's cup of tea. He stood still, eyeing her.

"What?" she said to him.

He raised his eyebrows. "I wasn't sure if I should come in or not. It sounded rather . . . heated in here."

Kate let out a sigh and folded herself back down into her chair. "I'm sorry," she said, looking from Simon to Nick and back again. "I'm just so frustrated with all of this. You're right, Nick. She's been dead for a century, and whoever did this died long ago, too. So, for me, this isn't about catching a killer and making him pay for his crimes."

"For all we know, he did pay," Simon said, setting the cup in front of Kate.

"What do you mean?" she said.

Simon settled into the other armchair. "We've got the body, but we don't know anything else," he said. "For all we know, somebody did pay for the crime, all those years ago."

Kate nodded. "You're right. I hadn't thought of that." Kate paused for a minute. "For me, it's about something else. I only know that I can't stop looking until I find out what that 'something else' is. But without a name, I don't know how I can find out anything online, and . . ." She let her thought dissolve into a sigh.

Kate took a sip of the tea that Simon had placed in front of her and found her hands were shaking.

Simon eyed her and then turned his gaze to the detective, who had also noticed.

"She's thought of nothing else since she arrived," Simon said to Nick. "It's taking its toll on her, physically and emotionally. I've been begging her to take a break. We both can see she needs it."

Kate set her teacup on the table. "Thank you for talking about me as though I'm not sitting right next to you."

Simon smiled at her. "Well, Grandma's not here, so that kind of slight is up to me now."

Nick leaned forward, toward Kate. "Listen," he said. "I think your cousin is right. I really shouldn't be doing this because the investigation is still technically open, but how about we go somewhere for a beer and talk about anything other than this case?"

"I think it's an excellent idea," Simon piped up. "You need something else to think about."

"Well . . . ," Kate began.

"Well, nothing," Simon said. "And you don't have to go anywhere, either. We've got no guests right now. There's an entire bar at your disposal. Charles isn't here to make you any dinner, but feel free to whip up anything you'd like to eat. And I will put a 'Closed' sign on the door on my way out."

"Since when are you going out?" Kate asked him.

"Since right now," he said. "Have fun, kids." He turned on his heel and walked out of the room.

Nick looked at Kate, smiling. "He gets his way all of the time, doesn't he?"

"You have no idea," she chuckled, pushing herself to her feet. "We had better get into the bar before he comes back and drags us in there himself."

CHAPTER TWENTY-TWO

Wharton, 1910

Addie and Jess walked toward the Connors' grand home, hand in hand. Jess had hired a car, but Addie never felt comfortable in those contraptions and told her husband that she wanted to walk in the cool night air.

"Not a good idea, darling." Jess had looked at her through narrowed eyes. "In your condition?"

"You act as though I'm fragile as a china teacup." Addie had smiled, putting on her coat.

"You are." Jess patted her growing belly. "You're carrying precious cargo, you know."

"Please?" she asked, making her way out the door and striding ahead of him down the street. "It's just a little walk."

"Are you sure you're up to this?" Jess stood in the doorway and called after her. "It's quite a climb. I don't think—"

"Nonsense." Addie kept walking. "With all the lying about I did today, I can use a bit of exercise."

"Follow us," Jess called over his shoulder to the driver as he jogged down the street to catch up with his wife. "If she gets tired, I want you close by."

He caught up with Addie and grabbed her hand. "You vex me, Miss Cassatt," he smiled at her.

"That's 'Mrs. Stewart' to you." Addie smiled back at him.

They walked in silence on the raised sidewalks for a bit, and then Jess said, "Darling, I'm so sorry about this morning."

"Let's not talk about it anymore," Addie said, squeezing Jess's hand. He squeezed back. She didn't want to think about the bitter words they had exchanged that morning, but they were still hanging in the air between them.

"I just don't understand why you cannot seem to make small talk with these people," Jess had said to her at the breakfast table. "It's just a dinner party, Addie. Once again I found you in the library instead of socializing with the wives of my colleagues. Why must you be so shy? Don't you understand how embarrassing it is for me?"

Addie looked down at her untouched oatmeal. "I didn't realize I was an embarrassment to you."

Jess pushed his chair back from the table with a huff. "That's ridiculous. You know you're not an embarrassment. It's just . . . Addie. Aren't you happy here?"

She met his gaze. "I love our home and the town of Wharton and especially the proximity to the lake. I love you! And I love Celeste and Harrison. But the parties and socializing . . ." Her words trailed off into a sigh.

"What is the problem, Addie? How difficult is it to make a little small talk with the wives of my colleagues? To laugh? Can't you even appear to be having a good time? I just don't understand why you can't bring yourself to be more helpful to me in this way."

With that, he had grabbed his briefcase and stalked out the door without even a backward glance.

It didn't help matters that he had come home from the office and found Addie swimming instead of dressing for the dinner party they were to attend at the Connors' that night. He didn't know—as she rushed onto shore and into the house after him—that it was the lake that soothed her after his outbursts.

Now they turned the corner and started up the hill. "It will be just Harrison and Celeste tonight, my dear," Jess let her know. "Celeste wasn't up to hosting a crowd."

"Darling, I've made a vow to myself to be better about all of these dinner parties," Addie said, squeezing Jess's hand.

He stopped and looked into her eyes. "Do you mean it?"

"Of course I do," she said. "I'd do anything for you, Jess. And as you say, it's only a little laughter and light conversation. It's just that I can never think of anything to say. But to solve this problem, I'll ask Celeste to give me some advice."

Jess put his arms around his wife. "That would mean the world to me, my dear." And then he pushed back and looked at her. "You and I could practice, also! I promised to guide you through these social minefields, and I daresay I have done a poor job. As I said, I've been through this. I've been in your shoes."

"How did you become so good at it?" Addie asked as they continued their walk.

"I'd have a few phrases at the ready whenever I entered a party," he said, squeezing her hand and remembering those carefree days. "Compliments are always a good way to break the ice. 'My, isn't your dress beautiful?' or, to complete strangers, 'I don't believe we've met. I'm Jess Stewart.'"

"I'll remember that," Addie promised, as much to herself as to Jess. She would never be an embarrassment to him again.

As they neared the house, Addie could see Harrison standing on the front porch. "Hello!" he called down to them, waving. Jess waved in return. Addie smiled broadly.

"My wife insisted we take advantage of the cool evening air," Jess said as they climbed the stairway to the Connors' massive porch. "I had hired a car . . ."

"What a wonderful idea." Harrison smiled and took Addie's hand, threading her arm through his. "I've long admired your athleticism, Addie. I wish my own wife would take more of an interest in the out-of-doors."

"Perhaps after the baby is born, she will feel more like exercising," Addie offered.

"Perhaps." Harrison continued to beam at her. Turning to Jess, he said, "Celeste awaits."

That the two women had conceived children at roughly the same time was a relief to Addie, who had been worried about how her fragile friend would take the news that Addie and Jess were going to have a child. Addie had, in fact, kept the secret to herself for weeks, and asked Jess to do the same, until she could find a way to tell Celeste about their upcoming arrival without sending her into a torrent of grief.

Addie knew that Celeste still fiercely mourned the loss of her baby daughter Clementine the year before. They couldn't encounter a pregnant woman on the street without Celeste dabbing at her eyes with a handkerchief and becoming still and silent. It was as though she was just going through the motions of a conversation, or shopping, or whatever they were doing. Outwardly, she was calm and collected, but Addie could see the firestorm that raged within.

When Addie discovered she herself was expecting a child, she knew that, soon, she would be the object of that simmering rage. Was there a gentle way to break this news to someone who would be broken by it? Addie wasn't sure there was and had fretted about it for weeks.

She was spared finding the answer to this riddle, however. Over dinner one night, Jess told her about a conversation he'd had with Harrison that afternoon at the office.

"He confided that Celeste is with child," Jess had said, raising his eyebrows. "He asked that we keep it under our hats for the moment. Don't let on that you know. Wait for her to tell you. Harrison wanted us to know right away because Celeste is going to be quite the china doll until the baby comes. No more picnics, no more walks in the country. She's going to slow down considerably. Take care of herself. They want to do all they can to ensure this one makes it."

"I completely understand." Addie hugged her husband. "Did you tell Harrison our news in return?"

"I did." Jess smiled. "He was so pleased. I told him to go ahead and tell Celeste. It'll be easier coming from him."

And indeed it was. The next day, Addie answered the knock at the front door to find the Connors' driver, hat in hand.

"I've been sent by Mrs. Connor to bring you up the hill to the mansion for lunch, ma'am," he said, handing her a note from Celeste. "If you're able."

Addie didn't much like automobiles, but she accepted the invitation, knowing that Celeste was going to announce her condition and the secret would be out in the open at last. When Addie arrived at the mansion, she was led into the parlor, where Celeste sat on the couch surrounded by freshly cut flowers.

"Addie." Celeste smiled, holding her arms out wide. "Harrison told me your wonderful news. We couldn't be happier for you." Addie crossed the room and hugged Celeste, as summoned.

"Thank you." Addie smiled, intending to say more about how thrilled she and Jess were about the baby, but something about Celeste's face silenced her. There was a darkness behind Celeste's eyes. Addie could see that her friend was not at all pleased with the fact that she was not the only expectant mother in the room. And then it hit Addie. *I've stolen her spotlight.* She didn't know what to say.

"I have happy news of my own to share," Celeste broke the silence.

"No!" Addie cried in mock surprise, grasping her friend's hands.

"It's true," Celeste said. "I've planned a little celebration lunch for the two of us. Imagine, both of us expecting babies at the same time!"

"Oh, Celeste, I'm so happy for you—for us!" Addie gushed. "You and I can go through this together. How wonderful!"

Over lunch, the pair talked about baby names and doctor visits, and gradually, Addie began to think that she had just imagined the animosity behind Celeste's eyes. *She's probably just worried about delivering a healthy baby.*

Celeste reached over and grasped her friend's hand, and just for a moment, the veneer that shrouded her real feelings vanished. "I hope— I believe—things will be different this time," she whispered. Her voice trailed off, and Addie could see the tears begin to well up in Celeste's eyes. Her friend would worry every day until the baby was born.

"Of course they will, my dear Celeste," Addie said. "Our children will grow up together, the best of friends."

She put her other hand on top of Celeste's and said a silent prayer.

Addie thought of that months-ago day now, as she and Jess entered the Connor house for dinner.

Throughout the meal, Addie could see that Celeste was pale and drawn and breathless. The men made conversation about work matters, mostly, but instead of her usually animated repartee, Celeste only quietly smiled, as though the expression was painted onto her face. It made Addie wonder why on earth her friend should be going to the trouble of arranging these dinner parties and luncheons, especially tonight when she clearly would have preferred to be curled up in her own bed rather than entertaining visitors. As the men adjourned to the porch for cigars after dinner, Addie took Celeste's arm and led her to the sofa in the parlor.

"You are not feeling up to this tonight, dear Celeste," she said.

"Nonsense." Celeste smiled. "We must maintain our social obligations. A man in Harrison's position—"

"—should know when his wife has had enough of company," Addie interrupted. Addie knew that she should end this evening now, for Celeste's sake. She patted her friend's hand, stood up, and said, "I'm going to find my husband and tell him it's time to go home."

"But the men haven't had their Scotch," Celeste protested.

"I, for one, am not feeling well," Addie stated, raising her eyebrows. "I am going to have to beg my hostess's kind indulgence and take my leave earlier than expected."

Celeste sighed and leaned against the back of the sofa. "You are such a dear," she said.

Addie followed the sound of the men's voices from the parlor through the big double doors and onto the porch. It was a beautiful, peaceful evening signaling the coming of spring.

"Darling," she said to Jess, "I'm sorry to interrupt, but we need to be going now."

"So soon?" Harrison protested. "But you've only just arrived! I do so enjoy your visits."

"I hope you won't think me rude, but the baby is dictating my actions these days." Addie took her host's arm and whispered, "On our way down the hill, we will stop at Dr. Maki's house. I think he should come up and have a look at Mrs. Connor."

"It's not . . . time?" Harrison looked from one to the other of his friends, his smile melting into a look of concern.

"Not yet," Addie said. "Celeste seems frightfully tired, however, and just as a precaution—"

"Yes, yes, good thinking." Harrison squeezed Addie's hand. "You are always so kind, my dear."

"We'll see ourselves out, Harrison," Jess said.

As they walked down the steps, Jess and Addie heard Harrison calling to his wife and assumed all was well.

They did not see her collapse into his arms, nor did they see him carry her upstairs to the bedroom. Jess and Addie had stopped at the doctor's house and were home, snuggling together in their own bed, talking of Jess's upcoming trip to Chicago—very ill timed, he thought—when Dr. Maki arrived at the Connor mansion. And later still, as Addie drifted off into sleep in the arms of her beloved, the doctor was giving Celeste something to quiet the raging fever that had overtaken her.

CHAPTER TWENTY-THREE

Kate had poured a glass of chardonnay for herself and a Scottish ale for Nick, and the two of them were sitting across from each other at a table near the window. It was after four o'clock already, and the sun was sinking low in the sky.

Nick took a sip of his ale and gazed out the window. "Photographers call this the golden hour," he said, pointing outside. "See how the light is illuminating everything so beautifully?"

Kate smiled, noticing for the first time that the trees, the grass, the flowers, and even the houses seemed to be glowing.

"It's the best time for shooting, when the world is bathed in that soft, golden light," he said.

"So, you're a—" Kate was about to say *photographer*, but the word stuck in her throat. The vision—or whatever it was—she'd had of her and Nick Stone, walking together in the woods, a camera in his hand, replayed in her mind.

"I'm a what?" He smiled.

She shook her head, trying to push the vision away. "Photographer," she said. "But it seems like I already knew that. It sounds familiar. Did you tell me about this before?"

"Not likely," he said and took a sip of his ale. "It's not something I broadcast to a whole lot of people. It's just a hobby, but I love it."

"Something to do when you're not chasing bad guys?"

"I think part of the reason I'm drawn to it is precisely because I chase bad guys for a living," he said. "I shoot landscapes, mostly. It reminds me of the beauty in this world. And other things."

"In contrast to the ugliness you must see every day on the job."

He held her gaze for a moment. His eyes had a clarity to them that Kate hadn't noticed before.

"That's exactly right," he said to her. "Not a whole lot of people get it, but you do."

Kate fidgeted in her chair but couldn't contain the smile that broke out across her face. "When did you take it up? The camera, I mean."

"My dad was a photographer," he said. "By trade. He gave me my first camera when I was about thirteen years old. An Instamatic."

Kate grinned. "I remember those! I think I had one, too. With the old kind of film—what was it called?"

"One-ten," he said, nodding.

"Wow," Kate said, thinking back to her middle school years, shooting photos of her friends with that same kind of camera. "The technology has changed so much over the years. Who even uses film anymore?"

"I do," he said. "I know everyone's a photographer these days with their cell phone cameras, but to me, there's just something about using an old camera that you have to set by hand."

"There's an artistry that has been lost," Kate agreed.

"I don't think Ansel Adams Photoshopped any of his images," Nick said, leaning forward. "That was all his eye, his skill as an artist."

The air between them began to electrify—Kate could feel the tingle on her skin. *Best to tone this down a bit,* she thought.

"So, your father was a photographer," she said, circling the conversation back to safe territory. "What did he think of you becoming a cop?"

"He never knew it," Nick said, a sad smile on his face. "My dad had his own photo studio. He did portraits to make a living, but he really loved shooting landscapes. And when I got out of school, I worked with him."

"He must have loved that," Kate said, thinking of her own father. "But—he died before you joined the force?"

Nick nodded, a sheen in his eyes. "It's the reason I became a cop, actually," he said, clearing his throat.

Kate felt the rush of Nick's emotion—grief—and reached over to touch his hand. The heat was palpable, jolting up Kate's arm and then all through her.

"I'm sorry," she said. "We can talk about something else."

"I was out of the shop," he said, his voice hoarse and low. "I came back to find him on the floor in a pool of blood. They got away with about seventy-five bucks in cash. That's all we had on hand."

"Oh, Nick."

"I know it's cliché, but that's why a lot of people become cops. I dedicated my life, then and there, to putting the bad guys behind bars."

They sat there, looking into each other's eyes for a moment, the intensity of the emotion flowing through both of them.

"Did you ever find the people who did it?" Kate asked, not knowing if she should.

He shook his head, a grimace of disgust twisting his lips. "I've never stopped looking." He cleared his throat and took a sip of his ale. "Man, how did this get so heavy?"

"Sharing life experiences will do that to a conversation." Kate smiled. "But do you know what I'd like now?"

"What's that?"

"Pasta," she said, giving his hand a final squeeze and pulling away. "Are you hungry? I know it's a little early, but I could whip up something for us."

Nick finished his ale. "A fabulous idea," he said, putting his glass down on the table. "But I'll help. I'm pretty handy with a spatula."

Kate smirked. "I'll bet you are."

Soon, Kate and Nick were in the kitchen, aprons on, knives in hand. She was slicing tomatoes, and he was chopping onions. Bacon was sizzling under the broiler, and chicken was cooking on the stovetop grill. A pot of pasta water was heating on one burner, a stainless steel pan was warming on another, and in a saucepan, butter was melting.

"What are we making, exactly?" Nick asked.

"Cheesy pasta with onion, bacon, tomato, spinach, and chicken," she said. "Comfort food. I thought we could both use a dose of it. My own famous recipe. Here, hand me those onions, will you? And get the milk out of the fridge?"

As the pasta bubbled in the water, Kate began sautéing the onions. "This'll be your job," she said to Nick, handing him the spatula and stepping away from her post in front of the pan. "Caramelize. Don't burn. And then add the tomatoes and, last, the spinach."

"Yes, ma'am." He smiled.

While he was doing that, Kate added a few tablespoons of flour to the melted butter in the saucepan and stirred to make a roux. To that, she added the milk and the shredded cheese.

Ten minutes later, they were back at their table with heaping bowls of pasta in front of them.

"This is incredible," Nick said, taking a bite. "Do you mind if I inhale it? I may not be able to talk for a while."

"I think in some parts of the world, that's a compliment to the chef."

"Only if it's followed by profuse burping. Which I'm not above, by the way."

Kate smiled, watching him. How long had it been since she'd had such an easy conversation with a man other than Simon? She couldn't remember the last time. Things had been so strained with Kevin over the past year or so, she had trouble recalling a time in which they were truly happy.

"What?" Nick said, taking a bite of his pasta. "You're staring at me."

She was out on a limb, and she knew it. "You're really easy to talk to, Nick Stone," she said, inching out onto that limb even further.

He smiled. "So are you," he said. "I haven't opened up like this to anyone at the precinct—nobody knows about my dad. And yet here I am blurting all of this out to you. This may sound like a strange thing to say, but it feels like I've known you forever."

Kate's stomach did a quick flip. "I'm the one dreaming about a dead woman, remember? Very little is going to sound strange to me."

Their conversation meandered through typical first-date territory—where they had spent their childhoods, college experiences, the roads each of them had taken to get where they were. They had so much in common—favorite movies, books they enjoyed, even where they liked to travel, and how they treated their dogs—Kate began to peek into the future and wondered if hers was going to include Nick Stone.

But she shook that thought out of her head. Now was not the time to even consider getting involved with another man. Her divorce papers weren't even signed. And she was involved in an investigation he was working.

After dinner, Nick and Kate took their drinks into the library and sat in front of the fire.

Nick's arm rested against the back of the sofa, inviting Kate to snuggle in. She didn't, fighting off every impulse she had to do so.

"I'm glad I took the afternoon off," he said finally, not looking at her.

"I'm glad you did, too," she said.

"I should probably get going," he said. But neither of them moved.

And then he turned to her, his outstretched arm pulling her shoulders in to him. Before she knew it, his mouth was on hers, and her arms were wrapping around his neck. She dissolved into him and wished the kiss would go on forever.

But then she pulled away, shaking her head. "I can't do this."

"I'm sorry," he said. "I just—"

"No, I just—too. But Nick, this is wrong. I'm still married. I'm in the process of getting a divorce, but technically . . ."

He nodded. "I understand. I should go."

"That might be best." She got up from the sofa on shaky legs and followed him to the door.

Before he left, he turned to her.

"I had a really good time tonight," he said. "I know you're still married. And you're part of an open investigation. The timing stinks. But when all of that works itself out, I hope we can do this again."

"I'd like that," she said and shut the door behind him as he walked out into the crisp, fall night.

CHAPTER TWENTY-FOUR

"So?" Simon said across the breakfast table the next morning. "I want to hear every last detail."

Kate could feel the heat rising to her cheeks. She had thought about nothing else but her evening with Nick Stone during her early morning walk with Alaska.

"That good?" Simon grinned.

Kate shook her head. "I have no business seeing another man," she said. "I'm still married to Kevin."

Simon set his fork down on the table. "Listen," he said. "You're not *seeing* him. You just had dinner. But Kate, this is me you're talking to. We both know you're not getting back together with Kevin. I saw it in your eyes the second you walked through the door."

Kate had to admit it to herself—he was right. The thought of seeing Kevin again filled her with revulsion.

Kate's phone ringing startled both of them. She looked at the number and whispered to Simon, "I think it's the good detective."

Simon took a sip of his coffee and leaned in.

"Hello?"

"Hi," said Nick Stone.

"Hi," Kate said, grinning.

"I know I said I was going to leave you alone until you got your life sorted out."

"I never asked you to leave me alone."

"Well, that's good," Nick chuckled, his deep voice sending a shiver through Kate. "Because I don't intend to. But I'm calling today because I was thinking about your brick wall."

"Were you now?"

"I was. And I think I have an idea for you."

Kate smiled and took a sip of her coffee. "Are you going to tell me this idea?"

"I thought I might. Yes."

"Today?"

He laughed. "Yes, today. Here it is. I was thinking about how you came up empty searching on the internet because you didn't have the name of the person you're looking for."

"That's right. And I'm not sure where to go from here."

"What about to the library?"

Kate furrowed her brow. "I don't follow you. What would I be looking for there?"

"Old newspapers," he said. "I'm sure the library has the Wharton daily paper on microfilm, all the way back to 1905. Even earlier. You'd have to physically look through them, but you wouldn't need a name. It's the headline you're after. If your lady and her husband were acquainted with your great-grandparents, and better yet, if they lived in Wharton, her murder would've been news."

Kate closed her eyes. "Of course," she said. "I've been so used to looking things up in an online database for so many years that I didn't even think of archives at the library."

"Forest for the trees," he said. "Sometimes the closest person to a case can't see the obvious. I'll tell you, when I got this idea, I thought it might be a way to crack this case, and then . . ."

"It's my case, not yours," Kate said.

"That's right. I can't send someone from my team to do research on a dead woman from a hundred years ago."

"So you called me," she said.

"Exactly."

Kate was silent for a moment, buzzing with excitement. Would this finally lead her to the truth?

"Thank you, Nick," she said. "Thank you so much. I'll head down to the library right after breakfast."

"Let me know what you turn up."

"I will," Kate said, clicking her phone off.

After telling Simon all about it while they finished their meal, Kate gathered up her purse and jacket.

"I have a strong feeling that I'm going to find something," she said to Simon. "I really do."

"You know what? I do, too." Simon smiled, squeezing her hand.

Simon walked her to the door and kissed her on the cheek. "Here's to fruitful hunting."

When she reached the library, Kate pushed open the big double doors carrying a purse heavy with quarters. She had stopped at the bank on her way down the hill and exchanged some bills for several rolls of coins, knowing that the temperamental microfiche machine at the library might require a good deal of coaxing before it agreed to print out any pages.

Even in this digital age, old copies of the town's daily newspaper, the *Wharton Tribune*, were still stored on rolls of film that looked something like old-fashioned home movie reels. As a reporter, Kate was familiar with the medium and the machine needed to read it, a cumbersome cube with a screen about the size of a standard-size television and a hand crank that was used to advance the film. She had researched many stories in this way over the years, threading the film through the machine and using a handle to spin through the issues, which appeared on the large monitor, until she reached the one she needed. The film represented actual photographs of the newspaper that had been reduced—Kate was able to see an entire page of the paper, sometimes two, at once on the screen.

To Kate, reading old newspapers on microfiche was a bit like time travel. Issue after issue appeared on the screen and then vanished. Then another, then another. The faster she spun the handle, the faster time would go by.

"Where do you store old copies of the *Trib*?" Kate asked the librarian, a twenty-something man with messy brown hair pulled into a man bun on the top of his head.

"How old?" he asked her.

"I'd like to start with the year 1905 and go forward from there," she said.

"Last couple of drawers on the right," he said, pointing to a shelf in the back of the library.

"Do all of these machines make copies?" Kate asked. She did not want to find herself staring at vital information with no way to print it out.

"Only the three nearest to the window," he replied, again, pointing. "You'll need quarters."

Kate thanked him and found the rolls she needed, chose a machine, one that could indeed print the page viewed on the screen, and settled in for what she knew would be a long day's work. Unlike the internet, there was no way to search a microfiche by subject. The newspapers appeared in their entirety and were arranged by date only. Did the woman die in 1905? 1910? Kate had no way of knowing exactly when it had happened. Grasping in the dark wasn't her favorite way of collecting information, but at the moment, it was all she had. Kate carefully threaded the first roll into the machine, January 1905, and flipped the power switch on.

Hours later, she had searched through nearly four years' worth of newspapers. An event like the death of a prominent woman would be front-page news, Kate reasoned, so she took the time to scan only the front pages of each issue. She found herself sidetracked, however, by other stories in the news—it was a glimpse into American life in a more innocent age. World War I hadn't yet occurred—a thing as horrible as a *world war* wasn't even imagined on the day that her great-grandparents had had a picnic with the beautiful, long-haired woman in Kate's dreams. Prohibition was not in full swing, though there were rumblings about it, immigrants were flooding into Ellis Island. Closer to Kate's home, the logging and shipping industries were dominating the news and refabricating the countryside.

Kate was startled to read that, in 1905, several severe storms hit the Great Lakes, including one so fierce and sudden that it froze men solid on the deck of their ship, which was stranded just far enough offshore to prevent their rescue, as horrified townspeople looked on. That storm created the call for more lighthouses to be built—ones that Kate herself had explored, and considered ancient, as a child. It was a time of incredible expansion and growth in the area, and the sense of optimism, not just in Wharton but in the country as a whole, was tangible, even to Kate, reading about it secondhand almost a century later. *What an exciting time to be alive,* Kate thought, *when the country was relatively new.* She saw her great-grandfather's name and grainy photograph in the news several times, always in reference to his business.

She looked at her watch and thought of taking a break to rest her eyes from the monitor's glare, but instead she decided to just keep plugging along. She was here now, and fatigued or not, she wasn't going to stop searching until she had some answers.

Kate threaded roll after roll, scanned page after page, worrying with every headline that passed before her eyes in a flash that perhaps she was mistaken, perhaps she would find no information about this woman's death, perhaps the woman on her beach was not the same woman in the photograph after all.

Then she came upon something that made her stop short. Kate held her breath and read:

LOCAL WOMAN MISSING

Mrs. Jess Stewart (née Adelaide Cassatt) has gone missing from her Front Street home. Mr. Stewart, vice president of Canby Lines, owned by local businessman Mr. Harrison Connor, returned home late Sunday, April 24, from a business meeting in Chicago to find his wife had vanished without a trace. She was last seen by a maid on Sunday afternoon.

Upon arriving home that evening and finding his wife missing, Mr. Stewart sent word to his wife's parents, Mr. and Mrs. Marcus Cassatt of Great Bay, who had not heard from their daughter. St. Joseph's Hospital has no patients who match her description. Mrs. Stewart's clothes, shoes, and suitcases remain in the home. Police reports indicate no evidence of foul play.

Mrs. Stewart is a young woman with long auburn hair. She is heavy with child, due to deliver at any moment. The frantic Mr. Stewart asks anyone with any informa-tion regarding his wife's whereabouts to contact the authorities.

Mr. Connor has offered a sizeable reward to anyone who provides information that will bring Mrs. Stewart home.

A photo appeared under the article. Small and inky though the shot was, there was no mistaking it. Kate's heart began pounding loudly in her chest, her body shaking with the reality of it. She was looking at proof of the impossible.

Adelaide Stewart—Kate caught her breath. *Addie.* That was the name of the woman in Kate's dreams. Jess Stewart was the husband. His name took root in her heart, as though it had been there all along.

Kate put three quarters in the machine, and through the tears that had begun welling up in her eyes, she hit the "Print" button.

Kate was a reporter; she knew there had to be more to the story. What happened to Addie? How did she wind up missing? What of the child? The story said she was "heavy with child," yet she washed up *with* a baby. And how did she end up in the lake in her nightgown? Kate turned the machine's handle slowly, twisting through the days and weeks that were held captive on the roll.

MAN ARRESTED! WIFE MURDERED!

Mr. Jess Stewart, vice president of Canby Lines, has been arrested in the disappearance of his wife, Adelaide. After a thorough police investigation, Mr. Stewart was taken into custody today and charged with her murder.

Mr. Harrison Connor, Mr. Stewart's employer, president of Canby Lines, proclaims Mr. Stewart's innocence, offering a sizeable reward to anyone providing information that will lead to his exoneration.

The piece included two photographs, the same one of Addie that had appeared in the earlier story and another of her husband. Kate had seen that face before in a dream. She knew this man. She had touched him, felt the love that Addie felt for him. She remembered his sweet words, the scent of the lilacs he had brought her. There was no way he killed her. At the sight of his photograph, Kate felt a gnawing in the pit of her stomach. Again, tears welled up in her eyes. She felt sick at the thought of it. Not him. Not Jess. But she remembered Nick's words: If a wife and baby are murdered, look to the husband first.

Kate stared at the story on the screen before her, at once marveling at the differences in the reporting style of the day—so biased, so many questions left unanswered—and wondering how this turn of events could possibly have taken place. She printed out a copy of the story and continued on her search, threading the next roll of film and turning the handle slowly, watching the days and weeks unfold before her in an instant. It didn't take long for Kate to find the next installment of the story. It was splashed across the front page, the headline in bold, uppercase type.

STEWART TRIAL BEGINS TODAY

The trial of Mr. Jess Stewart, formerly the vice president of Canby Lines, begins today at the courthouse in Wharton. Crowds began gathering on the courthouse steps early in the day, awaiting a chance to see the accused murderer arrive on the scene.

Mr. Stewart is accused of killing his wife. The crime is made all the more heinous by the fact that Mrs. Stewart was expecting their first child. Her body has not been found.

"I want to see him hang," said Wharton police chief Arnold Becker on the courthouse steps. "We've got a solid case against him. There's no doubt in my mind this man killed his wife."

Despite the police chief's statements, Mr. Harrison Connor, owner and president of Canby Lines, Wharton's largest employer, steadfastly maintains his belief in the innocence of his former vice president.

"I know Jess Stewart personally, and I do not believe he had anything to do with his wife's disappearance," Mr. Connor told this reporter this morning as he arrived at the courthouse. "This entire trial is a travesty. There is no proof the woman is dead. She may have simply run off. Her husband is devastated by this loss, as are we all. I am here today to support my friend and feel confident he will be exonerated at trial."

Kate threaded yet another roll of film into the machine and began to turn the handle. The trial was in full swing. Not a day went by without sensational headlines.

EYEWITNESS PUTS STEWART IN WHARTON ON SATURDAY!

During the first day of testimony in the trial of Mr. Jess Stewart, his assertion that he returned to Wharton on Sunday, April 24, to find his wife missing has been called into question.

The crowd was standing room only for the beginning of what is already being called the Trial of the Century. Mr. Stewart is accused of murdering his wife, née Adelaide Cassatt, and it seems that the whole town of Wharton has come to see for themselves whether or not this man is a cold-hearted killer. Along with the townsfolk, Mr. Stewart's mother, Mrs. Jennie Stewart, has been in attendance, as have the parents of the murdered woman, Mr. and Mrs. Marcus Cassatt, of Great Bay. Mrs. Stewart and the Cassatts were sitting together, no animosity apparent between them.

"My son is innocent," Mrs. Stewart declared before the trial began.

"We believe Jess had nothing to do with Addie's disappearance," said Mr. Cassatt, his wife too distraught to comment on the proceedings.

Mr. Johann Lange, a dockworker at Olsen's Fish Market, was the first witness called in the trial. He testified that he saw Mr. Stewart passing by the fish market on Saturday, April 23.

"He was angry, anybody could see that," testified Mr. Lange. "I know it was Saturday because the boats came in. Usually, the fishermen fill their nets and come back into port on Saturday, what with Sunday being the Sabbath."

Under questioning, Mr. Lange divulged that he saw Mr. Stewart angrily walking down Market Avenue past the fish market toward Front Street, where his home is located.

Mr. Stewart jumped from his chair upon hearing this testimony, shouting, "It's a lie! It's a lie!"

With that, the courtroom erupted into pandemonium, people shouting and tempers flaring. Finally, Mr. Lange exited the courtroom, yelling, "I hope you hang, wife killer!"

Judge Arvid Anderson quieted the crowd with threats of expelling the lot of them.

Tomorrow, the trial resumes.

CHAPTER TWENTY-FIVE

Kate's heart was beating hard in her chest. She printed out the story, but before she could thread the next roll, she noticed the librarian slouching over to her.

"We're closing for the day, ma'am," he said. "We close early in the off-season. You've got to finish up and go."

Was it so late already? "I'm sorry, I guess I lost track of time," she mumbled, gathering her papers and eyeing the enormous pile of rolls on her desk. "I'll put these away before I leave."

Kate pushed her way out of the library's heavy door and was taken aback by the twilight she encountered outside.

She dug her phone out of her purse and dialed.

"You won't believe it!" she said to Nick, nearly breathless. "You won't believe it! I can hardly believe it myself."

"You found something?"

"It took all day, but yes," she said, walking fast. "Can you meet me at the coffee shop? I can't wait to show you what I found."

"I'll be right there."

Kate crossed the street and hurried down the block to the coffee shop, ordering two coffees before settling into a table by the window. She opened the file folder she was carrying and pulled out the copies she had made at the library, strewing them across the table.

Nick arrived a few minutes later.

"Look at this!" she said, her eyes shining.

"I'll be damned," Nick whispered as he studied the grainy newsprint photograph of Addie. "That's the same woman in the photo you showed me yesterday. And her name—Addie. Didn't you tell me that was the name of the woman in your dreams?"

"They called it the 'Trial of the Century.'" Kate was talking fast. "Jess Stewart—he's the husband—was arrested and put on trial for the murder of his wife. My great-grandfather stood by him in a very public way. He even offered a reward to anyone who found the real killer. They were friends! Jess Stewart worked for him at Canby Lines."

Nick stared at Kate, open mouthed. In one afternoon of research, she had indeed produced evidence of the impossible.

"You're right about one thing," Nick said. "I can hardly believe this. It's just—" He sighed. "I deal with black-and-white issues. This is one hell of a shade of gray." Nick leafed through the copies of articles. "What happened with the trial?" he asked her. "Was he found guilty?"

"I don't know!" Kate cried. "The library was closing. I didn't get to the rest of the story."

"You're going back tomorrow, I assume," Nick said.

"As soon as the doors open."

"Let me know what you find," he said. "I won't be putting this in the case file, but now you've got me hooked."

Kate took a gulp of her coffee and gathered her copies back into their folder. "I've got to tell Simon about this," she said. "He's not going to believe it, either."

She stood up and Nick reached for her hand. "You know, Kate, I have no idea what to do with this information. But I'm really glad you took me along for the ride."

She smiled at him and squeezed his hand, electricity jolting through her as she did so. The truth was, Nick was the first person she'd thought of calling when she found out about Addie and Jess. She wasn't sure what that meant, but she knew it meant something.

"I'll be in touch," she said.

Kate hurried up the hill and burst through the doors of Harrison's House to find Simon in the library with a cup of tea.

"I found it!" she announced, tears stinging the backs of her eyes. "It's all true, Simon."

She opened the folder and fished out the copies, telling him the whole story.

"You know what I wonder?" Simon said, still staring at the articles. "She died more than a century ago. You're dreaming about her now. Why?"

"I don't follow you," Kate said.

"I think we're going from a whodunit to a whydunit and, from there, to a whyKate."

Kate wasn't sure what he meant.

"Think about it from your perspective," he said. "What would be so vital, so important, to compel *you* to come back from the dead and reach out from beyond the grave to someone living? Because that's exactly what I think Addie is doing."

"It sounds creepy when you say it like that." Kate grimaced. "Do you think it's that deliberate? You're making it sound like Addie herself is doing all of this somehow. Invading my dreams."

"If she's not doing it, who is?" Simon said. "And why?"

Kate felt a chill at the thought of it. All these events were becoming too starkly real, too tangible. The bodies, the photograph, the articles. Her own physical reactions. The whole situation was haunting—literally.

"Do you think I'm supposed to do something for her?" Kate wondered.

"You want to hear a flat-out guess?" Simon said. "I'll bet it has something to do with the trial."

"We don't even know if her husband was found guilty or innocent at this point," Kate said. "Still, like Nick said last night, what could it possibly matter now? She's been dead for almost a century. That trial is so long in the past that nobody even remembers it anymore."

"Addie does." Simon smiled.

As Kate settled in beneath her thick down comforter later that night, a confusion of thoughts swirled through her mind. It was difficult to process all that had happened during the day. A newspaper article confirming that the woman in her dreams was *real* and might have been *murdered* had produced a tightening in Kate's stomach that wasn't quieted by a good dinner, fine wine, or the companionship of the person closest to her in the world.

She couldn't get it out of her mind. It was breathtaking, literally. Kate had been having trouble filling her lungs with air ever since she had seen those black, typewritten words on the page, those grainy photographs confirming Addie's existence, and the fact that her death had resulted in the "Trial of the Century."

Now, as Kate punched her pillow and turned onto her side, she couldn't turn off those thoughts. Was Simon right? Were her dreams and Addie's sudden reappearance somehow tied to the murder and the trial? Kate wasn't sure, but whenever she thought of the notion of Addie's husband killing her, she was overcome by a feeling that was hard to define. It just didn't seem possible. The love that she had felt between them in her dreams—it was hard to imagine that kind of love curdling and ending in death.

Simon popped his head into Kate's room, breaking her train of thought.

"And how are we doing?" he inquired.

"*We're* doing just fine," Kate laughed.

"I'm going downstairs to Skype with Jonathan," Simon said. "If you need anything, just holler."

Kate could already feel the heaviness behind her eyes as she snuggled down into bed. "I have a feeling I won't be hollering. I'll be drifting off in very short order."

"Let me tuck you in," Simon said, pulling the covers up to her chin. He kissed her, turned off the light, and closed the door, leaving Kate alone with her thoughts as her eyes fell shut.

She found herself standing in the middle of a large room. She recognized it almost immediately—it was the ballroom on the third floor of Harrison's House. But it was different from how Kate remembered. It was cleaner, newer. All the shutters were open, and the windows were freshly washed. Candles lit the room—Kate saw their light flickering against the windowpanes.

Odd, Kate thought. *Someone must have been up here cleaning all night long. Would Simon have done that? Why?*

Then it occurred to her. *Oh, I'm dreaming.*

Then she heard the voices. Talking and laughing. Glasses clinking, high heels on the wood floor. The room was filled with people. Was this a party? Kate longed to turn around and see what was happening but could not direct her gaze away from the window. She felt a slight breeze on her face as she noticed that some of the windows themselves were open as well. The view was expansive and dramatic, but this, too, was different than she remembered it. Kate could see all the way down the road to the harbor, where two enormous ships floated lazily in the background and a cluster of smaller boats filled the slips at the town dock. People crowded the streets, walking into and among the shops. They congregated down at the harbor, and Kate noticed a group of young people—families, she thought—enjoying a picnic on a grassy hill overlooking the water. Green leaves adorned the trees, flowers were everywhere, and the sun was setting, turning the sky into an explosion of pinks and purples. *What a lovely day,* Kate thought. *It must be high summer, tourist season.*

She leaned out of the window to get a better look. The town itself was immeasurably smaller than Kate knew it to be. Where the Flamingo restaurant should have been, the whole block was taken up by what looked to be a warehouse. The bookstore and the drugstore, both gone. In their places, an open field with a large sign proclaiming FRESH BLUEBERRIES! PICK YOUR OWN!

Next to the water, the Dockside Café, too, was gone. An industrial building stood there, two stories high. Kate saw a sign on its wall but could not make it out completely. Only the word FISH was discernable. She saw no antique shops and no art galleries. There were stores on the streets, just not the ones that Kate knew. A grocer, what looked to be a restaurant. Was that a hardware store? Kate couldn't make out the rest of the signs.

Instead of the row of stately Victorian homes that Kate had come to know, one small, clapboard house with a decaying front porch stood between Harrison's House and the town center. Shabby though the house was, Kate noticed a magnificent garden that stretched into what looked to be two lots. Kate could make out stalks of corn, sunflowers, lettuce, beans, and a whole host of other vegetables ripening in the sun. *Beautiful,* Kate thought. She noticed that the roads were unpaved and entire blocks were simply undeveloped, grassy land. Lines of raised, wooden sidewalks snaked through town, so the ladies and gentlemen who lived there wouldn't soil the bottoms of their dresses and trousers on the muddy, dirty streets. The lakeshore looked rugged, untamed and dominant against such simple edifices.

It wasn't until Kate looked closer at the people on the street that she got it. Long dresses, three-piece suits and bowler hats, parasols. Model T cars. Horses tied to hitching posts here and there. No cell phone, power line, or music to be seen or heard. She was looking out the window into Wharton circa 1910.

Her other dreams had seemed just as concrete and real to her as this one did, but they had not contained such specific information. She learned a bit about Addie in those other dreams, to be sure, but she hadn't learned anything about her surroundings. This dream, this was all about experiencing Wharton as it was a century ago. Kate was joyous, wanting to take it all in. She consciously tried to remember every last detail. *I must not forget anything. Please let me remember it all.*

"Quite a sight, isn't it?" a voice jolted Kate out of her reverie. She had been staring intently out the window, but at the sound of the voice, she felt herself whirl around toward the interior of the room.

"It is indeed," Kate said, in a voice that was not her own. Kate was astonished to be facing Harrison Connor, her own great-grandfather, as young and vibrant as he looked in the photo Kate had found in that very room. He was wearing a tuxedo and flashed a sincere smile when their eyes met. Only then was Kate able to see beyond him into the sea of people in the ballroom. Women in floor-length dresses, men in tuxedos. The room was glittering with light and shimmering with laughter and music. Some people were dancing, while others stood in groups drinking cocktails and chatting. Servants wandered about carrying trays of hors d'oeuvres and drinks. Kate looked down at her dress, green taffeta, and then was able to feel it scratching against her legs.

Kate heard herself saying, "I'm so glad you invited us to this gala. It's quite lovely."

"Oh, don't be silly, Addie, I know you're no fan of these affairs." Harrison chuckled, taking her hand. "You're so good to come anyway."

Kate felt herself smiling at this man.

"I brought this up from the cellar especially for you." Harrison handed her a wine glass. "I know that the martinis we're serving tonight aren't to your taste, so I raided my private wine stock. It's from France. I thought you might enjoy it."

Kate smiled and thanked him as she brought the glass to her lips. She tasted the wine, cool and crisp on her tongue. "This is delicious, Harrison, thank you," she said.

"Your husband is a lucky man," Harrison said, raising his glass. "I don't believe he realizes exactly how lucky he is to have such an extraordinary wife."

Kate looked across the room and saw the man to whom Harrison was referring. Addie's husband, Jess Stewart. She recognized him from the dreams. And from the photograph, and the newspaper article about the trial. He was so effortlessly handsome, so alive there in the candlelight of a glittering ballroom, wearing a tuxedo as though he had been born in it. He was holding a martini glass, standing in the center of a gaggle of beautiful women. He said something Kate could not hear, which caused the women to erupt into laughter.

"I don't know how extraordinary I am." Kate felt herself smiling and shaking her head. "Jess loves these affairs—look at him over there, life of the party as usual. And me here, cowering in the corner. I never quite know what to say."

"Say? Darling Addie, you needn't say anything at all." Harrison smiled at her. "You're the most captivating woman in the room without speaking one word. But I understand your feelings. Sometimes I'd rather just stand here looking out the window at the harbor instead of entertaining all of these people, as well."

"Do we have a pair of wallflowers here *yet again*?" It was Celeste, sidling up to her husband. She hissed, "Harrison, mingle! And Addie, my goodness, can't you *ever* join in? Don't be such a stick-in-the-mud!" And then she flounced off, toward other people's conversations.

"She hath spoken." Harrison smiled to Kate. "So shall it be done." Harrison held out his arm, and Kate felt herself take it as he led her into the fray. They walked toward the group of women congregated around Addie's husband.

"Jess, old boy, I'm so sorry to have monopolized your enchanting wife this evening," Harrison said, a bit too casually considering the force of his gaze into Jess's eyes. "You must have been wondering what had become of her."

"Addie!" Jess gushed, embracing her and kissing her on the cheek. He smelled of alcohol. Was he drunk? Kate thought he was. "Darling, you must meet some old friends of mine. Sally Reade, Claire Thorson, and Helene Bonnet." He gestured toward the striking women standing next to him. "I've known these girls since my early college days. They're in town from the city this weekend."

Before Kate had a chance to respond, one of the women spoke. "I'm so pleased to make your acquaintance, Mrs. Stewart." Sally Reade bared her teeth—Kate supposed it was a smile—and extended her hand. "I've been longing to meet the woman who married our Jess Stewart."

The two other women giggled. "We all thought Sally was going to be the one who coaxed him to the altar," one of them said. "In college they were *quite close*." More laughter.

"We were never so surprised as when Jess came back to the city and announced he was *engaged*," said the other. "You must be quite something, my dear, to have won his heart."

These sort of catty women made Kate's skin crawl. She would have loved nothing better than to put them in their places with a few well-chosen words. But she could not speak. She simply looked from one woman to another and back to her husband again, with tears stinging her eyes. Then Sally Reade smiled broadly and put her hand lightly on Jess's forearm as she leaned in and whispered something in his ear, all the while staring into Kate's eyes. Kate did not mistake the woman's intent. This was a clear gesture of ownership.

"Oh, that's all ancient history, girls," Sally said, bringing Kate's eyes back into focus. "Jess is an old married man now! With such a *lovely* wife!"

The scene began to fade before Kate's eyes. Sally slowly vanished, as though she was evaporating. The other partygoers disappeared as the candles were extinguished and the room went dark. The wood and the floors and the doors and even the windows began to age, yellowing, cracking, gathering decades of dust in an instant.

She saw a man rushing into the turret at the end of the room, emitting an awful cry that sounded like a wounded animal on its deathbed. That scene swiftly faded into the picture of a child playing on the floor, growing up, and finally putting those childish toys away for good. Fires were lit in the fireplace and doused in rapid succession. Spider colonies came and went, mice were born, scurried about, and died, windows were opened, closed, and then shuttered permanently. All of it happened in an instant, in front of Kate's eyes. And then, just as it had happened in this room once before, when she was a child, the air seemed to be sucked from the room. Kate couldn't breathe.

"What's going on?" Kate cried, gasping for breath as she slumped to the floor in the darkness. "Help me!"

"Honey! Kate! Wake up!" It was Simon, holding her. They were on the floor of the dark and dusty ballroom.

Kate stared into his face with wild eyes. She was confused, remembering with such clarity the scene she had just experienced moments ago, here in this very room—gleaming, beautiful, and new—juxtaposed with the dusty, neglected reality of the present. She hovered between the two worlds for a moment, not knowing which was real and which was the dream.

"Simon?" she whispered.

"Come with me." He helped Kate to her feet. "We're getting out of here."

They didn't notice the dark figure hovering in one corner of the room, dissipating into wispy smoke before disappearing completely.

Moments later, they were back in Kate's room. Simon had retrieved a hot brandy from the bar, and she was crawling back into bed.

"Okay, now tell me what happened," she said to him. "How did I get upstairs?"

"I came to check on you a few minutes ago, and you weren't in bed," Simon told her. "I thought maybe you had gone downstairs to the kitchen—or to the bar—and so I started down there, but then I noticed that the door at the end of the hallway was open. I went up the stairs to find you standing in the middle of the room. Just standing there. You were asleep, I think."

"I've never been a sleepwalker," Kate said, taking a gulp of the brandy.

"There's a first time for everything, I guess," Simon said.

"You will not believe what I was dreaming about," Kate said. "You just won't believe it."

Simon's eyes grew wide. "Don't tell me it was another one of *those* dreams," he whispered.

"It seemed so real," Kate murmured. Her eyelids felt heavy and thick. "Harrison was in it. There was a gala party."

"You sound like Dorothy, post-Oz." Simon smiled, stroking her hair. "Listen, honey, there's no place like home. You need to get some sleep, for real this time. This sleepwalking is not a good sign. God only knows where you'll traipse off to next. Move over, kiddo. You just earned yourself a bed partner."

Kate obeyed, slumping down on her pillow, exhausted by the day's events. "I'll tell you all about it tomorrow," she mumbled. Within seconds of uttering those words, she fell into a deep sleep.

"I think he was cheating on her," Kate said, chewing a mouthful of eggs at breakfast the next morning.

"Who?"

"Addie," Kate said, surprised to find tears welling up in her eyes. "I think her husband might have been cheating on her." The words of betrayal scratched her throat as she verbalized them, just as they had when she'd arrived at her parents' house on the night of her birthday with the news that Kevin had been with another woman. Kate's head pounded.

"Okay, out with it." Simon leaned closer to Kate. "I've been dying to know. What in the world did you dream last night?"

Kate told him the whole story then—the party in the ballroom, the view of the town as it had been a century ago, Addie, standing in a corner like a wallflower. Harrison Connor, a dashing young man. The other woman.

"Jess was talking to another woman, and there was something about the way she was looking at me," Kate started. "At her. The way the other woman was looking at Addie. She touched Jess's arm like she owned him. And the things she said! Apparently she was an old girlfriend. It was all very subtle, and it could've been innocent, but it certainly seemed to me that something was going on between them."

"Right here in this house," Simon murmured.

"Right where we were standing day before yesterday."

"So, tell me more," Simon said, his eyes narrowing.

"I was looking out the window, and I could hear a party going on behind me," Kate explained. "I wanted to turn and look at everything— I was dying to—but I couldn't. My body, or more exactly, *hers*, wouldn't move that way."

They were silent for a while. "You know what I think?" Simon said. "If you really are dreaming about the past, then you're dreaming about what was. Literally. You're seeing, and living, what actually happened. You couldn't turn and look into the ballroom when you wanted to in the dream because she didn't in real life."

"That's exactly what I was thinking!" Kate said.

"But I have to tell you, last night's dream might have been nothing more than the product of your overactive imagination. You found those newspaper clippings yesterday, and we had been up in the ballroom wondering what it might have been like in Harrison's day. You had that weird encounter with . . . whatever it was that scratched your neck. That might be all it was."

"Agreed," Kate concluded. She stared out onto the street, remembering the detail of how it had been all those years ago. "But if that's the case, I've got a very accurate imagination. I saw the sun set on Wharton out of the windows in my dream. I know exactly what this town looked like one hundred years ago."

After breakfast, Kate walked out of Harrison's House with Alaska at her side into a rush of chilly air. It startled her—she had been expecting a warm, summer day. *No,* she thought, *that was what the weather was like in my dream. It's autumn now. Summer's over.* She turned and began making her way down the hill, the same hill she had climbed and descended yesterday and many times before that. Yet this time, she was struck by how much it had changed. Pavement, houses one after another, shops, restaurants. Cars. People. Cell phones. As Alaska sniffed here and there, Kate thought about the past.

Where was the blueberry patch? Where was the house with the magnificent garden? Kate looked around and tried to mesh the streetscape she had seen in her dream the night before with the modern-day version of the same. There, on the corner, the white wooden house with the big front porch. That's where the garden had been. Kate wondered if the people who owned that house ever found an errant carrot, a determined sunflower, a stubborn stalk of corn growing in their finely manicured backyard. Did they have any idea what had been there before their house was built? Did they know that someone had tended the earth, turned the soil, watered, and weeded and did it all to feed his family?

Kate walked in these two worlds, the present and the past, for an hour or so. And then it was time to take Alaska back to the house and start her day. She was anxious to get back to the library and learn the rest of the story.

CHAPTER TWENTY-SIX

Kate was waiting on the steep library steps when the scruffy librarian, the same one who had been there yesterday, slouched around the corner, headphones on his ears, enormous coffee cup in his hand. When he saw Kate, he smiled.

"Been here all night?" he teased.

"Not quite." She smiled.

"You're here to time travel again, aren't you?" he asked as he fumbled with his keys and opened the big double doors.

"That feels exactly like what I'm doing," Kate said. "Sometimes I don't know where 1910 ends and today begins."

"Tell me about it," he mumbled, flipping on the lights and setting his overstuffed shoulder bag on the counter.

"Okay if I just head to the shelves myself?" Kate asked.

"You know the way," he said.

Soon, Kate had gathered the next rolls, threaded her machine, and immersed herself in the past. After a few moments, she found the next article.

POLICE CHIEF OUTLINES CASE AGAINST STEWART

Wharton police chief Arnold Becker explained to jurors today how and why he came to charge Jess Stewart with the murder of his wife.

"It's simple, common-sense police work," Chief Becker explained on the stand. "In matters like this, things tend to stay very close to home. When a wife goes missing, we look to the husband first. Usually, that's the farthest we have to look."

"So, your case against Mr. Stewart is entirely circum-stantial?" asked prosecuting attorney Jeffrey Howard.

"No," the chief said. "The dockworker, Lange, came to us and said he knew Stewart's story about coming back on the Sunday train from Minneapolis was false because he had seen him in Wharton on Saturday. And we haven't been able to find a single witness on the Sunday train who remembers seeing Stewart. That means Stewart lied. Lying plus a missing wife generally leads to a murderer."

This wasn't good. They couldn't find one witness who would say that Jess was on the Sunday train? Kate wondered how hard they had looked, how many people they had interviewed. Her reporter's instincts kicked in, and she found herself thinking about the accuracy of passenger records and logs a century ago. Would the rail company have had information about who was on that train? People probably just bought their tickets with cash, she reasoned. No credit card receipts, no checks with one's name and address on them, no online reservations.

Police couldn't track someone's movements as accurately as they could today. It would be much easier to hide the truth of one's whereabouts, or fabricate an alibi, in that simpler time, Kate thought.

Kate desperately wanted to believe in Jess's innocence. But she had to admit that it was looking more and more like he was, indeed, guilty of this crime.

STEWART EJECTED FROM COURTOOM!

It was an emotional day in the courtroom as jurors heard from Mrs. Stewart's physician, Dr. Jonas Maki, who testified that Mrs. Stewart had come to see him for a routine appointment one week before she disappeared.

"She was ready to deliver her baby," Dr. Maki testified. "It could have come at any time."

When asked if Mrs. Stewart had ever confided in him regarding trouble in her marriage, Dr. Maki replied that she had not. "She was excited for the birth of her first child, and she reported Mr. Stewart was pleased about it as well."

The courtroom hummed and murmured as the doctor stepped down from the stand, but just at that moment, Mr. Jess Stewart rose up out of his chair and began screaming wildly. "Why isn't anyone looking for my wife? You've arrested the wrong man and left it at that! She could be alone, hurt, giving birth to our child! Why won't you go out and look for her?"

Mr. Stewart's lawyer and two bailiffs tried to restrain Mr. Stewart, who flailed his arms and knocked over his chair, continuing to rant and rave like a madman. He was ejected from the courtroom by the judge, who recessed the trial for the day, presumably to allow Mr. Stewart to regain control of his senses.

This reporter could see that the jury was shocked by the outburst of rage and anger, imagining, no doubt, what sort of dark and evil circumstance had caused Mr. Stewart to turn that rage on his poor wife.

Despite Kate's obsession with the trial itself, she continued to marvel at the differences in journalistic styles of a century ago. So much emotion. So much bias. *The reporter covering this trial obviously believes Jess is guilty,* Kate thought.

WITNESS FROM THE SUNDAY TRAIN COMES FORWARD!

Mrs. Elsie Johnson, widow of Elmer Johnson of Wharton, took the stand today to testify that she and her daughter, Mrs. John Potter of Wharton, saw Mr. Jess Stewart on the train from Minneapolis to Wharton on Sunday, April 24.

"My daughter and I had gone to the city a week earlier for some shopping," Mrs. Johnson testified. "We were coming back on the train that Sunday, and we saw Mr. Stewart."

"You're sure it was Mr. Stewart?" the prosecutor asked.

"I'm certain of it," Mrs. Johnson said. "I commented to my daughter how handsome he was. When I saw his picture in the newspaper and read that you couldn't find anyone to confirm that he was on the Sunday train, I knew I had to come forward."

"And you're sure it was Sunday?" the prosecutor wanted to know. "Sometimes when ladies are shopping, they can lose track of time."

A few members of the jury chuckled.

But Mrs. Johnson turned to the jury and said, "Mr. Stewart was on that train. It was Sunday. There is no doubt about it. I'll stake my life on it. I know because of that terrible fog. That was the day."

The packed courtroom gasped. Mr. Stewart's mother began crying and collapsed into the arms of Mrs. Marcus Cassatt. "Thank God," she was heard to say.

The courtroom also included prominent businessman Harrison Connor and his wife, Celeste, who was cradling their newborn baby in her arms.

Later, as they exited the courtroom, Mr. Connor told this reporter, "I have steadfastly maintained Jess Stewart's innocence. He is a victim here. The man lost his wife and child. There could be nothing worse than that for any man. Nothing worse."

Jess wasn't lying about coming to Wharton on Sunday! It didn't mean he didn't kill Addie, Kate reasoned, but at least he wasn't lying about his movements. It also meant the dockworker lied. Why would he do that?

Kate decided to keep searching the files to find out, once and for all, the outcome of the trial. When they knew what happened, then she and Simon could start dissecting everything she had learned. She threaded another roll into the machine and turned the handle.

WITNESSES TAKE STAND IN STEWART'S DEFENSE

A parade of character witnesses, including Jess Stewart's mother, Mrs. Stewart's parents, and local businessman Harrison Connor, took the stand today to defend Jess Stewart against these heinous charges that have been brought against him.

Hmm, Kate thought. *The reporter's tone is turning. Public opinion must be changing as well.*

"I have known Jess Stewart for a long time, since our days in college, and I can unequivocally state that he is not capable of murdering anyone, let alone his beloved Addie," Harrison Connor said on the stand today. "I believe in him so much that I have charged my personal attorney with defending him. My wife and I have spent countless evenings with the Stewarts, and we can both tell you that Jess and Addie were very much in love. He was fiercely protective of her and more than a little jealous. Who wouldn't be? His wife was one of the most beautiful women—inside and out—in this town or any other."

Something about this statement made Kate catch her breath. It sounded wrong somehow. It was almost as though her great-grandfather was planting seeds of doubt in the minds of the jury. *Jealous. Protective.* Why would he do that? Did he believe Jess killed Addie? If he did, why would he support him publicly? What did he really know? She read on.

> Mrs. Stewart's mother, Mrs. Marcus Cassatt, said on the stand that her daughter had loved Jess Stewart all her life, that they had been children together in Great Bay. Mr. Cassatt testified that Mr. Stewart had gone away to college promising to return and marry his daughter, which he, in fact, did.

> "My son has always been a good boy, a loving son, and a wonderful husband to his wife," testified Mrs. Jennie Stewart, widow of Mr. Phillip Stewart, through bitter tears. "He sends money home every month for me to live on. He worked hard to make something of himself, in order to give Addie something more than the life of a fisherman's wife. He loved Addie with all his heart, ever since he was five years old. He could not wait to be a father. There is no possibility that he killed her and that precious baby she was carrying. There's no reason. Why would he have killed them? There is no motive for him to have committed this crime."

But there was a motive, Kate thought. Stewart had been cheating on Addie. Judging by what had transpired in her dream about the ballroom, the way Harrison Connor pointedly steered Addie to break up the party between Jess and that woman, Sally, Harrison likely knew all about it. She threaded another roll into the microfiche machine and turned the lever gingerly, almost afraid to find what happened next.

STEWART UNFAITHFUL TO WIFE!

The jury heard about a different side of Jess Stewart during today's proceedings. Several rather damaging witnesses took the stand, eliciting gasps of disbelief from the packed courtroom.

Three women, Anna Jacobsen, Jill Jakes, and Helene Bonnet, all of Minneapolis, testified that they had relations with Mr. Stewart during and after his collegiate years, shedding doubt on Mr. Stewart's reported faithful intentions to marry Addie Cassatt.

The prosecuting attorney asked Miss Bonnet if she knew about a relationship between the accused and Miss Sally Reade, who, according to Miss Bonnet, is traveling in Europe at this time and could not be contacted for the trial. Miss Bonnet testified that Miss Reade, her self-described best friend, and Mr. Stewart shared an intimate relationship before and after his marriage. She claimed that Mr. Stewart had promised to marry Miss Reade, but broke it off suddenly because of his engagement to a girl from his hometown, Addie Cassatt. This threw Miss Reade into an emotional turmoil as breach of promise certainly would, and she did not see Mr. Stewart for several years. They were reacquainted last year in Wharton and, according to Miss Bonnet, resumed their intimate relationship.

"They were having an affair," Miss Bonnet stated. "Sally told me all about it."

Jess Stewart sat silently during the testimony, hanging his head.

Kate's stomach was turning. She threaded the next roll and read on.

JESS STEWART GUILTY OF MURDER

After ten hours of deliberation, in an unusual verdict, the jury in the Jess Stewart trial has found Mr. Stewart guilty of the murder of his wife, Adelaide, despite the fact that no body was found.

Mrs. Stewart was last seen on April 24 and is presumed to have gone missing from the couple's Front Street home shortly after that time. Mrs. Stewart was heavy with child, mere days away from delivery.

Prosecutors alleged that Mr. Stewart killed his wife to clear the way for him to marry his mistress, Miss Sally Reade, daughter of financier Preston Reade of Minneapolis and heir to his sizable fortune.

"I wouldn't have believed it if I hadn't heard it with my own ears," said prominent local businessman Harrison Connor, Mr. Stewart's friend and employer. "I guess this goes to show that we really don't know what anyone, even our closest friend, is capable of."

Sentencing will take place on May 15.

Kate printed the article. She felt a tightening in her chest, as though someone was pulling a rope around her. *He killed her. He really did it.*

She didn't want to read on, didn't want to know more, but she couldn't stop herself from threading another roll into the machine. She turned the handle, wincing with anticipation of what she might find on the next page.

JESS STEWART MURDERED ON COURTHOUSE STEPS!

As convicted murderer Jess Stewart was being led into the courtroom today to hear the judge hand down his fate, he was shot in the chest by Marcus Cassatt, the father of Mrs. Stewart.

"You bastard," Mr. Cassatt was heard to say. "You killed my little girl."

Mr. Stewart fell on the courthouse steps. This reporter heard him call out his wife's name as he took his last breath.

Kate stared at the page, tears spilling from her eyes. Her hands shook as she printed the article. She gathered up all the sheets she had printed over the past two days, put them together in a file folder, tucked it into her bag, and returned the rolls to their rightful resting places. She couldn't breathe. She couldn't wait to get out of that library and into the fresh air.

Kate burst through the double doors and onto the street, gasping as though she had been drowning. She made her way around the people, past the shops and restaurants, and out onto the town's main dock at the water's edge where she sat down, hard, and dangled her feet over the side toward the water.

The two people in her dreams were so alive, so in love, such good friends, laughing together, fighting, making up—and now they were dead, both of them, within weeks of each other. A family ruined, obliterated, not even given a chance to begin. A love denied, extinguished. Jess killed her. And his baby. Because of another woman. Addie's father probably ended up in jail himself, but Kate didn't read far enough to find out for sure.

And for what? *An affair?* How could it possibly be?

Kate fished a tissue out of her purse and dabbed at her eyes but couldn't stop the tears from coming.

"Hey." She felt a warm hand on her back. "Kate. What's wrong?"

Nick sat down on the dock next to her and put an arm around her shoulders. Kate put her head onto his chest and sobbed. He didn't say anything—he just held her and let her cry it out.

She drew back and blew her nose on a tissue. "I don't understand it," she said, her voice shaking. "These people lived and died a century ago. Had they not been victims of murder, had Addie and Jess lived out their entire lives to their natural conclusions, they'd still be in the ground right now. I couldn't possibly have saved them. I couldn't warn Addie about Jess's betrayal, no matter how desperately I wanted to. I couldn't warn Jess to keep his eyes focused on his family, or there would be dire consequences. I'm totally helpless. So, what is this all for?"

"I take it he was found guilty," Nick said.

She nodded, holding her file folder. "It's all in here."

"Why don't you show me what you found over a burger?"

Kate took a deep breath, not knowing what else to do. Nick stood up and held his hand out for Kate to take. She slipped her hand into his and let him help her up to her feet.

Inside the restaurant, Kate excused herself to use the ladies' room and splashed cold water on her face.

"Get a grip," she said to her reflection. She dug some moisturizer out of her purse, dabbed some concealer under her eyes, and ran a brush through her hair. Not ideal, but it would have to do.

When they had settled into a booth and ordered, Kate fished the copies of her newspaper articles out of her folder and handed them to Nick. She nibbled on french fries while she watched him read. Midway through, he looked up at her.

"This is wild," he said. "I've got to tell you—I've seen a lot of strange things in my years on the force, but nothing like this."

"Are you going to close the case?"

He grinned. "And put what in the case file? Victim murdered by husband. In 1910."

"I guess not," she said.

"You know, though," he said. "All of this is a start, but it really doesn't tell us what happened."

"How so?"

"Our lady—Addie—ended up in the water," he said. "With the baby. The last time anyone that we know of saw her—who was it? The maid on the day she went missing? She was pregnant and alive. How did she and the baby get in the lake?"

CHAPTER TWENTY-SEVEN

Later, when Nick was on his way to the precinct and Kate was back at Harrison's House, she and Simon sat together in the parlor as she filled him in on the events of the day.

As soon as she mentioned the possibility of a mistress to Simon, she felt tears stinging at the backs of her eyelids.

"It really makes you wonder," Kate said, dabbing at her eyes with a napkin. "That a man would commit murder, kill his own wife and child, for the chance of a life with a mistress. I just can't believe it. What a waste."

"Oh, honey, that's the oldest story on earth," Simon said. "It happens all the time. I don't suppose our dear great-granddaddy would've taken too kindly to one of his employees running around on a very pregnant wife. That likely would've gotten Jess Stewart fired, at the very least."

Kate rubbed her temples. Her head was beginning to pound.

"If Jess wanted to keep his life, his employer, his house, and his standing in the community and all of that, but just with a different wife—or without any wife, for that matter—he had one option," Simon said. "Make himself look like the grieving widower.

"It's really the perfect plan," he continued, studying one of the articles. "Coming back into town a day earlier than scheduled. Oh, but this witness testified that he was on the Sunday train."

"I just can't believe he cheated on her," Kate said, her voice wavering. "I know what I saw in the dream, but why would he do that? They were so much in love! He loved her his whole life. They were children together! I read it in the testimony of the trial. All their lives! Why would he do something so heinous and stupid?" A flood of tears overcame her, and she covered her face with a napkin.

"Katie, look at me," Simon said. "You've got to pull yourself together. I don't want to sound unsympathetic here, but you need to realize that this thing happened almost a century ago. To people you don't even know."

"But I do know her," Kate insisted. "I *am* her. I can't explain it. This is personal. It's me. I know that I need to put this thing in perspective, but I—" She stopped short, unable to continue.

"I think I know what this is about," Simon said. "It's Kevin, isn't it?"

Kate looked up from her tear-soaked napkin. "Kevin?"

"You're internalizing this whole thing because the husband cheated on Addie, just like Kevin cheated on you," Simon said. "Those tears you're crying, they're for your own marriage, your own dreams he shattered to bits."

Kate considered this and blew her nose. "I guess I'm lucky I didn't end up like Addie," she mused.

"Damn straight," Simon concluded, shuddering. "Listen, this is only natural. You're grieving. And you're exhausted. It seems to me that you need a long, hot bath. How would that be? I'll take Miss Alaska for a walk, and you just settle into a nice, hot tub."

Truth be told, Kate thought, a hot bath sounded like heaven.

"I'll do that," she said, pushing her chair back from the table.

Steam from the hot water filled up the chilly bathroom, and Kate leaned over the tub and breathed the vapor into her lungs. A slow breath in, a slow breath out. Calm down. Relax. Simon was right. It was all in the past. Almost a century in the past. It wasn't happening now. It wasn't happening to her. All this emotion was related to her own breakup. She slipped into the water and submerged herself.

Kate laid her head on the back of the massive tub, closed her eyes, and floated. Soon, she could feel her body rocking back and forth on the waves, undulating up and down, to and fro, taken with the whims of the wind and the tides. She was a seashell, a piece of driftwood, a loon floating lazily on the surface of the Great Lake. *Nothing can hurt you here. You are with me now. I will keep you safe, here, with me, my daughter of the lake, until it is time.* Kate was enveloped in loving arms and held close, wrapped in a watery blanket, falling down, down, down. *Sleep, my daughter, sleep, until it is time.*

Kate felt the water entering her lungs, but instead of stinging like a thousand knives, stealing her breath and suffocating the life from her, she felt as though she were a baby, prebirth, floating in the watery embrace of her mother's womb, remembering the comfort and warmth of breathing in the liquid that, once long ago, had surrounded and sustained her when she was a fetus awaiting the moment of birth. She opened her eyes, somewhere, in some other place, and saw, through the darkness, a billowing white gown. A baby cradled in her arms. A school of tiny fish swimming around and through the strands of her hair. She heard a heartbeat, a soft thudding in the distance.

CHAPTER TWENTY-EIGHT

Kate awoke to Simon shrieking as he pulled her up from under the water. Kate coughed and sputtered until the water cleared from her lungs. Simon sat down, hard, on the floor next to the tub. "Jesus H. Christ," he said, shaking his head. "You nearly gave me a heart attack."

"What happened?" Kate coughed some more.

"I poked my head in here to check on you—thank God—and you were submerged," Simon said. "Did you fall asleep or what? Kate, you could have died. If I hadn't come in here—"

Kate sat up and drew her arms around herself. "I don't know what happened, exactly," she said. The sensation she had felt was so peaceful, so wonderful. Not like drowning, not like death at all.

"You are the most troublesome houseguest I have ever had," Simon said. "Now, get out of there. I'll wait in the bedroom."

When Kate was dried off and in her pajamas, she found Simon sitting in one of the two armchairs by the fireplace in her bedroom. She slipped into the other one, and they both put their feet on the ottoman between them.

"You know what?" she said finally. "Something's wrong here. I don't think this is over."

"What's not over?"

"This whole thing," she said. "I thought once I found out who Addie was and what happened to her, all of these weird things would stop happening to me. The dreams, the strange sensations."

"Like your chill the other night."

"Right, and like just now. Simon, I closed my eyes, and it felt like I was drowning. But—and this is going to sound bizarre—not in a bad way. It felt really peaceful. It seems like I experienced what Addie experienced, at the end."

"I don't like this game anymore," Simon said. "Can we stop?"

"Yesterday we were wondering why I was having these dreams, why she washed up on my beach, why, why, why. Remember?"

"That's right," Simon said, slowly.

"It can't be for me to just find out about this trial," Kate said. "What would be the point? Lots of people probably know about this trial. It's local history, as you said. I'm sure Addie's relatives, if any of them are still living, know about it. There's no reason for all of this other stuff to be happening if the only conclusion to all of these dreams is for me to find out that Addie's husband killed her."

"Correction," Simon interjected. "That Addie's *cheating* husband killed her."

"And?" Kate didn't understand.

"Not to be indelicate, but you have a cheating husband, too."

Kate pondered what he was saying.

"You think Addie is coming to me in my dreams to warn me about what might have happened, or what still could happen, with Kevin?" Kate asked finally.

"It makes as much sense as anything else."

"I don't know," Kate mused. "Kevin's a lot of things, but he's no killer."

Simon leaned in toward her and lowered his voice. "And you've got a pre-nup that says he gets half of your money if you die. I'm sorry to say so, Kate, but I'm really glad you've got a hunky policeman and a steely-eyed cousin looking after you right now."

Kate looked unconvinced, but Simon made a mental note to tell Nick Stone all about Kate's pre-nup and his suspicions.

Later, after Kate had gone to bed and was sleeping a dreamless sleep, she was jolted awake by the sound of a siren. No, not a siren. She looked around to find herself standing in a kitchen that was not her own, watching a teakettle whistling on the stove. She felt two arms snake around her waist from behind and heard a soft voice in her ear. "How are the two most precious people in the world feeling on this fine morning?"

Two people? Kate saw nobody else in the room. Then she turned to the man behind her and saw the enormously handsome face of Jess Stewart. Addie's husband. The man who killed her. Kate was terrified but felt herself smiling. "I am feeling like taking a walk down to the market after you leave for the office," she heard herself say. "Your child is feeling like kicking her mother repeatedly."

Child. Mother. Kate put her hands on her stomach, gingerly. There was no denying it, Addie was pregnant. Kate closed her eyes and reveled in it. She had longed for this feeling herself for so many years. Tried so many times. She rubbed her hands across her belly—Addie's belly—and just then felt a small thudding inside. *My God. I feel the baby kicking. I can actually feel it moving inside of my body. This is what it feels like to be carrying a baby.*

"He's getting his morning exercise." Jess smiled at her. It was one of the warmest smiles Kate had ever seen. His eyes shone with love as he patted her stomach. "Running a race in there, little boy?"

"Yes, *she* is," Kate heard herself teasing. The moment between this husband and wife was so intimate, so loving, Kate felt somewhat embarrassed to be intruding on it. It wasn't the first time Kate had felt this way while dreaming about Addie's life.

"I wonder, darling, whether it will be a boy or a girl," Jess said as he sat down at the table for breakfast. "What do you think? You women always have a sense about these things."

Kate put two plates of scrambled eggs and toast on the table—*where did those come from? I must've been making them*—and sat down across from Jess.

"I'm truly not sure," Kate said. "I feel as though I know this baby so well now because it's a part of me, living and growing inside of me, but I do not have any idea whether it's a boy or a girl. Do you have a preference?"

"I know every man hopes for a son to carry on the family name." Jess chewed thoughtfully. "But I'd be just as happy with a little girl, as beautiful as her mother."

Kate felt herself smiling. "Can you imagine how spoiled a little girl would be with you as her doting father?"

"We'll need a bigger house for all of the dolls I'm going to buy for her." Jess smiled. He stood up and dropped his napkin on the plate before him. "I'll get right on that today. 'Earn more money. Needed to spoil child.'"

"Excellent," Kate said. "You do that, and I'll keep busy growing the baby."

Jess walked toward the door. "Don't forget, darling, we have dinner at the Connors' tonight." *At Harrison's House.*

"I remember," Kate sighed. "I don't think it's a good idea to go. I don't want to go."

Jess turned and looked at her. "Why ever not?"

"Will it be just the four of us, or will other people be attending as well?" Kate could feel tension begin to build up in the pit of Addie's stomach.

"I don't know," Jess said offhandedly. "Why do you ask?"

"I'm uncomfortable around some of the Connors' friends. One in particular."

"Which one?" Jess said casually.

"You know full well which one." Kate could feel Addie's determination to hold her husband's gaze. She would not be the first to look away. *She's talking about the woman in the ballroom! She suspects something is going on! She's confronting him!* An uncomfortable silence fell between husband and wife. Kate felt it in the air, as tangible as fog.

"I thought we were finished with those silly doubts of yours, Addie." Jess smiled at her. *He's too calm. Too collected. His wife is accusing him of infidelity, and he's cool as ice water. He's treating her like a child.*

"I thought we were finished with you taking me for a fool," Kate said, and walked away from him. She looked out the kitchen window toward the water. Kate could feel Addie's heart racing. Her eyes were quickly blinking back tears.

"Nothing happened between Sally and me, darling," Jess said, hurriedly gathering up some papers into his leather briefcase. "She's just an old friend, that's all. You're making much too much of it."

"I just don't want that woman anywhere near us. Not now. The fact that she keeps coming to Wharton—to visit whom? Why does she keep appearing at dinners and parties thrown by our friends?"

Jess turned away from Addie and ran a hand through his hair. He took a deep breath and turned back to his wife.

"Yes, I courted some women, including Sally, before we were married. That I didn't tell you about it myself—that was a mistake on my part. I know that now. And I'm sorry. I'm sorry for not telling you before, and I'm sorry for the way you found out about it, at that party in the Connors' ballroom, in front of everyone. She has treated you horribly. But refusing to go to the Connors'—"

"I'm not refusing to go," Addie said. "I've never refused to go. It's just that—" Her words dissolved into tears.

Jess dropped to his knees in front of his wife, putting his head on her stomach. "Addie, I'm so sorry. Let's not have angry words between us."

Addie didn't respond. She was looking the other way, anywhere but at her husband.

"Please, Addie. I'd rather die than hurt you. I love you more than you can imagine. You and our baby are my whole world, my whole life. You mean everything to me. And Sally? It's not even appropriate uttering her name in the same sentence as yours." His voice had a hint of desperation to it, Kate thought. As though he was trying too hard. "I will let Harrison know, discreetly, that you don't want to be at any of the same functions as that woman—that *we* don't want to be there. Would that make you happy?"

"And tonight? What about tonight?"

"Sally is not in Wharton at the moment." Jess seemed to stumble over his words. "Not that I know of, anyway. She will not be at Harrison and Celeste's tonight. It will be just the four of us. You like Harrison and Celeste well enough, don't you?"

"I do, yes," Addie admitted.

"Then, will you consent to go, or should I call it off?"

Addie sighed and smiled wearily at the man she had loved her whole life. "We can attend," she said, stroking his hair.

"Spend the day pampering yourself," Jess said. "Take a long walk on the lakeshore if you like."

"I have the washing to do. I can't be a lady of leisure today."

"No, you don't, and yes, you can, in that order." Jess smiled. "Starting today, Harrison is sending down one of his girls to help you twice a week until the baby is born, and after that, we'll talk about engaging her permanently."

"A maid?" Kate heard Addie saying. "Oh, Jess, I don't think—"

"That's right, don't think about it," Jess interrupted, laughing. "It's settled."

Kate walked Addie's husband to the door and felt his arms snake around her again. Kate felt herself wrapping her arms around his shoulders. She closed her eyes.

"Take good care of my baby today," Jess whispered into Addie's ear.

"Take good care of my husband today," she whispered. He wiped her eyes.

"I hate it when we fight," he said softly. "I hear myself sounding just like my father, and I hate it. I don't want to go anywhere today. I want to stay here with you and make you smile."

Kate looked into his eyes.

He kissed her deeply, murmuring, "I love you so much, Addie."

"I love you, too," she said. "It's all right. Now, off with you."

When the door closed behind Jess, Kate walked into the bedroom—the same white bedroom she had visited in her dreams when this all began—and smoothed out the comforter and pillows. She caught sight of the woman in the mirror, her auburn hair tangled around her shoulders, her belly swelling beneath her dress.

She has no idea what's coming. That man is going to kill her.

Then it occurred to Kate: *Maybe I can warn her.* Kate began screaming inside of her head: *Get away! Leave this place! Your husband is going to kill you and your baby!* Kate tried many times to speak the words aloud but could not. Kate was an invisible mute, trapped inside this scene, this body. Nonetheless, she kept trying, silently screaming the words as loudly as she could. *Get away! You're in danger!*

She approached the mirror, picked up the hairbrush, and, as she brushed that long, auburn mane, Kate stared into the eyes of the woman in the mirror. *Listen to me! I'm here to help you! You're in danger!* Kate screamed in her mind. But Addie simply brushed her hair. *Addie Stewart! Hear me! You are going to die on April 24 if you don't do something about it! Get away from this man!*

Addie dropped the hairbrush and stared deeply into the mirror. A look of confusion came over her face. Was there a flash of recognition?

Kate screamed louder. *I'm here! Listen to me! You are in danger! You will die if you don't leave this place! Save yourself! Save your baby!* Addie turned and looked behind her, this way and that. Kate felt her heart beating. Could she be reaching her? *Jess is going to kill you and your baby!*

Kate was astonished as Addie, staring at her own reflection in the mirror, began to silently mouth the words that Kate was screaming inside her head: "You are in danger." Kate shouted in time with Addie's lips: *You are in danger,* until the two women were repeating the words together, over and over.

Addie ran to the door, opened it, and looked outside. She saw Jess walking down the street—he was nearly three blocks away by now. Somehow he sensed her, turned and waved. She put up her hand in greeting, and then Addie—and Kate—watched Jess Stewart until he disappeared from view.

CHAPTER TWENTY-NINE

Kate awoke to a tear-soaked pillow and looked at the clock. Three thirty. She tossed and turned, trying to get comfortable enough to drift back into sleep, but soon she admitted defeat. There would be no more sleep for her tonight. She pulled on a robe and padded down to the living room, sat on the couch, and looked out the window toward the water.

Take good care of my baby today. The man who had whispered those words softly into Kate's ear was arrested for her—or rather, Addie's—murder. How could he have possibly done it? Why would this man have killed his wife and baby? For an affair? Images from the dreams bombarded her mind. The lilacs, the sweetness, the whispered words, the love. Sally, the other woman. Was all of it a lie? How did the life they shared go horribly wrong? Did he spin out of control and kill her in a moment of passion?

More images washed over her. The body on the beach. The white gown. The baby. Tears stung her eyes and clouded her vision.

"What a bastard," Kate said aloud in the dark. "His own wife and child." She heard a low yowl. It was Alaska, curled up in a ball in the corner of the room, tail covering her nose.

"Am I making too much noise, Lass?" Kate said softly, and walked over to her drowsy friend. "Did I wake you?" Kate scratched the dog's snout and behind her ears.

Kate felt like walking. She was restless and needed to clear her head, to shake off what she had learned in the library and especially this latest dream. That it was the middle of the night didn't concern her. Not even the most dangerous predator would be fool enough to try to do Kate harm with an enormous, fierce-looking dog by her side.

"Should we see what's happening in the outside world?" she whispered to her dog. Alaska's ears perked up at this familiar phrase. The dog unfolded herself from her sleeping position, stretched, and trotted off in search of her leash. A few minutes later, after Kate had pulled on a pair of jeans and a sweatshirt, she and Alaska stole quietly out the door and into the chilly night.

The night sky in Wharton never failed to amaze Kate, no matter how many times she saw it. Usually, in towns of any size at all, the stars were at least partially obscured by the lights of the city. But here, they were so bright, so big, and so tangible that it seemed to Kate the town itself was a bit closer to the heavens than the rest of the world. As Kate walked with Alaska down the sidewalk, she drew her breath in at the sight of the starry universe laid out before them. The deep blackness of the sky contrasted with the stars' brilliance. The sight of it obscured the day's events for Kate, and she lost herself in the vastness of space.

The streets were empty at that late hour, as Kate knew they would be. No lights flickered from any storefront or house that she could see, but the water shimmered brightly, reflecting the moon and stars. She walked down toward the lakeshore to get a better look. A street sign on the corner caught her eye. FRONT STREET. Kate had walked here countless times, but on this night, the sight of the sign stopped her. *She disappeared from their Front Street home.* Kate shivered.

"This is the street where Addie lived," Kate whispered to Alaska. "But in which house?"

Front Street was just three blocks long and so named because it ran directly in front of the lakeshore. The houses along both sides of the street were definitely old, but were they old enough? A century old? Kate wasn't sure. All the houses were wooden and of the same basic style, two stories with big bay windows on the main floor and generous front porches. Most of the houses were white, differentiated from one another only by a picket fence here, a flourishing garden there. One had a porch swing.

To Kate, it was an idyllic setting for a home, with the lakeshore in every backyard. She was wondering what kind of king's ransom it would take to own one of these houses today when she remembered that Canby Lines had built several houses in town for its upper management workers. It was a nice perk for young families—common a century ago but unheard of in modern times. Kate was proud that her great-grandfather had taken such good care of his workers, but she wasn't sure if these were the houses he had built or not. It made sense, however. One could see they had been constructed by the same builder.

She disappeared from their Front Street home. The line from the newspaper rang through Kate's mind again. Was Addie murdered in one of these houses?

Just then, she felt Alaska tug hard on her leash. She was staring in the direction of the house at the very end of the block. Kate had long admired that house because of its large sloping corner lot that ran down to the lakeshore. Alaska tugged again on the leash and growled low in her throat.

"What is it, girl?" Kate's voice trembled. She looked up and down the street. No lights shone from any of the houses. Everyone was asleep. Everything was still. But Alaska's growl told her there was a danger somewhere, hidden.

Being here on the street where Addie had likely disappeared—the reality of standing so near where the event had surely occurred—sent a shiver through Kate. What was she doing wandering around outside at this time of night? It was foolish to be out here when every other living soul was in bed. She wanted to turn and walk up the hill toward home, but Kate's feet were frozen into place. Why was Alaska growling? Why was she staring at that house?

"Quiet," she whispered to Alaska, not wanting to disturb the people who were, no doubt, sleeping inside the house at that very moment. She looked this way and that, and seeing nothing, felt compelled to look further. Kate stole into the backyard. She followed a path down to the lakeshore, where she found a small dock. Alaska's increasing growls told Kate to stop right there and not go any farther.

As she was standing there on the water's edge, a sense of knowing engulfed Kate. *This is the spot. This is where she died.* In that moment, Kate felt a sharp pain in her back. And then another, and another. She cried out in a whisper as she fell to her knees, bent in half. She whirled around on her knees, but nothing was there. Nothing but an empty yard on a deep, dark night. Then she heard it, clean and clear: A male voice, horrified, anguished, stricken. "Good Christ, what have you done? Addie, oh my God—" It was an otherworldly sound, a tinny, scratchy echo reverberating in the emptiness, as though it was a recording being played on a gramophone. The words hung in the air as heavy as fog on a damp afternoon.

Kate scrambled to her feet and began tugging at Alaska's leash, but the dog didn't want to leave this spot—she was transfixed, growling. Kate pulled harder and Alaska finally responded. They sped out of the yard, around the house and onto the street and didn't stop running until Kate had put several blocks between her and whatever hung there in the air of that backyard.

She slowed to a jog and then to a walk as she headed up the hill toward the house. All Kate wanted was to be back inside, in her bed, under the fluffy down comforter. She bent low, aching from the pain that still radiated in her back, panting as though she had just run a marathon, her heart beating as though she had just seen a ghost.

Back in her room, Kate pulled the comforter to her neck as Alaska curled up at the foot of the bed. She was relieved to feel the security and safety of being here, in this room, in this bed. Kate stared out the window until the first rays of dawn slivered across the dark sky.

CHAPTER THIRTY

Wharton, 1910

"This trip is very ill timed," Jess complained, hurriedly packing his suitcase. "I do not like leaving you right now."

Addie was sitting in the rocking chair in the corner of their white bedroom on Front Street, turning her silver hairbrush over and over in one hand, rubbing her enormous belly with the other.

"I'll be fine, darling." She smiled. "You are such a worrier. Women have been having babies for a while, you know. There's no mystery to it. It's not as though I'm giving birth to an ostrich."

"I just wish your mother could've come to stay with you while I'm gone," Jess said, disregarding his wife's attempt at humor. "This trip came up so quickly. There was simply no time to send for her."

"Again I tell you, I'll be fine." Addie rose with great difficulty, waddled over to her husband, and put her head on his chest. He wrapped his arms around her and there they stood awhile. She listened to his heartbeat and wondered if the baby could hear it, too.

"I'm not going," Jess said.

Addie laughed. "You're going to tell Harrison that you can't lead the meeting in Chicago because your wife is going to have a baby? I don't think so."

"But I want to be here," Jess complained. "For you. What if the baby comes early?"

"In that case, you will have a brand-new son or daughter to greet you upon your return." Addie smiled. "Don't worry, Jess. It's not like we're living in the wilds of Great Bay—we're in a city. If the baby comes early, the doctor is just a few steps away. I could crawl there on my hands and knees if necessary."

"Harrison has promised that he will look in on you," Jess said. "And Ginny will be here every day for at least a few hours to do the washing and the marketing."

"A whole legion of people to look after me." Addie grinned. "I may even go up to visit Celeste. I haven't yet seen the baby."

"Don't you dare," Jess warned her, wagging his finger. "I don't want you trudging up that hill like a turtle."

"A turtle!" Addie slapped him on the chest. "So that's what I am now?"

"It wasn't so long ago that you were a tiger, my dear," he laughed. "That's how you got into this situation, if I'm not mistaken. All kidding aside, Addie, promise me you're not planning to go visiting in your condition. Even if you took a car, it's just not proper. You should be home, resting. We can go see Celeste and the baby when I return, when we have one of our own to show off. Harrison told me she isn't taking visitors now, anyway. I think, after so many disappointments, she wants to make sure this baby is healthy and well before . . . well, you know what I'm trying to say."

Addie could see the wisdom of this. They had just received word that Celeste had delivered, weeks ahead of schedule, but even Harrison wasn't talking too much about it. Because of what happened with Clementine, Addie reasoned, they were in seclusion with this one, not wanting anyone to intrude on their all-too-fragile family. Addie understood the notion of holding something so precious closely, carefully, as though the idea of exposing this new little life to the outside world might cause it to flee from its harshness. She didn't even know whether the new Connor baby was a boy or a girl. Ah well, she'd find out in time.

Truth be told, Addie was glad for the admonishment to stay home. She didn't feel much like expending the effort to make a social call. She had been so tired for the past few days. Although she was trying to convince her husband not to worry about this trip, she was filled with trepidation about being left alone. She couldn't forget that odd sensation when a voice inside her head had told her that she was in danger. *Leave this place! Addie Stewart! Hear me! You are going to die on April 24 if you don't do something about it!* That date was but one week away.

It has to be some odd reaction to impending childbirth, Addie tried to tell herself. It was simply too horrible to be true. She could shrug it away; that voice in her head hadn't recurred. She held Jess tightly and prayed to her great-grandmother's spirit to give her peace. Now that he was leaving, she dreaded the lonely nights ahead.

"I'll stay right here, reading by the fire," Addie promised her husband. "I'll not even go to the market. Nor to the library. I'll simply count the days until you get home."

"As will I," Jess said to her.

Soon enough, he was gone to catch the train, and Addie felt very much alone in the house. She sat in the rocking chair, the one they had purchased for the baby, and rocked back and forth, back and forth, rubbing her belly and wondering.

Two days passed without incident, then three, then four. For Addie, the nights were filled with worry, but the days seemed soft and effortless and peaceful, as though the light of day evaporated the demons that arose when the sun went down.

Ginny, the maid from the Connor household, arrived faithfully at ten o'clock every day and did the washing, the cleaning, the marketing, and even most of the cooking, always setting a simmering pot of something on the stove for dinner when she left promptly at three. One day, she even brought a basket of hot bread, jam, and several books for

Addie to read, with the Connors' compliments. Her visits were enough company for Addie, who tired easily and wanted nothing more than to sit in her rocking chair, reading and staring at the wide expanse of water that lapped at the edges of their sloping backyard.

On the seventh day, Addie arose from her bed with great difficulty, letting out a monstrous moan as she heaved her body to its feet. She was more than ready for this baby to arrive, unwieldy and unbalanced as she felt now. She smiled as she thought that it had been only two weeks since she and Jess had trekked up the hill to the Connor mansion for dinner. There was no way she could have attempted that journey now.

Ginny arrived promptly at ten o'clock, filled with chatter about the town, the market, and the weather.

"Something's in the air, Mrs. Stewart," Ginny said as she was washing the supper dishes from the night before. "Amos at the market says all of the fishermen are staying off the lake today. Might be a storm, he says."

Addie opened the kitchen door and stared down the long slope to the lake. There was a humidity in the air that was unusual for that time of year. Springtime in Wharton was usually a muddy, rainy affair, quite unlike spring in her hometown of Great Bay, which, although it was not so far away from Wharton, was typically still covered in a soggy, sloppy layer of snow in early April. Addie wasn't quite used to the seasons in her new home, the warm winds of winter preventing much snow from accumulating, and the crisp zephyrs of summer sucking all the humidity out of the air.

But today, the air felt different, as though it had been displaced from another season, lost on the wind and unsure of where to turn. It hung, heavy as a blanket, over the lake. Where water and air met, it seemed to sizzle and crackle like a thousand invisible bolts of lightning were hitting the water's surface, just out of sight. The sky above was an unsettling shade of blue, but in the distance it looked angry, threatening, and green.

Addie waddled out to the backyard to sit on the bench on the crest of the hill. Here, away from the bustle of the city docks, the lake was as still as a sheet of ice. Indeed, it looked so solid that Addie felt sure she could walk on it. She knew, from her lifelong love affair with this lake, that its waters would soothe and protect her on a day such as this—oh, how her aching muscles were crying out for a swim—but she had long since promised her husband that she wouldn't go into the water until after the baby was born. Silly, superstitious man that he was.

"I thought I'd make a pot of stew for you tonight, ma'am," Ginny called out from the kitchen doorway.

"Oh, don't bother, Ginny," Addie called back. "I'm not in the least bit hungry. In fact, I still feel full from breakfast. Please don't trouble yourself."

"Are you getting on all right, ma'am?" Ginny walked outside to where Addie was sitting on the bench, a concerned look on her face. "Is your time coming?"

Addie smiled and rubbed her belly. "No, my time's not coming. This baby is still warm and safe and snug just where she is. She's not wanting to come into this world just yet."

"*She*, said you." Ginny smiled. "You think it's a girl, then?"

Addie nodded. "I do. I just have a feeling." Then, turning to look at Ginny, she asked, "Is the Connors' new baby a boy or a girl?"

"I don't know, ma'am," Ginny said. "None of us in the house know, excepting Martha, Mrs. Connor's maid. And she's not saying."

"Whyever not?"

"Superstition," Ginny said softly, looking up and down the lakeshore and drying her hands on her apron. "Whispers around the house are that the baby is a little wisp of a thing, blue when it was born, fragile as a snowflake. Martha won't repeat its name, nor nothing about it, lesting that the devil come in and steal its soul."

"Oh no." Addie shook her head. "You know that's just a silly superstition, don't you, Ginny?" The girl shook her head, and Addie continued, "In any case, I pray that the poor thing grows stronger."

"As do we all," Ginny said. "We're all on pins and needles up at the big house, everyone deathly quiet, as if a noise would disturb the baby's slumber. Even Mr. Connor is padding around silent as a lamb. Me, if I had my way, I'd be banging and clanging and getting that baby to cry as hard and loud as it could. My mam always said that crying gives a baby strong lungs and a strong spirit. Strong enough to keep death away. Maybe that's why I chatter so much."

Addie smiled. It was true this girl had the gift of gab. And a strong spirit to go with it.

"Mrs. Connor is lucky to have you." Addie took Ginny's hand. "As am I. I've been so grateful for your help, Ginny."

"It's a pleasure, ma'am, to work for someone as kind as you are," Ginny said. "Now, you're sure I can't make you something to eat before I go?"

"Truly, Ginny, I'm in need of nothing," Addie said. "I'm dreadfully full. I couldn't eat a bite. And later, if I want something, I've still got some of that wonderful bread and jam you brought for me. And I think there is some soup left over on the stove as well. That will do."

"If you say so," Ginny said, nodding. "If there's nothing else you need, I'll be on my way. I don't like this weather. Best to get home safely before something kicks up." She scanned the horizon, squinting. "Let me help you back into the house now, yourself, before I go." Ginny extended her hands to Addie. "It wouldn't do to have you stuck out here, unable to get up off this bench, when the rain comes."

Addie smiled as she let Ginny pull her up. The girl was right, standing was quite a production. It might have been a problem for her to navigate it alone. "Mr. Stewart says I'm like a turtle," she laughed.

"Not for long, ma'am," Ginny said. "Soon, you'll have your own baby to hold, just like Mrs. Connor."

Later, Addie tried to read a book inside by the fire that Ginny had stoked before she left. But it was no use. Addie was antsy, edgy. Although she had been tired all day, she had an overwhelming urge to straighten things up and clean the house. She took the rag that Ginny had left in the sink and began cleaning the already-spotless kitchen, wiping off the stove and the table. Next, she swept the kitchen floor, moving out into the living room and then up the stairs and down the hallway toward the bedrooms. She opened the door to what would soon be the baby's room and straightened the crib, fluffed the blanket, and dusted the dresser and chest that had only recently come from a fancy furniture store in Minneapolis. She ran her fingers over the rocking horse in the corner, remembering the winter day, months ago, when Jess had brought it home, triumphantly announcing that he had purchased his child's first toy.

"The rocking chair should be in here, not in our room," Addie said to no one, imagining the countless nights she would spend by her child's crib, rocking her to sleep. The thought of her baby coursed through Addie like a heat wave. She was anxious to feel her child's warm body, to hold the little bundle that was so close now, so near.

She went into her bedroom and dragged the rocking chair, in fits and spurts, first pushing, then pulling, across the hallway to the baby's room. She positioned it next to the window, and as she did, she looked out over the lake at the coming storm. *Night is falling,* she thought. *Time to get out of these clothes.*

With great difficulty, she waddled across the hall, changed from her dress into her nightgown, and, having expended her last bit of energy, Addie returned to her child's room, and sat down in the rocking chair, finally, exhausted.

Nesting, that's what her mother called what Addie had just been doing. It was the unshakeable urge some women have to "ready the nest" for the coming baby. It meant, among the old wives who believed in such things, that the baby was readying itself to come into the world. The movement toward birth signaled the mother to ready the world for the baby. Addie remembered that, as a child, Marie and her friends would talk among themselves about such things as babies and childbirth and old wives' tales. Now, something inside Addie longed for her mother, wishing she could feel Marie's soft hand on her forehead, comforting her.

She sat in the chair, rocking back and forth, looking out over the lake. The soft to-and-fro motion, along with the soothing sight of the water, lulled the exhausted Addie into such a relaxed state of mind that she fell into a light sleep. It felt good to let go and drift away from her worries.

She did not see the fog as it rose up from the lake, born on the place where the humidity and heavy air met the cool water. She did not see it take shape and hover over the still, calm surface, breathing like a living thing would, growing and expanding with each exhalation. She did not see the fish, poking their heads out of the water, one after another after another, each hoping to get a taste of the velvety, living fog before it dissipated into the air, taking all the goodness with it.

Addie was rocking back and forth slowly, in a dreamless sleep, as the fog obliterated all the light in the darkening sky. She was sleeping as the fog enveloped the house on Front Street, wrapping its body, all its hundreds of tentacles, around the wooden structure and clinging to it, cradling it. She awoke only when she heard the singing.

It was a strange sound, one that traveled through her ears and around her heart and, finally, deep into her soul to a place that was familiar, though she could not remember how or why. She had heard this sound before, on the day of her birth, but of course she could not recall it. She only knew, as she was pulled from a deep sleep by the delicate sound, that it was calling her name.

Addie opened her eyes in the dusky room, but could see nothing outside the window but a solid wall of white. It startled her so much that she cried out, wondering if the world itself had been obliterated while she slept. Was she dreaming? She shook her head, still groggy from sleep, and realized that it was simply the fog, a consuming fog, that was rapping at her window.

With great difficulty, she pushed herself up from the rocking chair and walked to the window, pressing her face against the pane. There was nothing. She could not see more than an inch beyond the glass. As she pulled back a bit from the window, Addie was surprised to see her own reflection. She turned, faster than she should have, thinking someone was standing behind her in the room. But it was simply her own face reflected in the glass. Nothing menacing was there. Nothing at all.

"I expected rain," Addie murmured to herself, touching the windowpane, confused by the sight of the fog. Earlier in the day, it had indeed seemed as though rain was coming. The sky in the distance had been a threatening shade of green. Fog didn't usually appear on days such as this one, but Addie was coming to realize that, in her new home in Wharton, the weather took strange and unusual turns.

Darkness was descending upon the house, and quickly. Addie decided to make her way downstairs, where the fire was still burning in the fireplace. She lit a few candles and sat on the sofa in front of the fire. She was unnerved, looking this way and that, from one whitewashed window to another, wishing Jess was home. Why wasn't he here? Where was he?

Her thoughts dove into the ocean of her mind, and memories flooded forth, a whole lifetime, lived there, on the sofa in front of the fire. She thought of her childhood in Great Bay, with Jess, Polar, and Lucy. She remembered her father's warm smile and mother's gentle touch. She drifted to her wedding—all candlelit and resplendent, everyone singing Christmas carols. Her thoughts swirled from there to a bicycle ride, and then to a kiss on the platform in the train station, steam from the engine rising up and circling around them just as this fog now encircled the house.

The pains began. Erratic at first, and then coming in waves, every few minutes. There was no denying it; the baby was coming. Addie knew she should leave the house to find the doctor. She stumbled to the door, but just as her mother had done on the day Addie was born, she opened her front door to find a punishing wall of white. It terrified her. She knew the way to the doctor's house, it was just a short walk down the street. Surely she could find it, even in this fog. Surely. The length of one city block to the intersection, a left turn, and then four storefronts would lead her to the doctor. Or at least to someone who could help her get the rest of the way.

But that one city block before the intersection was completely empty. There were no other houses between their home and the main street. It was a grassy field on both sides. When she assured Jess that she could find the doctor when the baby was on its way, she didn't realize she would have to do it blindly.

"I must go or have this baby alone," Addie said aloud. She reached for her coat that was hanging behind the door and wrapped it around her. She stood there for a good, long while, but no matter how hard she tried, she could not force herself to step beyond her own threshold. The words she had heard in her head two weeks before were still ringing in her ears. *You will die on April 24.* That was today's date. Was this some sort of dark prophecy fulfilled? Would she lose her way in the fog and die giving birth? She had no wish to find out. She would not creep out into that dense, white, living thing.

The pains were coming regularly now, and they were so intense that she doubled over with the force of it. Addie closed the door, made her way back to the sofa, and lay down. There was no choice now. It was beyond her control. She knew she would have to get through the birth of this baby completely alone. *I can do this. Women have done this for generations. My mother did this. She was alone when I was born. Mama, where are you?*

Addie watched the flames dance and tickle the logs and lost herself in their power to mesmerize. *If only Jess were here.* He would find the doctor. He would bring him to the house. He would make sure she wasn't alone when the baby came. Addie had heard stories, whispered among the women of Great Bay, of children who died trying to come into the world feet first, and their poor mothers, who died trying to push them free. Would such a thing happen to her? *Calm down. I can do this. I am strong. I'll get through this.*

Despite the calming thoughts she kept replaying in her mind, Addie knew she was at the mercy of nature, at the mercy of her own body. She could not stop this baby from coming. She could not stop these pains long enough for the fog to lift. She could not summon the doctor with the sheer force of her will. Her life, and her baby's life, were now out of her hands.

The pain became so intense that Addie felt herself begin to hover above her own body. As she lay on her back, she took note of her belly, her legs, and her arms, but it was in a detached sort of way, as though she was watching it all occur from elsewhere. The only thing that was real was the pain, the incredible flood of intensity that began in her belly and radiated out into every cell of her body; every inch of her being was pulsing and vibrating with a pain so enormous that it engulfed the whole world.

She felt a coolness between her legs. Water, a flood of it. Somewhere deep inside, beneath all that pain, Addie's mind was screaming that the baby was coming, it was very near. But Addie didn't hear it. She wasn't a thinking being at that moment, she was only the pain. Pain was all there was. It was as though Addie herself were an infant, she was the baby being born, unable to think or reason or articulate her wants, needs, and desires. She was simply a mass of pain that existed for one thing—relief. An end to this suffering.

A song, then, an ancient, familiar song, calling her name, beckoning her near.

Addie summoned all her strength, rose from the sofa, and stumbled toward the kitchen door. *Relief.* She opened the door. *A warm hand, comforting me. A soothing embrace. Relief. An end to the pain. I'm coming. Water.*

In the firm grasp of childbirth, Addie had no way of knowing that three people were, at that very moment, on the way toward her house. One was worried about her, so near her due date, with fog shrouding the city. One was drawn there by something unknown. The third was coming to kill her.

CHAPTER THIRTY-ONE

Kate stumbled down a foggy path toward the lake, doubled over in pain. *Childbirth. This is what it must feel like.* She could not stand upright, the pain was so great. Kate turned and looked up the hill behind her—she could make out a house hovering there, in the fog. *Addie's house.* She could see no other houses anywhere in the distance. She was alone, in the fog, at the water's edge.

Kate watched herself dunk her feet in the water, which she expected to be freezing cold. She braced for the chill but didn't feel it. To Kate, it felt like scented, oiled bath water, warm, almost velvety to the touch. It felt so wonderful, in contrast to the pain that was raging through her body, that Kate wanted nothing more than to submerge herself in that comforting, soothing bath and float away.

She felt it then, a sharp pain in her back, then another, then another. Addie turned to look into the face of her murderer. *This should hurt more than it does* were the first words that went through Kate's mind when she realized what had occurred. Addie had been stabbed. Kate was witnessing the last moments of Addie's life.

No, not the baby. Save the baby. I've got to save the baby.

She slumped into the water and felt a delicate warmth, like feathers massaging her legs. Somewhere, outside of herself now, she felt the baby was coming, but Kate didn't care, she only knew that she needed to lie back. She turned and stretched out onto the surface of the water, as though she were reclining onto a bed. Its warmth overtook her and held her, suspended, on the surface of the lake. *This is what it feels like to die. This really isn't so bad.*

Kate felt her eyelids, heavy, so heavy, closing, then opening again with every twinge of pain. She wasn't thinking clearly, but she was present enough to know that Addie was vacillating between consciousness and sleep, or what seemed to be sleep. *The baby is coming.*

Kate was roused, for a moment, from this vague stupor when she realized that Addie was wearing the white, billowing gown that Kate had seen before, in her dreams, and on the beach that horrible day. *She's dying! She'll die if I don't do something!* Kate tried to wake Addie up, screaming inside of her head, *Wake up! Wake up! Your baby is coming! You're both going to die if you don't get up!* But the heaviness of her eyelids was too great, the warmth and comfort of the water was too soothing, the soft motion of her body undulating up and down on the waves was too calming. Kate gave in and was immersed in darkness.

Then, her eyes opened again. She was cold and shivering. She was out of the water now, on the beach. *I want to go back in the water. Take me back to the water.* Kate wanted very much to look around but found that her head did not move. Her eyes, she noticed, were barely open. She was looking through slits. She felt, too, that she was empty. The punishing pain that was ever present had ceased. *What's happening? Where is the baby?* Then, a voice. *Jess? Is that you?*

"I can't imagine what you're doing here on the lakeshore, Addie." It was not a man's voice.

What's the matter? Why isn't she helping me? Kate tried to look at who was speaking, but could only see the hemline of a skirt. She still could not move her head. Kate tried with all her might to open her eyes but couldn't. *Where is the baby? What's happened to the baby? Why aren't you helping me?*

"You were lucky that I came to see you, to introduce you to my beautiful baby," said the voice, singsongy now, like that of a child. "Your baby might have floated away on the tides if I hadn't been here. Come, let's get you up."

Kate listened, and heard a soft crying, far in the distance. *Her baby. Addie's baby. It was alive, then.* Kate felt herself slipping down again, eyelids heavy.

"What are you doing here?" A male voice boomed through the darkness, and Kate opened her eyes once again. "Thank God I found you. What are you thinking going out in this fog? Where is—" Kate felt an electricity in the air. "Oh my *God*. Oh my good Christ, what have you done?" Kate felt hands on her arms, saw a face come into her line of vision. Her eyes couldn't focus.

"My God, Addie, my God. Dear God. Is she—dead?" Kate felt a head on her chest, listening for her heart. He picked up her hand, felt for a pulse, and dropped it again. "I can't hear anything. Her heart's not beating. She's dead, good God in heaven. Did you—did you kill her?"

"Why would I kill her? That's a stupid thing to say."

"Where's the baby?" The voice was frantic. "Where's Addie's baby?"

"I put it in the carriage. Over there."

"What?" More panic, rising. Moans, tears. "What in heaven's name have you done? Why are you here? Why?"

"I came down here to show Addie the baby. Hadley wouldn't stop crying, you know how she gets. So I went out for a walk. You know how that calms her. And I found myself here."

"A walk? Celeste, what are you talking about? In this fog? Slow down and tell me exactly what's going on."

Celeste. Oh my God.

"Hadley is crying all the time."

"Hadley? My dear—"

Hadley. That's Grandma. Kate remembered well her father's mother. *They're talking about Grandma.*

"Listen, she's crying now."

"Where is Hadley, Celeste?"

"In the carriage, silly, where she always is. I put Addie's baby in there with her. I found the poor thing in the water, floating away. She was in the water! Can you imagine?"

Kate tried desperately to get a look at what was going on, but she couldn't see anything from where she was lying. *Addie must be near death,* Kate thought. *She's drifting in and out of consciousness.* Silence. *What's happening?*

"Celeste," the voice said, with great tenderness. "You know Hadley is dead. Honey? Remember? She died a few hours ago. Look at me, Celeste."

But Hadley lived. Kate was confused. *Hadley is Grandma.*

"Hadley isn't dead. What are you talking about? She wouldn't stop crying. So I put her in the carriage and went for a walk. I came down here."

Kate heard a gasp. She heard Celeste, in a singsong voice, cooing, "Rock-a-bye, baby, on the tree top, when the wind blows—" Crying, in the distance. Muttering.

"Jesus Christ, Celeste. Wait here, for Christ's sake. Don't move."

Several moments later, Kate felt a tugging on her legs. And then a thudding. She was in the bottom of a rowboat now. She saw a face appear in her line of vision, Harrison's face.

"Addie, I'm so sorry." Kate saw the tears flowing from his eyes. "Celeste had no idea what she was doing. She didn't mean to hurt you. She's not a bad person. Please forgive her. She has been insanely protective of Hadley—you know how she's been—and when the baby passed away today, she must've snapped. Lost all her senses. How I wish I had been here to stop this abomination."

Kate felt the motion of the boat on the waves. But she couldn't move. She couldn't turn her eyes, or her head. Addie was slipping away.

Was she bleeding to death? Kate wasn't sure. She tried with all her might to move her hands, even her fingers, but it was no use.

"You are so beautiful, so perfect. Jess, that bastard. He had the most perfect wife a man could hope for."

Kate was undulating with the waves as the boat traveled farther out into the bay.

"It's too late for you now, and it's too late for Hadley, but your little girl is still alive. You understand, Addie, nobody can know my wife is insane. Nobody can ever find out she did this to you. It would ruin us. I promise you, Addie, that we will take good care of your baby just as I know you will take good care of ours." More crying then.

Kate felt a bundle being tucked tightly under her arm, the folds of her nightgown wrapped over its lifeless face.

It wasn't Addie's baby that we found with her, after all. It was Harrison and Celeste's.

"May God forgive Celeste for what she has done, may God forgive me for what I now do, and for what I will do. Rest in peace, Hadley Connor. Rest in peace, Addie Stewart. May this lake never give up our secret."

And with that, Kate felt herself being shoved over the side of the boat and into the lake, where an enormous wave—there suddenly, from a glassy, calm surface—engulfed her. Undulating up and down, up and down in the soft, velvety water, taken with the whims of the wind and the tides. She was a seashell, a piece of driftwood, a loon floating lazily on the surface of the Great Lake. *Nothing can hurt you here. You are with me now. I will keep you safe, here, with me, my daughter of the lake, until it is time.* Kate was enveloped in loving arms and held close, wrapped in a watery blanket, falling down, down, down. *Sleep, my daughter, sleep, until it is time.*

CHAPTER THIRTY-TWO

Wharton, 1910

As Addie's body was enveloped into the arms of the lake, many things were happening on land.

Harrison had left Celeste murmuring and cooing into the baby carriage on the lakeshore and dashed into Addie and Jess's house, not sure what he was doing once he found himself inside. He was panicked, repeating Addie's name, over and over again, in a whisper. The sight of her body sinking under the water would haunt him for the rest of his life. Damn that Celeste. How could everything have gone so wrong in just a moment? How could this possibly be happening?

His decision to switch the babies was, perhaps, ill conceived, but he did it in a moment of terror. A live baby for a dead one. How could the existence of Addie's baby be explained without the mother? How could he possibly have found the baby without having murdered Addie? So many questions would be asked. Could Celeste be trusted to keep her mouth shut? No, it was easier this way. Both mother and baby gone. A clean break. Nobody, not even the household help, knew that Hadley had died that afternoon. An easy switch, no loose ends. It was as if fate had set things up perfectly.

Evidence. He should look for anything that might implicate Celeste in this crime. Was there any blood in the house? Where was the knife? He dashed around in a panic. Nothing. The house looked calm and peaceful, as though Addie and Jess might come walking inside at any moment. Nothing was out of place.

"Addie, your child will want for nothing," he promised her, there in the darkness. "I will spend the rest of my life making up for what my wife has taken away."

All this took just a few moments. Outside once again, he pushed past the still-murmuring Celeste and grasped the handle of the carriage. "Let's go, Celeste," he said, and the three of them walked into the fog, looking for all the world like an ordinary family taking a stroll together, instead of a woman who had lost her mind with grief, a misguided, deluded man who had committed, and would subsequently commit, the biggest sins of his life, and a baby who would go to her grave adoring a man who had stood by and watched her own father be convicted of a crime he did not commit.

When they reached their house that night, Celeste simply went to bed in blissful ignorance, remembering nothing but their delightful family walk on a cool evening. Harrison, after putting the wriggling baby into a crib where another had died just a few hours before, walked slowly up to the third-floor ballroom and into the turret. He closed the door and, satisfied that none of the household help would hear him, he sunk to his knees, finally allowing the unimaginable horror of what he had seen and done to wash over his body like a wave. He cried out with a primal sound of such desperation, need, and futility that his very being, every cell in his body, threatened to burst apart with the force of it.

Harrison did not know that at the very same moment, Jess Stewart had come home to an empty house. He would spend hours looking for his missing wife that night and the next day, knocking on Harrison's door, running all over town in an increasing state of panic, sending cables to her parents and his, talking to everyone they knew and finally to the police. Jess Stewart would make the very same sound alone in his bedroom as the sun went down on the first day without his wife, taking his hope and will to live with it.

Harrison also did not know that Jess, who was consumed with guilt about his brief, ill-advised, alcohol-fueled affair with Sally Reade, at first suspected that his wife had left him because of it. He imagined that, in his absence, Sally had come to Addie with proof of the affair. But as the days passed and Addie was still nowhere to be found, Jess became more and more frantic that something terrible had happened to her. Was Sally involved? That woman, despite all the fun and life in her, was unstable. He confessed his affair to the police—in retrospect, not the smartest move—in the hopes that they would look to Sally Reade for answers. They did, briefly. When her father and her best friend confirmed that she was in Europe for a short vacation, the police looked instead in one direction for Addie's killer. Directly at Jess Stewart.

Harrison hadn't intended to implicate Jess in this mess, though he did nothing to stop it. He knew about his friend's affair with Sally Reade and despised him for it. How could he possibly cheat on Addie? He deserved to lose his wife and child—just not that way. Harrison was simply consumed with covering up his wife's crime. When the investigation began to focus on Jess, Harrison had to choose. He chose his wife, or more exactly, the life he had carefully cultivated.

Harrison didn't count on, and indeed, did not know, that Celeste was beginning to remember things about that night. Snippets came back to her, a voice here, a scene there, as though she were remembering a dream. She became convinced that one of them, either she or Harrison, had killed Addie. She was not so unlike her husband, because she, too, chose to cover up what she suspected. So she called upon one of the dockworkers who had always provided similar "services" for her father, a man she could trust to do her bidding, and paid for his testimony implicating Jess Stewart. Not that Celeste had anything particular against Jess. But it wouldn't do to have Harrison go to jail. Let alone herself. They had a baby to care for. They were the richest couple in town. The largest employer. She would not betray her father's memory, erase all his hard work and sacrifice, with that kind of scandal. No. Jess had to take the blame for this. It was the only way.

During the trial, Jess Stewart became so despondent that his lawyer didn't dare put him on the stand. He did not know what became of his wife, he did not know how she died or who had killed her. He did not know that his baby was the gurgling, cooing bundle in Celeste's arms every day at the trial. He only knew that Addie and the baby were gone, his life was gone, his reason for living was gone. He felt that he was the cause of it all. In some sort of morality play of retribution for wrongdoing, his ill-fated affair, his betrayal of his best friend and soul mate, had somehow set this in motion, causing Addie and the baby to simply disappear, to vanish into the fog, taken away from an undeserving husband, never to be seen again.

When Marcus Cassatt confronted him on the courthouse steps, Jess was relieved to see the man and his gun. He turned his chest toward his murderer so Addie's father could get a clear shot, and he smiled. One moment after his body hit the ground, he was in Addie's arms.

"I will right this for you, my love," she whispered to him.

CHAPTER THIRTY-THREE

Kate opened her eyes with a start. She sat up and reached around to her back—and exhaled. It had seemed so real that she wasn't quite sure if she, herself, had been stabbed.

She threw back the covers and jumped out of bed, pushed her feet into slippers, grabbed her robe, and tied it around her as she ran down the main staircase toward the dining room.

Not seeing her cousin at his usual breakfast table, she called out for him. "Simon!"

He emerged from the kitchen with a pot of French-press coffee and two cups. "Kate, my God, what—" But she held a hand up, stopping his words.

"I know what happened," she said as the two of them sat down at a table and Simon poured.

Kate took a deep breath and began to talk. She told him all about the dream—Addie's death, Celeste's insane, terrifying voice, Harrison's panic, the final push out into the lake, a dead woman holding a dead baby that wasn't even her own, locked together in a watery grave.

"Addie was our great-grandmother," Simon whispered. "And Jess Stewart was our great-grandfather."

"He was innocent," Kate said, her voice trembling. "He was an innocent man, framed for his wife's murder."

"Why would Harrison do such a thing?" Simon asked. "He framed his best friend. Or, at the very least, stood by and watched him go down for a murder he knew the guy didn't commit. I can't believe it."

"I know, it's pretty low," Kate said. "I guess in the end, his wife and family and business and reputation were too much to lose."

"So, what did Harrison do?"

"To me, it seemed as though he panicked. Even if Addie and the baby had washed up the very next day, there would be no evidence whatsoever tying him or Celeste to their deaths."

"It's all so pointless," Simon mused. "Addie's husband wasn't guilty of anything but having an affair. They got away with it. What a nightmare. You know, our family will go insane when they hear about this," Simon went on. "Will they even believe us?"

"I know one way," Kate said, softly. "If we really want to see this thing through to its bitter conclusion, we should test our DNA with Addie's. By now, the police have probably figured out that the baby isn't hers. Nick didn't mention anything about it, but I was still a suspect until recently."

Simon was staring out toward the water. "That's one hell of a reason for Addie to come back from the dead," he said. "To set things right. To make sure people—her people at least—knew what really happened."

"And who they—we—really are," Kate said, hoping that was all there was to it. But the knot in her stomach told her there might be more to come.

CHAPTER THIRTY-FOUR

After she and Simon ate breakfast, Kate retreated to her room to shower and change. When she came downstairs again, she found Nick sitting with Simon in the living room, a fresh pot of coffee and two cups between them.

"Hi," she said to him, her stomach doing a flip at the sight of their grave expressions. "Is something wrong?"

"I called him," Simon admitted. "Kate, he really needs to hear this. From you."

Kate settled onto the sofa next to Nick while Simon retrieved a cup from the sideboard and poured.

"Jess didn't kill Addie," Kate said to Nick. "I saw it all last night in my dream. Nick, I saw her murder. I was there. It wasn't her husband, even though he was convicted of the crime."

And then she told him the whole story, everything she saw, and experienced, in her dream. After hearing it, he whistled, long and low. "That's quite a tale."

Kate bristled at this. "Do you believe me?"

"Every word," he said. "I don't know how, and I don't know why. But I believe you, Kate. I think you're right about how that murder went down. It certainly explains one of the myriad of puzzling things about this case."

"That the baby's DNA doesn't match the mother's?"

He raised his eyebrows. "Exactly. We've been wondering about it from very early on. And we knew the baby didn't die from drowning, so that only added to the mystery."

"Why didn't you tell me?" she wanted to know.

"It's called police work," he grinned. "We don't tell people everything."

"I guess I can see that," Kate chuckled. "But I'd sure like to know whether my DNA and Addie's show a relationship."

"Are you saying you want me to run your DNA against hers?"

"I would really like to know, once and for all."

The results of the DNA test were conclusive. Addie was indeed related to Kate and Simon. The baby was not. Now there was no doubt that the events Kate had dreamed about for the past several weeks were real.

Armed with this information and her stack of newspaper articles about the trial, she and Nick sat down with Johnny Stratton for what she knew would be a rather strange conversation. He had agreed to Nick's request to run the DNA test for Kate without an explanation as to why she had requested it—on the condition that they tell him everything once the results were in.

"In all my years on the force . . . ," he murmured, shaking his head as he paged through Kate's articles. He looked up from the newsprint and held her gaze for a few moments as if he were trying to see through her eyes and into whatever place had brought this hidden secret from the past to light. "It does seem to add up. These photos do indeed look like our lady, and there's no doubting those DNA results. It's just . . ." He sighed. "I have no idea what I'm going to write in my report to close this case."

Kate gathered up the articles that were strewn across the tabletop. "I know the feeling."

"Told your father any of this?" Johnny asked.

Kate thought of the conversation she would soon have with her dad. "I'm on my way there now. Finding out that Grandma Hadley—his mother—was actually the child of someone else and a stolen child at that? I'm not sure how he's going to take it. Simon hasn't told his dad, either. We toyed with the idea of just keeping this to ourselves. Letting sleeping dogs lie, as it were."

"Those sleeping dogs have a way of waking up and biting you when you least expect it," Johnny said, patting Kate's hand. "Honey, you're doing the right thing. The truth needs to come out, no matter how painful or confusing that truth might be. Otherwise, what was the point of it all? You've been through quite a lot so this lady's story could be told. Now all that's left for you to do is tell it to those who need to hear it."

Kate stood up and held the file of articles to her chest as Johnny enveloped her in a bear hug. "I'll tell you what," he said. "There's never a dull moment in police work."

She and Nick exchanged a quick glance, and she was out the door.

A week later, Kate and Simon, along with Kate's parents, Simon's parents, and Jonathan stood with Nick Stone and Johnny Stratton on the deck of a Coast Guard cutter, more than a mile offshore in the greatest of lakes. Kate hugged an urn close to her chest.

"Does anyone want to say a few words?" Johnny asked.

Simon nudged Kate. "He's talking to you, if there was any doubt," he whispered.

Kate cleared her throat.

"I'm not quite sure what to say," she began. "But I know Addie better than anyone here. In my dreams, I saw an incredible love story between Addie and her husband, Jess, I saw my great-grandfather in his heyday, I saw insanity, and, finally, I saw a murder. I was with Addie during the last moments of her life. I learned that her beloved husband was the victim of justice gone wrong. I learned that everything we thought about our heritage was wrong. I learned that she and her husband live on, through our family."

Her father slung his arm across his brother's shoulders and squeezed, as her mother dabbed at her eyes.

"Thank you, Addie, for coming to me in my dreams," Kate went on. "Thank you for putting right the wrong that was done to your husband all those years ago and letting me get to know him like you did. And thank you for letting us know that we're your family. We will never forget you."

And with that, Kate sprinkled the ashes over the side of the boat. They floated for a moment before a small whirlpool appeared on the lake's glassy surface and swirled the ashes down toward points unknown.

"Rest well, Addie," Simon called out. "We heard you. Please know that your photograph will hang in our house, where your daughter grew up. She knew nothing about you, but her children do. And so do we."

Kate's father, Fred, and her uncle Harry both fought back tears.

Simon wrapped his arm around Kate's waist. "You did good, kiddo," he said, and they gazed out over the lake's calm surface, which reflected the clouds hanging in the late autumn sky.

He squinted into the distance where a dark figure poked its head out of the water and slapped its tail against the surface, creating enormous ripples that extended in concentric circles all the way to the boat. "What's that?" he asked.

"It couldn't be a beaver, way out here," Kate mused. "Otter?"

CHAPTER THIRTY-FIVE

Winter came. Kate stayed on in Wharton, helping Simon and Jonathan publicize the inn. Her divorce came through, uncontested by Kevin, who had already moved on to another job in a new town. And, no doubt, another woman. He and Kate met at Harrison's House to sign the papers, against Simon's advice. But she was strong enough to do it, over the initial pain, and secure in the knowledge that it was, indeed, best to go their separate ways. Not only because of Nick, to whom she was getting closer and closer, but also because Kate and Kevin's relationship was not right for either of them.

Kevin finally admitted to the affair and confessed that, perhaps, married life just wasn't for him. He had been itching for something new soon after they had walked down the aisle, and Valerie had not been the first.

In the end, they parted—if not as friends, then as friendly as possible. Kate's heart was still bruised by their failed love story and by his actions, but she knew, down deep, that it was simply his way. That's who Kevin was—a man who loved the thrill of a new relationship but got bored with maintaining one. She couldn't ask him to be someone he wasn't, nor could she be surprised when his true nature came out.

He stood to leave, and Kate threw her arms around him, pulling him into a hug. "I loved you, Kevin, I really did," she said, her voice wavering. "And I wish nothing but the best for you."

"I'm sorry," he whispered into her ear, his own voice cracking with emotion.

They stood there for a long moment, holding each other. And then he walked away, Kate watching until he disappeared from view, not knowing if she would ever again see the man she, at one time, believed she'd grow old with. She didn't know what the future would hold, and she never knew that he wouldn't marry again until very late in life, and that on his deathbed, Kate's name would be on his lips.

Meanwhile, renovations had begun in earnest on the third floor. As the workmen were refinishing the wood floors, installing bathroom fixtures, painting, and coming and going with furniture and window treatments, Kate was busy finding and framing photos of the past.

Simon had taken the photo of Addie, Jess, Harrison, and Celeste— the one that had ultimately led them to the truth about what had happened all those years ago—to a local artist, who painted a portrait of Addie and Jess using the photo as a guide. Simon intended to hang it over the fireplace on the third floor, newly dubbed Addie's Ballroom.

One snowy night, Kate opened the door to find Nick holding a bottle of wine in one hand, a bouquet of flowers in the other.

"Wherever did you get lilacs at this time of year?" Kate asked, taking the flowers from him and lifting them to her face to drink in the scent, which would forever remind her of Addie and Jess.

"I have my ways." Nick smiled and pulled Kate into a kiss. They lingered there, on the doorstep, snow lightly falling around them, the delicate chill in the air caressing their cheeks.

"I like your ways," Kate said, wrapping her arms around his shoulders.

"I knew we'd be christening Addie's Ballroom tonight, and I thought lilacs would be a nice way to honor her," Nick said.

Kate's eyes lit up. "Wait until you see it," she said. "I'm so glad I didn't let you up there during renovations until the big reveal tonight. It's really gorgeous."

She took him by the hand and led him inside the house, where they found Simon and Jonathan in front of the fire in the living room.

"The long arm of the law has arrived," Simon said, flashing Nick a smile. "Welcome, Detective."

"Thank you, citizen," Nick said. "But I have to tell you, I've been here for all of two minutes, and I do not have a drink in hand. I think that's a felony in some counties."

"Shoddy hosting," Jonathan said, crossing the room to pour a pint of Scottish ale and handing it to Nick with a wink. "It'll get you two to four years, hard time."

And the evening had begun. The four of them chatted over drinks for a bit, then retreated to the dining room for a dinner of salad, *boeuf en croûte*, roasted brussels sprouts, and red potatoes. Dessert and champagne were to be served upstairs in the ballroom.

A feeling of celebration wafted through the air—the inclusion of Addie and Jess in the history of Harrison's House with the completion of Addie's Ballroom just felt right.

But not all the occupants of Harrison's House felt the same. As Kate, Simon, Jonathan, and Nick made their way through dinner, a storm was brewing on the third floor.

CHAPTER THIRTY-SIX

"I can't wait for you to see it," Kate said to Nick as the four of them made their way up to the third floor. "It all came together so—" But her words stopped and hung in the air as they all walked through the doorway into the ballroom.

Most of the photos that Kate had painstakingly chosen and had framed were now on the floor, their glass panes shattered. Furniture was upended. Champagne bottles, which had been chilling on ice, were cracked and lying in a pool of still-bubbling liquid. One had been thrown against the wall, a wet stain spreading out over the fresh paint. Several of the new window shades were torn down, and the doors to the turrets were standing open, signaling that the carnage had spread there.

"No!" Kate cried as she noticed the portrait of Addie and Jess sizzling in the fireplace, their faces melting in the flames. She rushed toward it and grabbed the frame, only to drop it again, its heat burning her hands.

Nick was at her side in an instant with the ice bucket. "Here," he said, guiding her hands into the slush.

Kate could sense a presence, the same one she had encountered in this room weeks before, a malevolence that seemed to permeate every corner, every alcove. It was a blackness that seemed to grow as her fear grew, stronger with every beat of her heart.

None of them was able to find any words. It seemed that they were frozen, looking around the room that was in shambles, unable to process what they were seeing. It wasn't until the only photo still hanging on the wall flew across the room and hit Kate directly in the forehead that they were startled out of whatever it was that entranced them.

"Okay, we're getting out of here," said Nick, pushing Kate toward the stairs and dropping the ice bucket in the process. He turned to Simon and Jonathan, still staring in stunned silence. "Move, you two."

The four of them hurried out of the room, almost tripping over each other, and didn't stop until they were on the first floor, breathless and panting.

"My God," Simon said, staring at Kate's forehead. "Jonathan, run and get a washcloth."

As Nick guided her to the sofa in the living room, Kate reached up to her forehead and felt a trickle of blood with her shaking, stinging hands.

"What was that all about?" Nick said, taking the cloth from Jonathan and holding it to Kate's forehead. "What happened up there?"

Simon sat down in one of the armchairs next to the fireplace with a thud, shaking his head. He opened his mouth to speak but closed it again, unsure of words to describe what he had seen.

"Obviously, somebody broke in," Jonathan mused. "But who? Who would do such a thing?"

"When is the last time any of you were up on the third floor?" Nick asked, looking from Kate to Simon to Jonathan and back again.

Kate just shook her head. Simon ran a hand through his hair.

"It was earlier today," Jonathan said. "For me, at least. I ran up there to put some champagne on ice not long before you got here. Five o'clock, maybe?"

"And everything was—"

"Fine. Perfect. Just as it should be."

"Was anybody coming and going since then? Workmen? Employees? Hotel guests? Nobody heard anything?"

Jonathan shook his head. "Nobody. Charles left as soon as the dinner was served, and we don't have any guests, not tonight."

Nick stood up. "Can you show me the back or side doors?" he said to Jonathan. "Any other entrances, first floor and basement windows, that sort of thing. Fire escapes."

Nick rubbed Kate's shoulder as he examined her wound. "I don't think it needs stitches. You just stay here and tend to that head. I'm going to take a look around."

She covered his hand with hers. "Thank you," she said.

When Nick and Jonathan had left the room, she turned to Simon. "I think we both know this wasn't any workman."

Simon leaned forward. "Do you think it's that same—whatever it was—that attacked you on the third floor?"

"What other explanation could there be?" Kate said.

They exchanged glances. "You said that the only spirits in this house are family," Kate said. "You don't think—"

"Yes, I do. I was thinking exactly the same thing." Simon lowered his voice. "Celeste . . . ?"

"She's the only one who would be upset that Addie's memory is being kept alive, that the truth about the babies and Addie's death is finally out in the open. We can't be sure, but I think it's her."

Simon let out a sigh. "I haven't told Jonathan about your experience up there while he was away," he mused. "I guess now's the time."

"The portrait of Jess and Addie," Kate wailed, covering her face with the washcloth.

"He's just going to have to paint another one, that's all there is to it," Simon said. "I didn't think he captured her eyes, anyway."

Kate dabbed at the cut on her forehead and noticed the blood was lessening. "I don't know what we're supposed to do now," she said.

"Well, I know one thing," Simon said, pushing himself to his feet and walking to the sideboard to pour himself a Scotch. "We can't have that hateful shrew up there wreaking havoc with our new ballroom. What if it happens when it's full of guests? I just won't have it, Kate. She has to go."

"Agreed," Kate said, setting the washcloth on the end table and joining him at the sideboard, her stomach tightening. "But how in the world do we go about getting her out of here?"

"Getting who out of where?" It was Jonathan, along with Nick, back from their tour of the house.

"Did you find anything?" Kate asked, knowing that what had just happened was not the result of a break-in.

Nick shook his head. "This place is tight as a drum. There's no way anyone got in or out, unless they walked through the front door. And we'd have seen or heard them if they did."

Kate shot Simon a look. "Then I think you guys had better sit down," she said.

An hour later, Kate and Nick were walking in clockwise circles through the ballroom, carrying a smoldering bunch of sage, which was giving off a thick, aromatic smoke.

Kate had explained her previous paranormal experiences to Nick and Jonathan, who had jumped onto the computer to research "how to get a ghost out of your house." He found a treasure trove of ghost-busting information, and they decided to use it all.

While Kate and Nick were dealing with the sage, Jonathan was spreading salt across the doorways, windowsills, and stairs leading to the third floor, and Simon was anointing those same areas with oil. Kate would've preferred to have Alaska by her side, but she decided to keep the dog downstairs, away from the smoke, the salt, and the oil.

When they had done it all, Kate looked around the room. "Now what?" she said.

"This one's new to me, kids," Nick said, shrugging.

"Is this all there is to it?" Simon wanted to know. "Are we supposed to do anything else?"

Jonathan was squinting at the screen on his phone. "It says here we should address her. The spirit."

"Address her?" Simon furrowed his brow.

"Talk directly to her," Jonathan said, still looking at the phone. "Tell her what you want."

"Just like that? Evict her like a troublesome houseguest?"

Jonathan looked up. "That's what it says here."

"I think it should be you," Simon whispered loudly to Kate.

"Me?"

Simon pointed to her forehead. "You're the one experiencing all of this weirdness. It's all directed at you, Kate. You need to be the one to tell her to go."

She knew he was right. "Okay," she said. "Here goes." Kate cleared her throat. "Great-Grandmother Celeste Connor, who lived and died in this house, please leave us in peace. We've put a lot of work into restoring this house to the beautiful mansion you built. Please know that we will honor your memory in this place."

She shrugged, not knowing what else to say. Kate looked around the room.

"Does anybody feel anything?" Kate asked. "Any presence at all?"

"Like I said, this is new to me," Nick said. "I'm still thinking about a real-life intruder, if you want to know the truth."

Jonathan and Simon exchanged a glance. "I don't feel anything," Simon said. "Is she gone, do you think?"

"No idea," Jonathan said, putting a hand on Simon's shoulder. "But maybe we should call it a night."

As Kate flipped off the main light switch and the foursome descended the stairs for the second time that evening, nobody noticed Harrison sitting on the turret steps, his arm around a young Hadley's shoulders.

"Sage, smudging." Harrison sighed. "If only it were as simple as that, Hadley, my dear." He shook his head. "I think it's time we call in the big guns. Death hasn't changed her at all. She's still as stubborn as she always was."

CHAPTER THIRTY-SEVEN

Kate opened her eyes with a start and took in a quick breath. What was that noise? Scratching? She sat up and listened, but all she heard was the soft hiss of the steam radiators, which had come to life because of the chill in the air.

She looked around the room—nothing was amiss. The fire that Simon had set in her room's fireplace had burned down, and all that was left now were gently glowing coals casting a soft light around the bedroom and strange shadows on the walls.

Her door was slightly ajar. *Alaska,* she thought. Sometimes the dog nosed out of the room at night in search of her water dish or to patrol the house, both of which were fine with Kate.

Nick was sleeping in the next room. When they had finished "ghost-busting," he had called the precinct and asked a squad on duty to watch the house, still convinced a real-life intruder had trashed the ballroom. As he was readying to go, Kate tugged on his jacket and asked if he would spend the night.

Nick looked slightly stunned. "I thought we were taking it slow."

Kate laughed, and Simon and Jonathan muffled their own chuckles. "I wasn't giving you keys to the fantasy suite," she said. "I was just thinking we all might feel safer tonight with a big, strong policeman under our roof."

"Oh." Nick ran a hand through his hair. "In that case, I—"

"We have an entire house full of empty guestrooms," Simon said as he turned Jonathan toward their master suite. "If you choose to stay, feel free to take your pick. Charles will be here to make breakfast in the morning for all of us. Good night, kids."

"I can make a call to get someone to walk Queenie," Nick said, a slight smile on his face.

And with that, Kate and Nick were alone. They had spent the next hour or so in the living room, talking about the evening, sharing kisses, and staring into the fire that was blazing away in the fireplace. When Kate had started to nod off, Nick's arm around her, her head on his shoulder, he nudged her awake.

"I think it's time to go up," he said, stealing one last kiss by the fire.

He led her up to her second-floor room, Hadley's Suite, and they stopped at the door, Nick leaning against its frame.

Kate draped her arms around his neck. "I'd love to invite you inside," she whispered.

He smiled. "I'd feel better about it if I knew Mr. and Mr. Busybody weren't down the hall."

"I suppose you're right." Kate smiled. "If we emerged from the same room in the morning, they'd demand a play-by-play."

"We would not!" came a voice from down the hallway.

Kate and Nick shared a laugh, and he kissed her good night. "If you hear anything, I'm in the next room."

"Okay," she'd said and slipped inside her room, shutting the door behind her.

Now, Kate snuggled back down under the covers and exhaled, thinking of the man in the next room and wishing he was lying beside her. She watched the shadows play on the walls for a bit and then closed her eyes, not realizing that the coals in her fireplace were too small to cast shadows.

∾

An hour later, Nick found Kate cowering in the corner of one of the turret rooms above the third floor, a massive dog standing over her, growling. Nick had awakened because of Alaska's barking and followed the sound up to the third floor. Jonathan and Simon pounded up the stairs a few moments later.

"Alaska!" Nick yelled. "Down! Down, girl!"

But the dog didn't move. Her yellow eyes were trained on Kate's face, a fierce snarl coming from the dog's throat, her teeth bared.

Nick tried to reach Kate, but the dog stood in his way, a low growl warning him off.

"Kate! What—"

It was then he noticed Kate's demeanor, as though she didn't even know the dog—or he—was there.

Instead of the bright hazel in her eyes, Kate's pupils were black. She was staring off into space, her arms crooked as though she was holding a baby.

"She cries so," Kate said, in a paper-thin voice not her own. "I cannot get her to stop crying! Why won't she sleep?"

"Kate," Nick called to her. "Kate, it's me. Look at me, Katie."

"That's not Kate," Simon whispered, reaching for Jonathan's arm. "Alaska would never growl at Kate."

"Hush, little baby, don't you cry . . . ," Kate sang in a whisper.

"Let me try," Simon said to Nick. He nodded.

"Celeste," Simon said, his voice wavering. "Celeste, what have you done?"

At this, Kate's head snapped in Simon's direction. "What have *you* done?" she said to him, slowing pushing herself up to a standing position. "This is all your fault." But she wasn't looking at Simon. She was looking beyond him, down the turret steps into the empty ballroom below. Simon didn't realize Harrison was standing there. "You brought her into this house. My house. I want her out. She's not a Connor."

Simon, Nick, and Jonathan watched as Kate tumbled—or more exactly, was thrown—down the turret steps, Alaska barking ferociously at her heels. Kate landed with a thud on the ballroom floor.

"Alaska, move aside!" Nick yelled, pushing the dog and risking a broken arm in the process. But the dog didn't bite, allowing Nick to get to Kate and lift her to her feet.

"Kate, honey, wherever you are in there, it's Nick," he said. Kate's head was lolling to the side, her black eyes wild, a terrifying grin across her face.

Kate got to her feet, a low chuckle escaping her lips. "Hush, little baby, don't you cry . . ."

The air around them began to swirl and thicken, as though they were standing in the center of a windstorm.

"Tell her to go to the light," Jonathan whispered to Simon.

"Go to the light?" Simon hissed in a whisper. "Is that really a thing?"

Jonathan shrugged. "No idea. But what else are we going to do? Invoke somebody! Your relatives?"

Simon cleared his throat. "Great-Grandfather Harrison, if you're here, help us send Celeste to the light. Take her away, Harrison. Help her cross over. I know you don't want this, and she can't stay here with us."

"Mama's going to sing you a lullaby . . ."

"I've summoned your great-grandmother, boy," a voice whispered in Simon's ear. "Call Addie. I've got someone of my own to call."

"Addie!" Simon called out, louder than before. "Great-Grandmother Addie Stewart! We call upon you to help us rid this place of this dark spirit, to free your great-granddaughter Kate from her grasp."

And the windstorm around them became more violent, blowing photos and furniture across the room, whirling and swirling with a feverish, frantic energy. Cries and howls emanated from nothingness, filling the room and their very bodies with the wails and regrets of the dead.

"All of us love Kate, Celeste," Simon shouted above the din. "Every living thing in this room loves Kate to the very depths of our souls. That is stronger than you. We are stronger than you. Kate is stronger than you. The truth is stronger than you. Go to the light, Celeste. It's over. It's time for you to go home."

Silence, finally, when Harrison stepped close to Celeste, carrying a baby in his arms.

"What are you doing here when it's her feeding time?" he said, his voice gentle and soft, holding Clementine close to his chest. "Stop tormenting this poor girl and tend to your daughter. That's what a loving mother should do."

And with that, Kate fell to the ground in a heap. Alaska was on her in an instant, licking her face. Standing next to the dog's great head, too faint for any of the men to see her, was Addie. She reached down and stroked Kate's hair, her violet eyes shining.

"My darling girl," she whispered into Kate's ear. "She's gone. She can't hurt you. She never could. Never really wanted to. It was the madness, the grief."

Kate murmured and reached for the great-grandmother she didn't consciously know was there.

"I'm so proud of you," Addie said. "Thank you for all you've done for me. For us."

And with that, Addie turned to her beloved Jess and took his hand.

"Look at her, darling," she said to him. "Our great-granddaughter."

"She's beautiful, Addie." Jess smiled at her. "Just like you. Just like Hadley. Now that this is done, what shall we do today, my love?"

"They'll be fine now." Addie straightened. "The whole world awaits." They turned and walked hand in hand into forever.

Kate reached up to stroke her dog's soft fur. And then she noticed the three men standing above them.

"What's going on?" she asked, coughing.

Nick reached down, took Kate's hand, and helped her to her feet. He pulled her into a hug and held her close. She could feel his whole body shaking. "Thank God," he whispered, tears of relief escaping from his eyes.

CHAPTER THIRTY-EIGHT

On one particularly windy, chilly day, Kate and Simon, along with Nick and Jonathan, drove up the rocky shoreline to Great Bay, where Addie and Jess had spent their childhoods. Kate had spent the last few weeks doing research into their lives—birth and death records existed, but not much else. She knew both Addie's and Jess's fathers had been fishermen, as had their fathers before them. But no relatives existed. Neither Addie's nor Jess's parents had more than one child. Both families lost everything that horrible, foggy night on the shores of the lake in Wharton—or believed they had. Young Hadley remained, though out of their view and their knowledge. She had children and grandchildren—a family blossomed out of all that devastation. And nobody knew until now.

Great Bay was not the thriving fishing village that it was when Addie was born. Instead it had become a sleepy tourist town, filled with inns and restaurants dotting the craggy, windswept shoreline. Old houses were torn down, new ones took their places, and time went on, despite the great tragedies that had occurred here.

While Jonathan and Nick checked into the hotel, Kate and Simon visited a small fishing museum that they had heard was there. It contained relics of the fishing village that the town had once been—photographs, mementos, and ships' logs, as well as items from the town itself. They wandered through the museum's rooms, soaking in the history, searching for a familiar face among the old, weathered photographs of fishermen displaying their catches, town picnics, and celebrations—life in the once-thriving community.

The curator, a man of at least seventy years of age, his boyish face belied by his graying hair and gnarled hands, approached. "Looking for anything special?" he asked.

"We've just learned we had relatives that came from Great Bay," Kate explained. "We were hoping to . . . I don't know . . . get a sense of the town as it was a century ago. Maybe find out some more information about our family."

"What was the family name?" the curator asked.

"There are two," Simon said. "Cassatt and Stewart."

The curator shot them a look. "Not the Cassatts and Stewarts involved in the trial . . . ?"

Kate nodded. "The same."

"But . . ." The curator squinted at Simon and Kate, obviously knowing the Cassatts and Stewarts had no children other than Addie and Jess. Kate held up her hand as if to stop his next words from forming.

"I know," she said, shaking her head. "It's complicated, but we *are* related, there's no doubt. And we're really hoping you've got some information that will help us find out more about our ancestors. We're very interested in knowing them."

The curator nodded his head in the direction of the museum's back room. "In that case, I think I have something that you might like to see." He led Kate and Simon to a display of old fishing gear and photos of men with boats full of fish.

"Marcus and Gene Cassatt," he said, pointing to one of the photos. "They were known in these parts as the best fishermen to ever set their nets on this lake. Legend had it they never came up empty-handed, never had a bad day, never were in danger. Of course, that was before all of the . . . unpleasantness of the trial and such."

Kate looked from the grainy photograph to Simon's face and back again. "I can see the resemblance," she said.

Then she had a thought. "What happened to him after the trial? He shot Jess Stewart in cold blood on the courthouse steps. Did he go to jail, too?"

The man nodded. "Would have if not for the stroke. Had it right after the shooting. He was in the hospital for a bit but finally died."

The curator continued, pointing toward a glass case. "His wife, Marie, donated something as well. My father told me about her coming in here that day. She was an old woman then, her daughter and husband long dead.

"She handed my dad a book and said that at some future time and place, people would come here and be interested in what it had to say. Said she had seen it in a dream—I'll never forget that."

Kate shot Simon a look. A dream?

"It made an impression on me as a young lad, you might say," the curator continued. "She wanted us to be the guardians of the book, until the time came. And then we were to hand it over to its rightful owners. I've worked here my whole life, and you're the first people to ask about the Cassatts. So I guess the people she was talking about are you, and I guess that time is now."

He shuffled over to the glass case, opened it, and reached inside. He handed Kate a slim volume with a leather cover. She read the title aloud: "Daughter of the Lake."

"It's quite a good story." He smiled. "You'll enjoy it. We took the liberty of copying it and adding it to the book of ancient lore we're putting together about this area."

On the way back, Kate stopped the car, and she and Simon walked down the rocky embankment toward the water, where they sat, staring out into the Great Lake. They had no way of knowing that, more than a century ago, Addie Cassatt had been born at that very spot. Just a few hundred yards away, Jess Stewart had seen baby Addie for the first time and plucked her from the watery embrace.

Back in those days, the lakeshore was a mystical, holy place, full of legend and lore. A place where water spirits could come to life, where ancient gods and goddesses swam freely among the salmon and trout, confounding unworthy fishermen and boaters and singing out in mysterious voices to children and mothers and murderers on foggy days, luring them to come, come to the water's edge. The lakeshore was magical then, in those days, and so it remained. But people had grown too noisy, too preoccupied, too sophisticated to listen to its song.

Kate and Simon sat on the shore and watched as the waves crashed against the rocks, over and over again, covering them with spray. Instead of stinging their faces, as the tiny shards of water should have on that cold, blustery day, it felt to them, for all the world, like velvet.

CHAPTER THIRTY-NINE

Wharton, 1910

Sally Reade couldn't believe her good fortune as she walked through the fog to the Cassatt house. The lake, the weather, even God himself seemed to be conspiring to help her do what she had to do! Oh, it wasn't going to be pleasant, she knew that outright. But it had to be done. Jess Stewart had made her the fool a second time. For the same woman, no less.

When they were younger, reliable, stable Jess had always been there, waiting for her to attend the next cocktail party. After graduation, he was clever enough to secure a wonderful job with a large firm. A solid foundation on which to start a life, her father had said. Sally agreed. It was all going so well. She was expecting his proposal any day. That was why it was such a shock when Jess returned from that visit to his hometown with the unthinkable news that he had become engaged. Engaged! Sally did not take the news well. Who would? She sank into a melancholia deeper than she had ever known.

Years passed before they saw each other again, as Sally had always known they would. She made it happen by traveling to Wharton for a party at the Harrison Connors'. So many old friends were there! Just like old times. And then, there was Jess. As handsome as ever. As charming as ever. Sally could tell that he still cared for her. Wasn't it obvious? Didn't everyone see it? The way he laughed so easily. The way he touched her shoulder when he spoke. Sally felt it then, the whole world vibrating with energy and life. Did everyone else feel it, too? She led Jess up into the turret—the perfect place for a clandestine fling!— threw her arms around him, and kissed him. He did not object. Yes, he had been drinking, perhaps too much, anyone could see that. But it didn't matter to Sally. Why should it?

That wife of his. What a country mouse she was. None of their old friends could quite believe he had married her. None of the women, anyway. The men seemed entranced, fools that they were. It was true, she was beautiful, but beauty only took one so far. No matter. Sally's plan was progressing, wife or no wife. That was the important thing.

After that night, Sally arranged to be in Wharton to see Jess whenever she could. A quick trip on the train from the city, no trouble at all. She was confident in her power to lure this man away from his wife. Sally would have what was rightfully hers. Didn't he love her? Hadn't he always loved her? Wasn't he hers?

A secret lunch here, a stolen kiss there. *Men are so easily swayed, especially if they've been married for a few years.* She took him to her bed a few times, after serving him one too many strong martinis. She knew this man, she knew what he liked, she knew his weaknesses. He could not resist her.

It was all going so well until the night he broke things off. Again! It was inconceivable to Sally. He was becoming a father, he told her. There was the welfare of a child to consider. He needed to straighten up, he needed to be the kind of person a son or daughter would be proud of. He needed to be the kind of person his wife deserved. He loved his wife and always had. As things were, he said, their affair had to end. Couldn't she see that?

She saw. Clearly. Jess Stewart had made a fool of her once again. But this time, Sally was not the same fragile young girl he had left years before. She was stronger now. Fiercer. This time, his sin was unforgivable. He had denied her the thing she most desired. It was only right for her to deny him the thing he most desired. Turnabout was fair play.

It was a perfect plan, really. She knew Jess was in Chicago for business that week. His wife would be alone when the nastiness occurred—Sally didn't like to think of the word *murder*, it sounded so evil, so wrong. This wasn't wrong, Sally knew. It was difficult, but it was the right thing to do. So many things in life were like that.

She imagined him coming home and discovering the body. Oh, how he would suffer. How he would grieve. Just as Sally had suffered and grieved. After it was over, Sally and Jess would be on even ground, one facing another. He had hurt her; she had hurt him. Fair. Perhaps she would even be there to comfort him. Perhaps he might turn to her, then, realizing how wrong he had been.

Further evidence of her cleverness: She had told that chatterbox Helene Bonnet that she was going to Europe for several weeks. She often went abroad. If her whereabouts that night were questioned, she would have an alibi as well, if the police didn't bother to check Helene's story.

And the fog! If Sally needed any confirmation that she was doing the right thing, that the very universe wanted what she wanted, it was the fog, shrouding the city, concealing her movements as she stole to Front Street that night, knife in hand.

Sally's thoughts were racing, here, there, and everywhere, as she crept around the side of his house. She hadn't counted on Jess's wife being outside, in the backyard near the lake, when she arrived. But no matter. The task could be performed just as easily there. Better, actually. No blood in the house. It was perfect!

She found his wife stumbling toward the lakeshore moaning and crying—clearly she was having the baby. This surprised Sally. She hadn't counted on that, either. Again, however, it was a fortuitous turn of events. In the throes of childbirth, his wife wouldn't be able to put up much of a struggle as Sally did what she had to do. She smiled at her good fortune and followed Addie down to the lakeshore. It all told Sally that she was doing the right thing. The trees and the grass and the fog were nodding in agreement. Sally could see it clearly, the way nature itself was cheering her on.

Then it was time. Could she go through with it? Could she end the life of another human being? *You've come this far, don't back out now. It's almost over. You're nearly there.* Sally could smell the lake and the sweet scent of the fog. Lilac on the night air. She looked behind her to the flickering lights coming from the house, blazing through the whiteness. The scene didn't seem real to Sally, there, on the lakeshore, dancing lights in the background, a knife in her hand.

She crept closer to Jess's wife. Closer still. Then, directly in front of her eyes, red seeped across a field of white. She didn't even realize she had done it. Sally stared as the red stain spread farther and farther onto the white nightgown. Jess's wife didn't even look at her. She fell into the shallow water. Sally stared at the bloody knife that she was holding and knew she had done what she came to do. There was no undoing it now. A few minutes later, Sally watched as the baby slipped from its dying mother's womb.

She ran to the side of the house and watched as another figure appeared out of the fog, which was lifting a bit. Impossibly, it was Celeste Connor, pushing a baby carriage. Sally watched as Celeste fished the baby out of the lake and put it in the carriage. Then another voice. Harrison. Sally heard it all, then—Celeste's crazy ramblings, Harrison's horror at what he thought she had done. A smile sliced across Sally's face. *He thinks his wife killed her. This is perfect.* She watched as Harrison put the body of Jess's wife in the rowboat.

Unbelievable. Then and there, in front of her eyes, Harrison had just absolved Sally of the crime she had committed. She had always liked that man. He put the guilt squarely on his wife's shoulders. The blame lay elsewhere, not with Sally. She hadn't expected such benevolence, not after what she had done. It was a good day.

Sally turned and headed back to her room, then. Her task was nearly finished. But there was still the matter of this knife. A tiny detail. She knew enough to know that she should get rid of it. She decided to take it to the shipyards and hide it in the trash. No one would notice it there among the fish entrails and battered boxes. Then she would return to her hotel and wait for the future to unfold.

She heard it as she walked past the city dock. Was it someone singing? It was a noise the likes of which Sally had never heard before. A song with no melody, no words. Was it human? Sally wasn't sure. But she was so captivated by the sound that, against her better judgment, she followed it to the end of the dock, the knife still in her hand. And then it dawned on her. She didn't need to find her way to the shipyards after all. She dropped the knife into the water and smiled as she watched it twirl downward, out of view. This night had gone so well.

The singing was louder now. Sally squinted out into the fog and thought she saw the outline of a creature in the water. An otter, perhaps? A beaver? What was it? Was this creature making the sound? Whatever it was, it locked eyes with Sally in that moment, and she was frozen there, at the end of the city dock, held captive by the intensity of the creature's gaze. Like prey in the sights of a cobra.

Sally did not have children, so she did not understand the fury of a grieving father. She could simply not foresee the blinding, vengeful rage that she had elicited with her actions that night. Poor Sally was so captivated looking into the eyes of the creature that she did not see the enormous wall of water moving toward her until it burst out of the fog and engulfed her, smashing the dock into pieces with its wrath.

The lake plucked Sally off her feet in its fury and twisted its tentacles around her as tight as a noose, plunging her body under the surface, forcing so much water into her lungs that they burst apart, killing her in an instant. It carried her lifeless body for miles to a faraway, desolate shore and spat her out in disgust.

To this day, on that faraway beach, where her bones had been picked clean and carried away by wolves, an aura of madness remains. Animals other than the fearless wolves stay away, sensing danger and destruction. But humans aren't as in tune with nature as animals are. Families congregate on that beach to take a dip in the cool water on steamy summer days, armed with picnic baskets and blankets.

But something is just not right about the place. Their otherwise well-behaved children always seem to run wild on that beach with a kind of frantic energy that gives parents pause, sending a shiver down their spines even as they resolve to limit the sugary treats in their children's lunches the next time. Friends and lovers argue, the anger seemingly coming from nowhere. Wives grow testy and annoyed with their husbands, who seem withdrawn and depressed, despite the blue sky and clear water.

And nobody lingers there too long, for fear that the madness is catching.

ACKNOWLEDGMENTS

Readers ask me if I base my characters on real people, and usually the answer is no, not entirely. Snippets of someone's conversation here, a description there. And that's true with this book, too, but as I was writing Simon, I couldn't get the voice of my darling friend Ken Anderson out of my head, as though he demanded to be written into the story. (He'd totally do that, by the way.) Simon has a whole lot of Ken in him. It was so gratifying to hear my agent and my editors, the first readers of this book, say: "Simon is so much fun! I love him!" I do, too.

Speaking of my agent and editors . . . I am profoundly lucky to have my wonderful, delightful agent, Jennifer Weltz, and her amazing team at the Jean V. Naggar Literary Agency representing me. Jennifer has been my invaluable sounding board, champion, lioness, and friend throughout the years. Plus she makes me laugh every single time we talk. Jennifer, I adore you.

To my stellar team at Lake Union: Danielle Marshall, Faith Black Ross, Kelli Martin, Alicia Clancy, Gabriella Dumpit, Ashley Vanicek, the amazing copyeditors (I bow to your superb attention to detail), and everyone else who works on my behalf, thank you for your faith in me, for your hard work, and for loving this story as much as I do.

To the independent booksellers who carry my books, get them into the hands of new readers, and graciously invite me into your stores to meet them, you have made my career, and I am eternally grateful to you.

And to my readers. Thank you so very, very much for coming along for the ride. Get in touch, send me an email with your thoughts, follow me on Instagram or Facebook and let me know how you liked this tale.

Finally, readers of my last book, *The End of Temperance Dare*, may have picked up on the fact that I set this story in the same community of Wharton, a small portside town of my own invention on Lake Superior. Wharton exists in my own imagination, and now, yours, but a real place is the inspiration for it. Bayfield, Wisconsin.

To me, Bayfield is a mystical, magical place steeped in Lake Superior legend and lore, overlooking the magnificent Apostle Island National Lakeshore, a string of twenty-one islands of indescribable beauty in my beloved harsh, powerful, and awe-inspiring inland sea.

Every summer I make sure to get to Bayfield at least once, most often for my birthday in August. For a very significant birthday, I rented out my favorite place, a Victorian inn called Le Chateau Boutin, and hosted my closest friends and family for a weekend none of us will ever forget. Le Chateau is the inspiration for Harrison's House—if you google it, you'll recognize it from my descriptions. It's not similarly haunted . . . that I know of . . . and there are no dark secrets lurking in any of the corners. It's simply wonderful and relaxing and lovely, and I highly recommend it to anyone who wants to experience Wharton for real.

About that inland sea, Lake Superior. It's a character in this book, much more so than in any of my others. You should know a few things if you're a newcomer to the greatest of lakes. Lake Superior, the largest freshwater lake in the world, is an ancient, powerful, vengeful, and, by turns, peaceful, calming, healing body of water unlike no other on the face of this planet.

The native peoples who lived on its shores called it Gitche Gumee (a rough translation) and believed that the lake itself was a great spirit, to whom the people gave offerings and gifts before setting out on any journey by boat. They knew the lake could be protective and welcoming and also murderous and sly, and they knew the lake was fickle. Best to appease it at the outset.

The creature young Jess saw when he discovered baby Addie is a real Lake Superior legend, Michi Peshu, an underwater deity. Ancient pictographs around the lake depict him, especially on the Canadian side.

By the way, this isn't just an ancient, old-fashioned belief. People who live on Lake Superior to this day, myself included, will tell you it really does seem to be a living thing.

DAUGHTERS OF THE LAKE

DISCUSSION QUESTIONS

1. The lore and legend of Lake Superior centers on the lake being a great spirit, Gitche Gumee. What are your thoughts on nature and the divine?

2. Addie exhibits pure love while Jess blunders his way through. Is he ultimately to blame for her death?

3. What would you come back from the dead to set right?

4. Do you believe love lives on after death?

5. Were Addie and Jess meant for each other? Did the lake choose him for her?

6. Did Celeste lose her mind, or was she calculated when she went to Addie's that night in the fog?

7. Both Harrison and Jess are deeply flawed but, at the same time, sympathetic characters. Is ambition the reason

for their downfalls? Could you live with such a flawed partner?

8. Who is the angry spirit in the house?

9. Why does the lake choose this time to allow Addie to wash up on Kate's beach? Is it to finally right the wrong of Jess's trial, or is it to save Kate?

10. Fog envelops Addie the day of her birth and the night of her death. What is the significance of this?

11. When Kate becomes ice cold and starts shivering, what is happening to her?

12. What is it about Wharton that invites otherworldly happenings?

13. Would you vacation at Harrison's House if you could?

14. The character of Simon is based on a real-life friend of Wendy's. Who would you put into a book, and why?

15. If you could ask Addie and Kate each one question, what would it be?

16. If you could ask Wendy one question about this book, what would it be?

DAUGHTERS OF THE LAKE
AUTHOR Q&A

I wrote these discussion questions to spark conversation in book clubs—I love my loyal book club readers. Then I thought it would be fun to answer these questions myself. So here are my thoughts. But my answers are no more valid than yours. This story is open to your interpretation, too.

1. The lore and legend of Lake Superior centers on the lake being a great spirit, Gitche Gumee. What are your thoughts on nature and the divine?

I lived on Lake Superior for sixteen years, and I can tell you without a doubt that there's something otherworldly and divine about that lake.

2. Addie exhibits pure love while Jess blunders his way through. Is he ultimately to blame for her death?

Jess's infidelities are ultimately the cause of Addie's death, but she doesn't blame him, so I won't, either.

3. What would you come back from the dead to set right?

Any wrong involving someone I loved. My beloved wrongly accused of my murder? I'd be back here in a nanosecond.

4. Do you believe love lives on after death?

My mom recently passed after sixty-three years of marriage to my dad. He still talks to her every day. So, yes. I believe it. I've seen it with my own eyes.

5. Were Addie and Jess meant for each other? Did the lake choose him for her?

Yes, the lake chose Jess for Addie the day she was born.

6. Did Celeste lose her mind, or was she calculated when she went to Addie's that night in the fog?

I was imagining she lost her mind and couldn't accept the death of her baby.

7. Both Harrison and Jess are deeply flawed but, at the same time, sympathetic characters. Is ambition the reason for their downfalls? Could you live with such a flawed partner?

To a certain extent, looking back on it, ambition is a big contributor, but it's not the only reason. I think there is an inflated sense of pride and entitlement that both men exhibit, too. Harrison covers up what he believes is Celeste's crime and allows his good friend Jess to take the fall for it. He also raises Jess and Addie's daughter as his own. Had Jess not been killed at the courthouse, Harrison would have let him believe his own child had died. But on the other hand, he was an excellent father to Hadley, and he was kind to and, in his own way, in love with Addie. Jess, too, was guilty of an affair even though he loved Addie with his whole heart and soul. Entitlement? Lack of character? Both?

Could I live with a flawed partner? I think we all do, to a certain extent. We're human, every last one of us. We all are guilty of doing foolish things. To me, that's what love is there for, to allow us to look beyond the mistakes and missteps our partners make, to forgive. That's what I believe "to err is human, to forgive divine" means.

8. Who is the angry spirit in the house?

When I was writing it, until I got about halfway through, I was thinking it was Celeste's mother, the angry woman in the portrait. But closer to the ending, I thought, no. It's Celeste herself.

9. Why does the lake choose this time to allow Addie to wash up on Kate's beach? Is it to finally right the wrong of Jess's trial, or is it to save Kate?

Both.

10. Fog envelops Addie the day of her birth and the night of her death. What is the significance of this?

I think fog is creepy, first of all, but to me it's the lake rising up.

11. When Kate becomes ice cold and starts shivering, what is happening to her?

She is experiencing what Addie experienced during the last moments of her life.

12. What is it about Wharton that invites otherworldly happenings?

To me, the veil between this world and the next is very thin in Wharton. It allows both good and evil to come and go.

13. Would you vacation at Harrison's House if you could?

Absolutely. The house is based on a real place, Le Chateau Boutin in Bayfield, Wisconsin. I go there every year.

14. The character of Simon is based on a real-life friend of Wendy's. Who would you put into a book, and why?

I've named characters after real people in my life. I put my dogs in my books, too.

15. If you could ask Addie and Kate each one question, what would it be?

For Addie: What is it like on the other side?
For Kate: Is Nick the great love of your life?

16. If you could ask Wendy one question about this book, what would it be?

I'll leave this one to you. Follow me on Instagram, Twitter, and Facebook @wendywebbauthor, and ask away.

ABOUT THE AUTHOR

Photo © 2010 Steve Burmeister

Wendy Webb knew from the minute she read *A Wrinkle in Time* at age eleven that she was destined to be a writer. After two decades as a journalist, writing for varied publications including *USA Today*, the *Huffington Post*, the *Star Tribune*, *Midwest Living*, and others, Wendy wrote her first novel, *The Tale of Halcyon Crane*. When it won the 2011 Minnesota Book Award for genre fiction, she started writing fiction full-time. Her second and third novels, *The Fate of Mercy Alban* and *The Vanishing*, established her as a leading suspense novelist, whom reviewers are calling the Queen of the Northern Gothic. She lives in Minneapolis and is at work on her next novel. Visit her online at www.wendykwebb.com and on Facebook, Twitter, and Instagram as wendywebbauthor.